TOMMYSAURUS REX

DOUG TENNAPEL
WITH COLOR BY KATHERINE GARNER

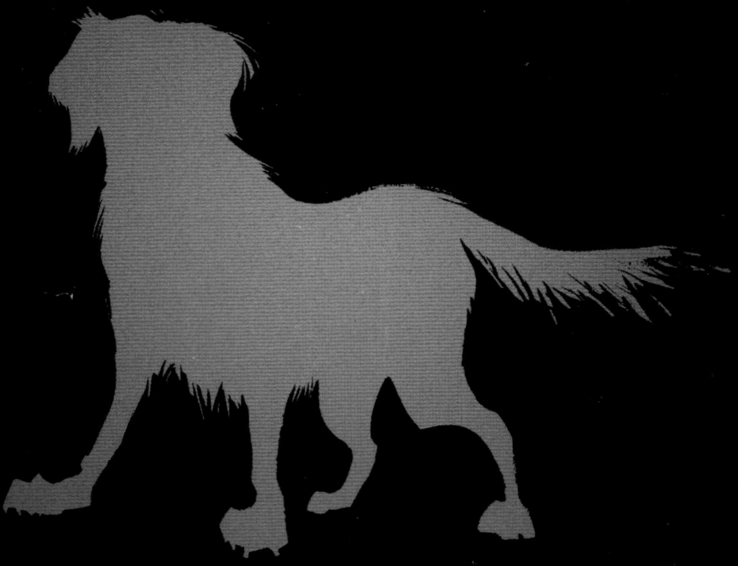

graphix
An Imprint of
SCHOLASTIC

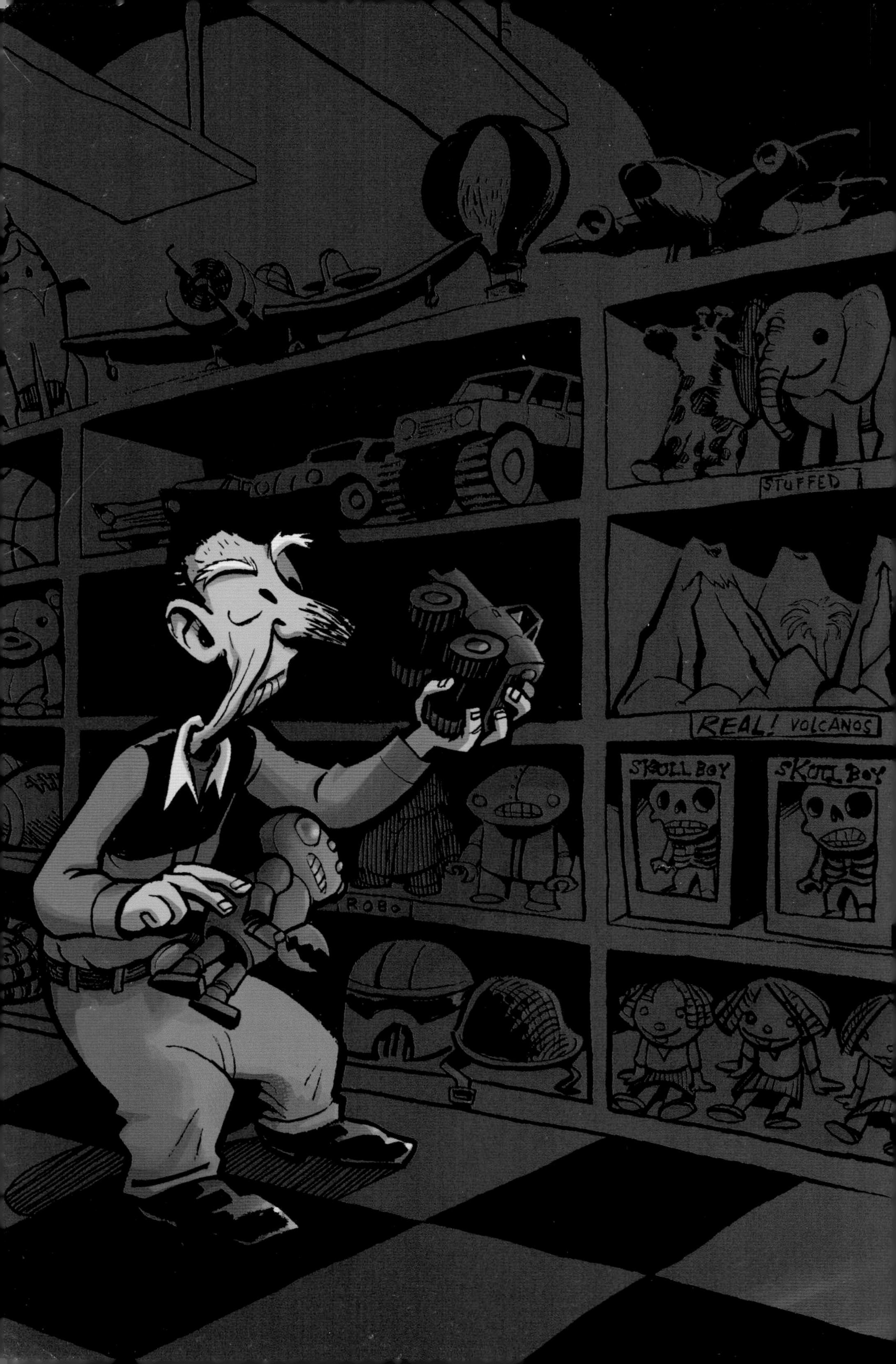
STUFFED
REAL! VOLCANOS
SKULL BOY
SKULL BOY
ROBO

I wish to thank Hugh Speed for rendering borders, Tony McVey for the cool dinosaur reference, Ray Harryhausen for the inspiration, and Philip Simon for helping me find paper. To Katherine Garner for the great color work, and to the beloved Mrs. TenNapel, you make me happy.

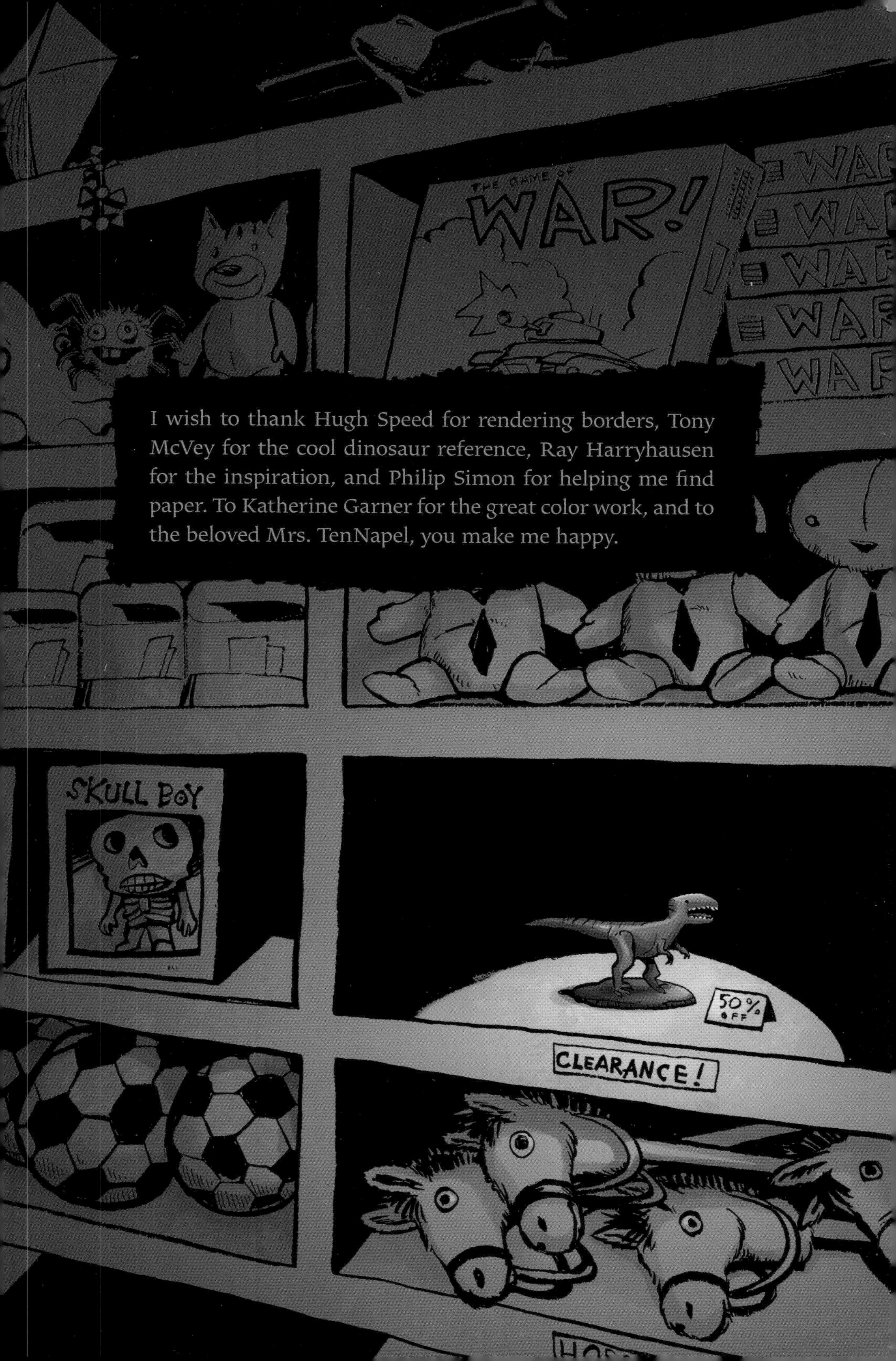
THE GAME OF
WAR!
SKULL BOY
50% OFF
CLEARANCE!

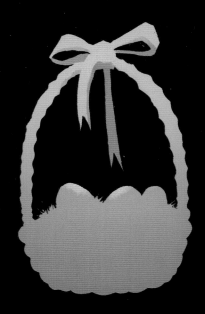

Library of Congress Control Number: 2012945113

ISBN 978-0-545-48382-7
ISBN 978-0-545-48383-4 (paperback)
10 9 8 7 6 5 4 3 2   19 20 21 22 23
Printed in China   62

First edition, June 2013
Edited by Adam Rau
Book design by Phil Falco
Creative director: David Saylor

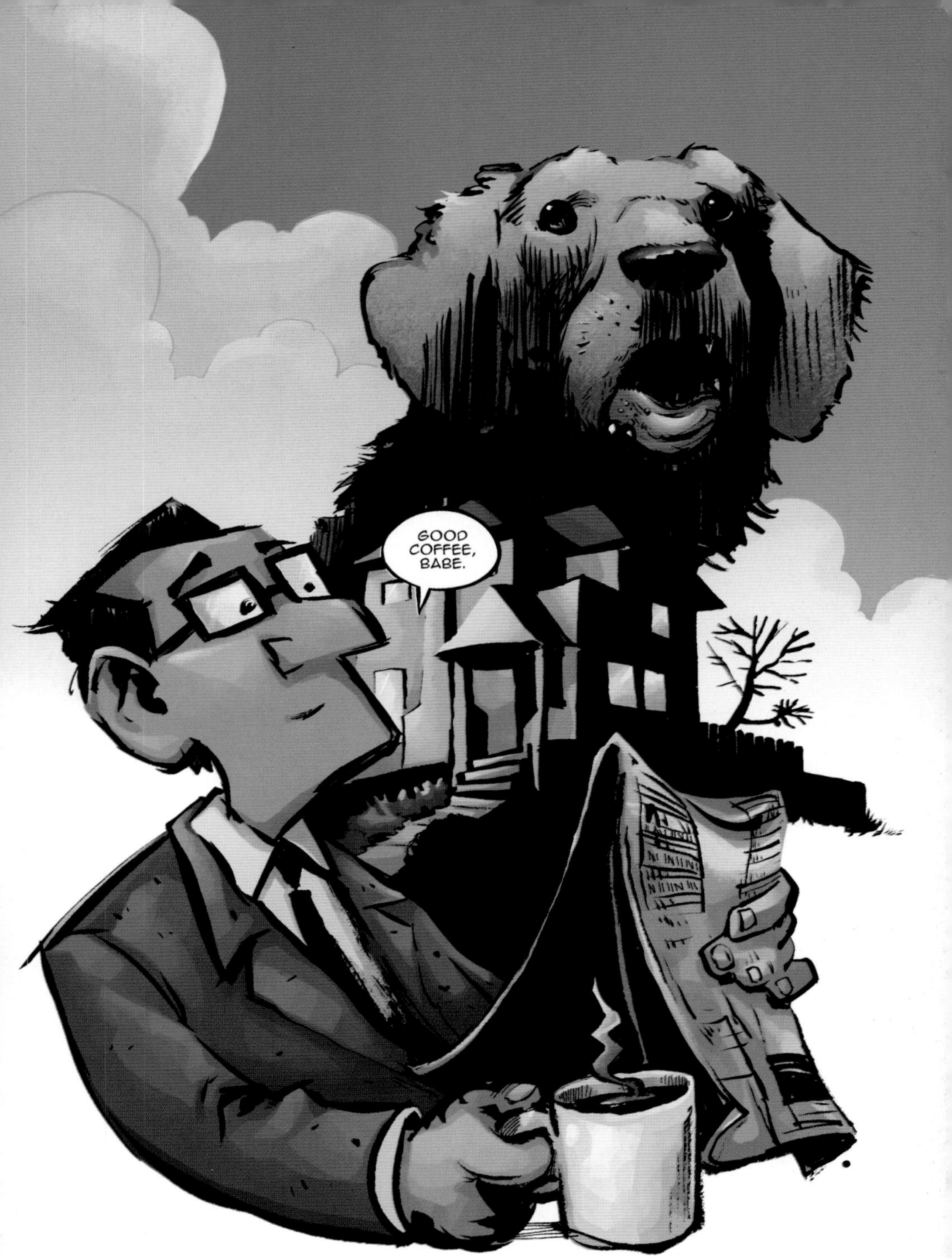
GOOD COFFEE, BABE.

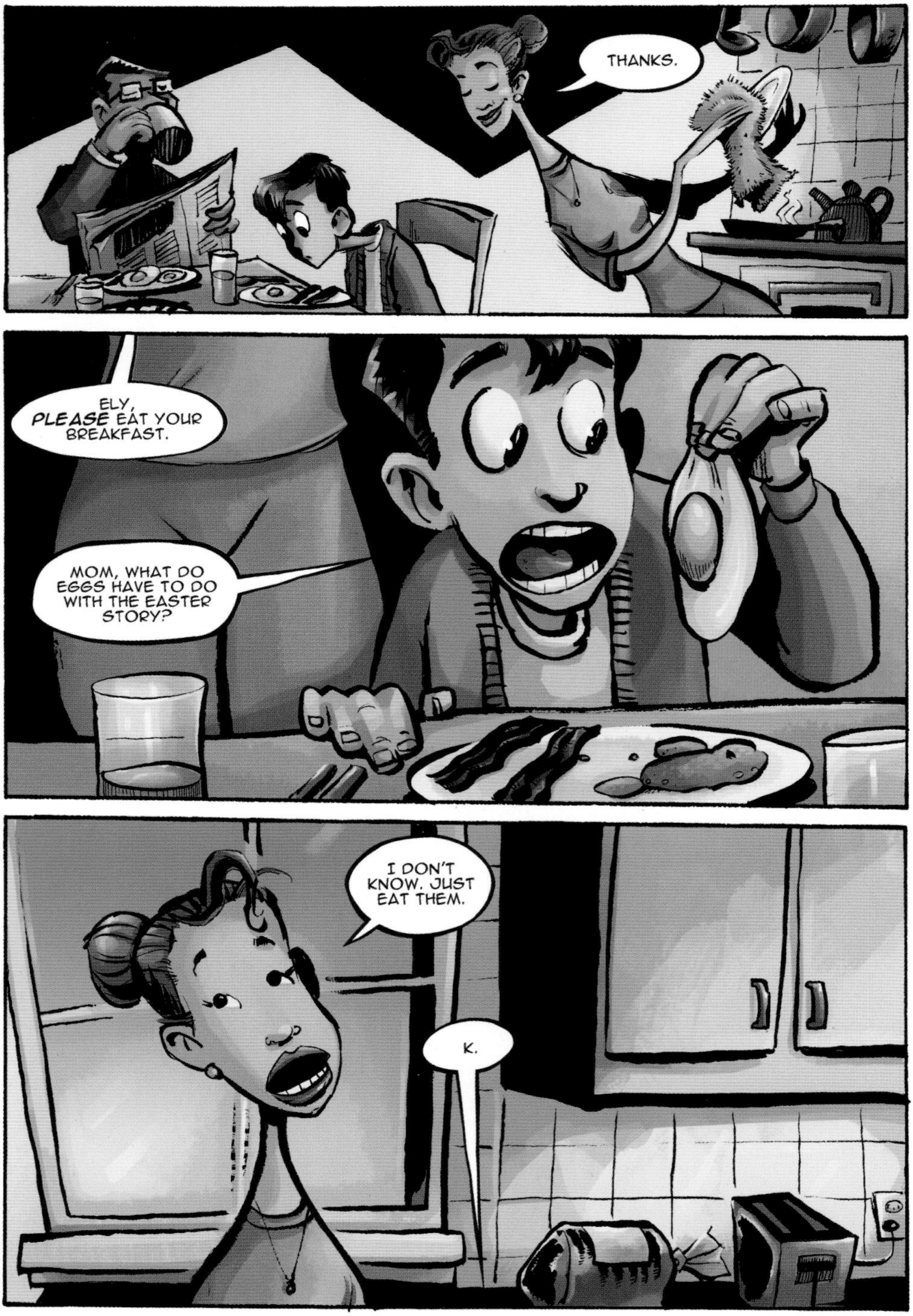
THANKS.
ELY, *PLEASE* EAT YOUR BREAKFAST.
MOM, WHAT DO EGGS HAVE TO DO WITH THE EASTER STORY?
I DON'T KNOW. JUST EAT THEM.
K.

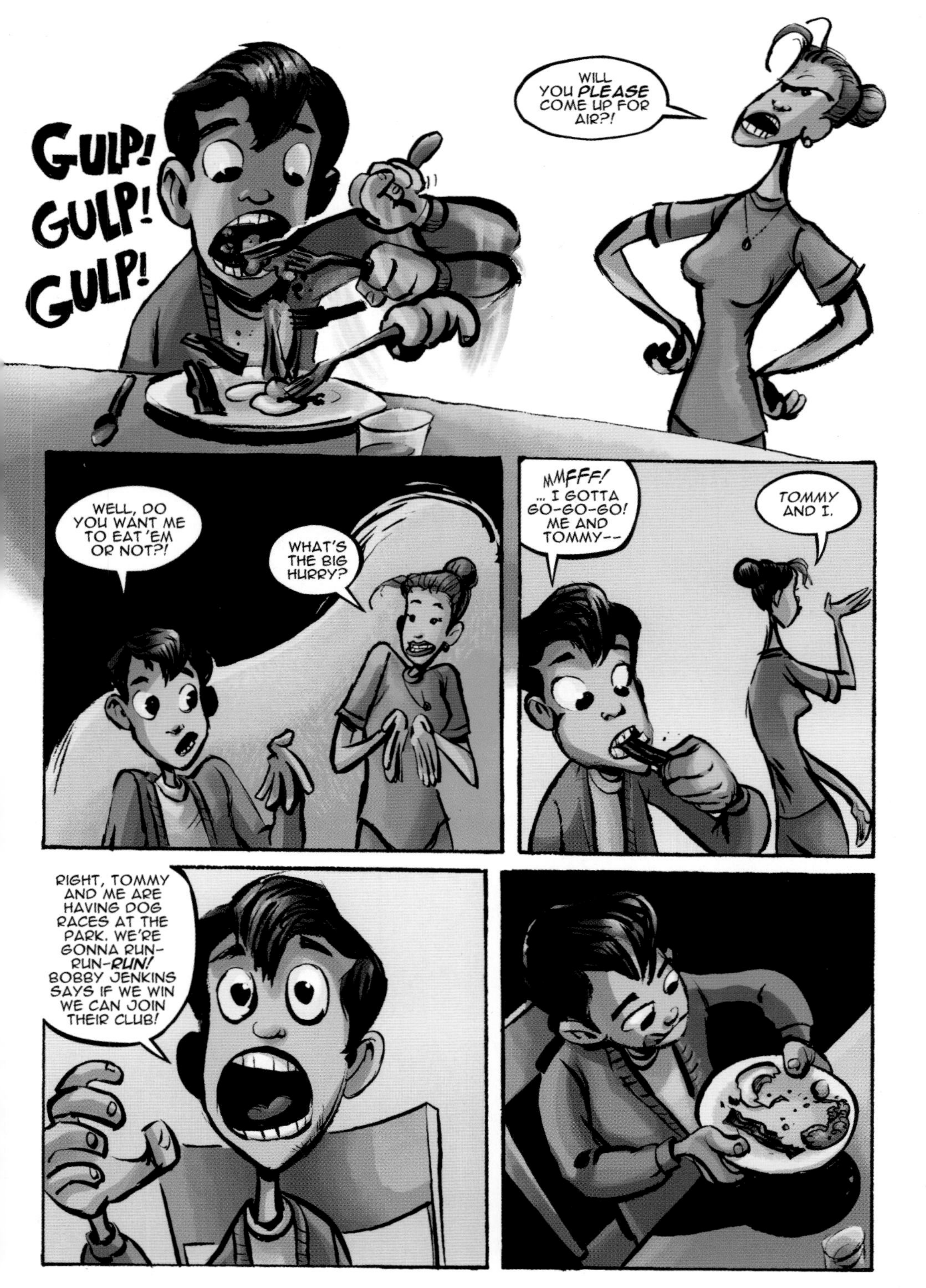
GULP! GULP! GULP!
WILL YOU PLEASE COME UP FOR AIR?!
WELL, DO YOU WANT ME TO EAT 'EM OR NOT?!
WHAT'S THE BIG HURRY?
MMFFF! ... I GOTTA GO-GO-GO! ME AND TOMMY--
TOMMY AND I.
RIGHT, TOMMY AND ME ARE HAVING DOG RACES AT THE PARK. WE'RE GONNA RUN-RUN-RUN! BOBBY JENKINS SAYS IF WE WIN WE CAN JOIN THEIR CLUB!

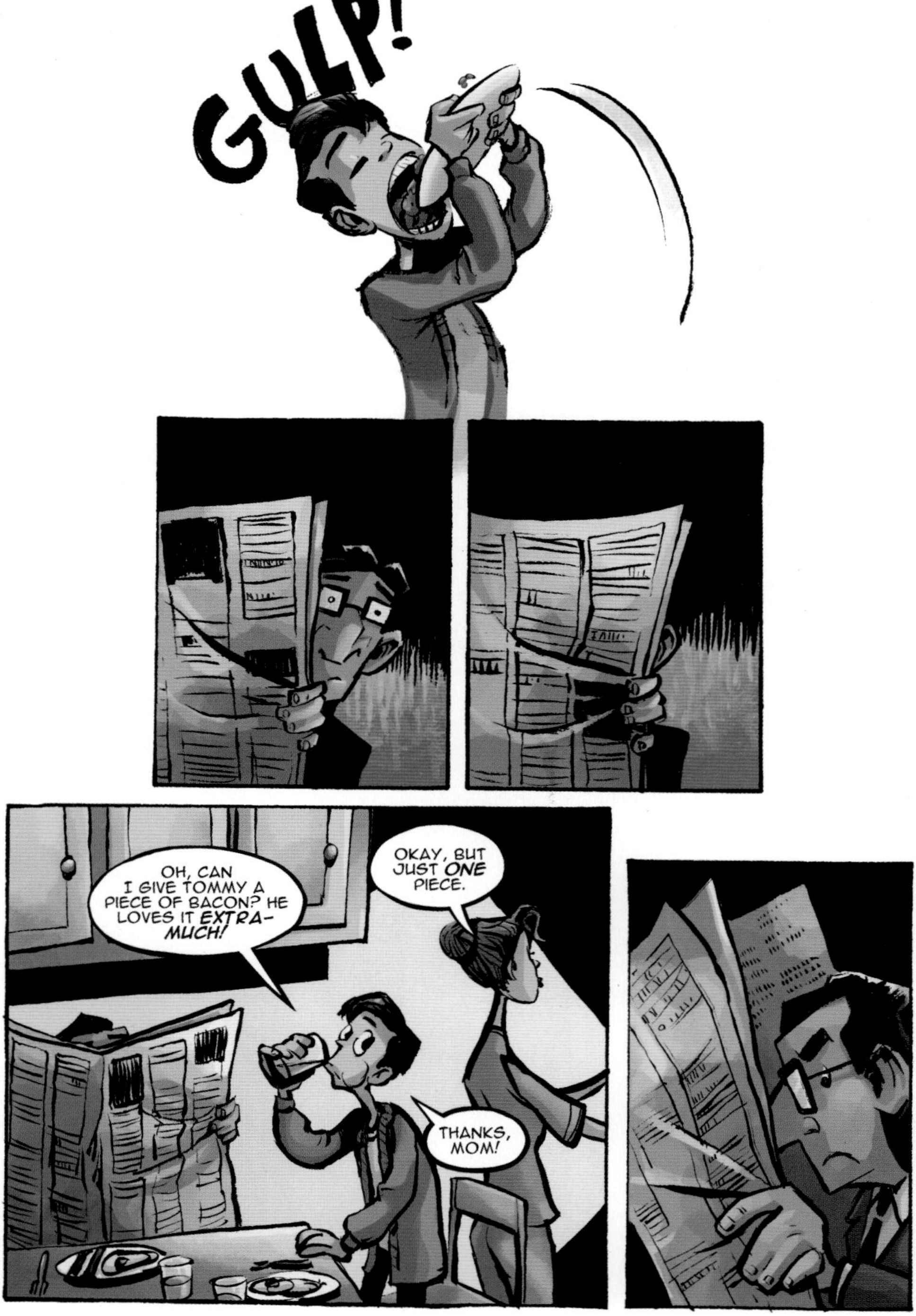
GULP!
OH, CAN I GIVE TOMMY A PIECE OF BACON? HE LOVES IT *EXTRA-MUCH!*
OKAY, BUT JUST ***ONE*** PIECE.
THANKS, MOM!

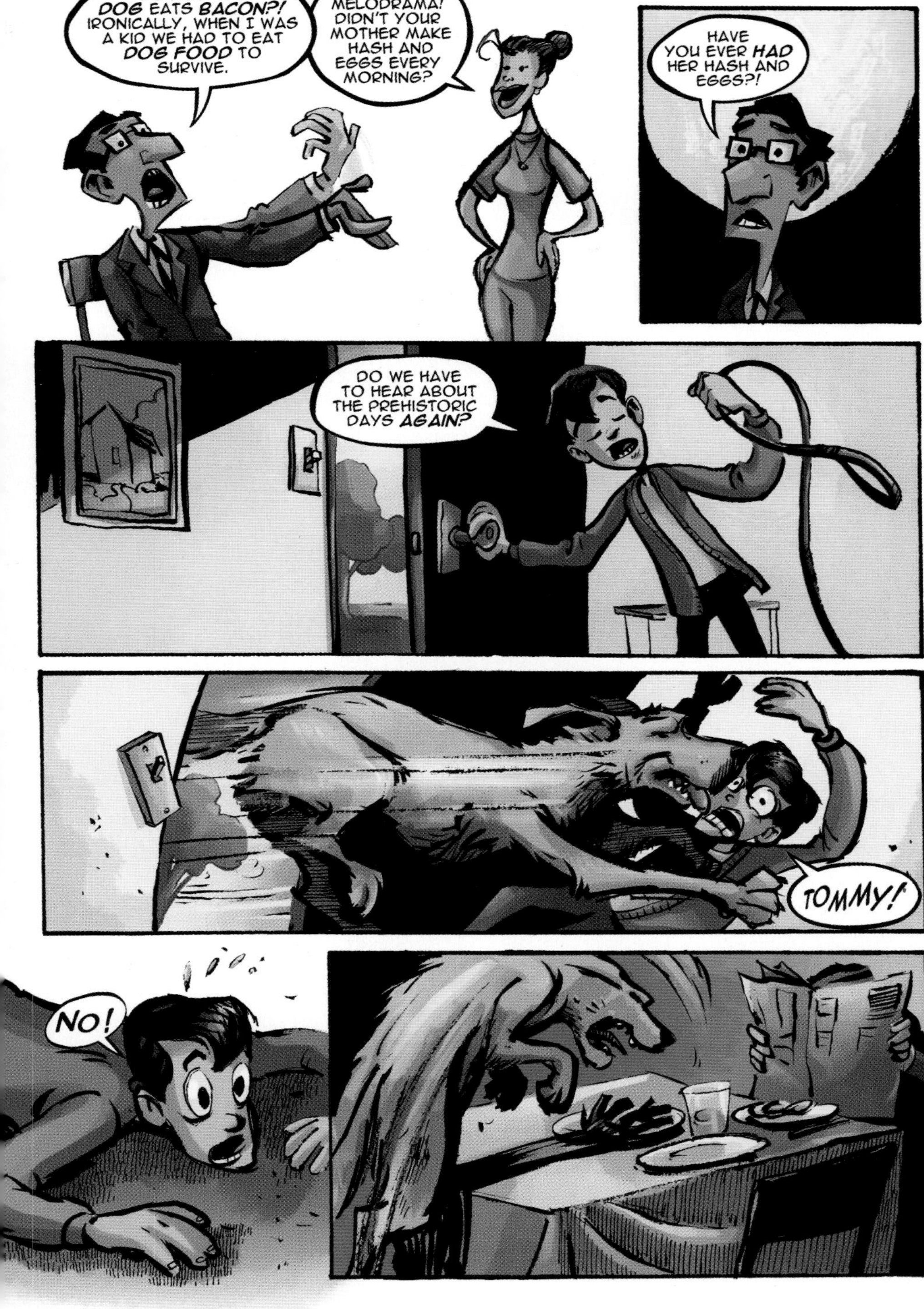
SO NOW THE DOG EATS BACON?! IRONICALLY, WHEN I WAS A KID WE HAD TO EAT DOG FOOD TO SURVIVE.
HEY, MR. MELODRAMA! DIDN'T YOUR MOTHER MAKE HASH AND EGGS EVERY MORNING?
HAVE YOU EVER HAD HER HASH AND EGGS?!
DO WE HAVE TO HEAR ABOUT THE PREHISTORIC DAYS AGAIN?
TOMMY!
NO!

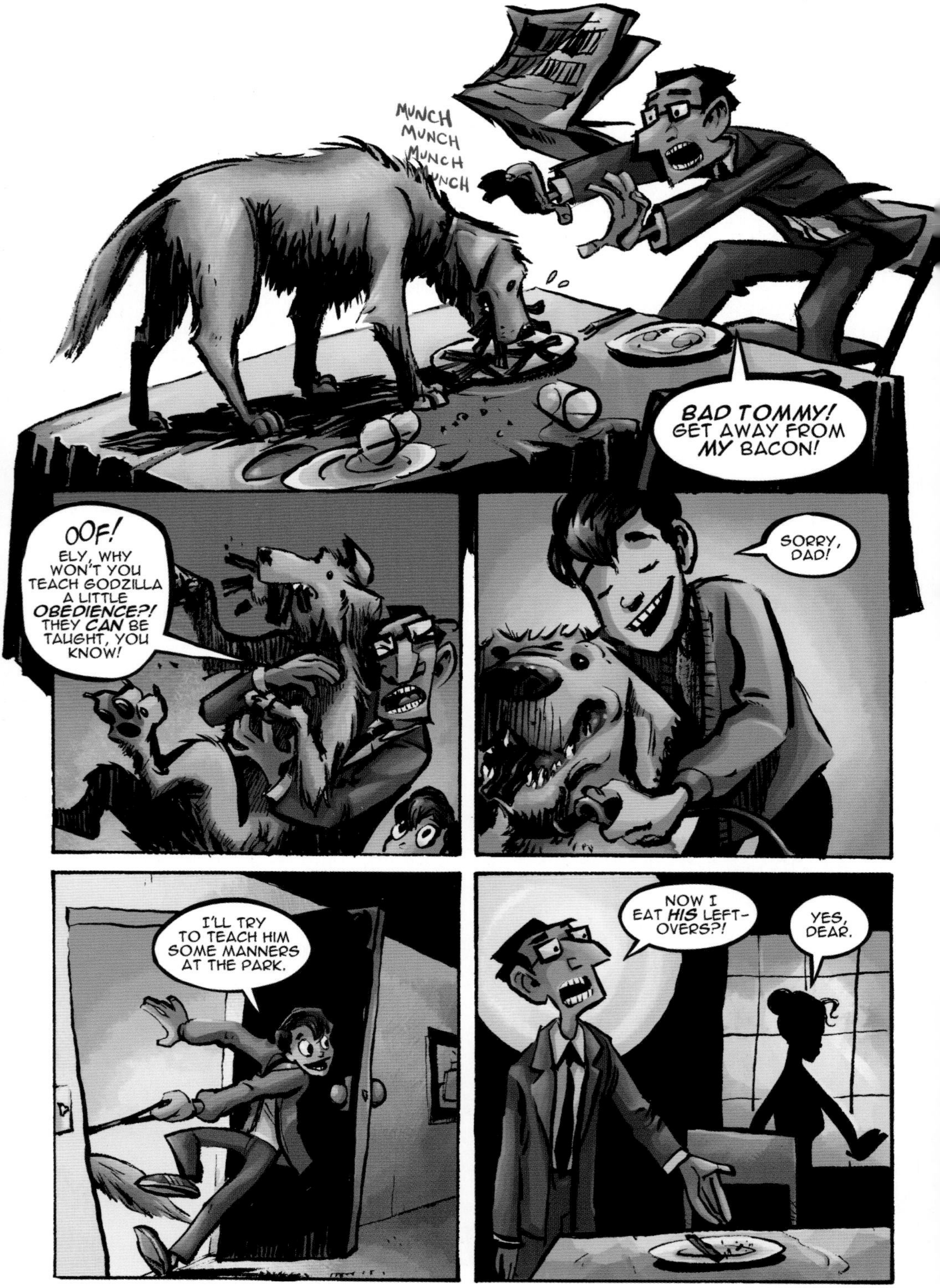
MUNCH
MUNCH
MUNCH
MUNCH
BAD TOMMY! GET AWAY FROM MY BACON!
OOF! ELY, WHY WON'T YOU TEACH GODZILLA A LITTLE OBEDIENCE?! THEY CAN BE TAUGHT, YOU KNOW!
SORRY, DAD!
I'LL TRY TO TEACH HIM SOME MANNERS AT THE PARK.
NOW I EAT HIS LEFT-OVERS?!
YES, DEAR.

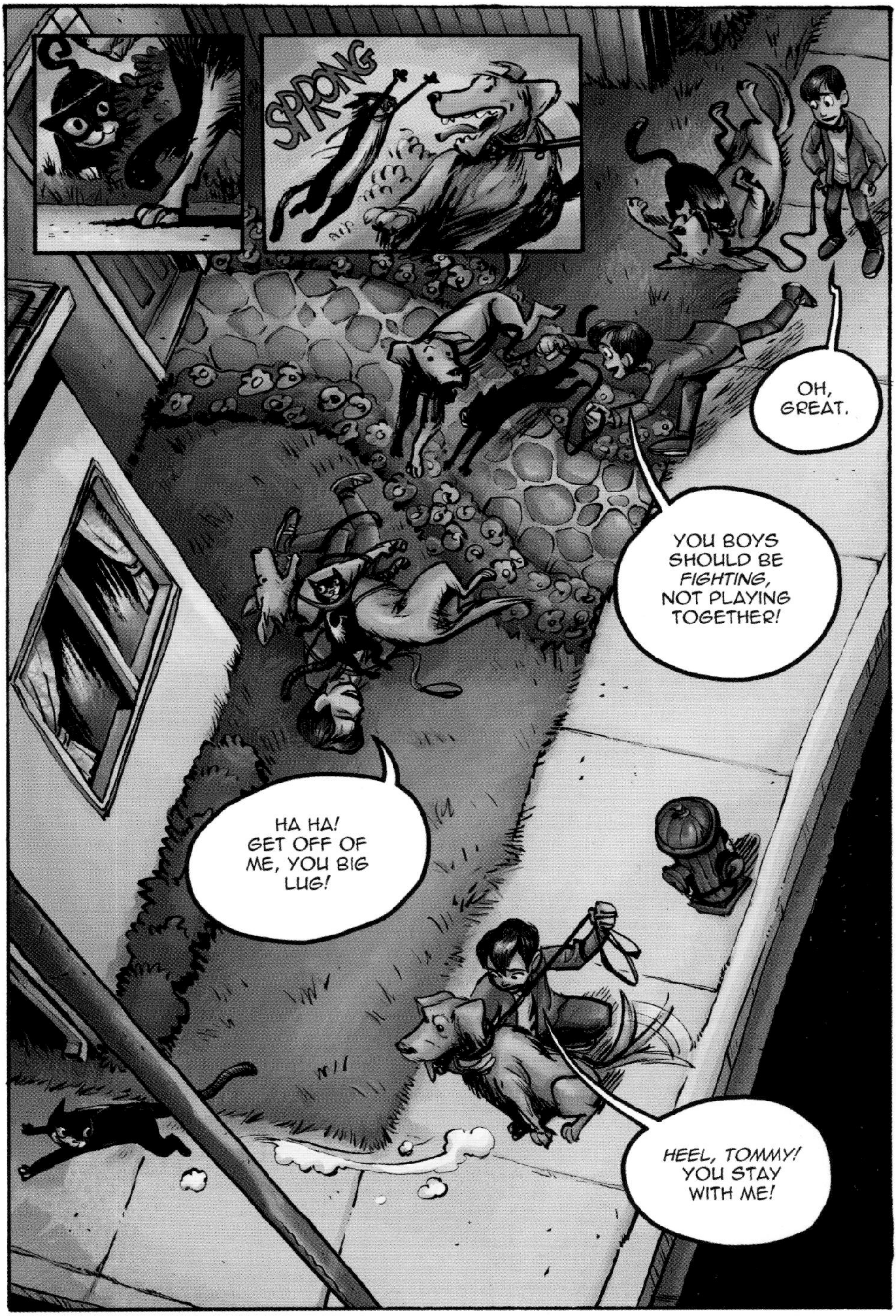
SPRONG
OH, GREAT.
YOU BOYS SHOULD BE *FIGHTING*, NOT PLAYING TOGETHER!
HA HA! GET OFF OF ME, YOU BIG LUG!
HEEL, TOMMY! YOU STAY WITH ME!

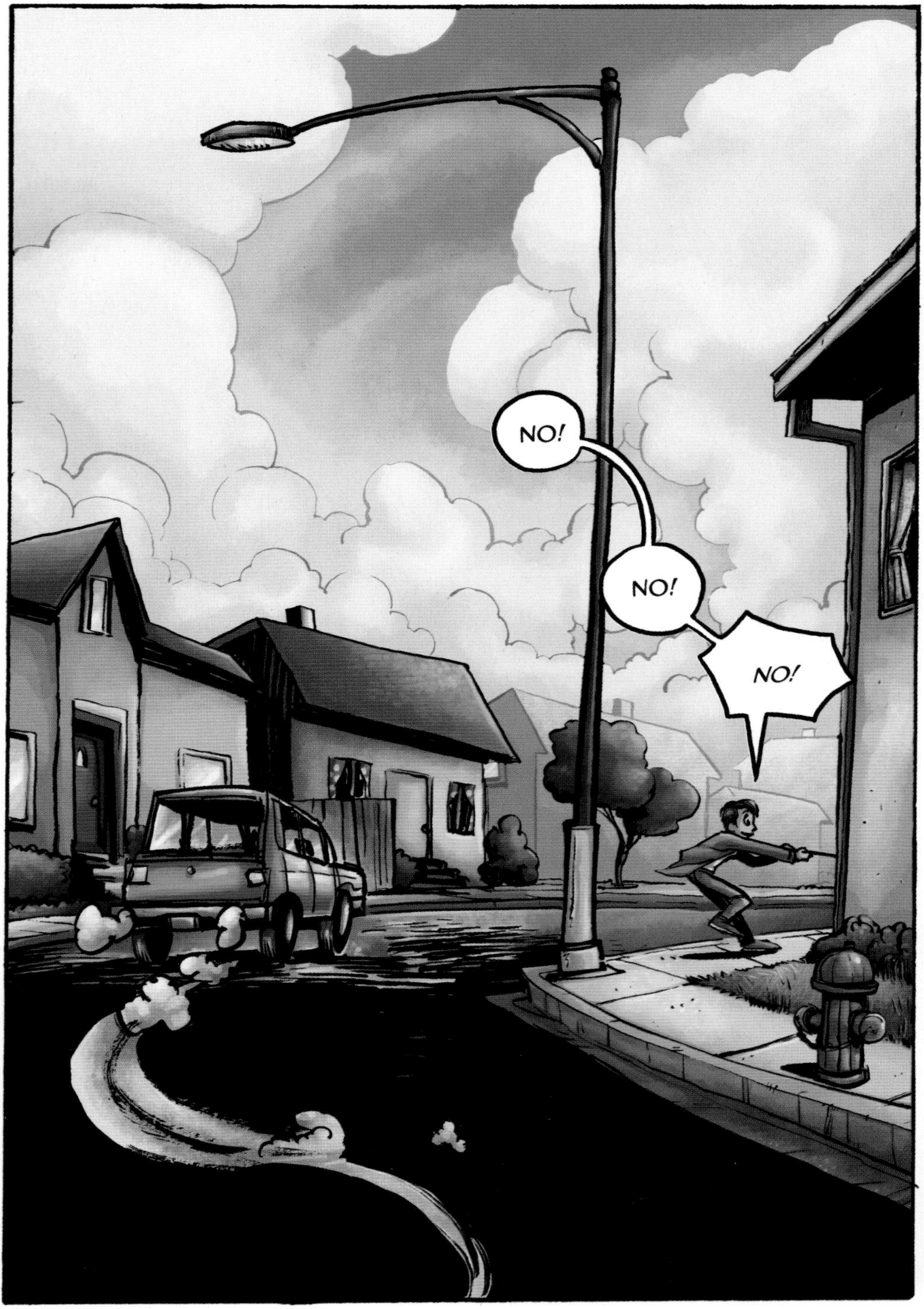
NO!
NO!
NO!

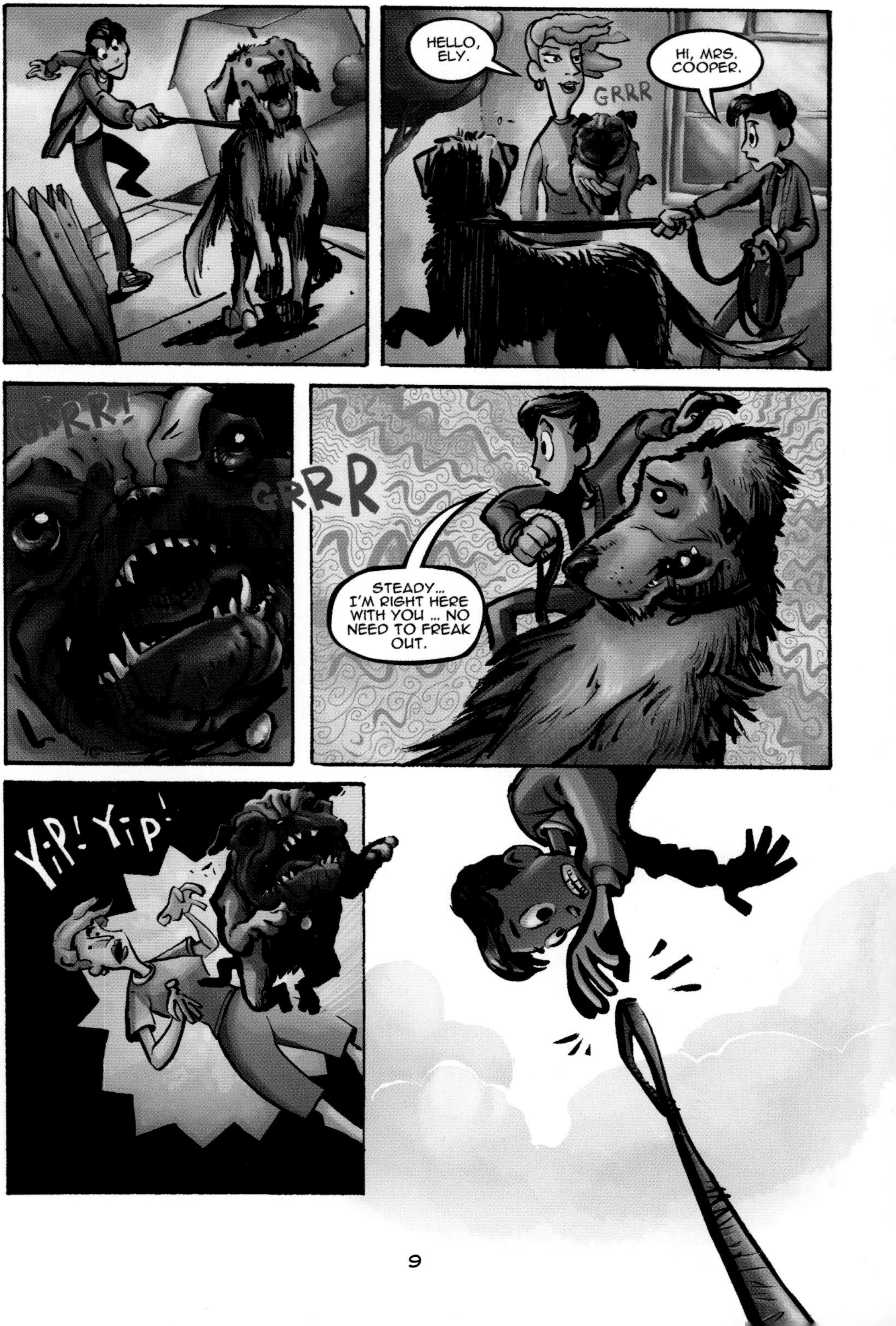
HELLO, ELY.
HI, MRS. COOPER.
GRRR
GRRR!
GRRR
STEADY... I'M RIGHT HERE WITH YOU ... NO NEED TO FREAK OUT.
YIP! YIP!

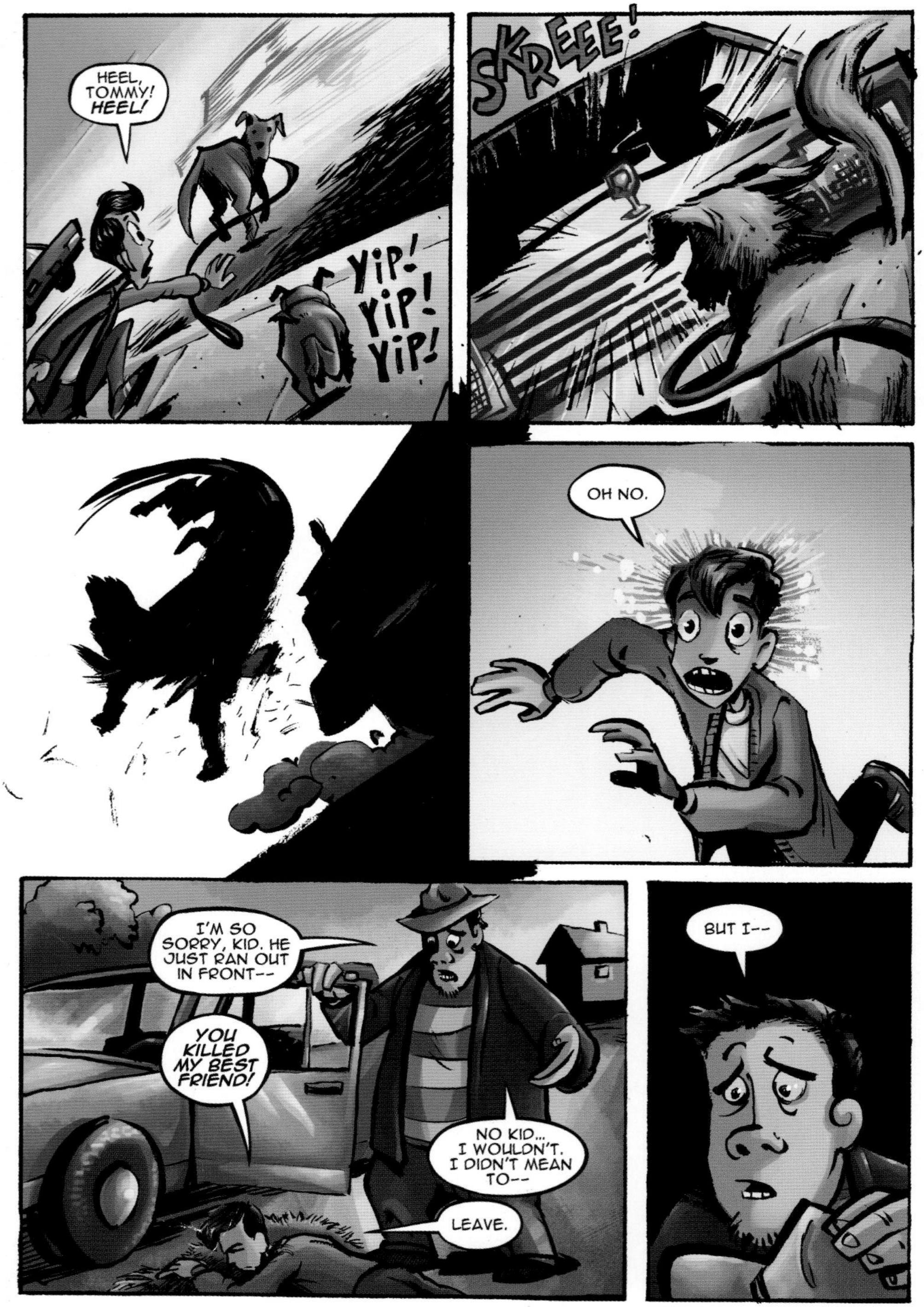
HEEL, TOMMY! HEEL!
YIP! YIP! YIP!
SKREEEE!
OH NO.
I'M SO SORRY, KID. HE JUST RAN OUT IN FRONT--
YOU KILLED MY BEST FRIEND!
NO KID... I WOULDN'T. I DIDN'T MEAN TO--
LEAVE.
BUT I--

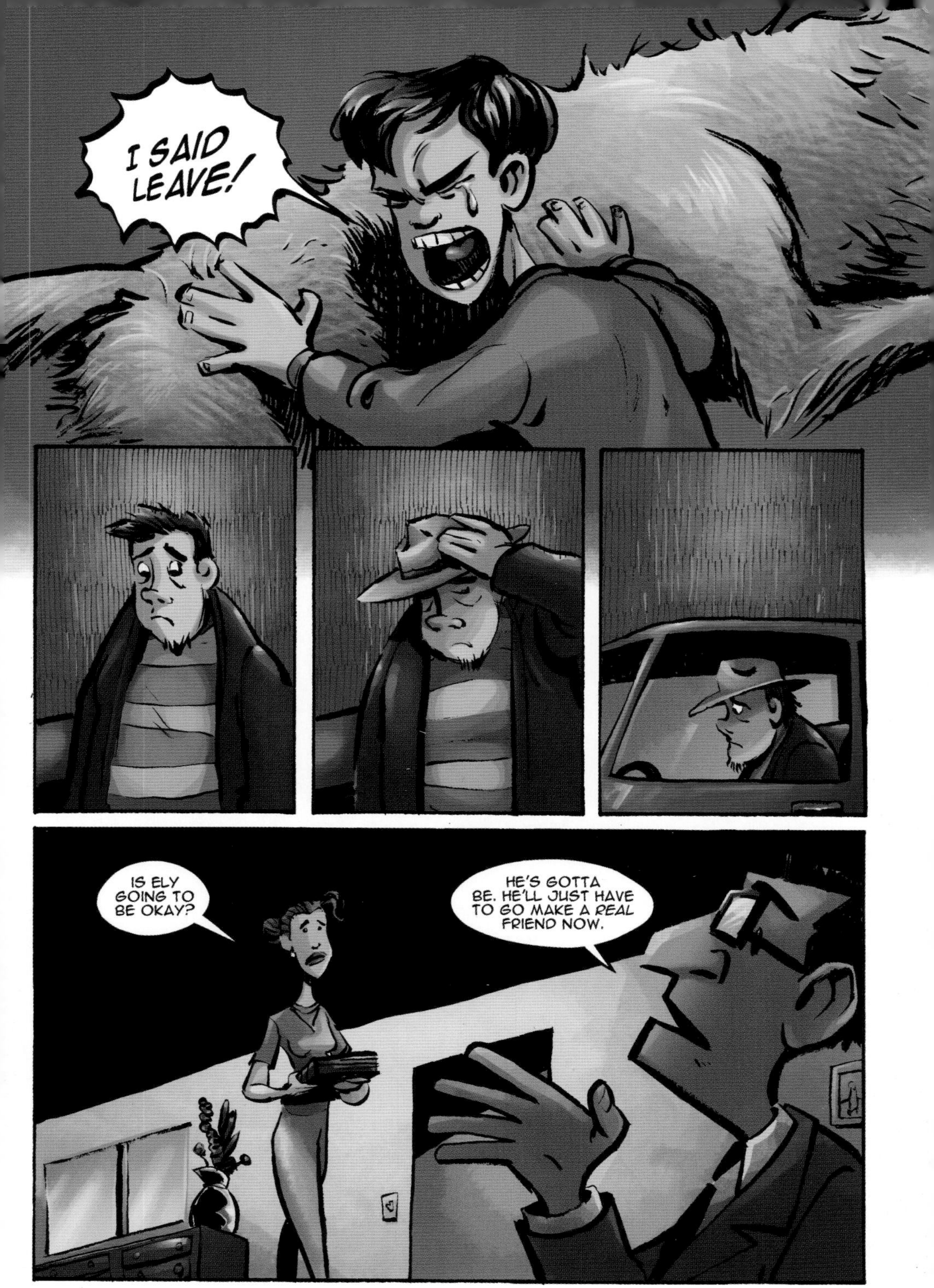
I SAID LEAVE!
IS ELY GOING TO BE OKAY?
HE'S GOTTA BE. HE'LL JUST HAVE TO GO MAKE A *REAL* FRIEND NOW.

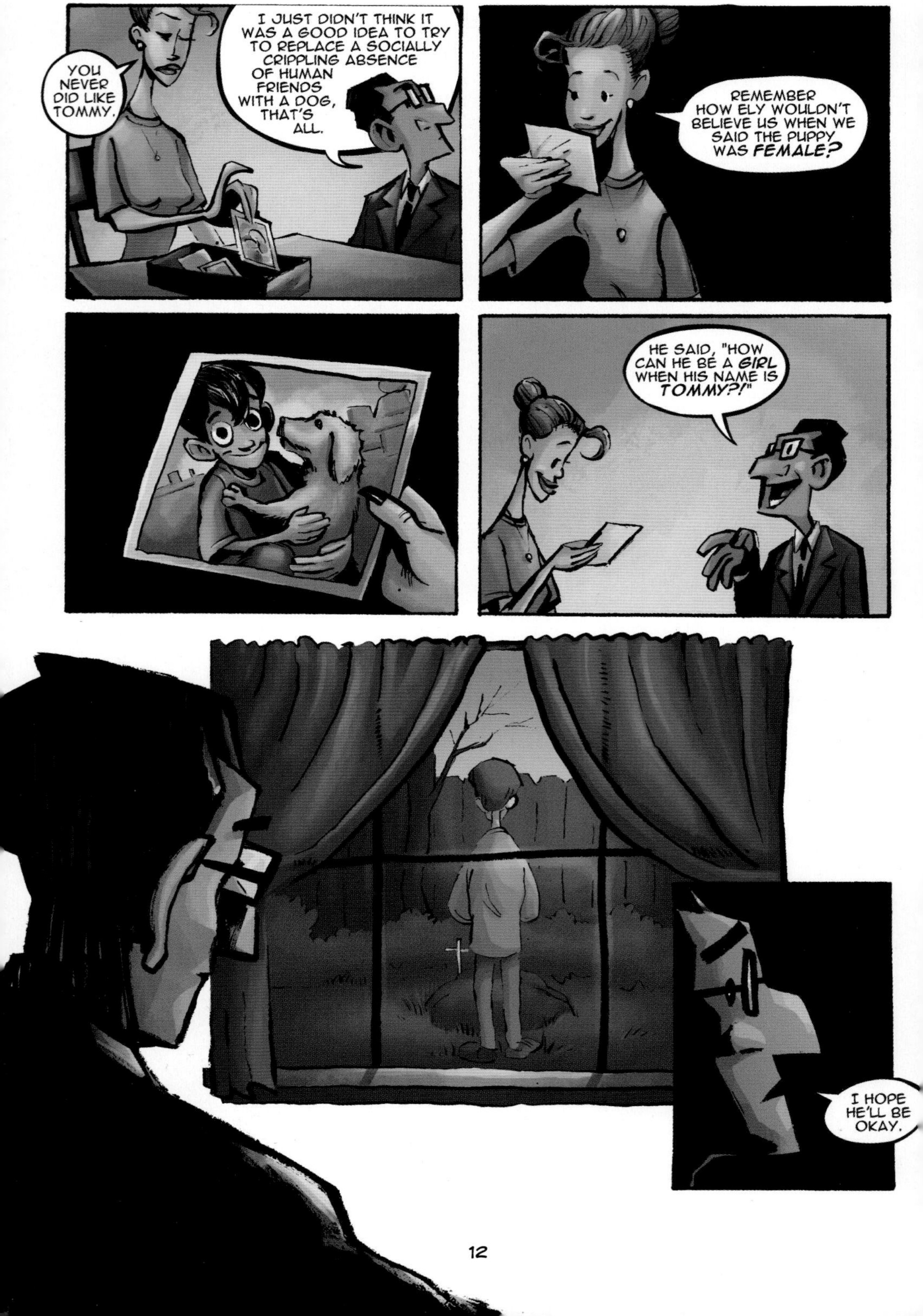
YOU NEVER DID LIKE TOMMY.
I JUST DIDN'T THINK IT WAS A GOOD IDEA TO TRY TO REPLACE A SOCIALLY CRIPPLING ABSENCE OF HUMAN FRIENDS WITH A DOG, THAT'S ALL.
REMEMBER HOW ELY WOULDN'T BELIEVE US WHEN WE SAID THE PUPPY WAS FEMALE?
HE SAID, "HOW CAN HE BE A GIRL WHEN HIS NAME IS TOMMY?!"
I HOPE HE'LL BE OKAY.

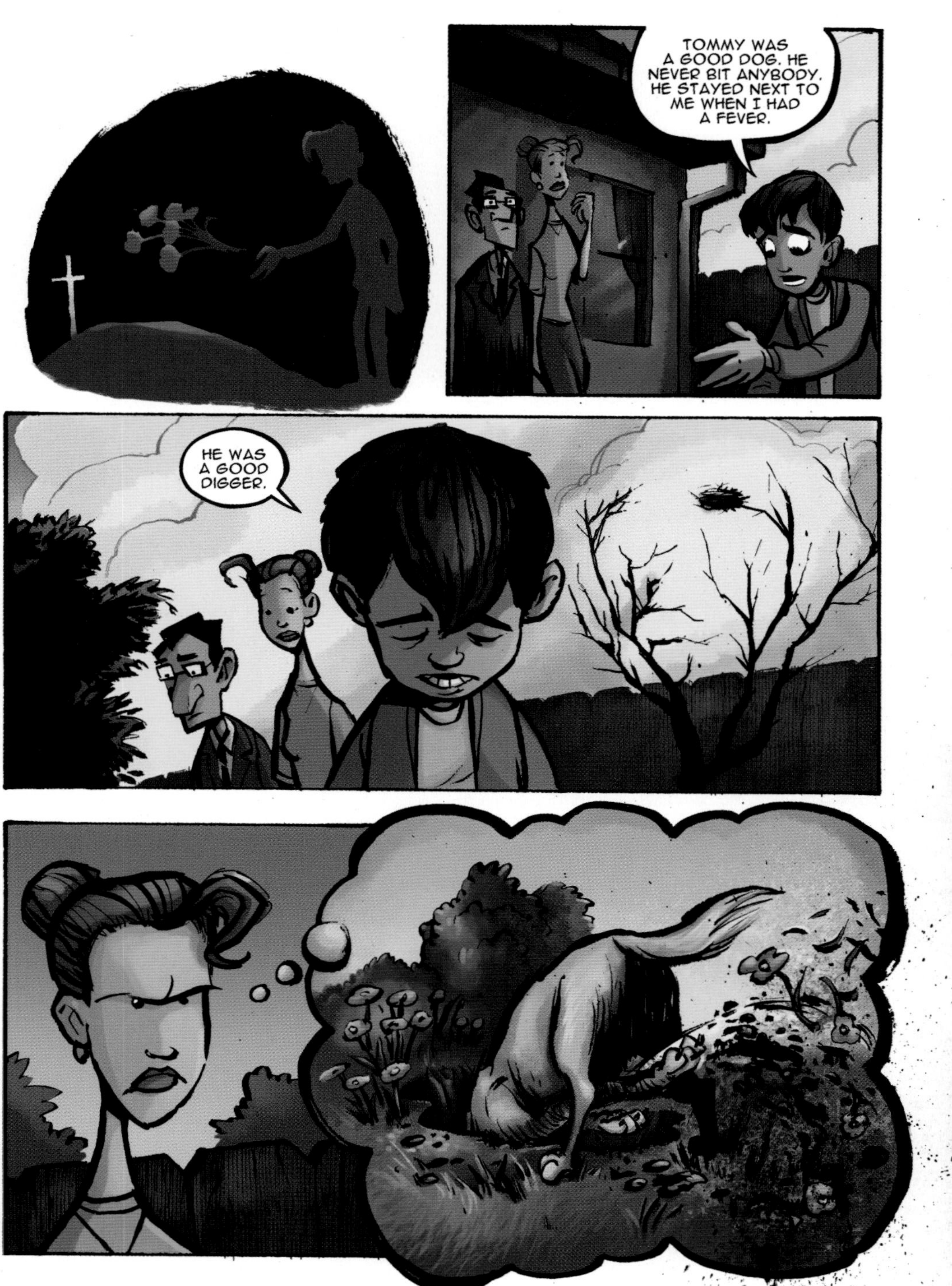
TOMMY WAS A GOOD DOG. HE NEVER BIT ANYBODY. HE STAYED NEXT TO ME WHEN I HAD A FEVER.
HE WAS A GOOD DIGGER.

HOW'S IT GOING, SON?

I SHOULD HAVE HELD HIS LEASH TIGHTER! HE'D STILL BE ALIVE!

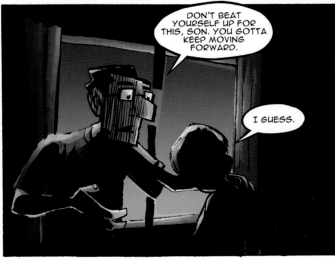

DON'T BEAT YOURSELF UP FOR THIS, SON. YOU GOTTA KEEP MOVING FORWARD.

I GUESS.

I HAVE A SURPRISE FOR YOU.

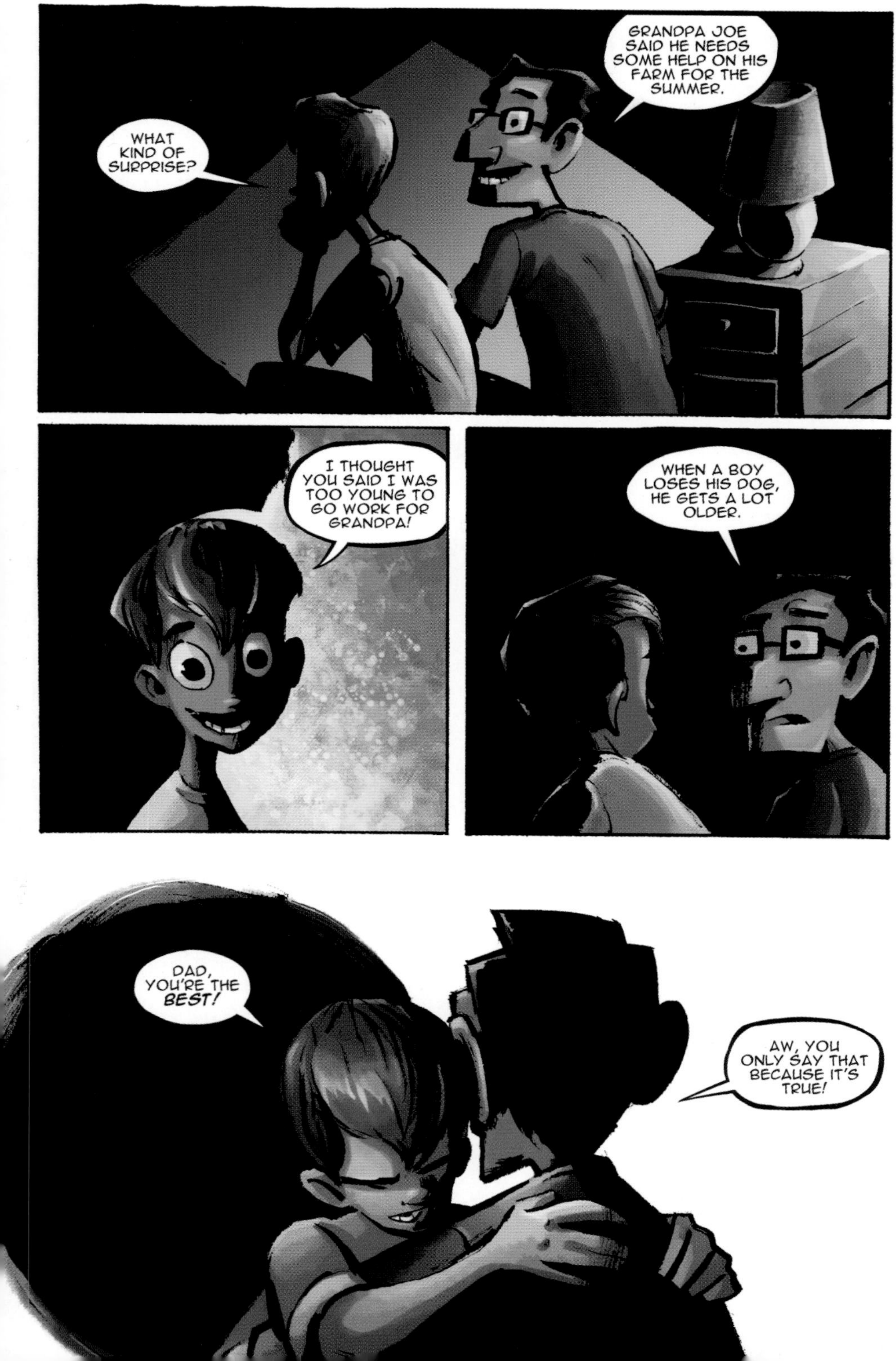
GRANDPA JOE SAID HE NEEDS SOME HELP ON HIS FARM FOR THE SUMMER.
WHAT KIND OF SURPRISE?
I THOUGHT YOU SAID I WAS TOO YOUNG TO GO WORK FOR GRANDPA!
WHEN A BOY LOSES HIS DOG, HE GETS A LOT OLDER.
DAD, YOU'RE THE *BEST!*
AW, YOU ONLY SAY THAT BECAUSE IT'S TRUE!

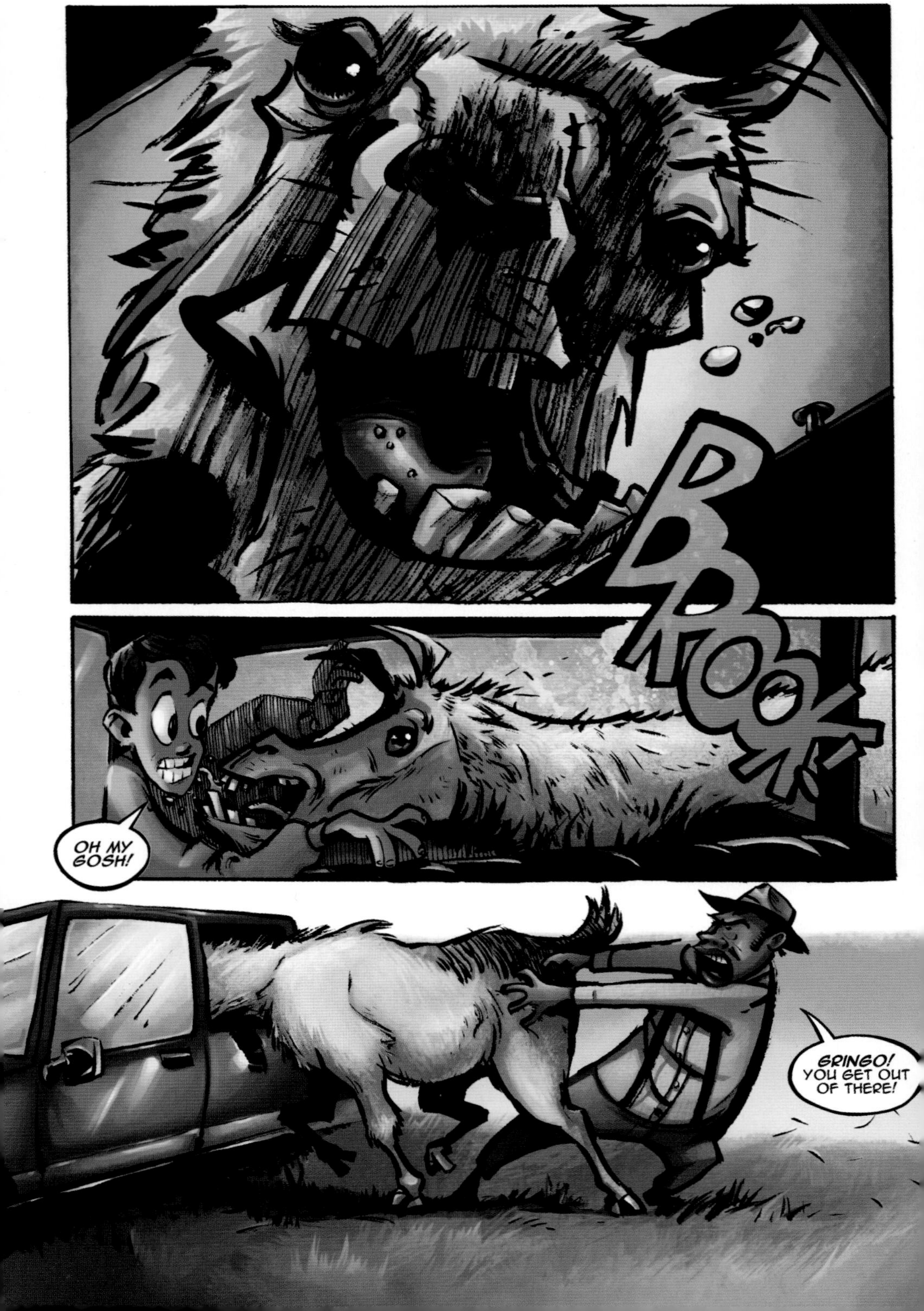

BROOK
OH MY GOSH!
GRINGO! YOU GET OUT OF THERE!

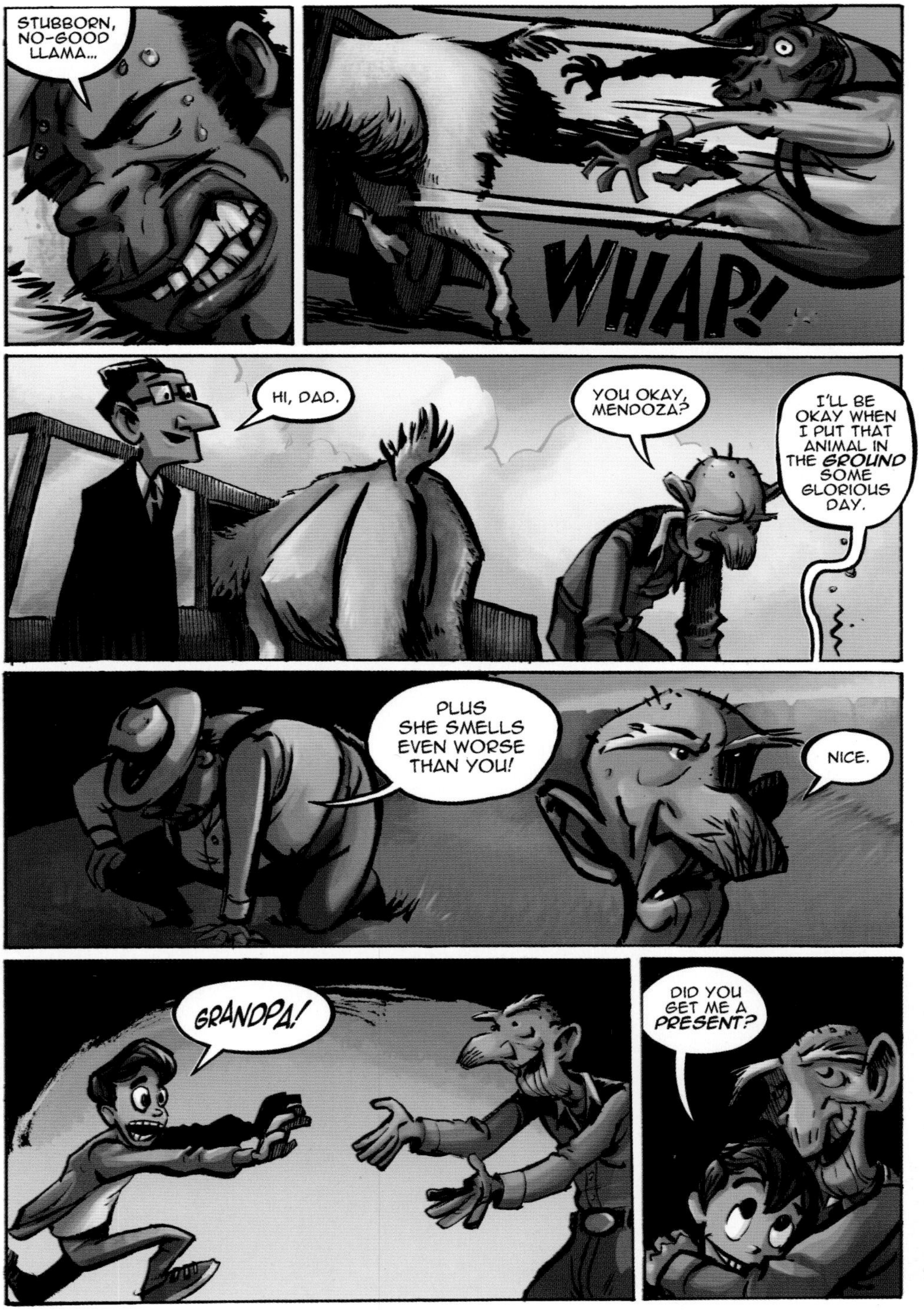
STUBBORN, NO-GOOD LLAMA...
WHAP!
HI, DAD.
YOU OKAY, MENDOZA?
I'LL BE OKAY WHEN I PUT THAT ANIMAL IN THE GROUND SOME GLORIOUS DAY.
PLUS SHE SMELLS EVEN WORSE THAN YOU!
NICE.
GRANDPA!
DID YOU GET ME A PRESENT?

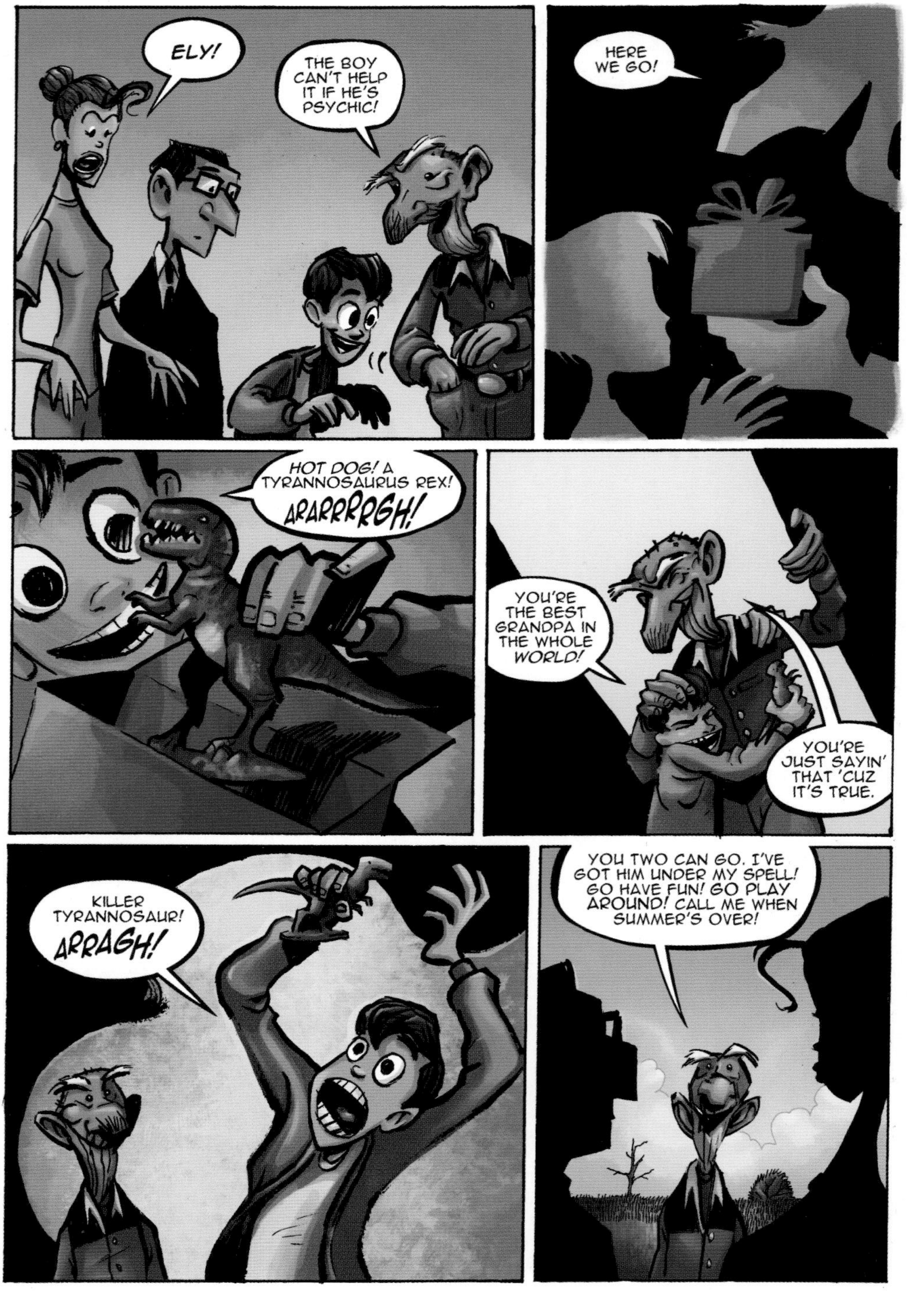
ELY!
THE BOY CAN'T HELP IT IF HE'S PSYCHIC!
HERE WE GO!
HOT DOG! A TYRANNOSAURUS REX! ARARRRRGH!
YOU'RE THE BEST GRANDPA IN THE WHOLE WORLD!
YOU'RE JUST SAYIN' THAT 'CUZ IT'S TRUE.
KILLER TYRANNOSAUR! ARRAGH!
YOU TWO CAN GO. I'VE GOT HIM UNDER MY SPELL! GO HAVE FUN! GO PLAY AROUND! CALL ME WHEN SUMMER'S OVER!

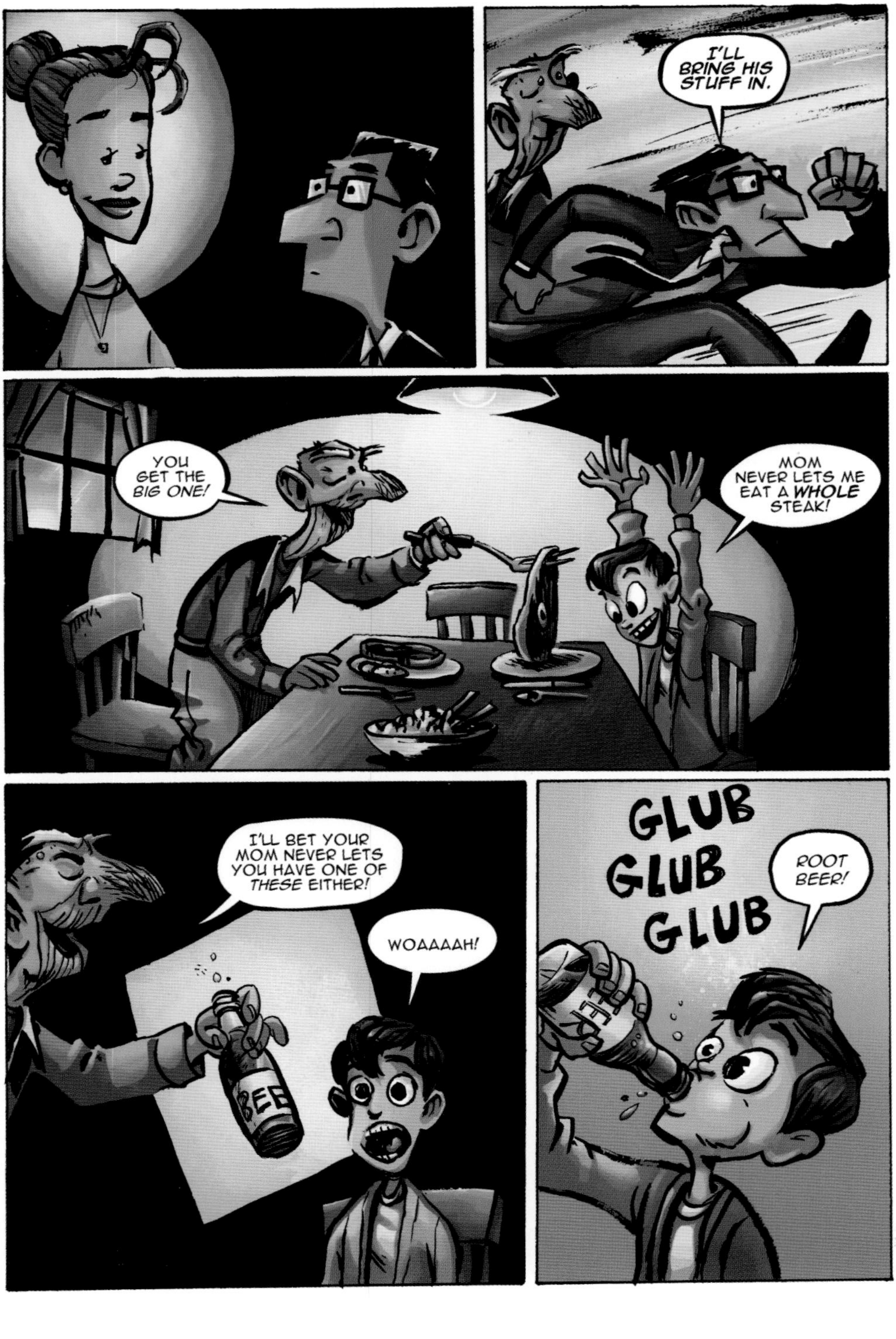
I'LL BRING HIS STUFF IN.
YOU GET THE BIG ONE!
MOM NEVER LETS ME EAT A WHOLE STEAK!
I'LL BET YOUR MOM NEVER LETS YOU HAVE ONE OF THESE EITHER!
WOAAAAH!
GLUB GLUB GLUB
ROOT BEER!

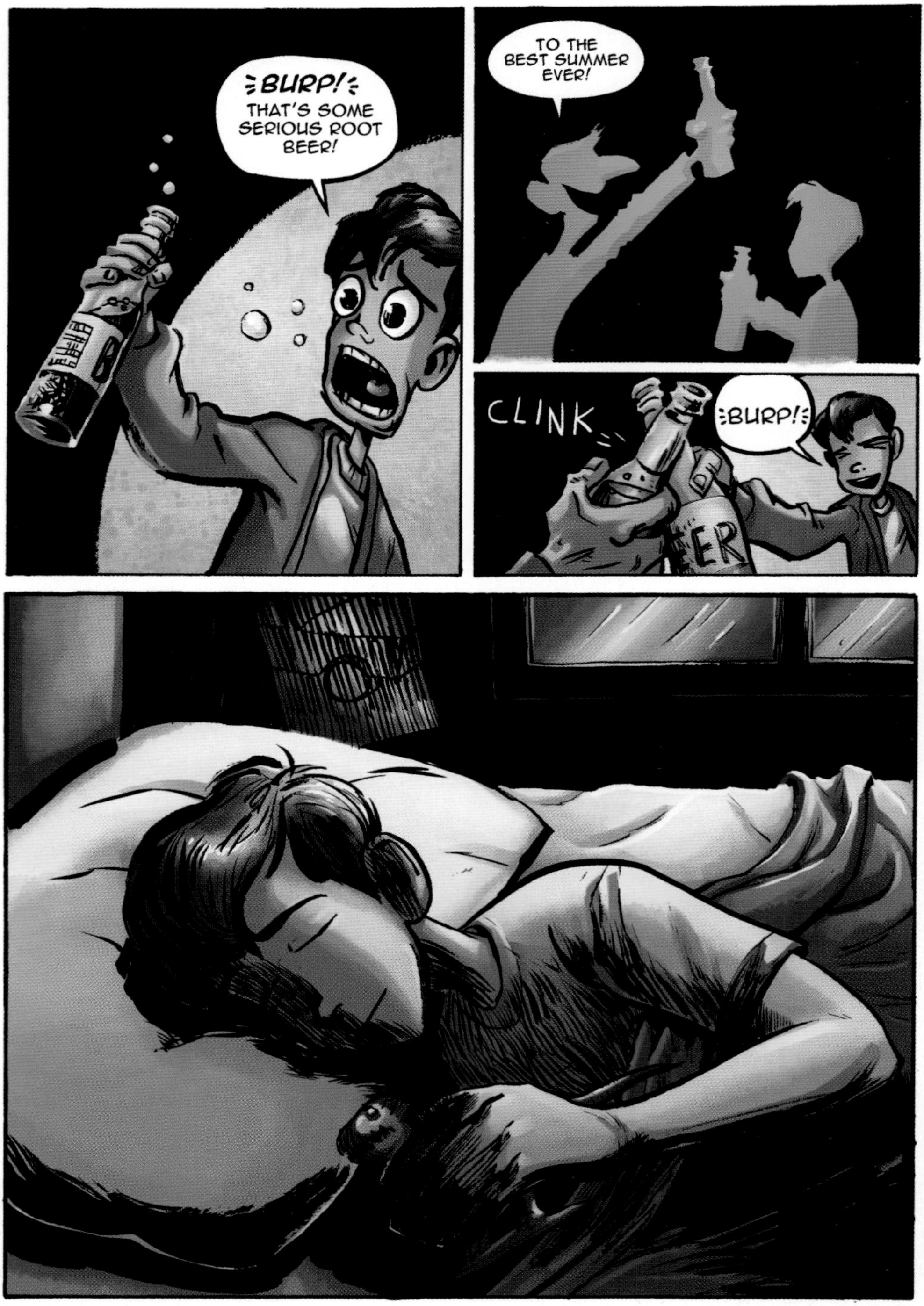
BURP!
THAT'S SOME SERIOUS ROOT BEER!
TO THE BEST SUMMER EVER!
CLINK
BURP!
ER

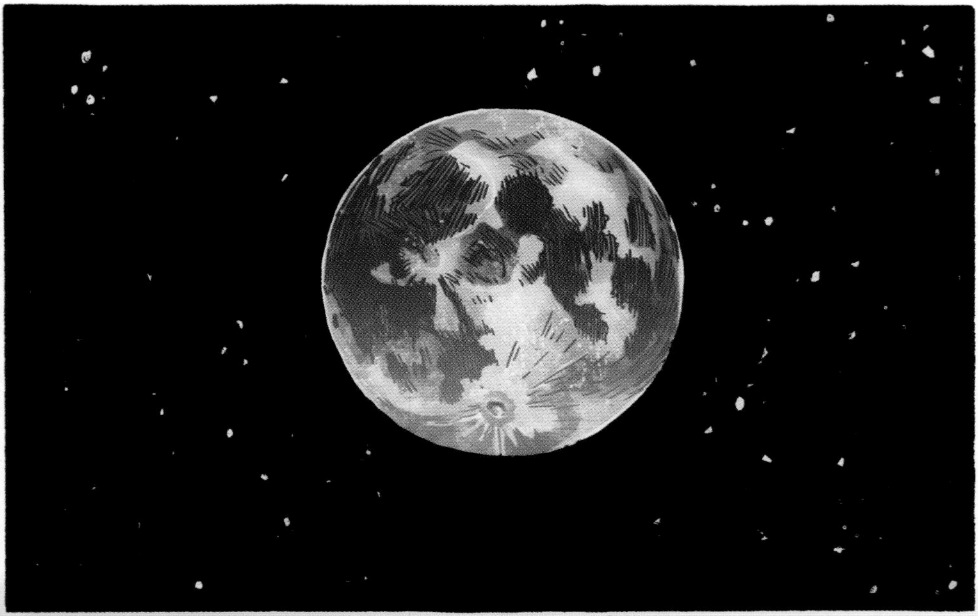

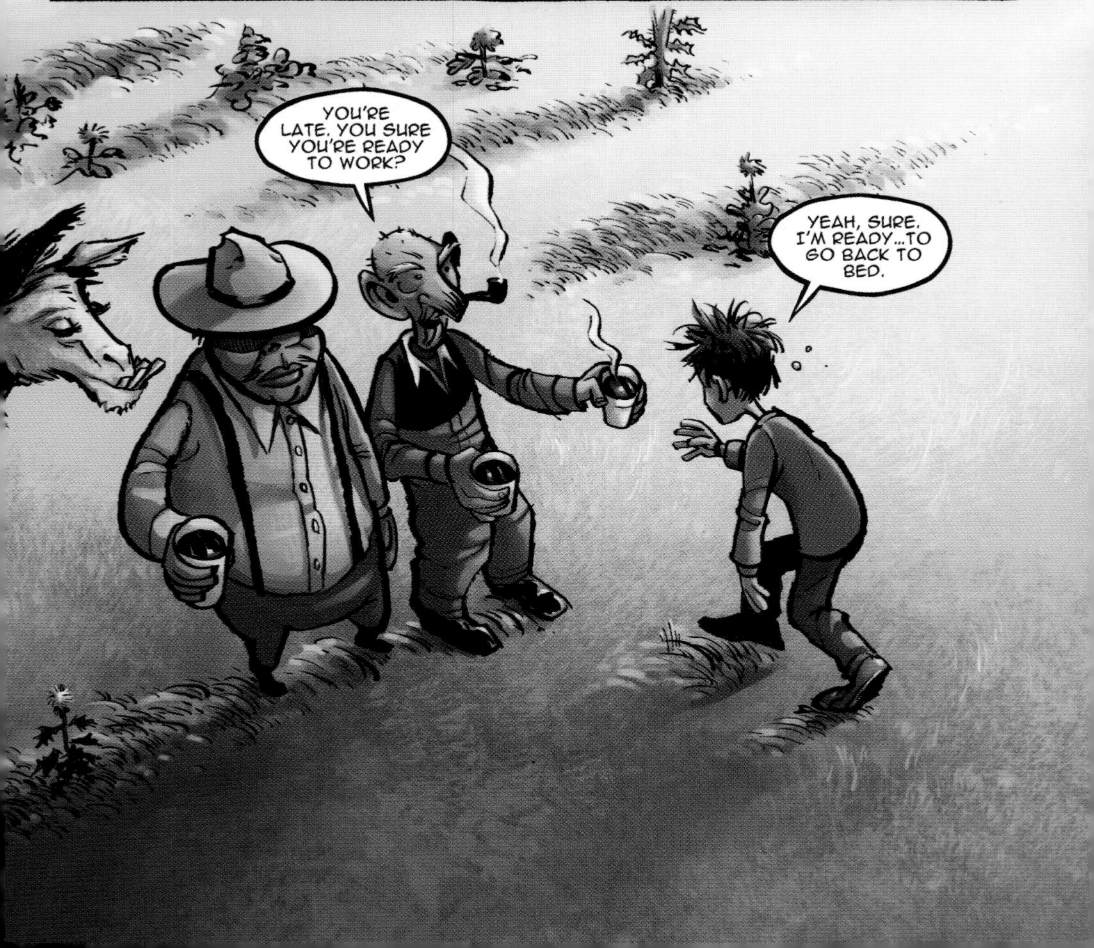
YOU'RE LATE. YOU SURE YOU'RE READY TO WORK?
YEAH, SURE. I'M READY...TO GO BACK TO BED.

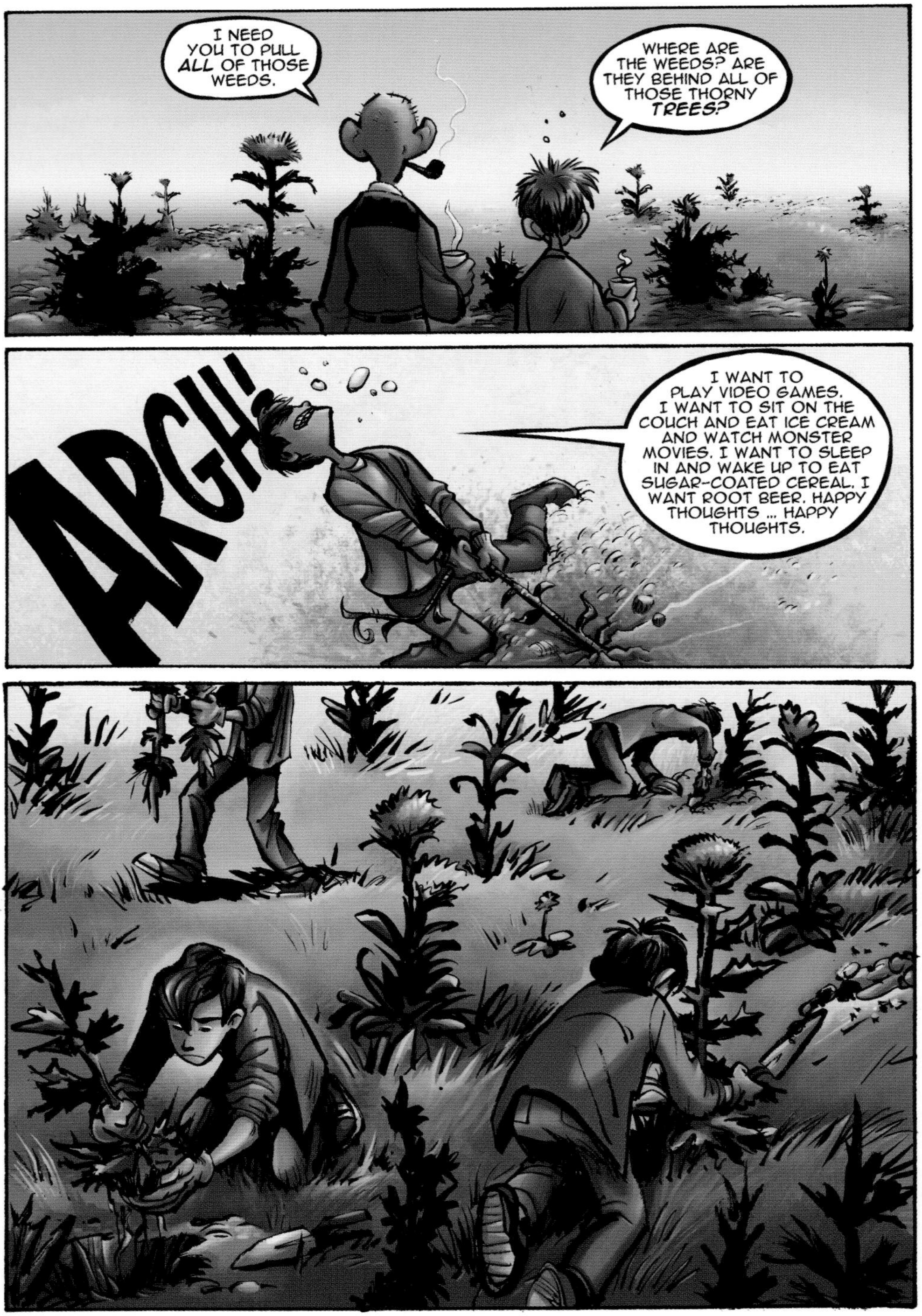
I NEED YOU TO PULL ALL OF THOSE WEEDS.
WHERE ARE THE WEEDS? ARE THEY BEHIND ALL OF THOSE THORNY TREES?
ARGH!
I WANT TO PLAY VIDEO GAMES. I WANT TO SIT ON THE COUCH AND EAT ICE CREAM AND WATCH MONSTER MOVIES. I WANT TO SLEEP IN AND WAKE UP TO EAT SUGAR-COATED CEREAL. I WANT ROOT BEER. HAPPY THOUGHTS ... HAPPY THOUGHTS.

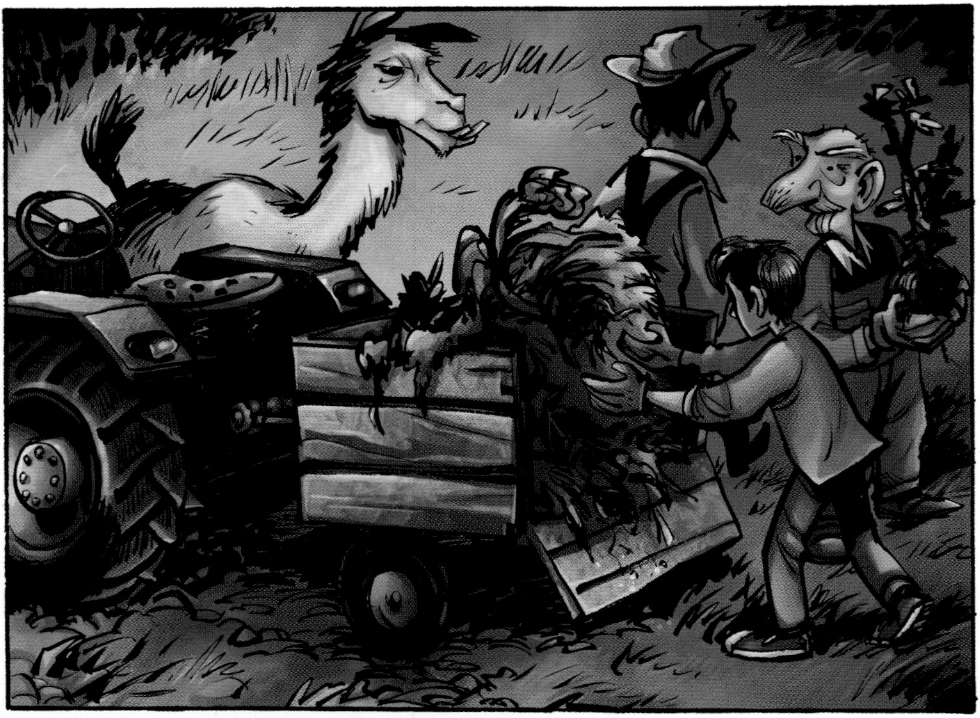

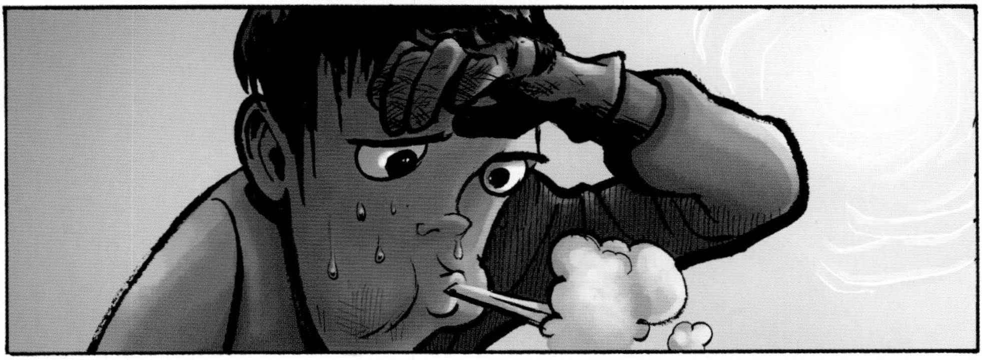

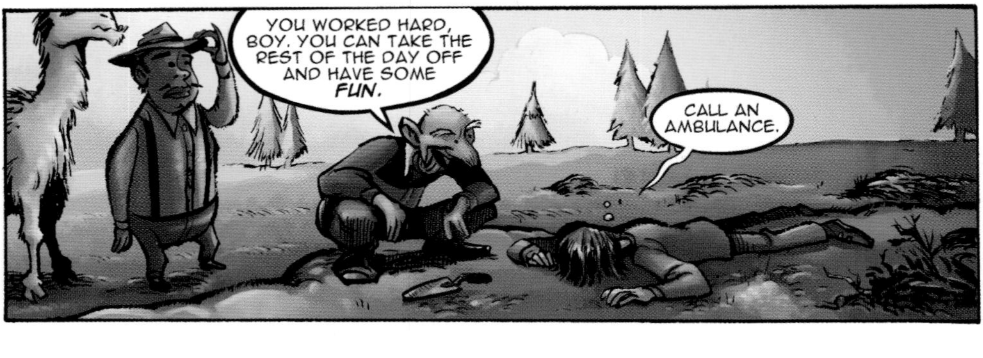
YOU WORKED HARD, BOY. YOU CAN TAKE THE REST OF THE DAY OFF AND HAVE SOME FUN.
CALL AN AMBULANCE.

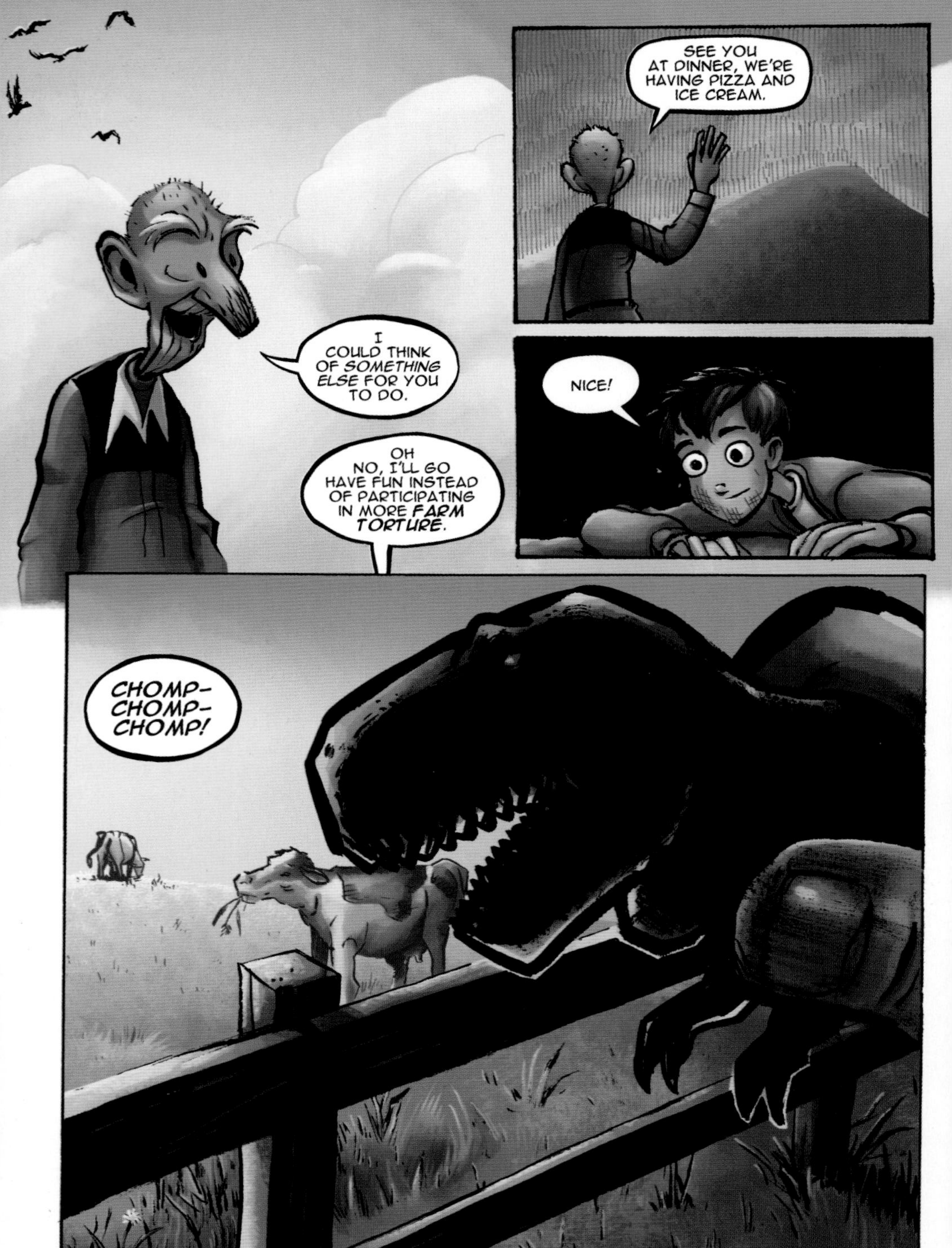
SEE YOU AT DINNER, WE'RE HAVING PIZZA AND ICE CREAM.
NICE!
I COULD THINK OF *SOMETHING ELSE* FOR YOU TO DO.
OH NO, I'LL GO HAVE FUN INSTEAD OF PARTICIPATING IN MORE ***FARM TORTURE***.
CHOMP-CHOMP-CHOMP!

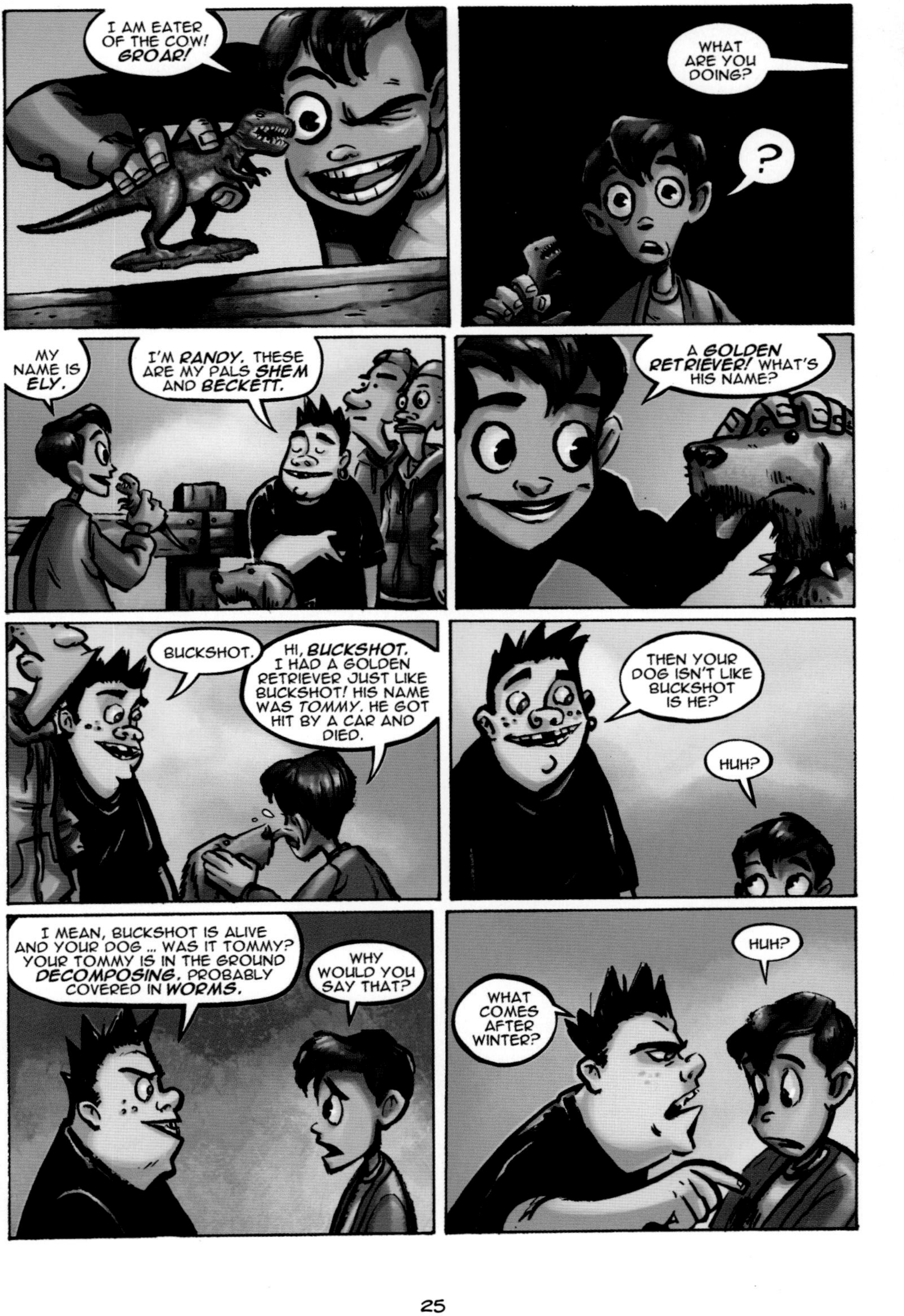
I AM EATER OF THE COW! GROAR!
WHAT ARE YOU DOING?
?
MY NAME IS ELY.
I'M RANDY. THESE ARE MY PALS SHEM AND BECKETT.
A GOLDEN RETRIEVER! WHAT'S HIS NAME?
BUCKSHOT.
HI, BUCKSHOT. I HAD A GOLDEN RETRIEVER JUST LIKE BUCKSHOT! HIS NAME WAS TOMMY. HE GOT HIT BY A CAR AND DIED.
THEN YOUR DOG ISN'T LIKE BUCKSHOT IS HE?
HUH?
I MEAN, BUCKSHOT IS ALIVE AND YOUR DOG ... WAS IT TOMMY? YOUR TOMMY IS IN THE GROUND DECOMPOSING, PROBABLY COVERED IN WORMS.
WHY WOULD YOU SAY THAT?
HUH?
WHAT COMES AFTER WINTER?

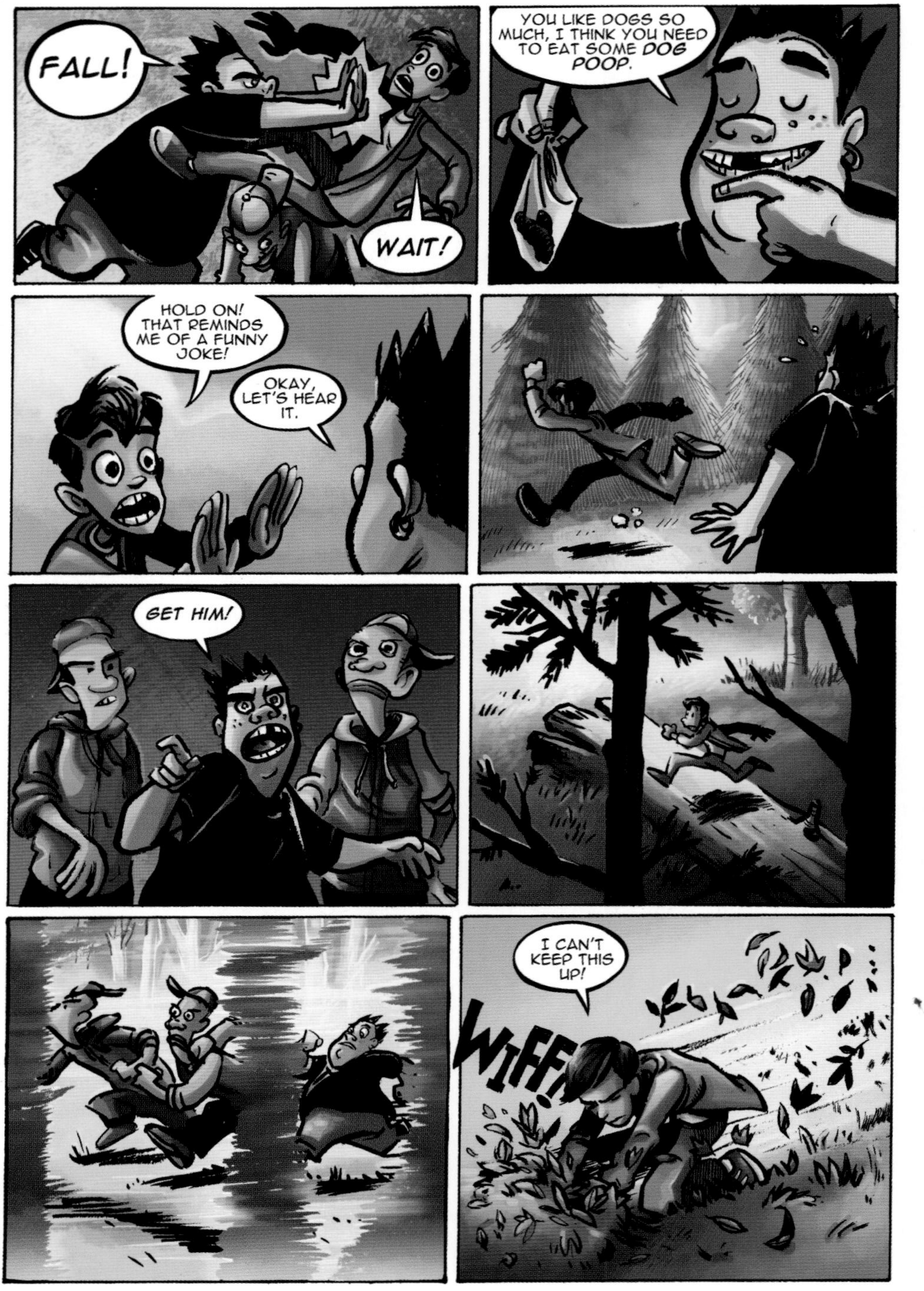
FALL!
WAIT!
YOU LIKE DOGS SO MUCH, I THINK YOU NEED TO EAT SOME DOG POOP.
HOLD ON! THAT REMINDS ME OF A FUNNY JOKE!
OKAY, LET'S HEAR IT.
GET HIM!
I CAN'T KEEP THIS UP!
WIFF!

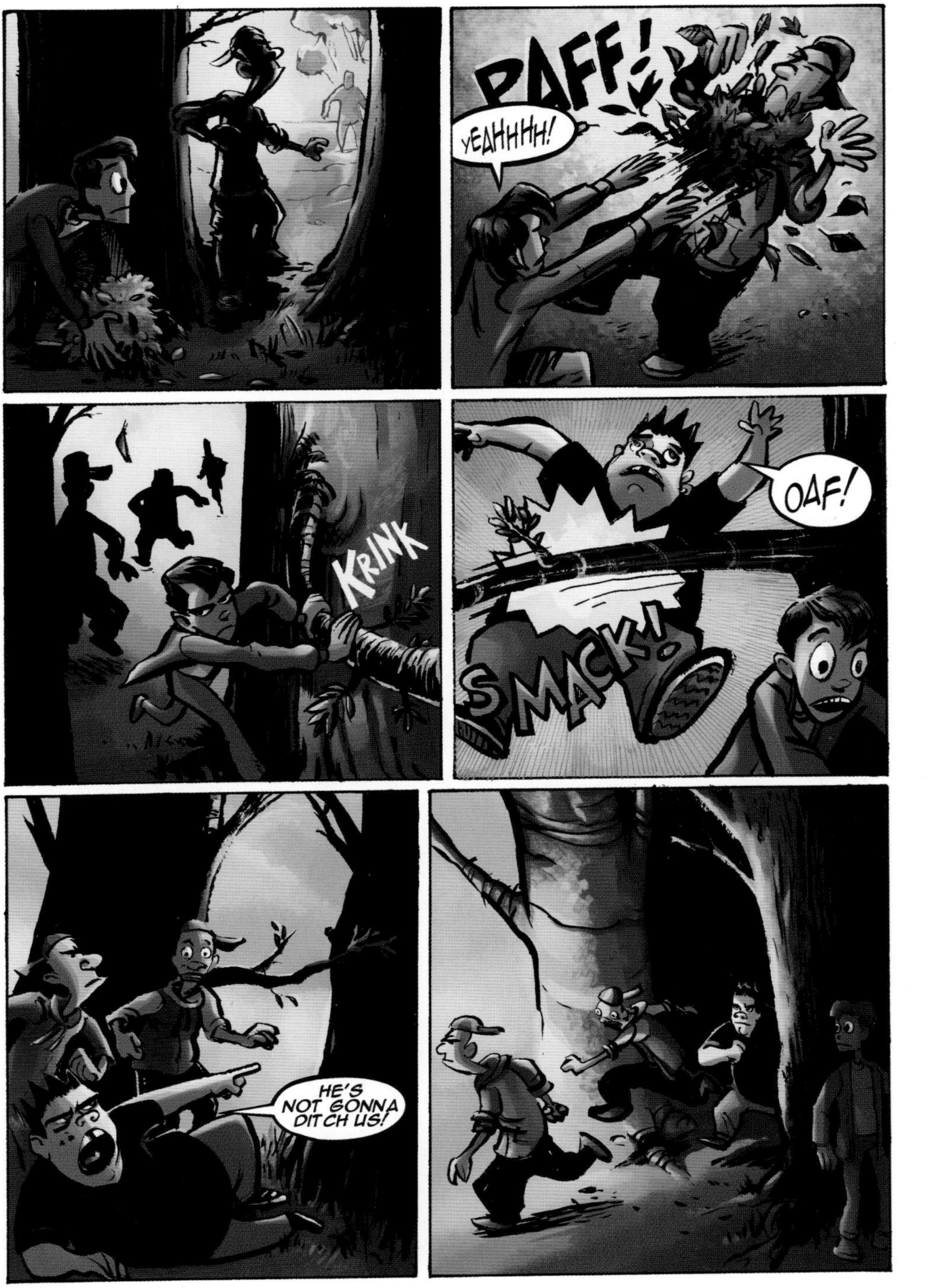
PAFF!
YEAHHHH!
KRINK
OAF!
SMACK!
HE'S NOT GONNA DITCH US!

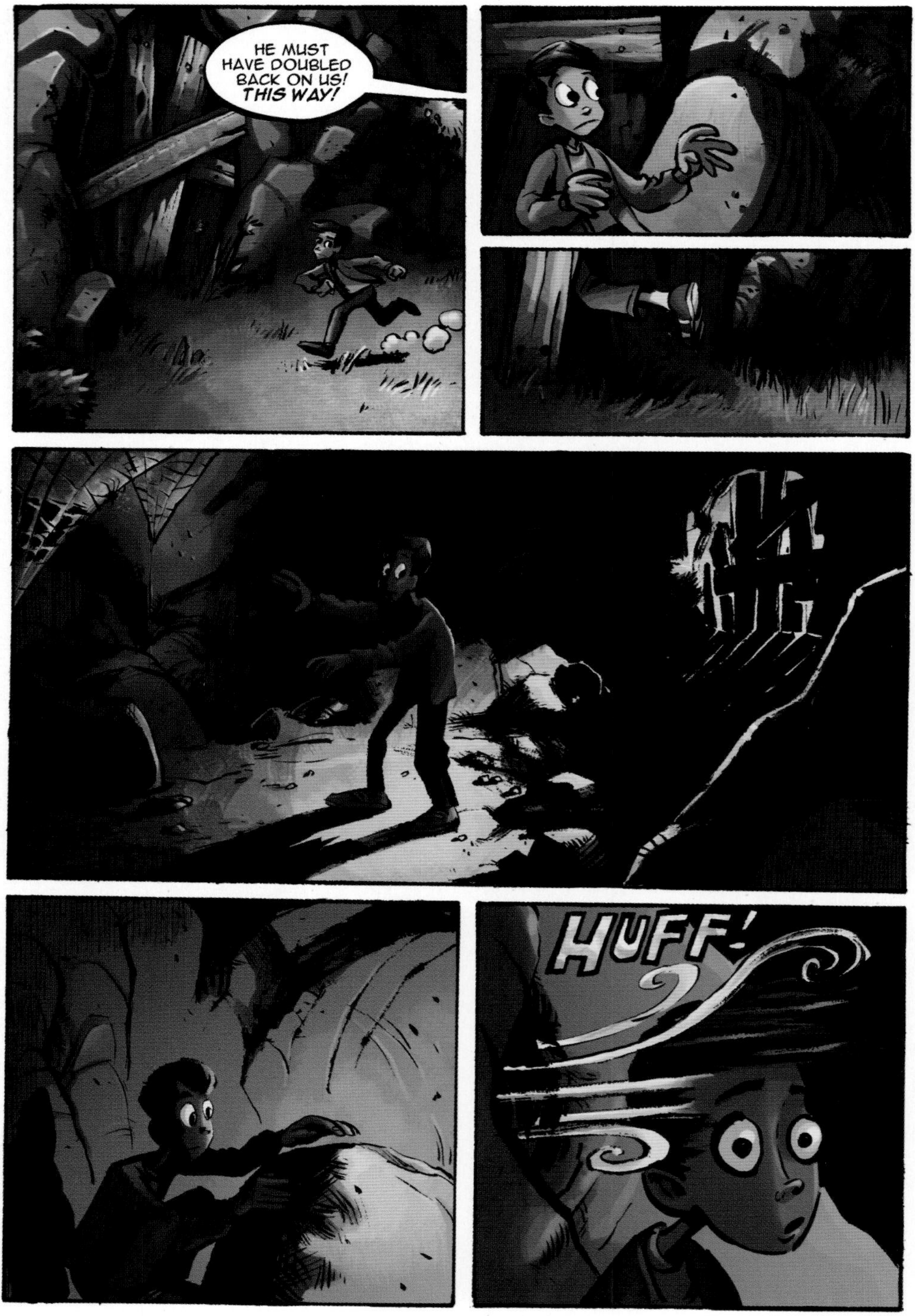
HE MUST HAVE DOUBLED BACK ON US! THIS WAY!
HUFF!

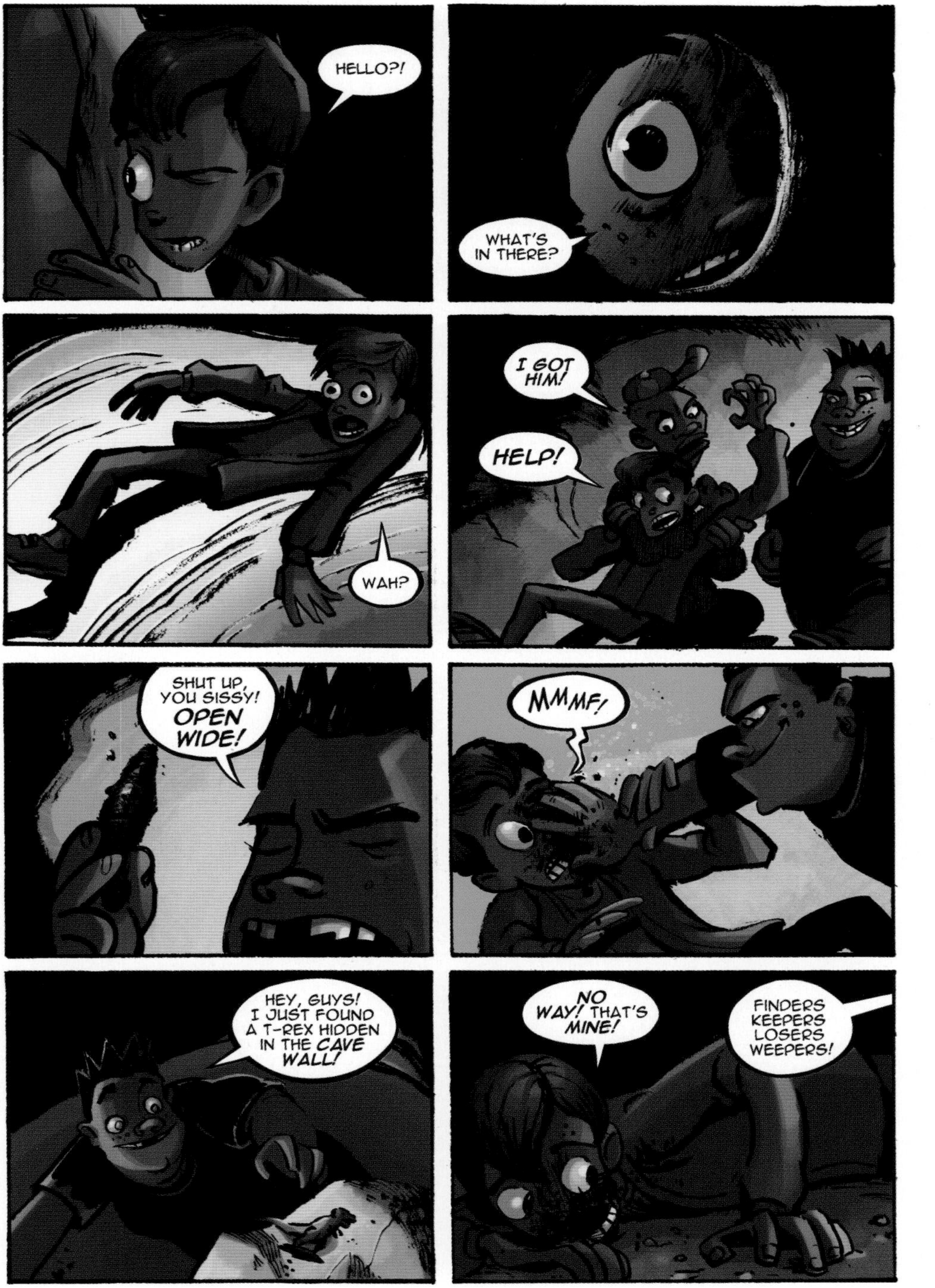
HELLO?!
WHAT'S IN THERE?
WAH?
I GOT HIM!
HELP!
SHUT UP, YOU SISSY! OPEN WIDE!
MMMF!
HEY, GUYS! I JUST FOUND A T-REX HIDDEN IN THE CAVE WALL!
NO WAY! THAT'S MINE!
FINDERS KEEPERS LOSERS WEEPERS!

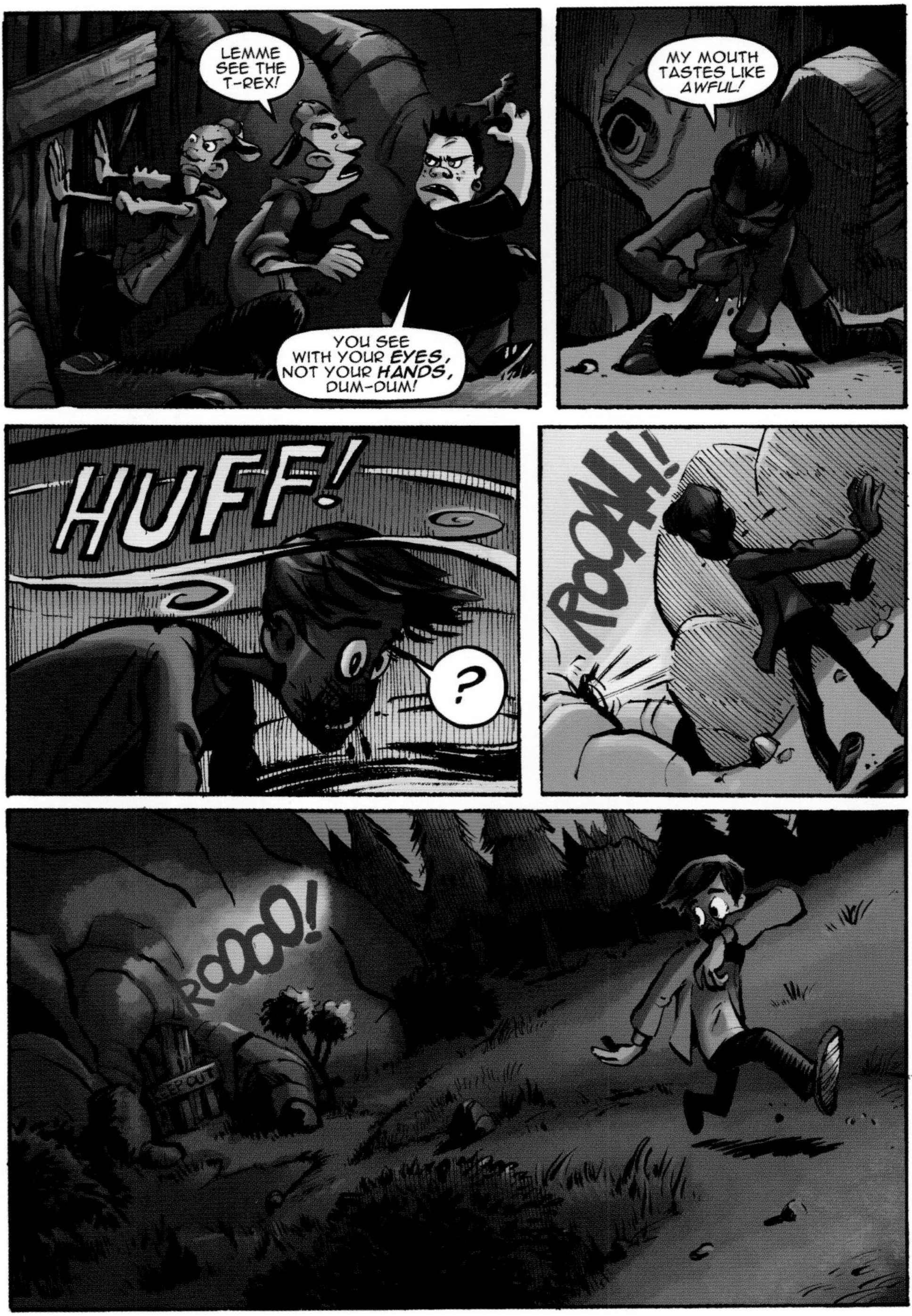
LEMME SEE THE T-REX!
YOU SEE WITH YOUR *EYES*, NOT YOUR *HANDS*, DUM-DUM!
MY MOUTH TASTES LIKE *AWFUL!*
HUFF!
?
ROOAH!
ROOOO!

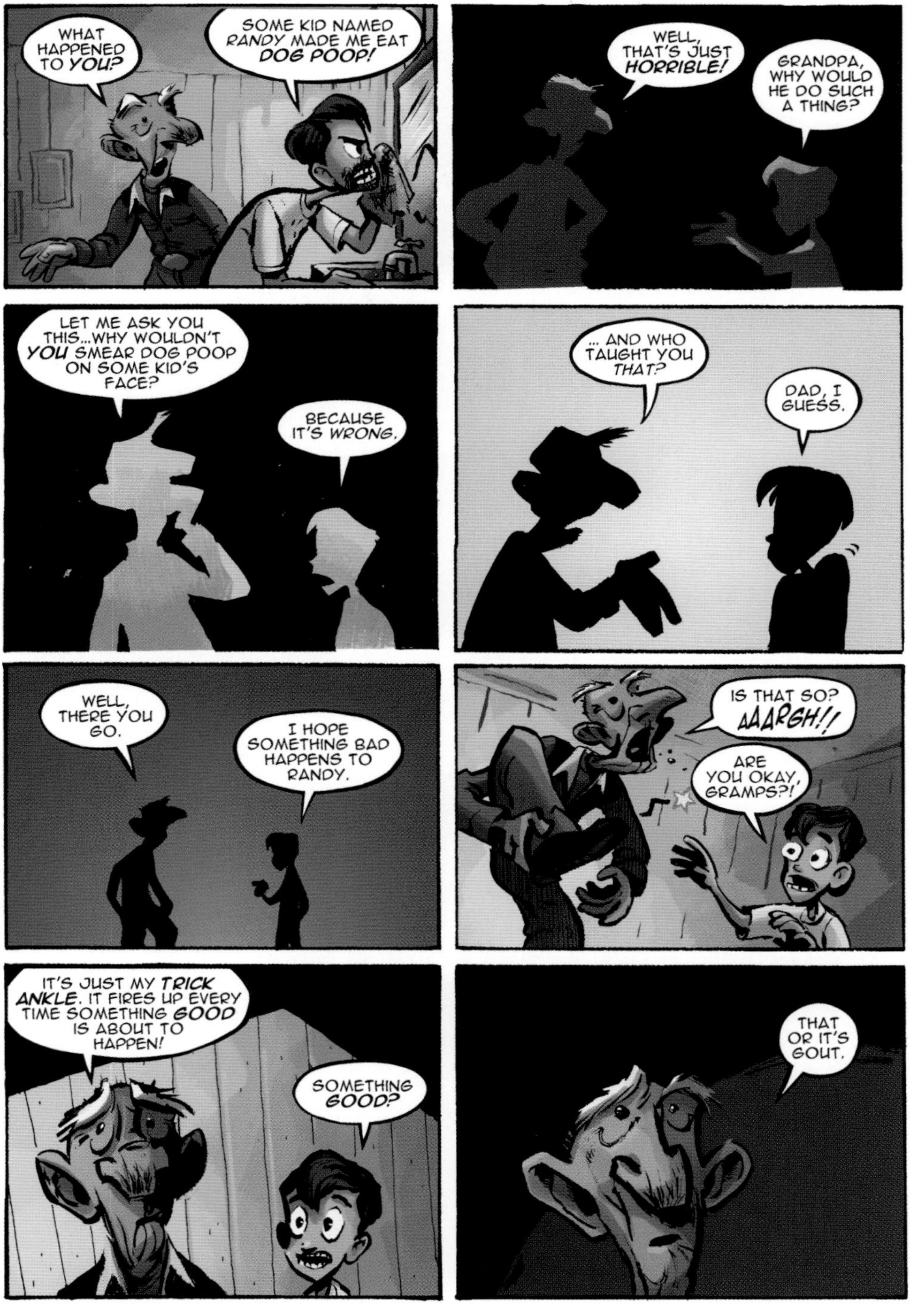
WHAT HAPPENED TO YOU?
SOME KID NAMED RANDY MADE ME EAT DOG POOP!
WELL, THAT'S JUST HORRIBLE!
GRANDPA, WHY WOULD HE DO SUCH A THING?
LET ME ASK YOU THIS...WHY WOULDN'T YOU SMEAR DOG POOP ON SOME KID'S FACE?
BECAUSE IT'S WRONG.
... AND WHO TAUGHT YOU THAT?
DAD, I GUESS.
WELL, THERE YOU GO.
I HOPE SOMETHING BAD HAPPENS TO RANDY.
IS THAT SO? AAARGH!!
ARE YOU OKAY, GRAMPS?!
IT'S JUST MY TRICK ANKLE. IT FIRES UP EVERY TIME SOMETHING GOOD IS ABOUT TO HAPPEN!
SOMETHING GOOD?
THAT OR IT'S GOUT.

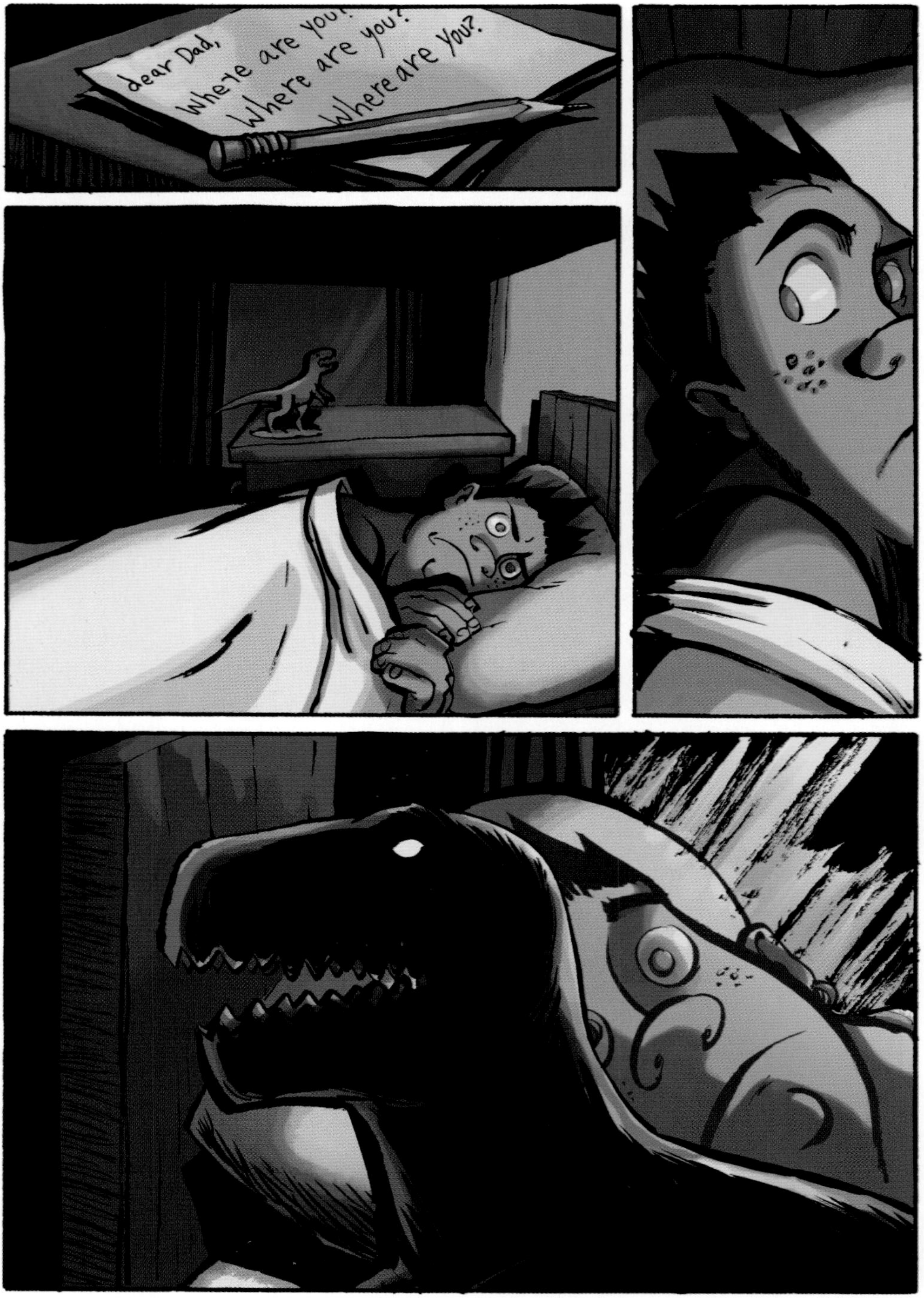
dear Dad,
Where are you?
Where are you?
Where are you?

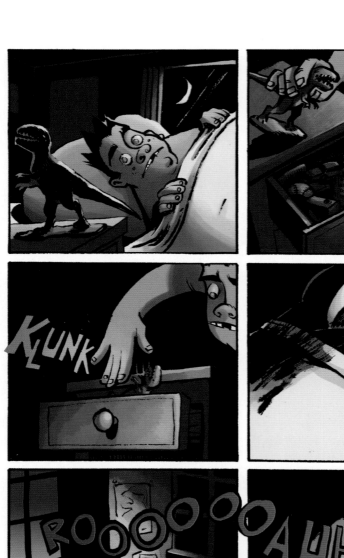

KLUNK

ROOOOOOOAHHH!

TOMMY?

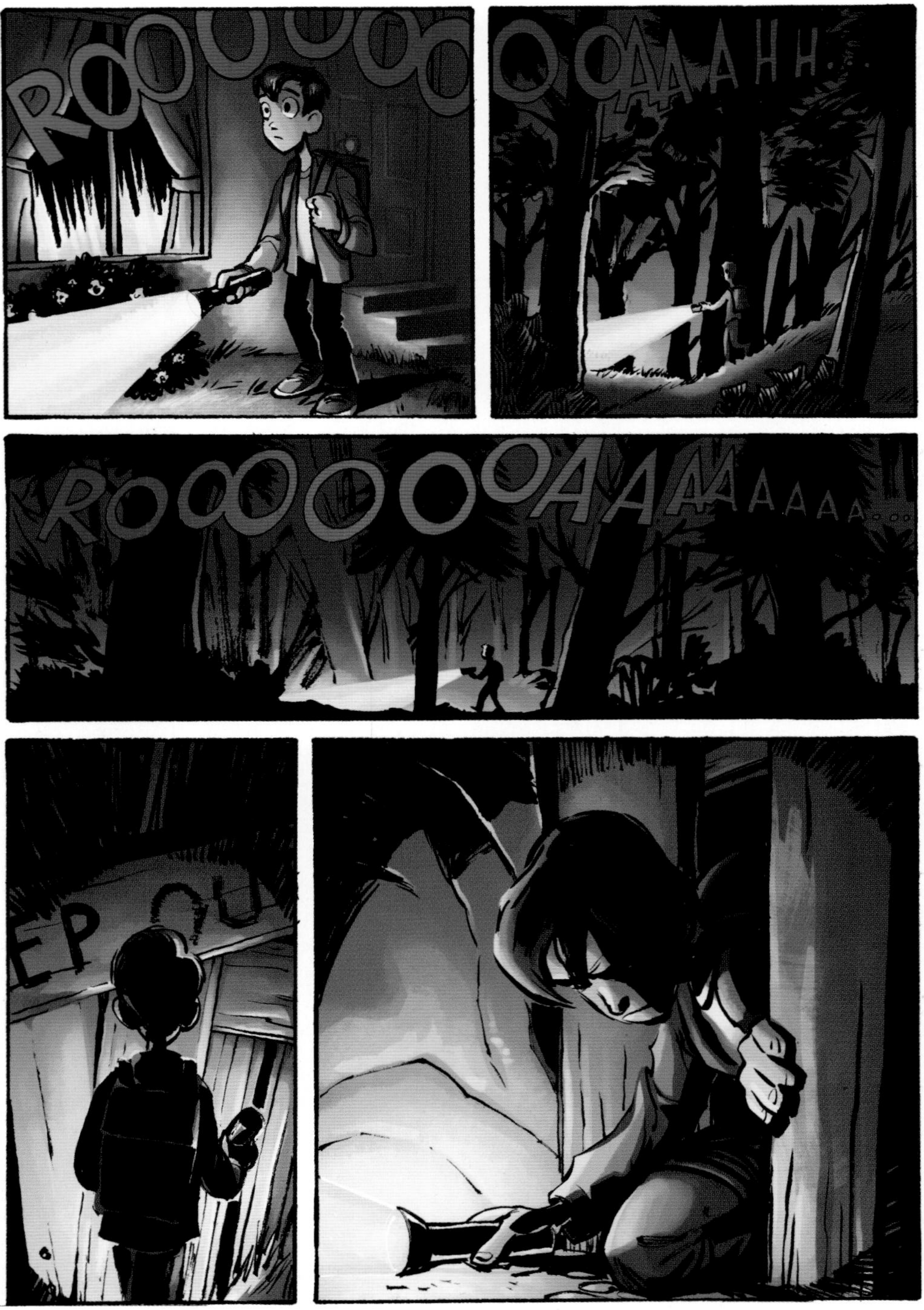
ROOOOOOOOOOAAAAHH...
ROOOOOOAAAAAAA...

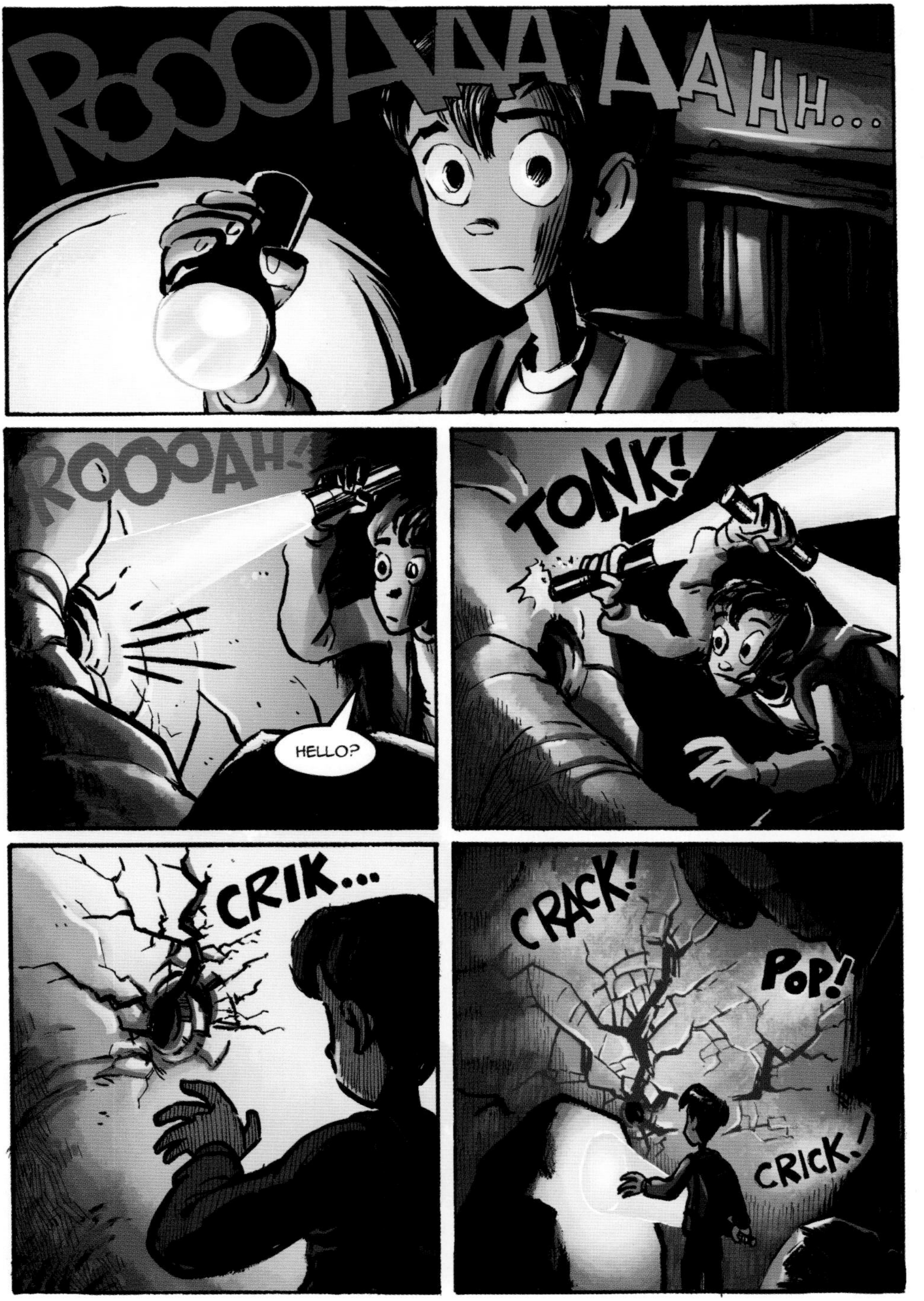
ROOOAAAAAHH...
ROOOAH!!
HELLO?
TONK!
CRIK...
CRACK!
POP!
CRICK!

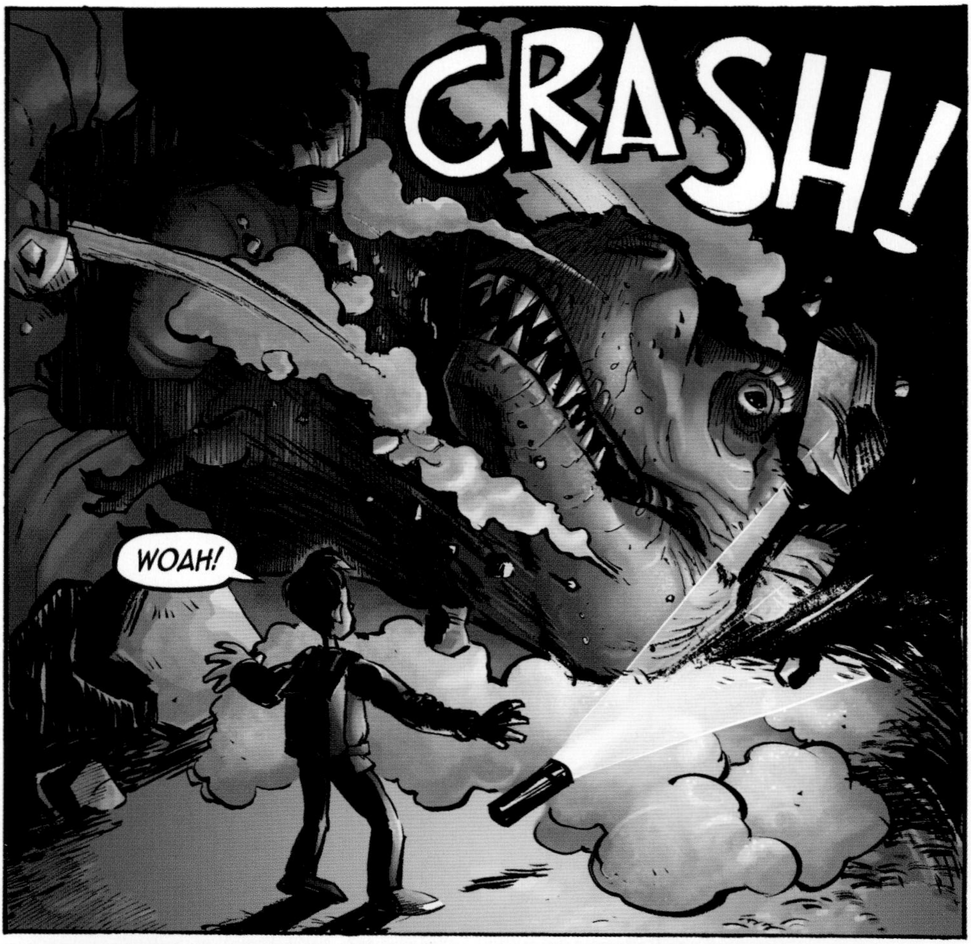
CRASH!
WOAH!

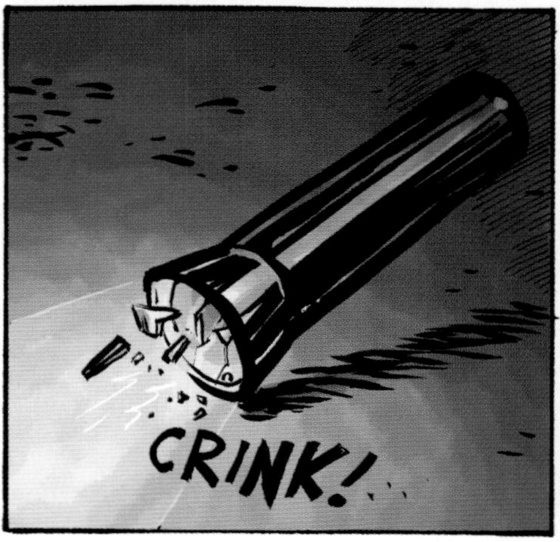
CRINK!

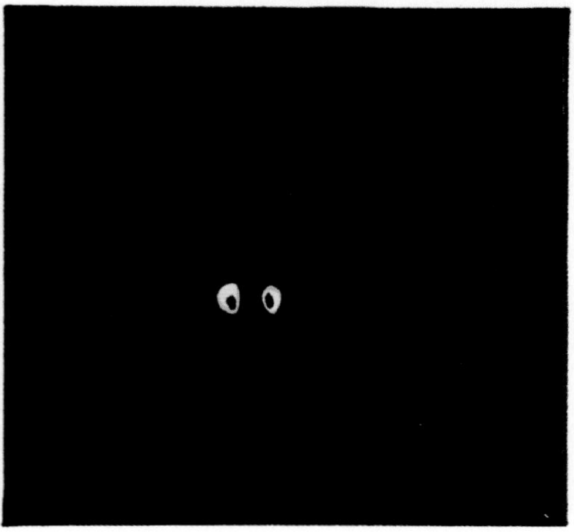

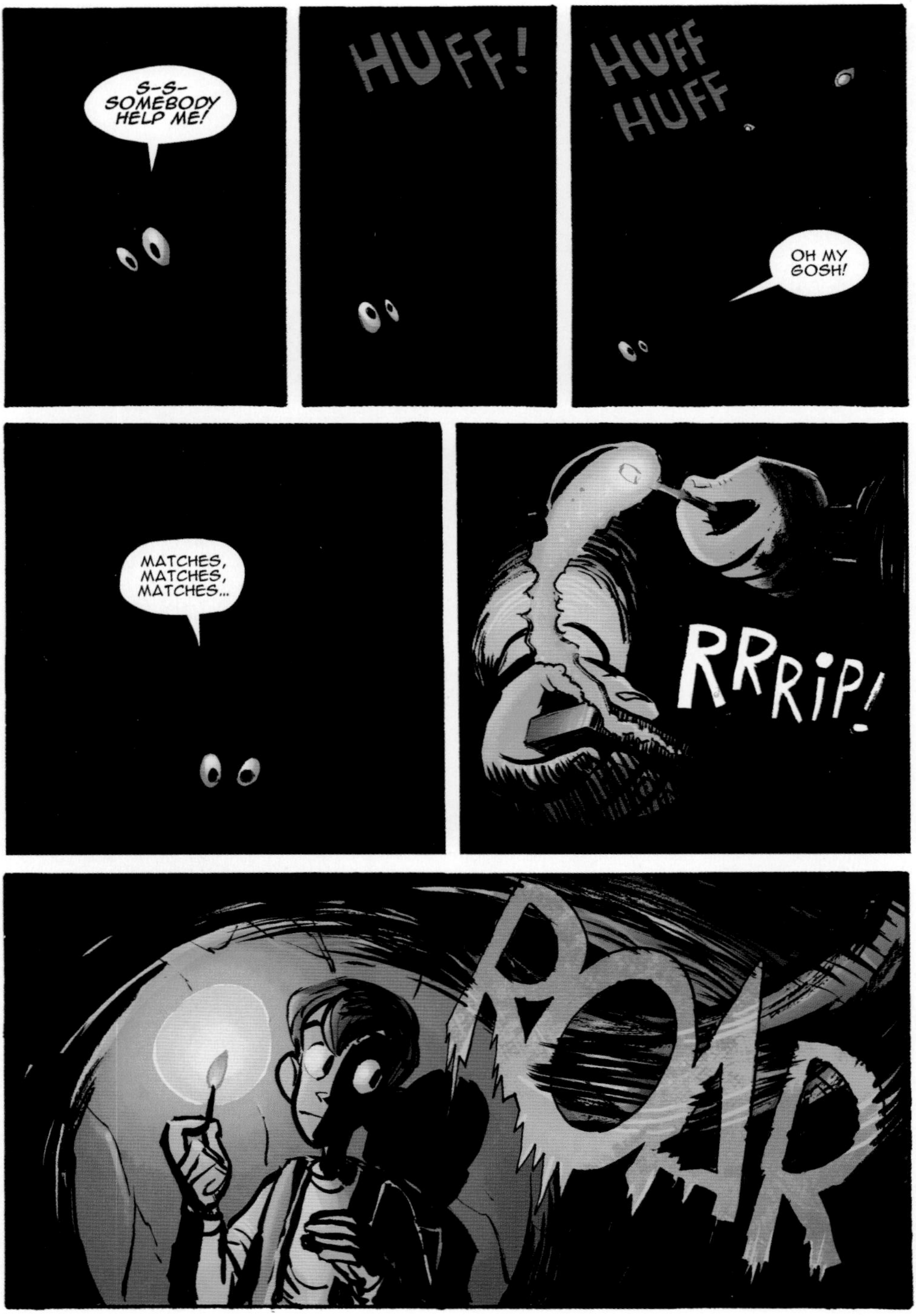
S-S-SOMEBODY HELP ME!
HUFF!
HUFF HUFF
OH MY GOSH!
MATCHES, MATCHES, MATCHES...
RRRIP!
ROAR

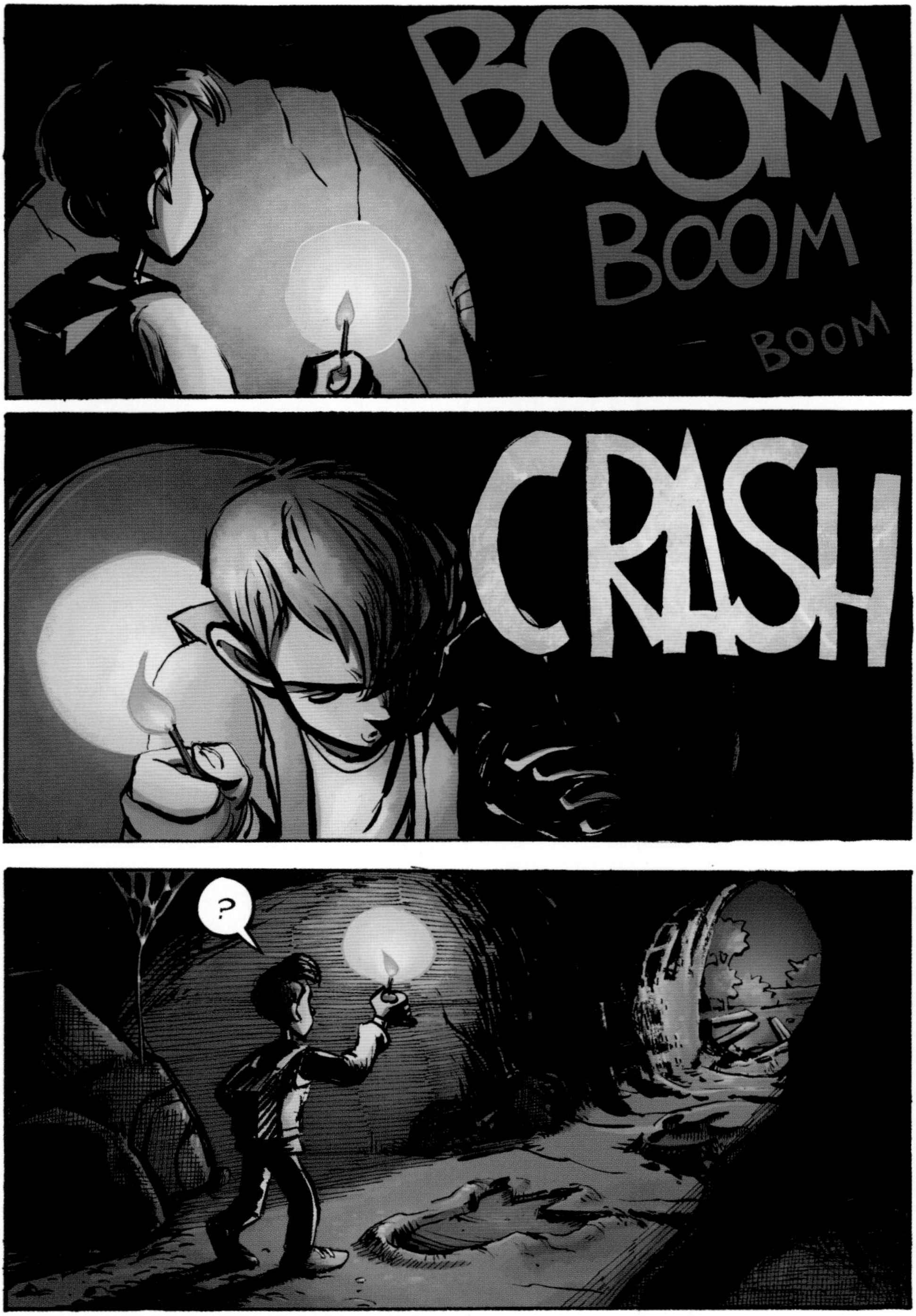
BOOM
BOOM
BOOM
CRASH
?

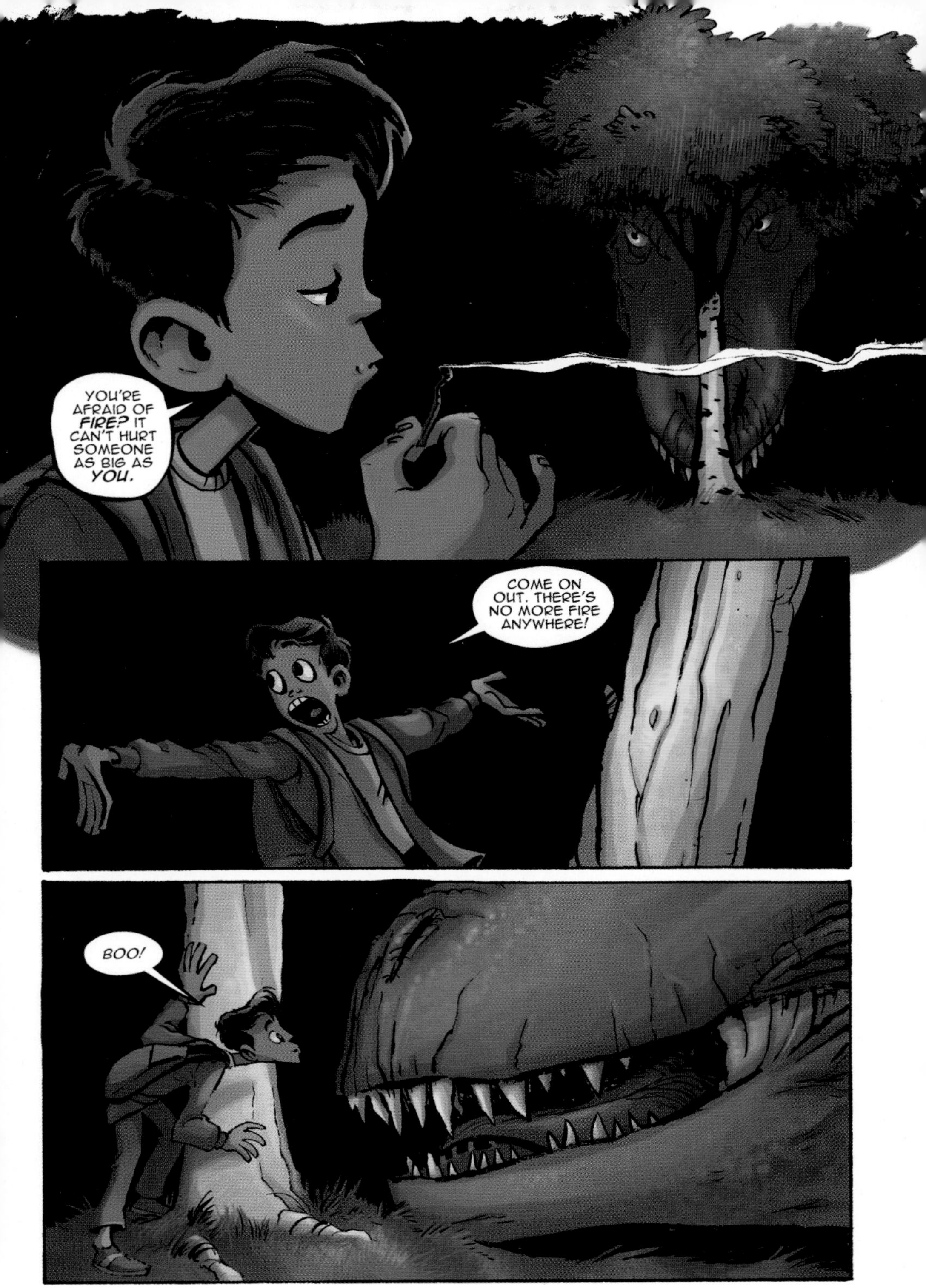
YOU'RE AFRAID OF FIRE? IT CAN'T HURT SOMEONE AS BIG AS YOU.
COME ON OUT. THERE'S NO MORE FIRE ANYWHERE!
BOO!

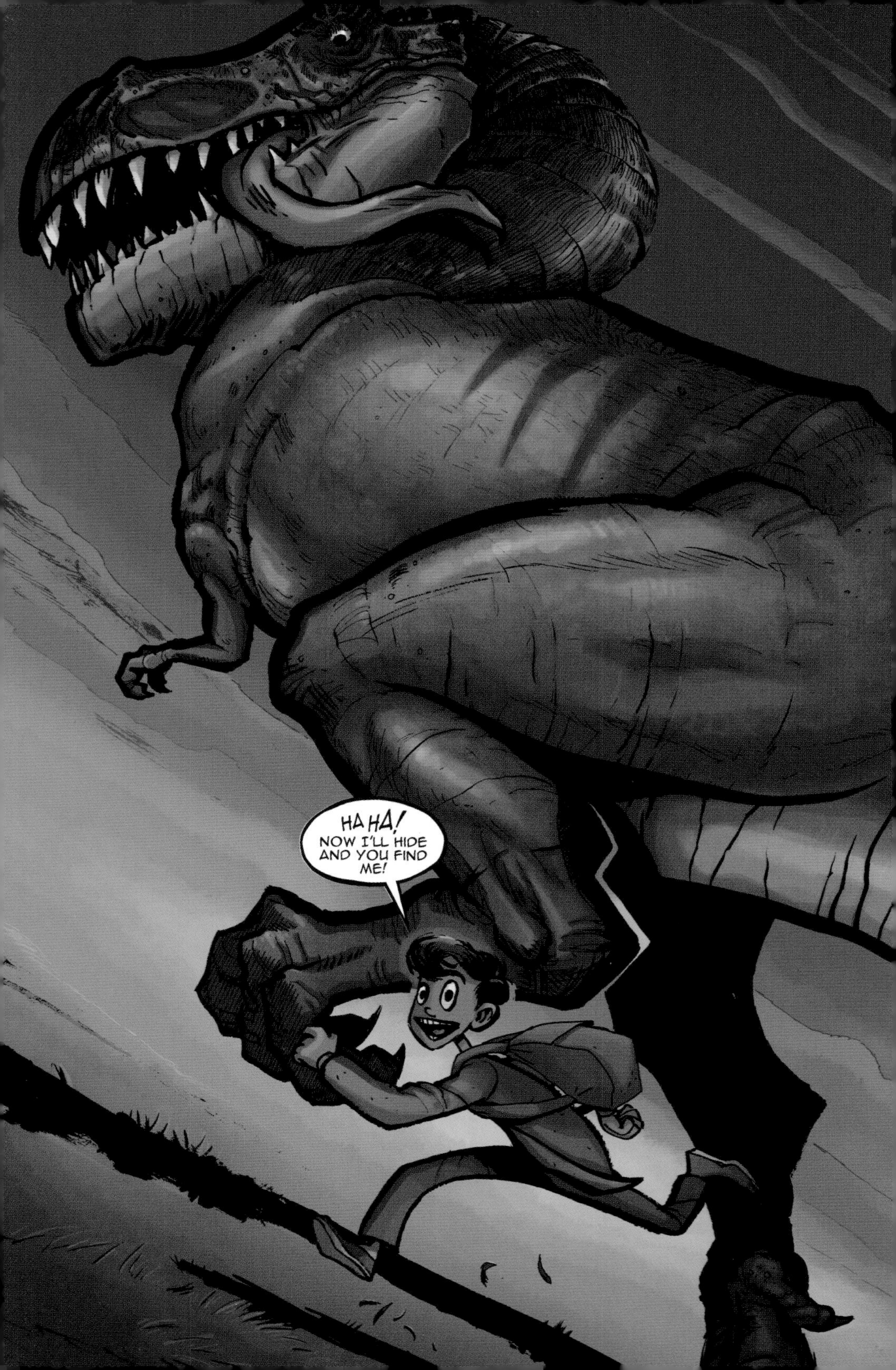
HA HA! NOW I'LL HIDE AND YOU FIND ME!

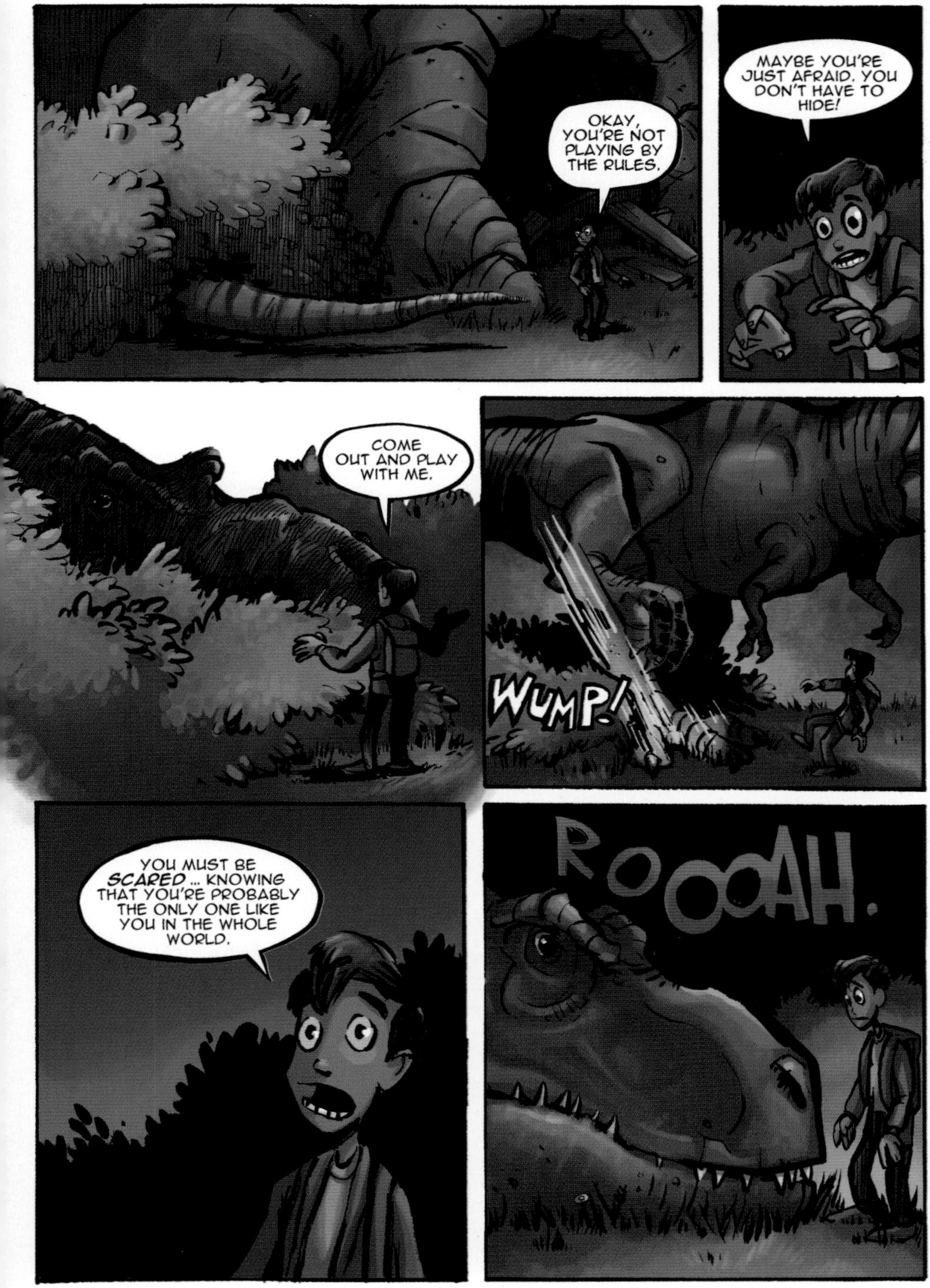
OKAY, YOU'RE NOT PLAYING BY THE RULES.
MAYBE YOU'RE JUST AFRAID. YOU DON'T HAVE TO HIDE!
COME OUT AND PLAY WITH ME.
WUMP!
YOU MUST BE SCARED ... KNOWING THAT YOU'RE PROBABLY THE ONLY ONE LIKE YOU IN THE WHOLE WORLD.
ROOOAH.

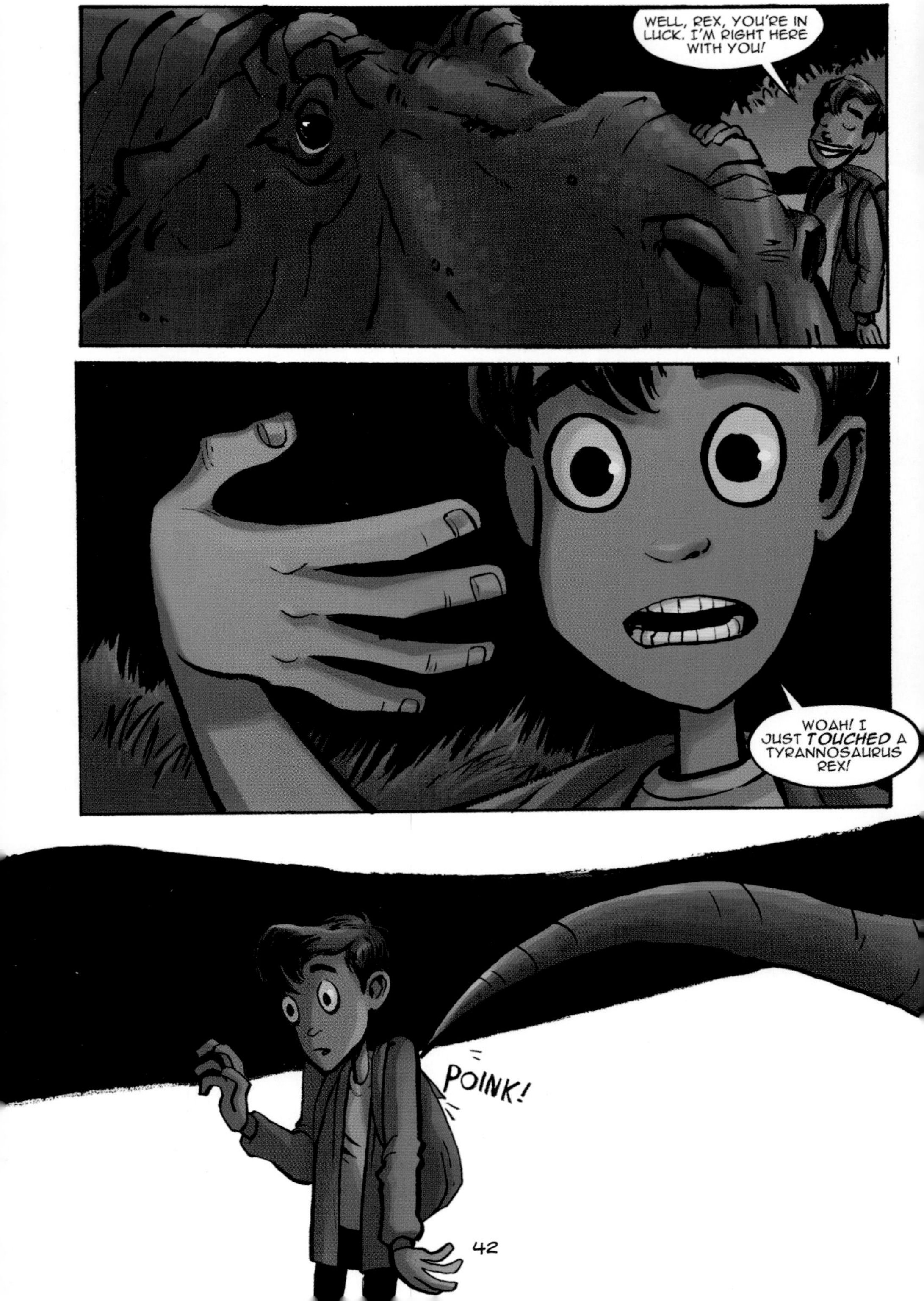
WELL, REX, YOU'RE IN LUCK. I'M RIGHT HERE WITH YOU!
WOAH! I JUST TOUCHED A TYRANNOSAURUS REX!
POINK!

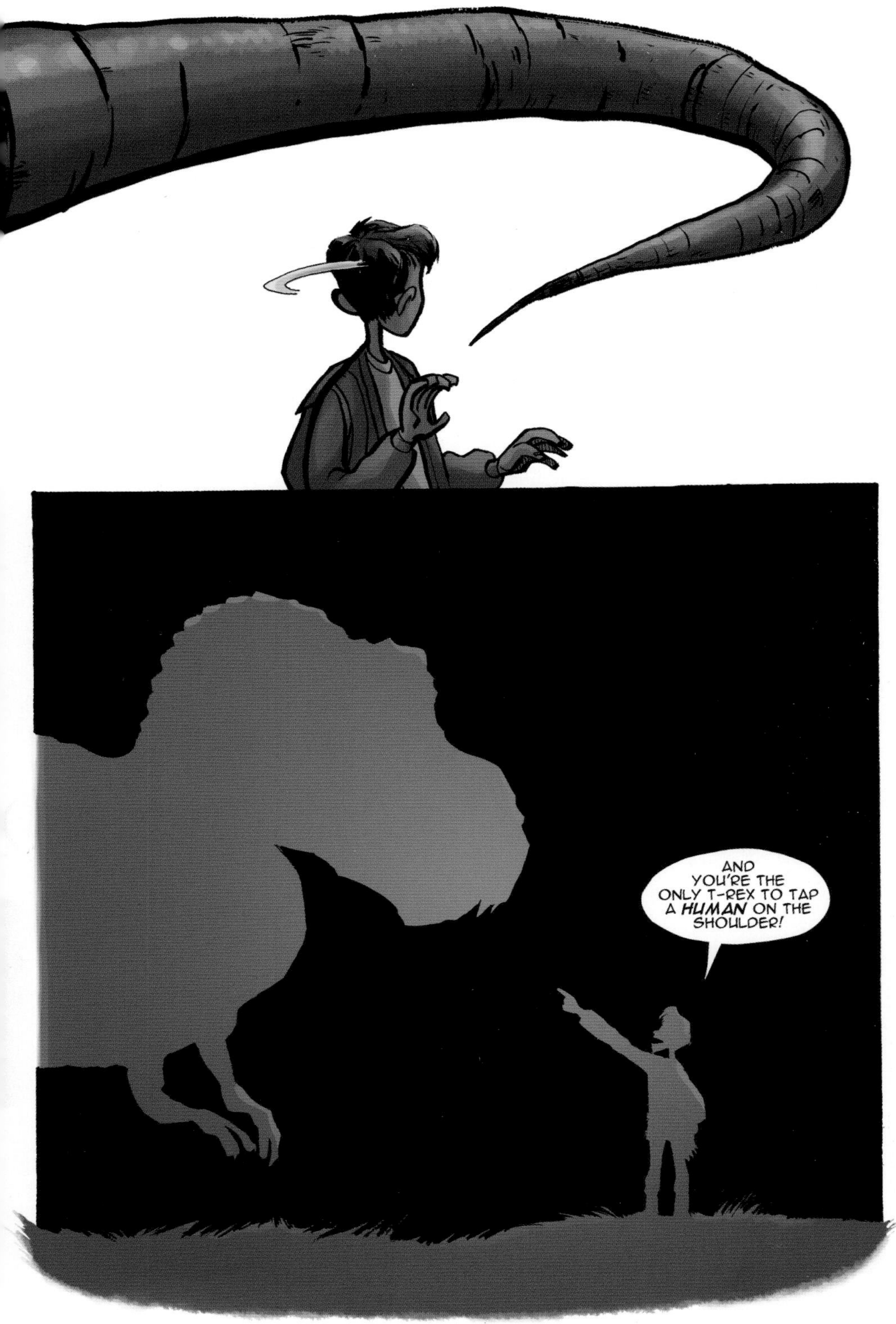
AND YOU'RE THE ONLY T-REX TO TAP A **HUMAN** ON THE SHOULDER!

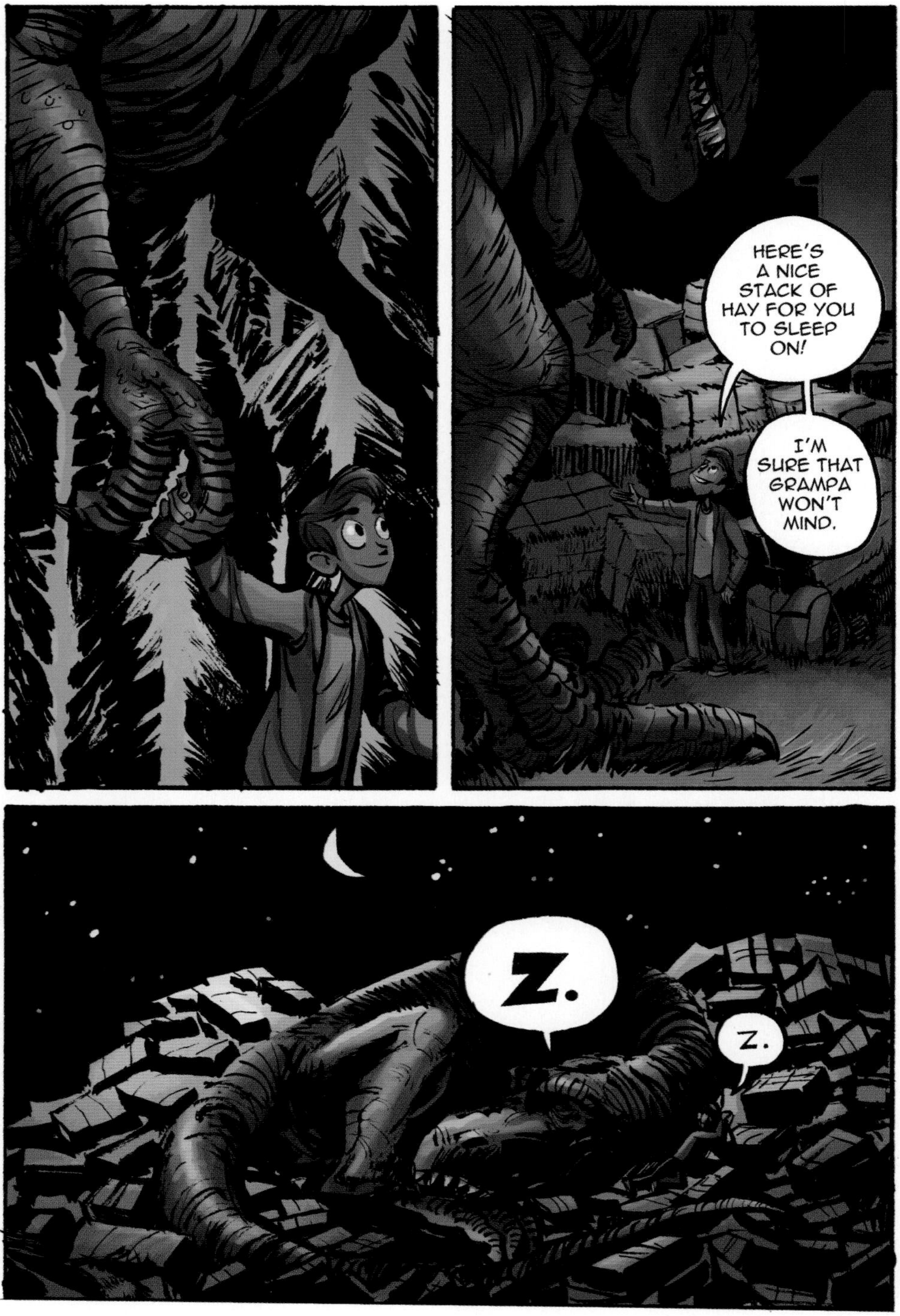
HERE'S A NICE STACK OF HAY FOR YOU TO SLEEP ON!
I'M SURE THAT GRAMPA WON'T MIND.
Z.
Z.

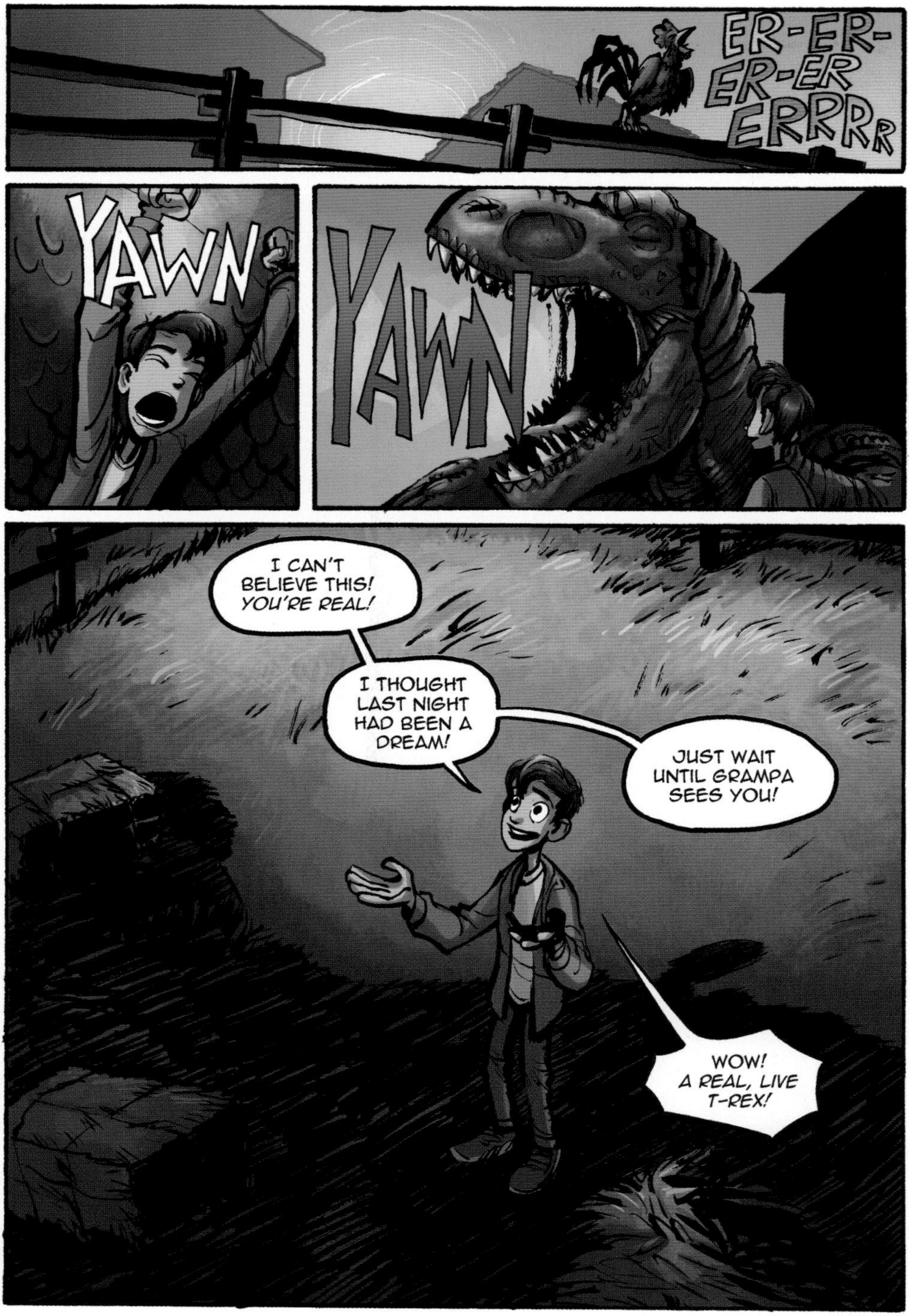
ER-ER-ER-ER ERRRRR
YAWN
YAWN
I CAN'T BELIEVE THIS! YOU'RE REAL!
I THOUGHT LAST NIGHT HAD BEEN A DREAM!
JUST WAIT UNTIL GRAMPA SEES YOU!
WOW! A REAL, LIVE T-REX!

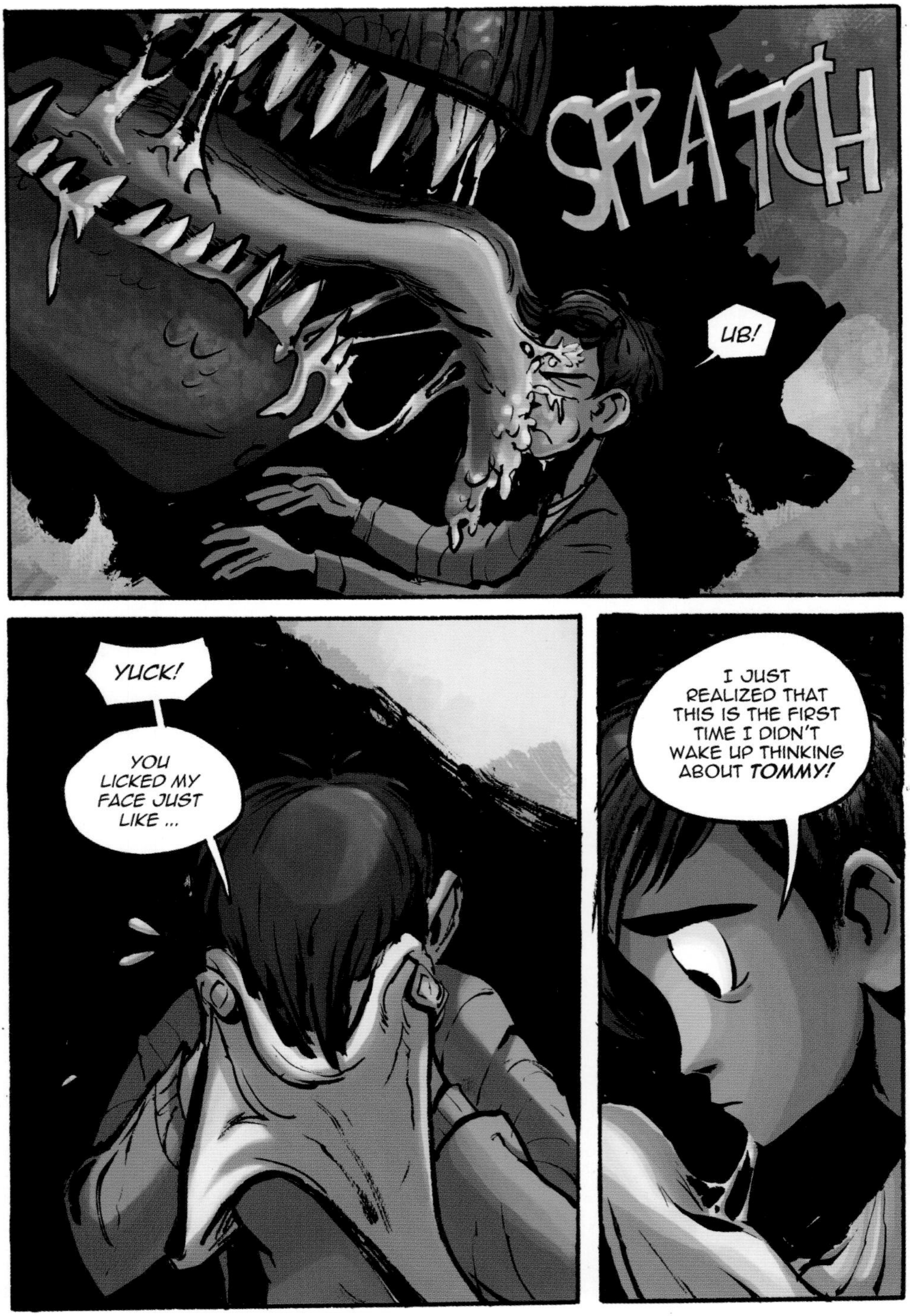
SPLATCH
UB!
YUCK!
YOU LICKED MY FACE JUST LIKE ...
I JUST REALIZED THAT THIS IS THE FIRST TIME I DIDN'T WAKE UP THINKING ABOUT *TOMMY!*

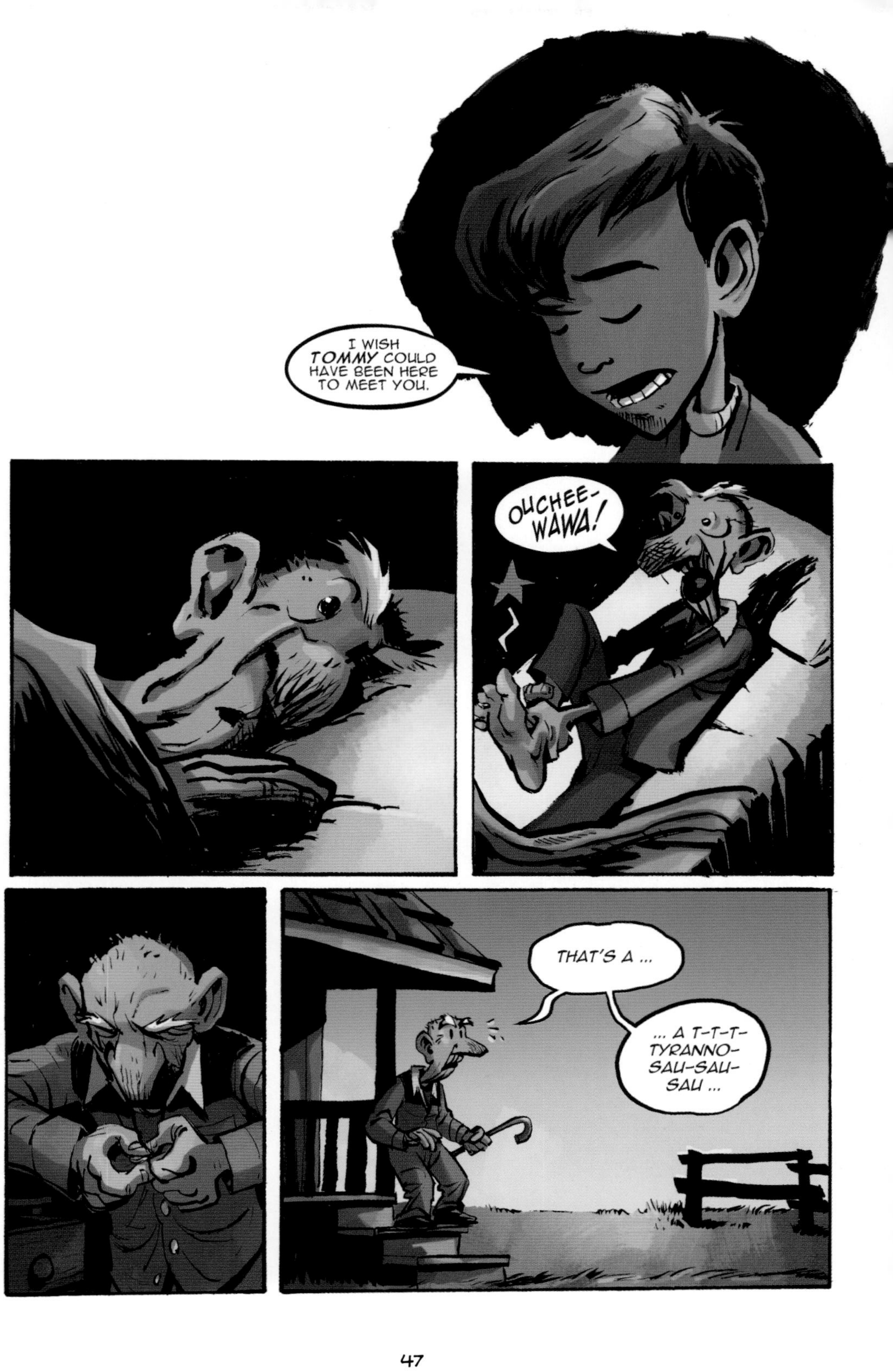
I WISH *TOMMY* COULD HAVE BEEN HERE TO MEET YOU.
OUCHEE-WAWA!
THAT'S A ...
... A T-T-T-TYRANNO-SAU-SAU-SAU ...

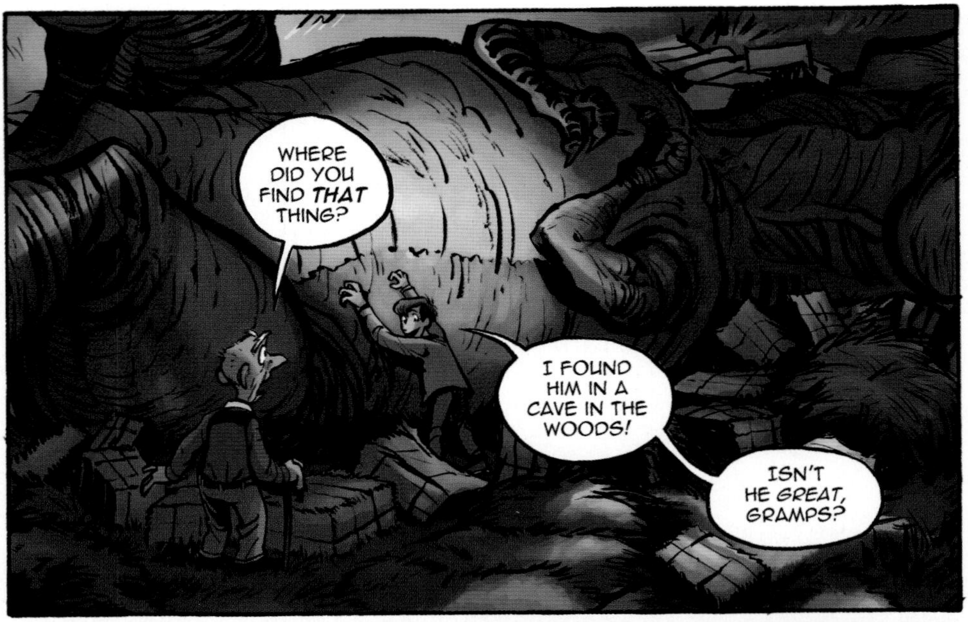
WHERE DID YOU FIND *THAT* THING?
I FOUND HIM IN A CAVE IN THE WOODS!
ISN'T HE *GREAT*, GRAMPS?

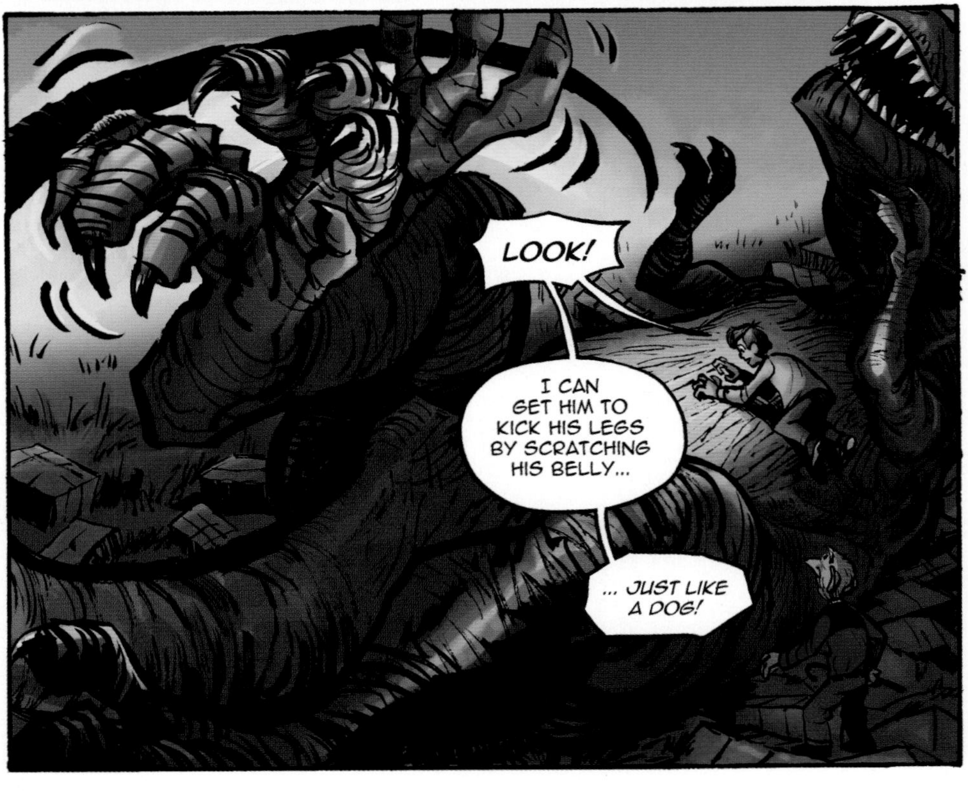
LOOK!
I CAN GET HIM TO KICK HIS LEGS BY SCRATCHING HIS BELLY...
... JUST LIKE A DOG!

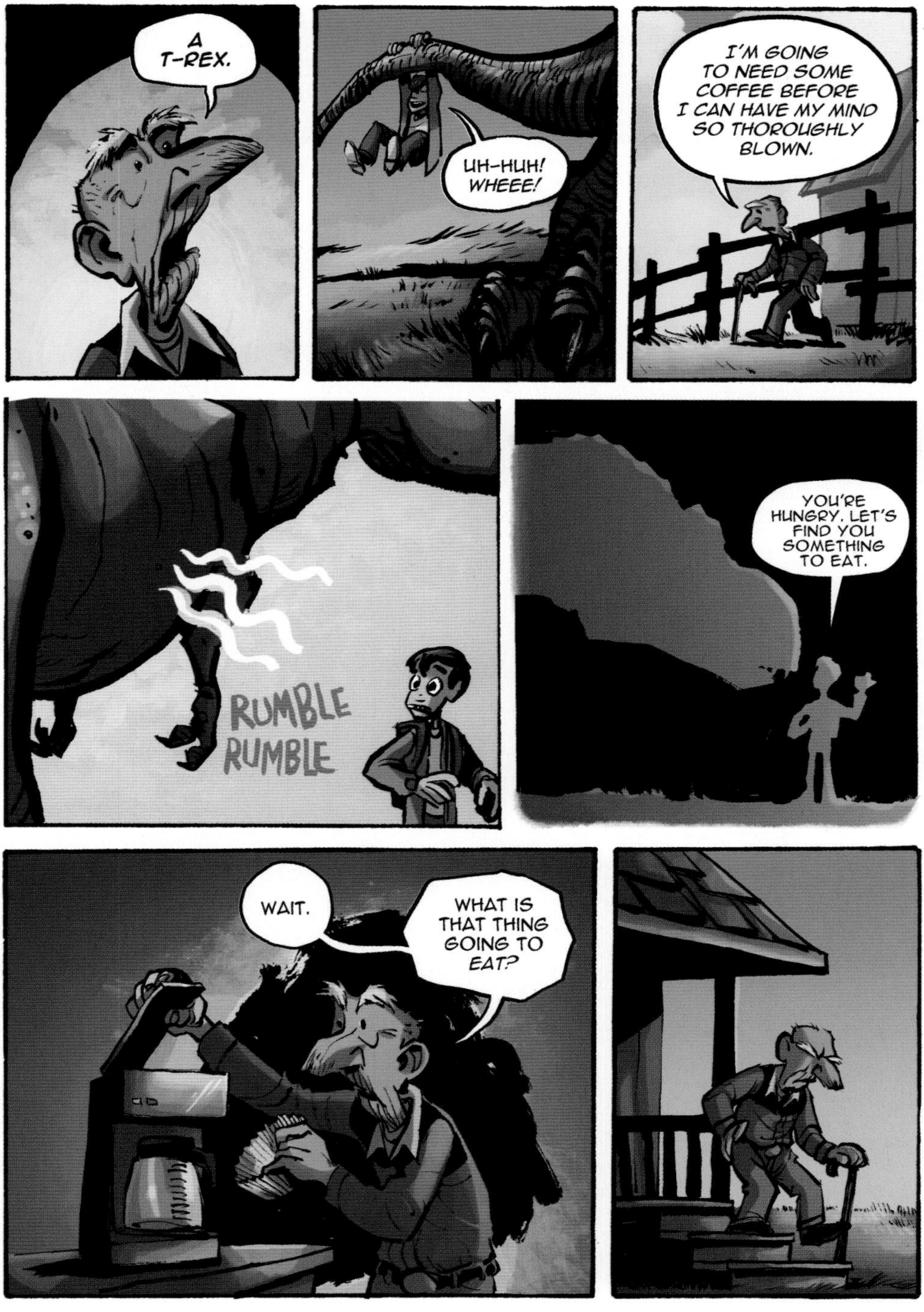
A T-REX.
UH-HUH! WHEEE!
I'M GOING TO NEED SOME COFFEE BEFORE I CAN HAVE MY MIND SO THOROUGHLY BLOWN.
RUMBLE RUMBLE
YOU'RE HUNGRY. LET'S FIND YOU SOMETHING TO EAT.
WAIT.
WHAT IS THAT THING GOING TO EAT?

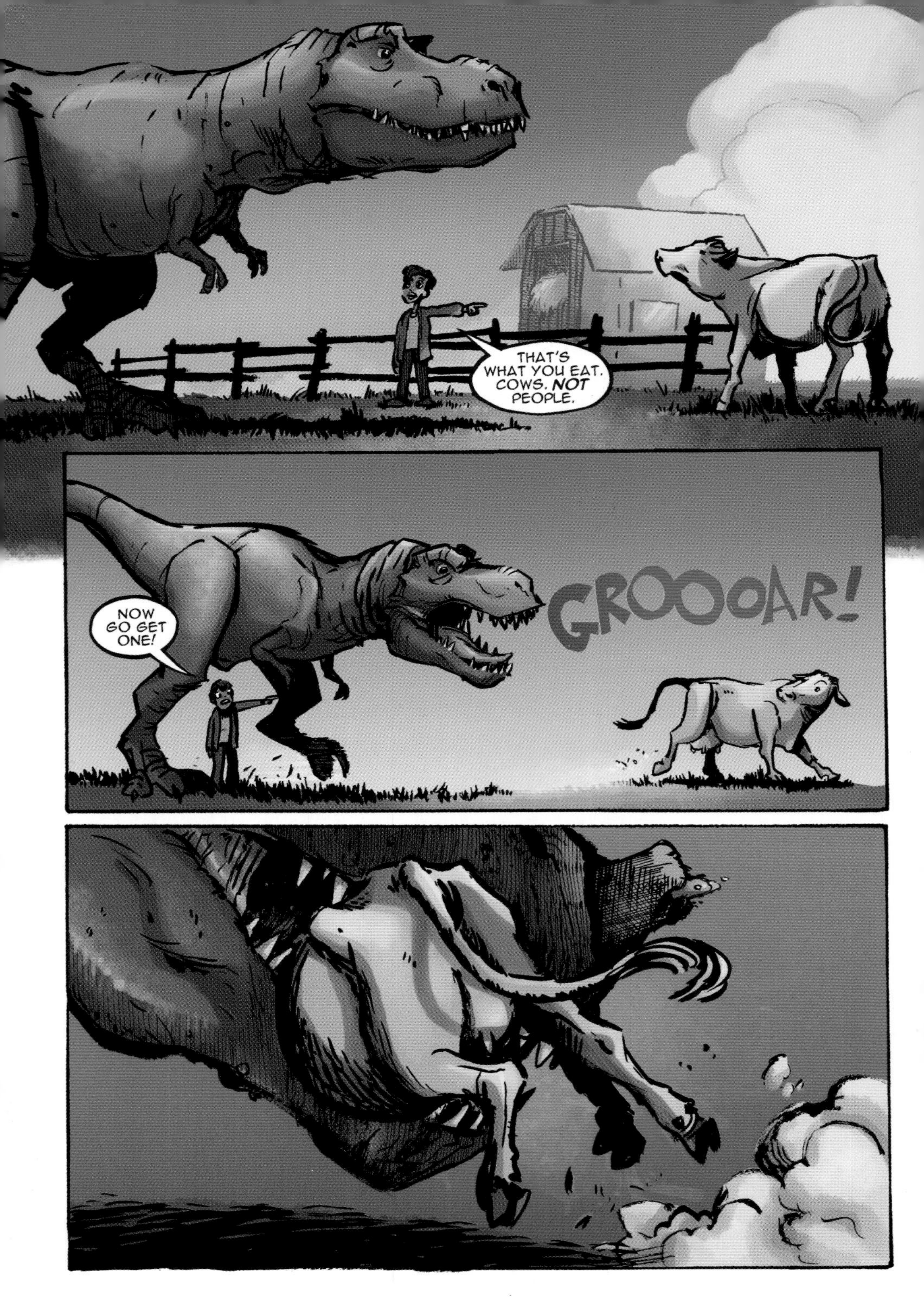

THAT'S WHAT YOU EAT. COWS. NOT PEOPLE.
NOW GO GET ONE!
GROOOAR!

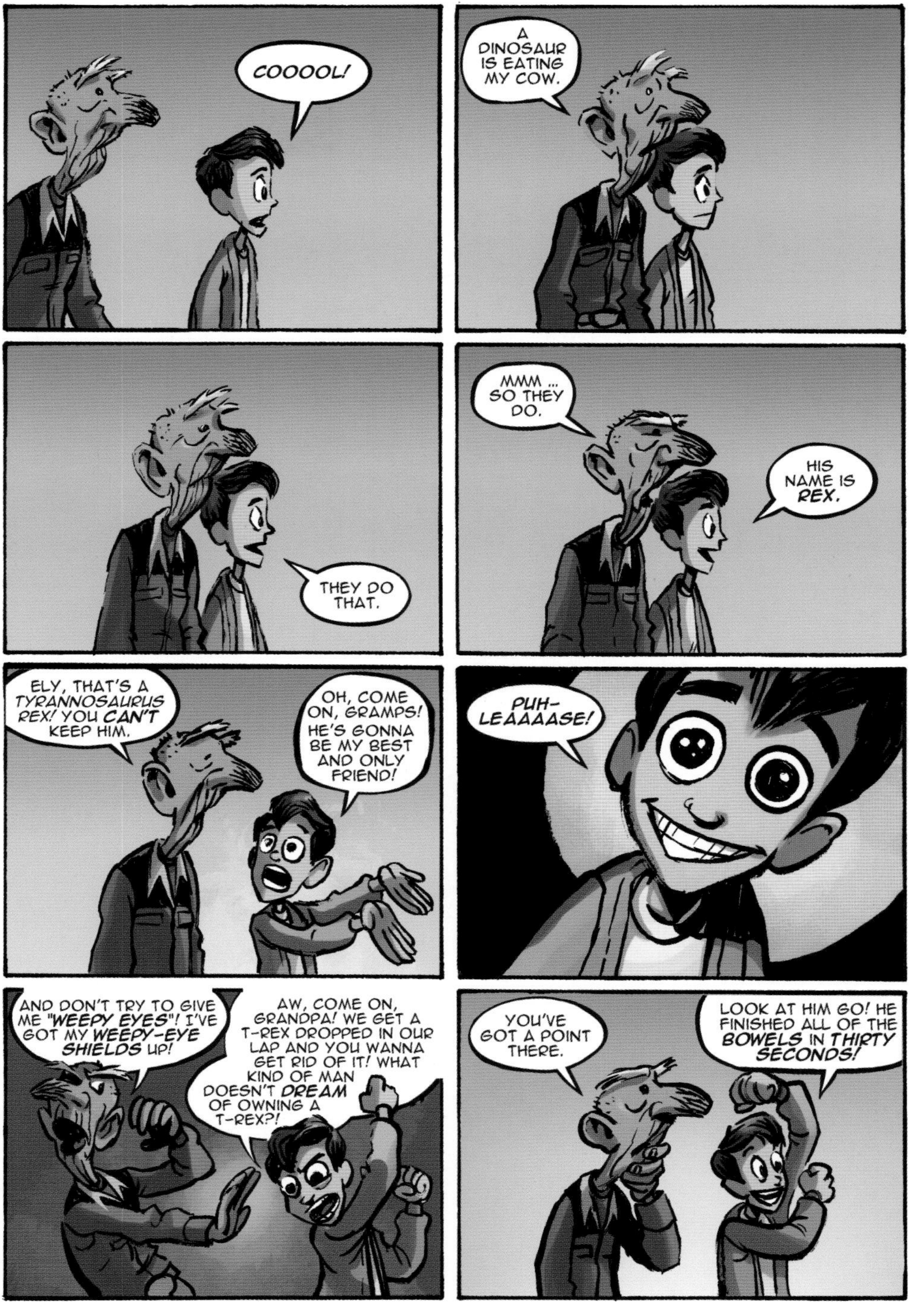
COOOOL!
A DINOSAUR IS EATING MY COW.
THEY DO THAT.
MMM ... SO THEY DO.
HIS NAME IS REX.
ELY, THAT'S A TYRANNOSAURUS REX! YOU CAN'T KEEP HIM.
OH, COME ON, GRAMPS! HE'S GONNA BE MY BEST AND ONLY FRIEND!
PUH-LEAAAAASE!
AND DON'T TRY TO GIVE ME "WEEPY EYES"! I'VE GOT MY WEEPY-EYE SHIELDS UP!
AW, COME ON, GRANDPA! WE GET A T-REX DROPPED IN OUR LAP AND YOU WANNA GET RID OF IT! WHAT KIND OF MAN DOESN'T DREAM OF OWNING A T-REX?!
YOU'VE GOT A POINT THERE.
LOOK AT HIM GO! HE FINISHED ALL OF THE BOWELS IN THIRTY SECONDS!

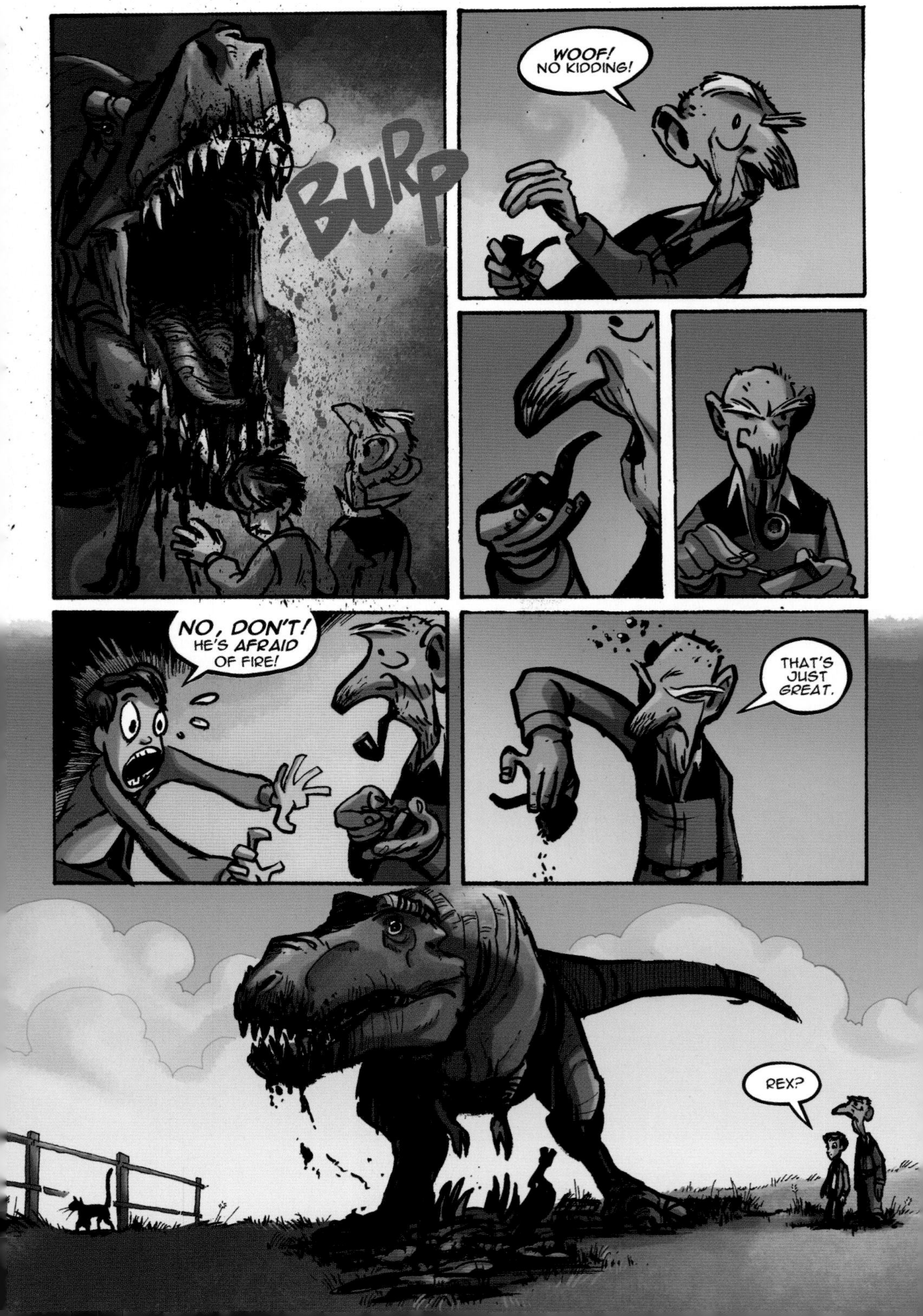
BURP
WOOF! NO KIDDING!
NO, DON'T! HE'S AFRAID OF FIRE!
THAT'S JUST GREAT.
REX?

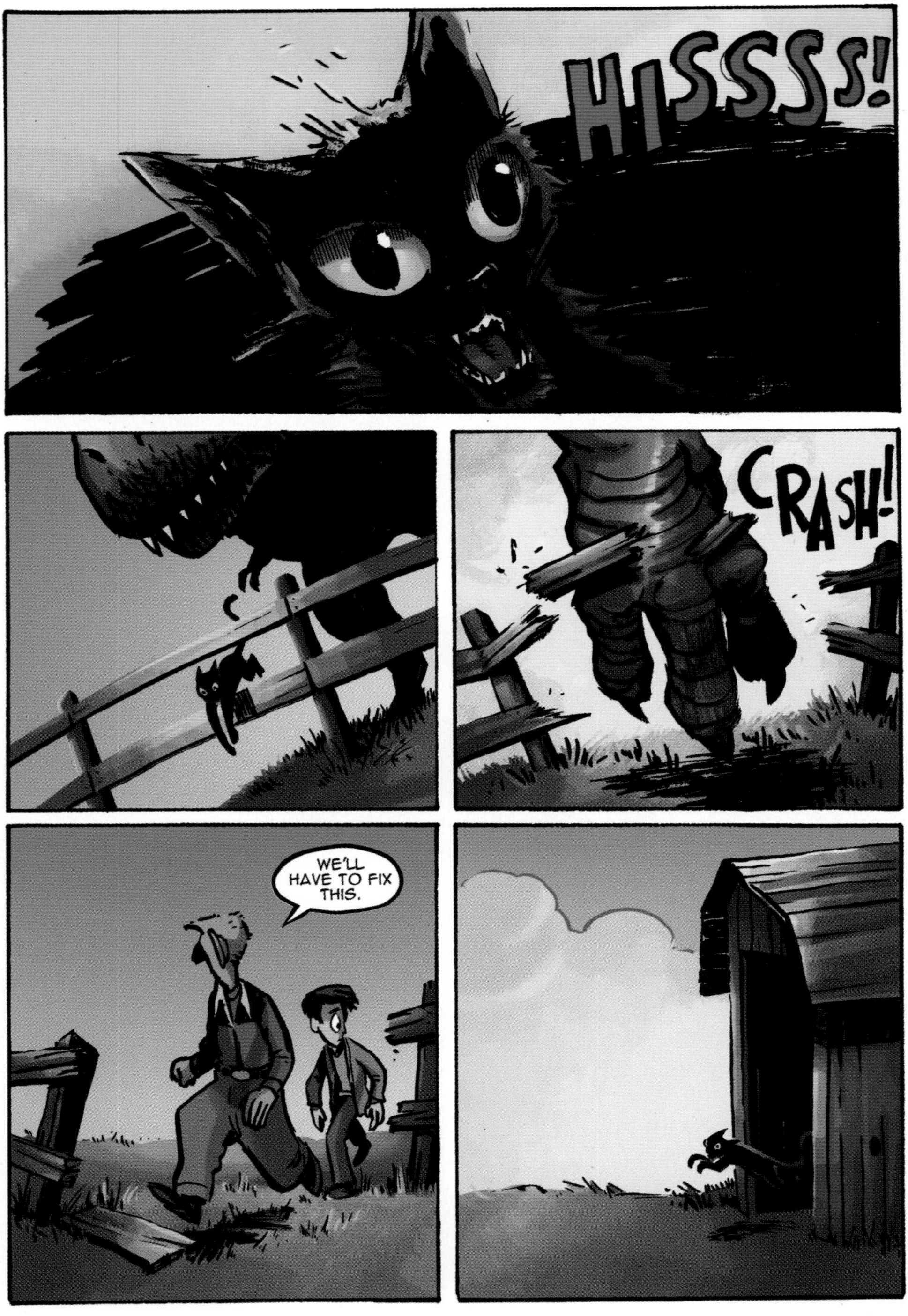
HISSSS!
CRASH!
WE'LL HAVE TO FIX THIS.

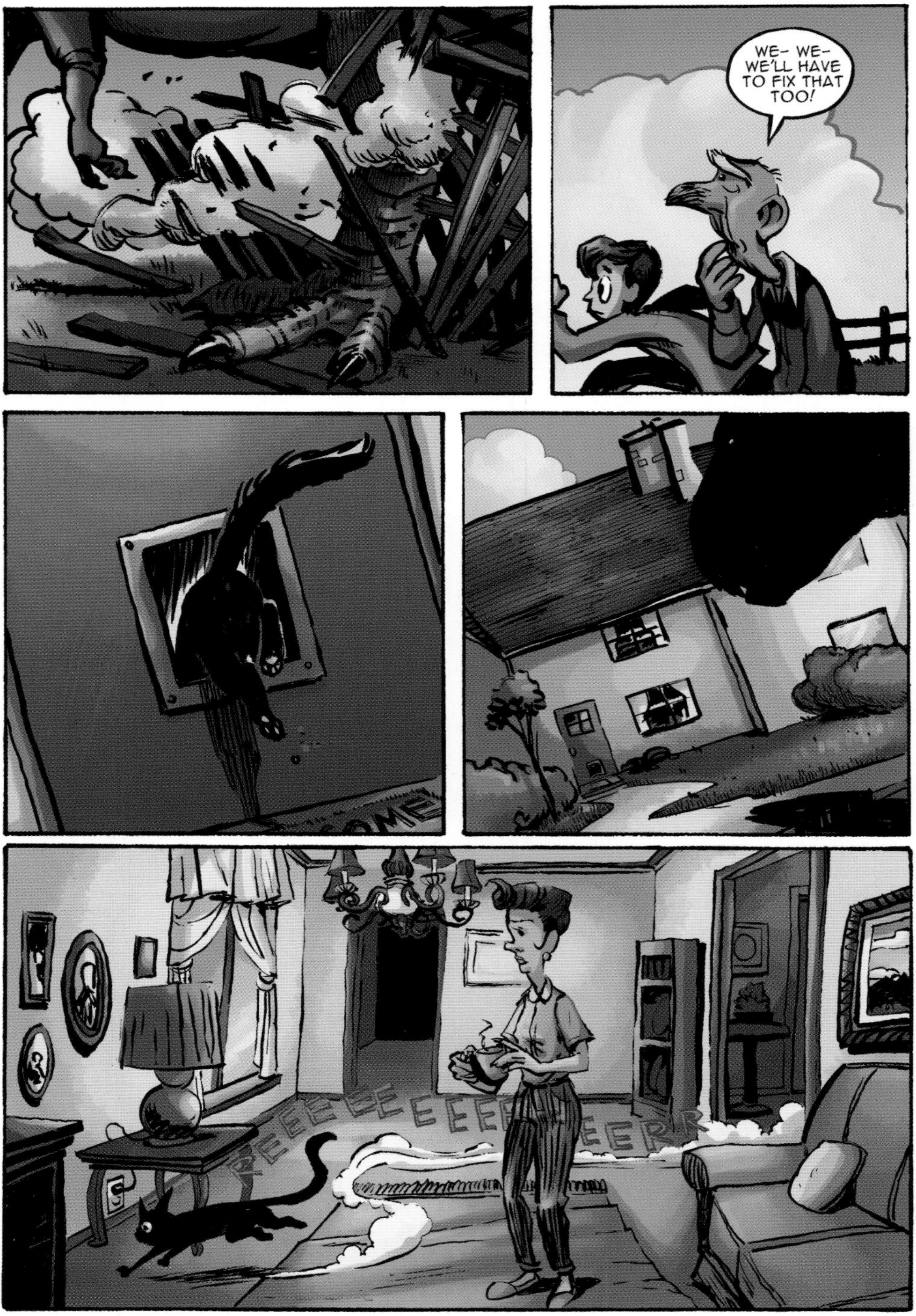
WE- WE- WE'LL HAVE TO FIX THAT TOO!
COME

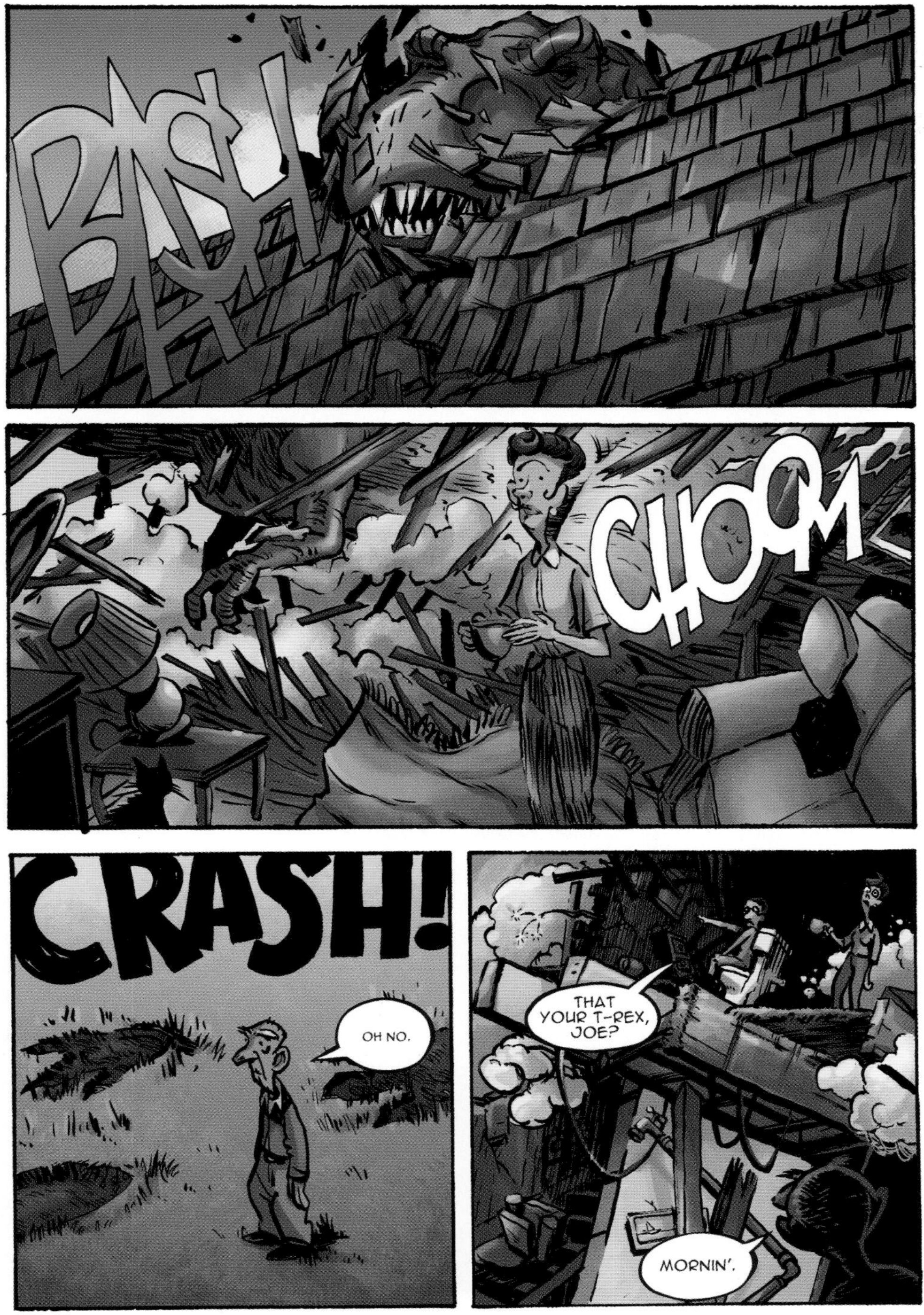
BASH! BASH!
CHOOM
CRASH!
OH NO.
THAT YOUR T-REX, JOE?
MORNIN'.

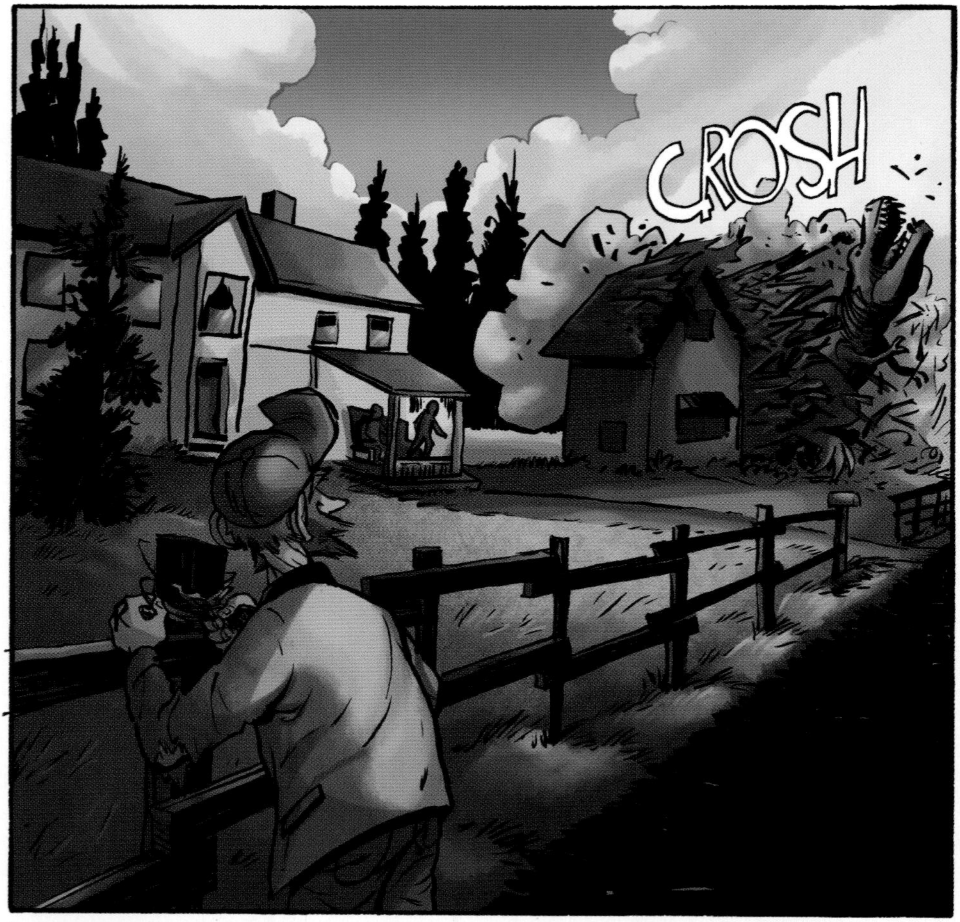
CRASH

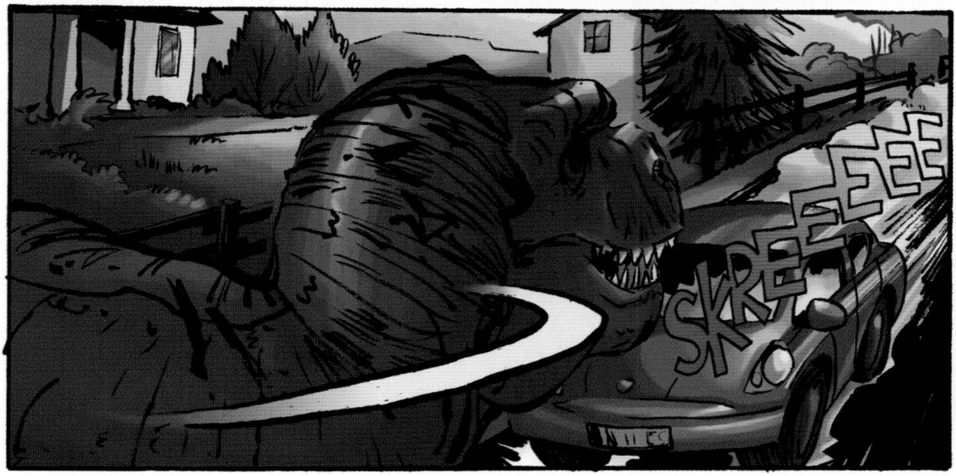
SKREEEEEEE

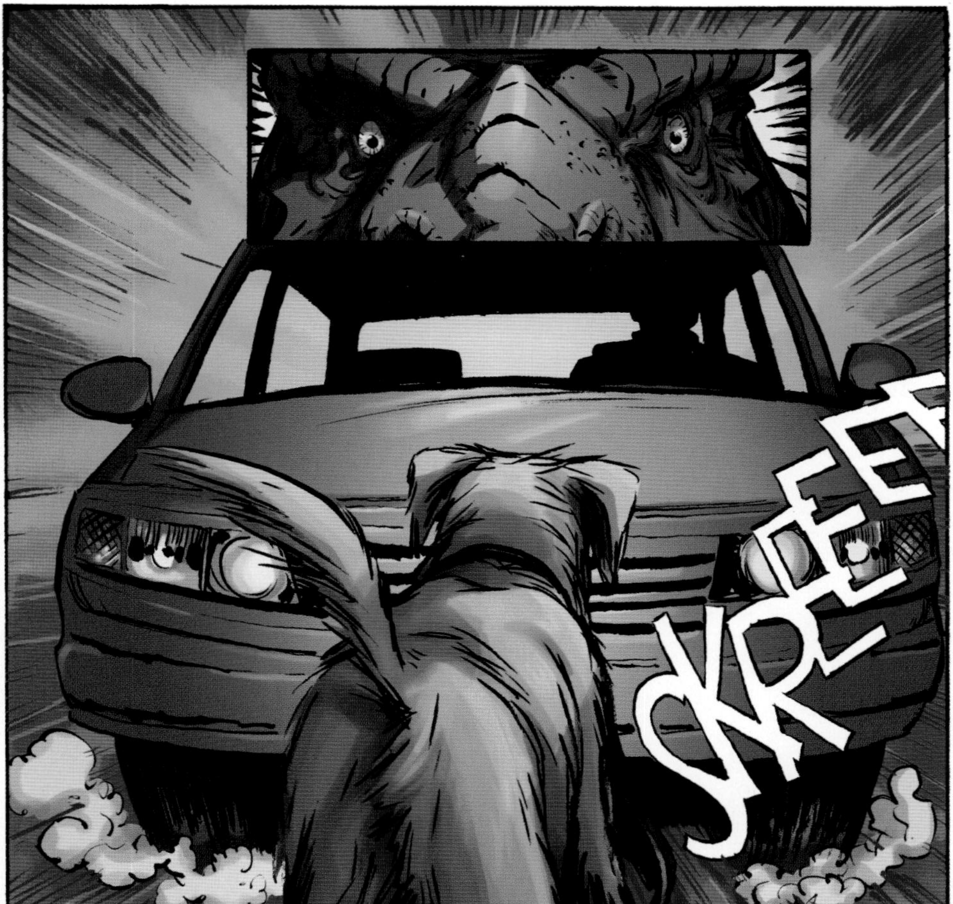
SKREEE

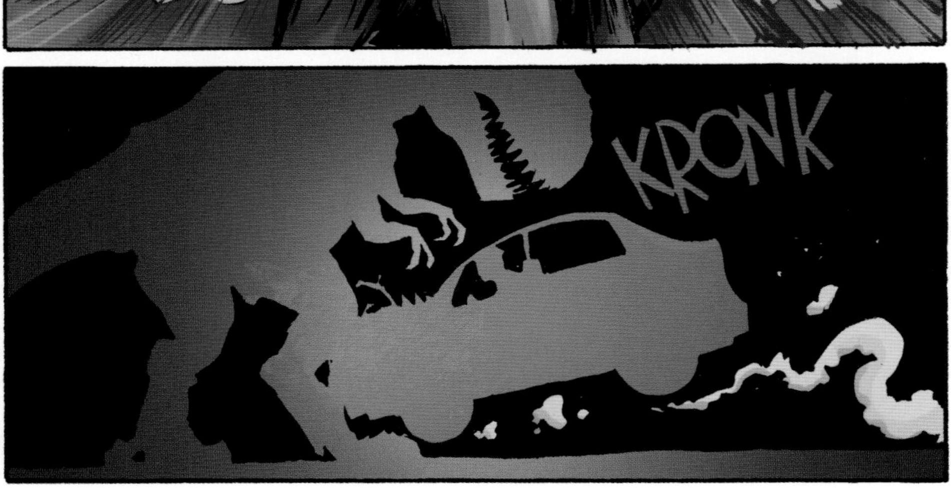
KRONK

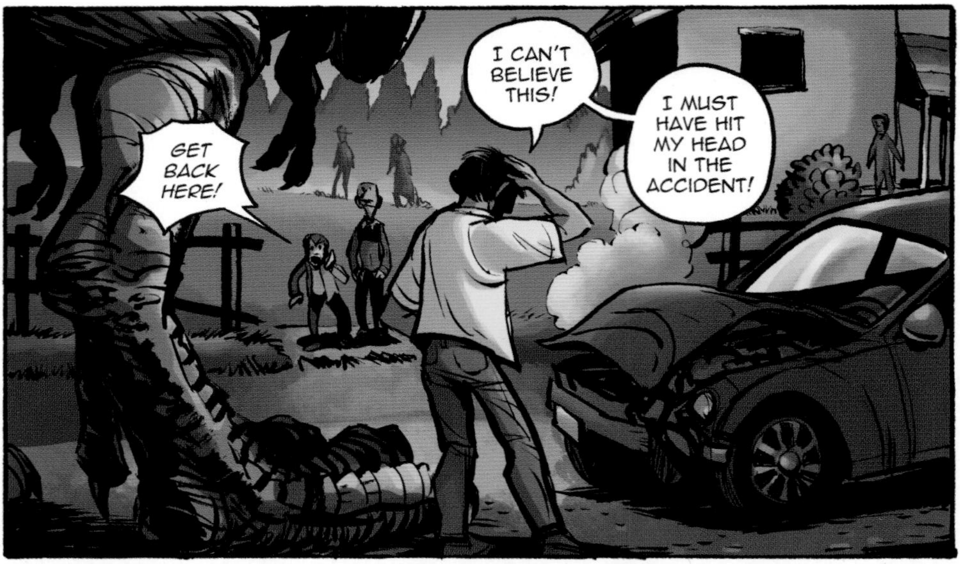
GET BACK HERE!
I CAN'T BELIEVE THIS!
I MUST HAVE HIT MY HEAD IN THE ACCIDENT!

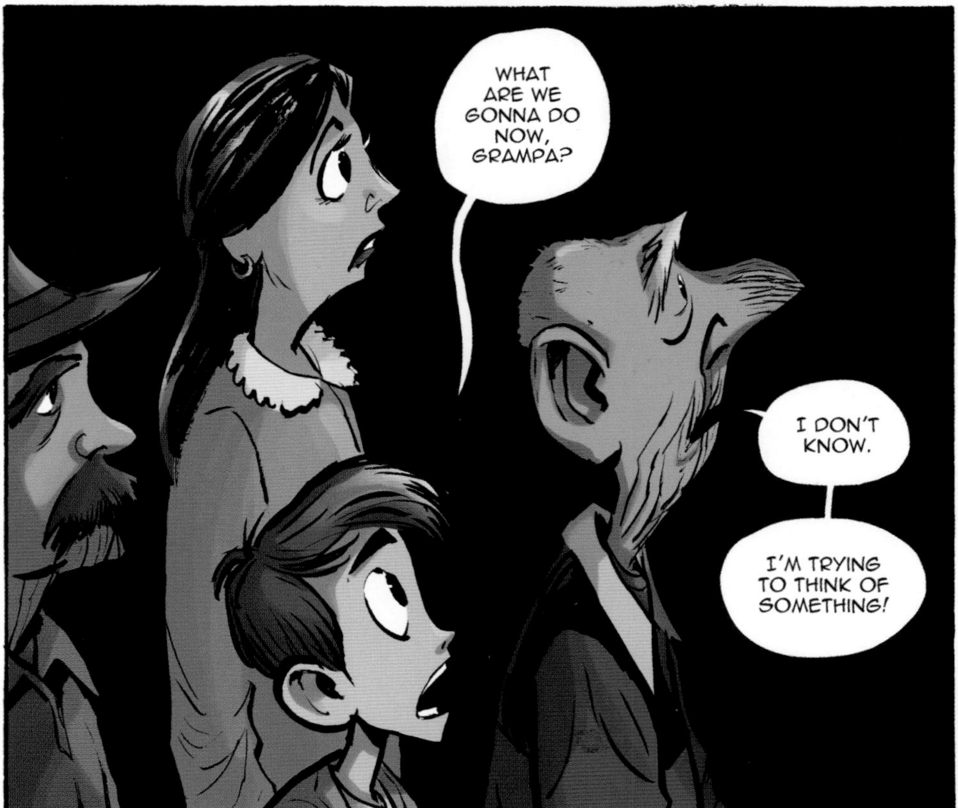
WHAT ARE WE GONNA DO NOW, GRAMPA?
I DON'T KNOW.
I'M TRYING TO THINK OF SOMETHING!

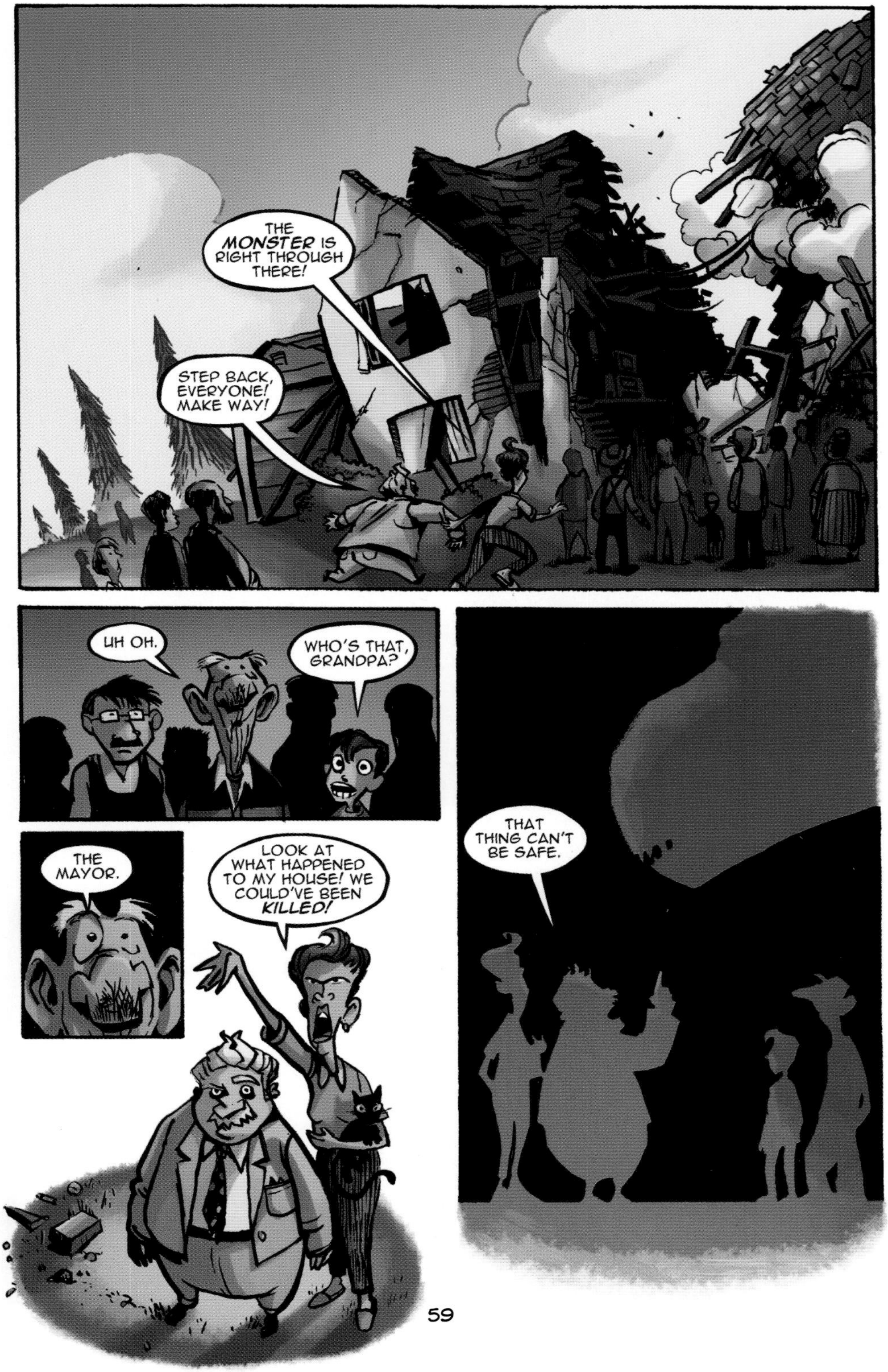
THE MONSTER IS RIGHT THROUGH THERE!
STEP BACK, EVERYONE! MAKE WAY!
UH OH.
WHO'S THAT, GRANDPA?
THE MAYOR.
LOOK AT WHAT HAPPENED TO MY HOUSE! WE COULD'VE BEEN KILLED!
THAT THING CAN'T BE SAFE.

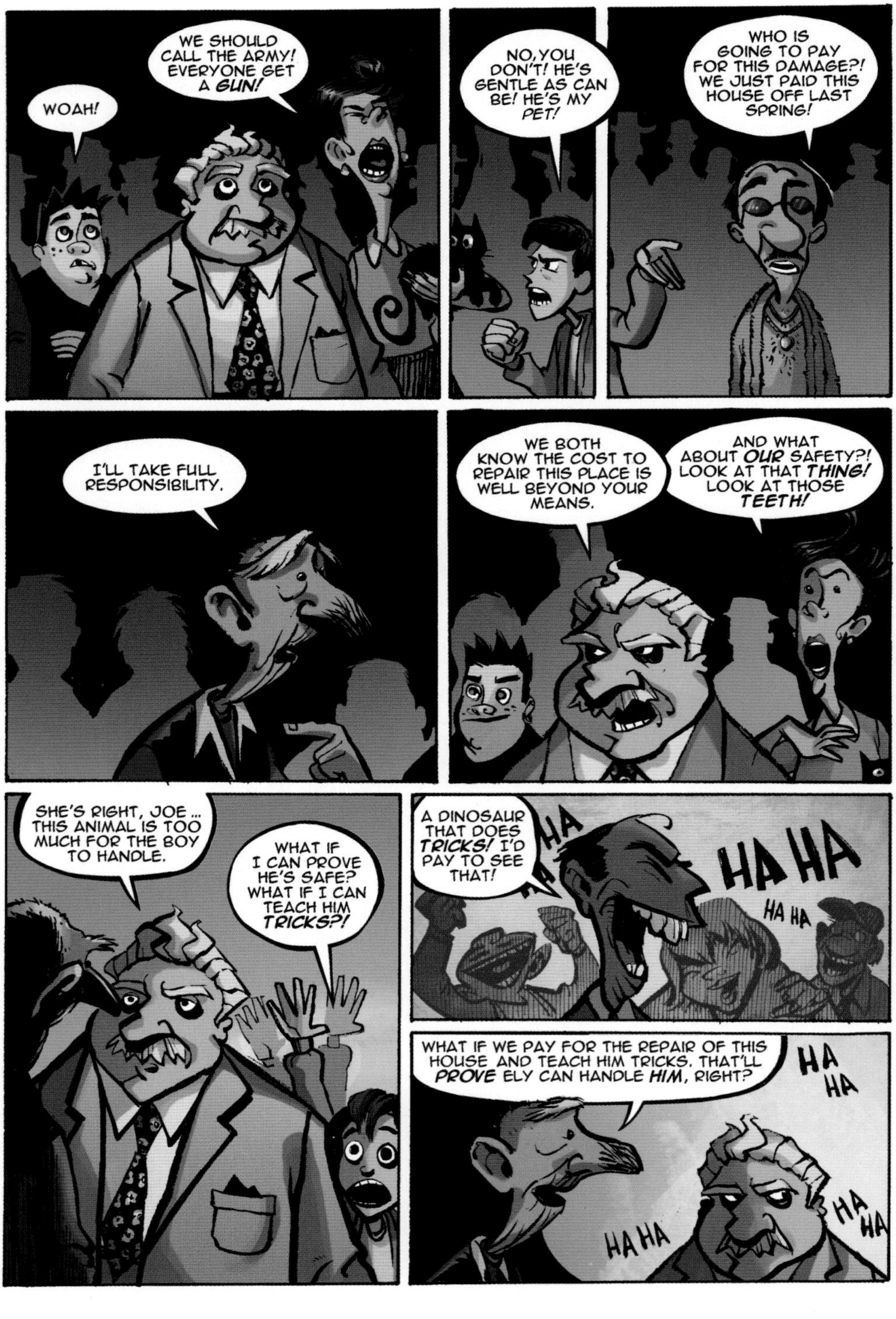
WOAH!
WE SHOULD CALL THE ARMY! EVERYONE GET A GUN!
NO, YOU DON'T! HE'S GENTLE AS CAN BE! HE'S MY PET!
WHO IS GOING TO PAY FOR THIS DAMAGE?! WE JUST PAID THIS HOUSE OFF LAST SPRING!
I'LL TAKE FULL RESPONSIBILITY.
WE BOTH KNOW THE COST TO REPAIR THIS PLACE IS WELL BEYOND YOUR MEANS.
AND WHAT ABOUT OUR SAFETY?! LOOK AT THAT THING! LOOK AT THOSE TEETH!
SHE'S RIGHT, JOE ... THIS ANIMAL IS TOO MUCH FOR THE BOY TO HANDLE.
WHAT IF I CAN PROVE HE'S SAFE? WHAT IF I CAN TEACH HIM TRICKS?!
A DINOSAUR THAT DOES TRICKS! I'D PAY TO SEE THAT!
HA HA
HA HA
HA HA
WHAT IF WE PAY FOR THE REPAIR OF THIS HOUSE AND TEACH HIM TRICKS. THAT'LL PROVE ELY CAN HANDLE HIM, RIGHT?
HA HA
HA HA
HA HA

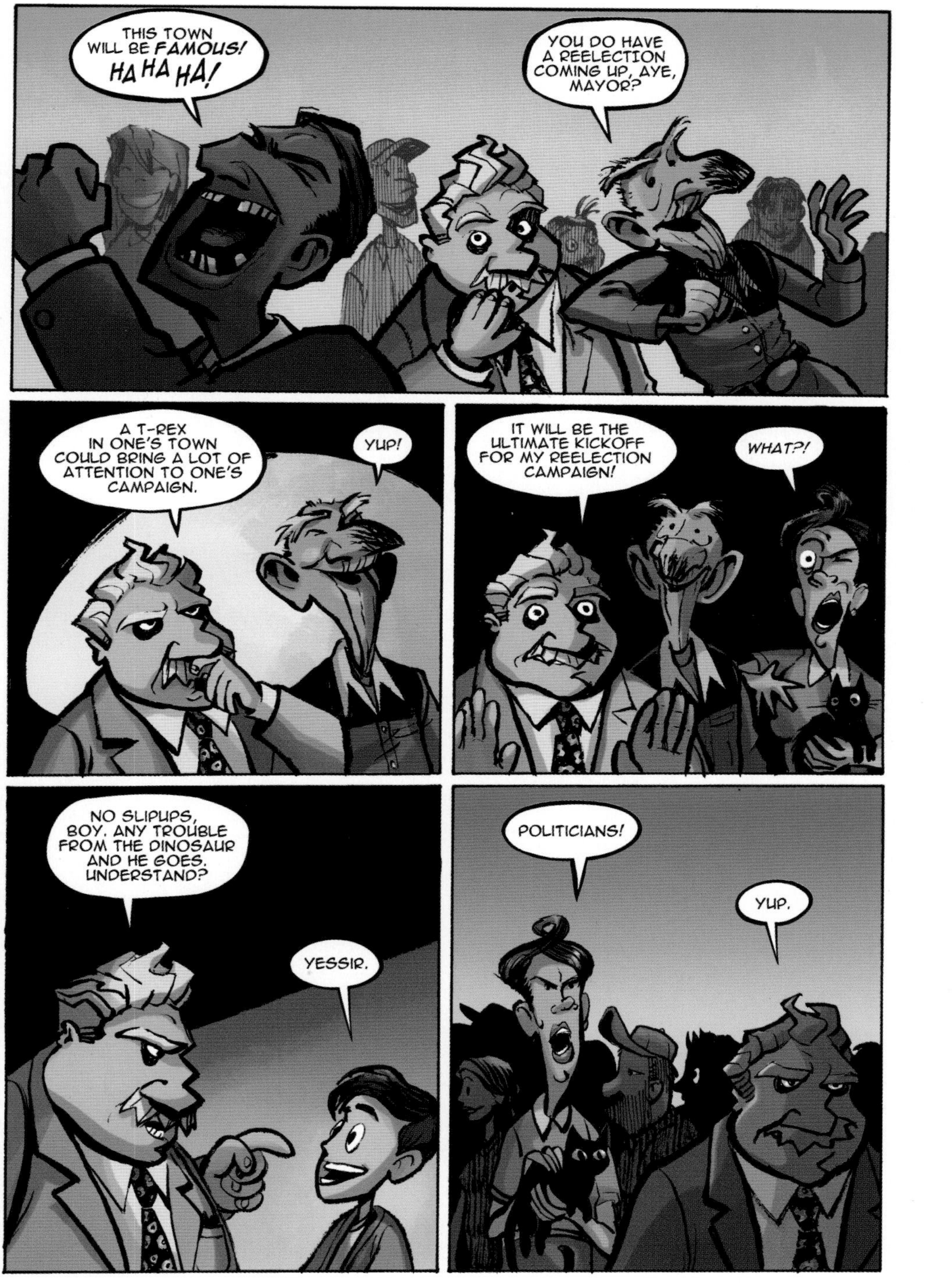
THIS TOWN WILL BE *FAMOUS!* HA HA HA!
YOU DO HAVE A REELECTION COMING UP, AYE, MAYOR?
A T-REX IN ONE'S TOWN COULD BRING A LOT OF ATTENTION TO ONE'S CAMPAIGN.
YUP!
IT WILL BE THE ULTIMATE KICKOFF FOR MY REELECTION CAMPAIGN!
WHAT?!
NO SLIPUPS, BOY. ANY TROUBLE FROM THE DINOSAUR AND HE GOES. UNDERSTAND?
YESSIR.
POLITICIANS!
YUP.

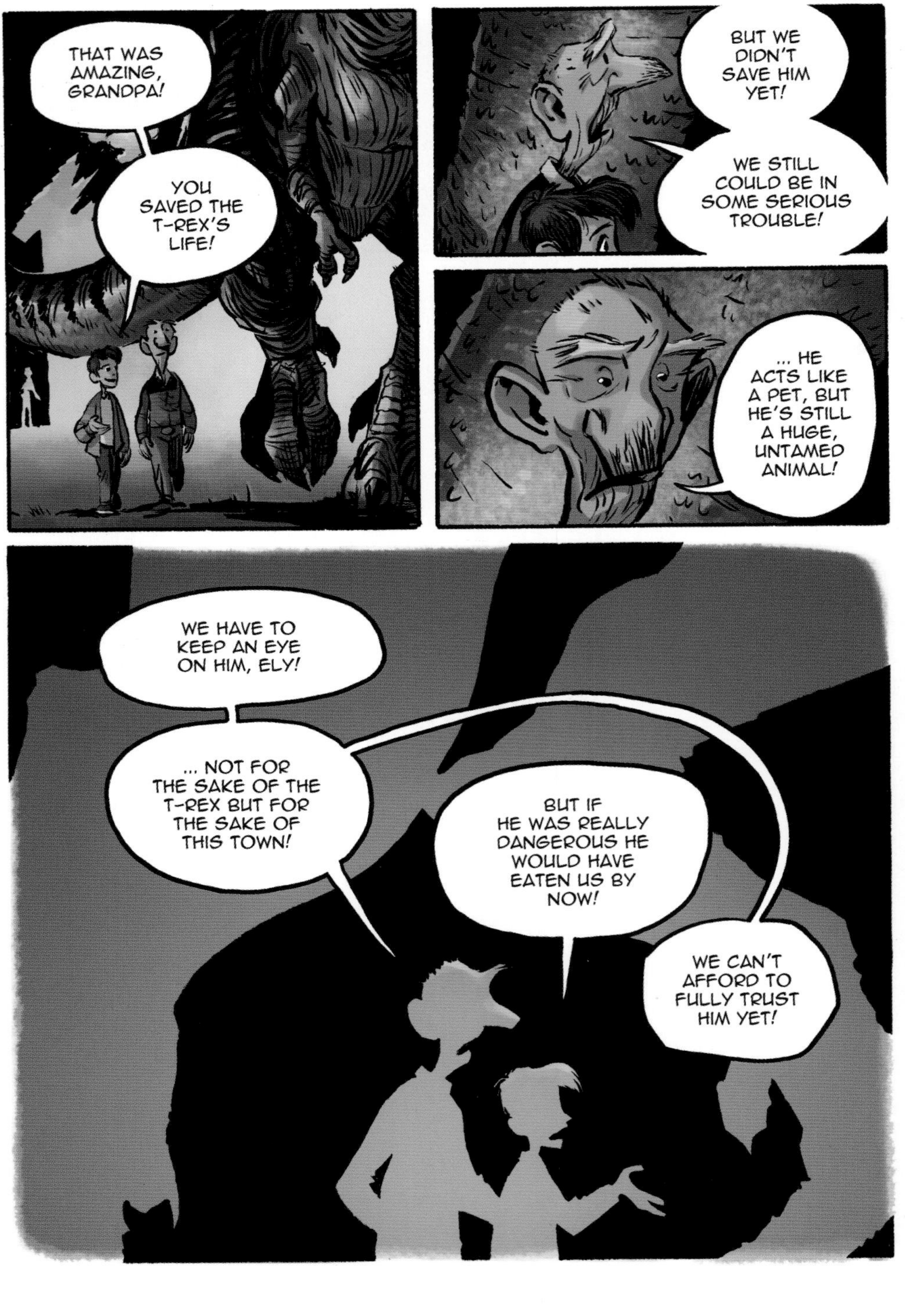
THAT WAS AMAZING, GRANDPA!
YOU SAVED THE T-REX'S LIFE!
BUT WE DIDN'T SAVE HIM YET!
WE STILL COULD BE IN SOME SERIOUS TROUBLE!
... HE ACTS LIKE A PET, BUT HE'S STILL A HUGE, UNTAMED ANIMAL!
WE HAVE TO KEEP AN EYE ON HIM, ELY!
... NOT FOR THE SAKE OF THE T-REX BUT FOR THE SAKE OF THIS TOWN!
BUT IF HE WAS REALLY DANGEROUS HE WOULD HAVE EATEN US BY NOW!
WE CAN'T AFFORD TO FULLY TRUST HIM YET!

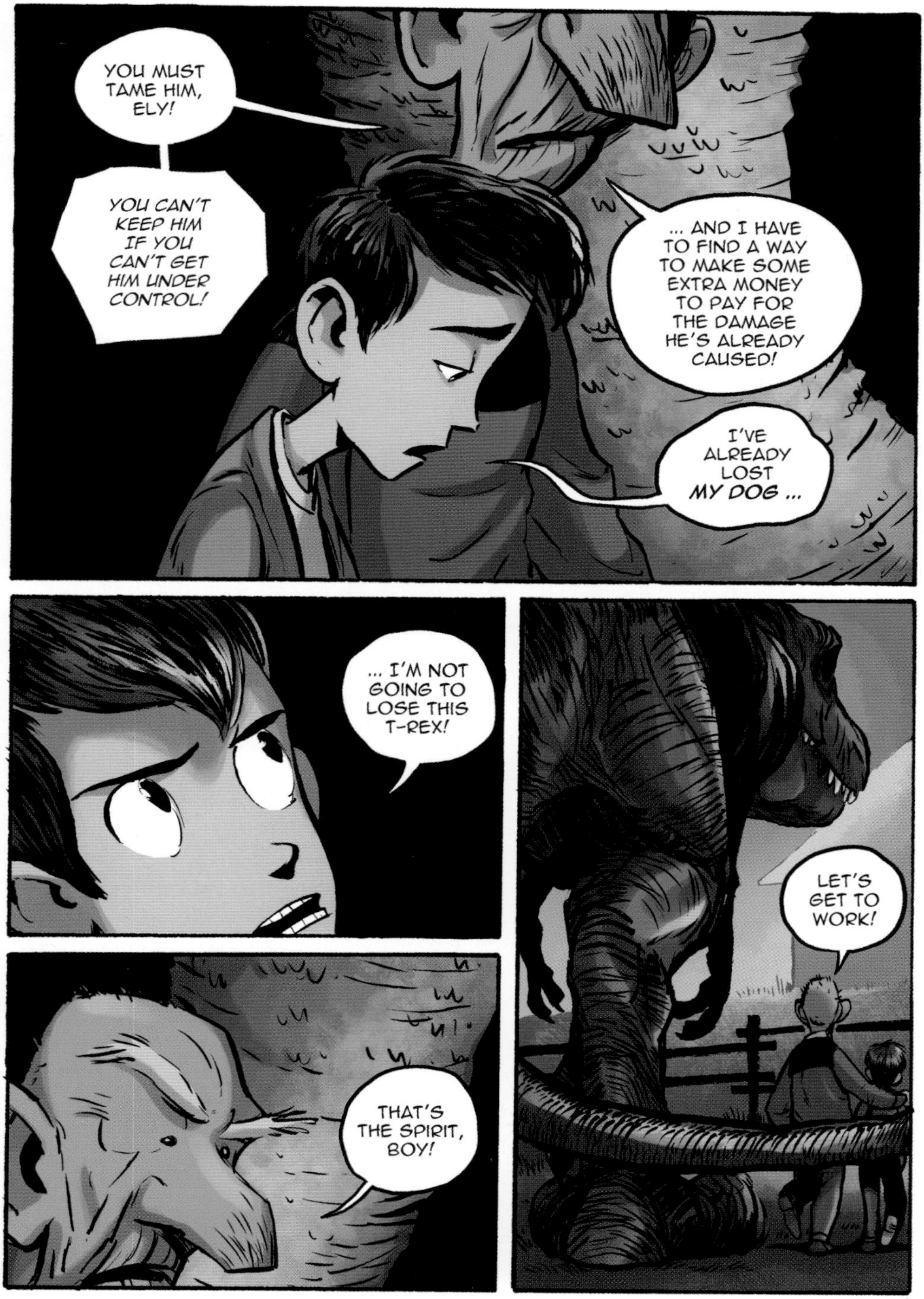
YOU MUST TAME HIM, ELY!
YOU CAN'T KEEP HIM IF YOU CAN'T GET HIM UNDER CONTROL!
... AND I HAVE TO FIND A WAY TO MAKE SOME EXTRA MONEY TO PAY FOR THE DAMAGE HE'S ALREADY CAUSED!
I'VE ALREADY LOST MY DOG ...
... I'M NOT GOING TO LOSE THIS T-REX!
THAT'S THE SPIRIT, BOY!
LET'S GET TO WORK!

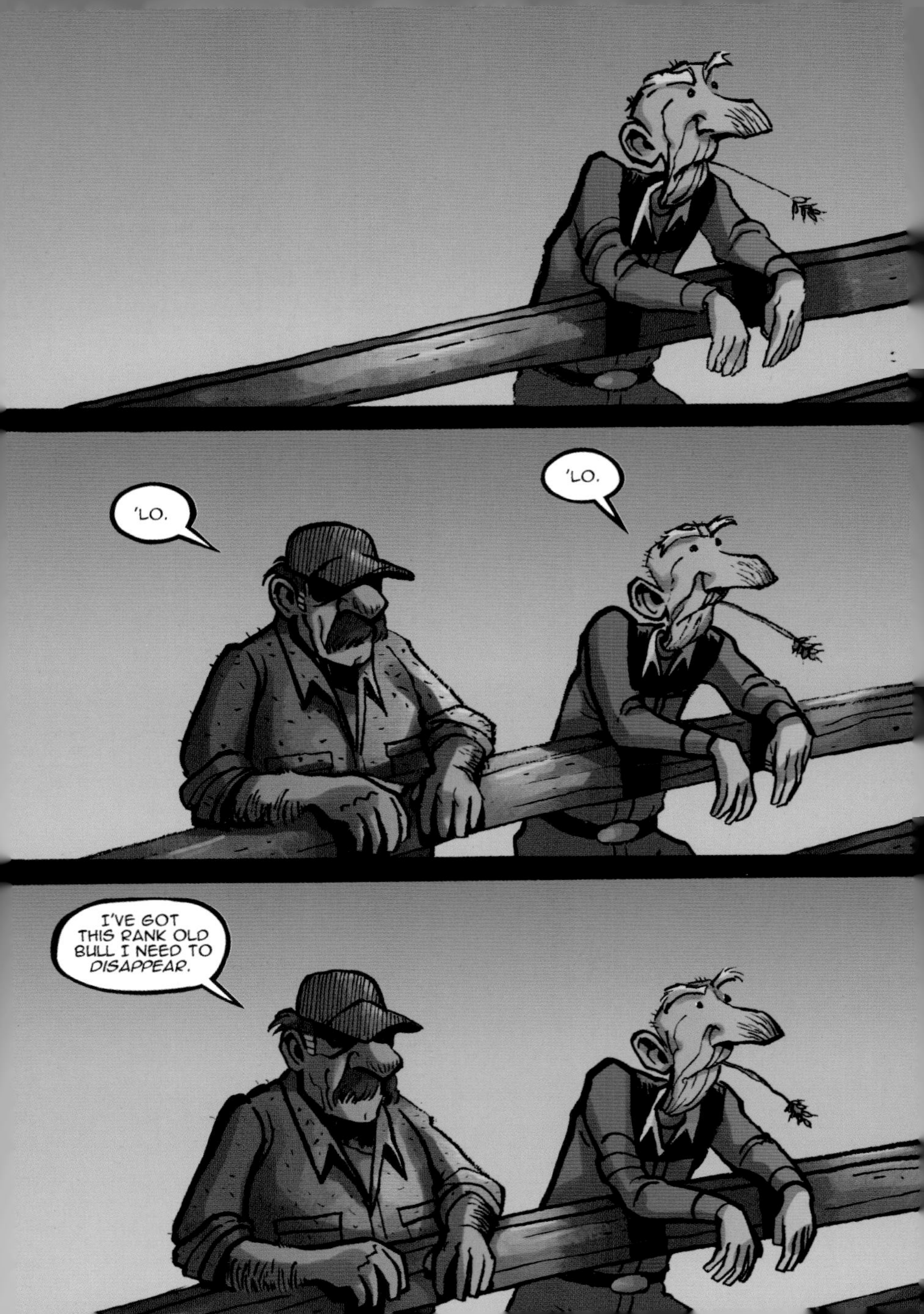
'LO.
'LO.
I'VE GOT THIS RANK OLD BULL I NEED TO *DISAPPEAR*.

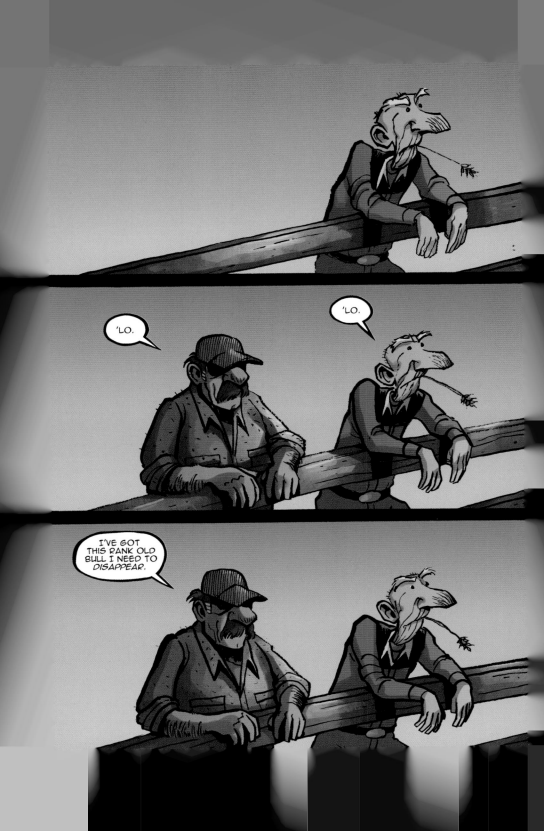

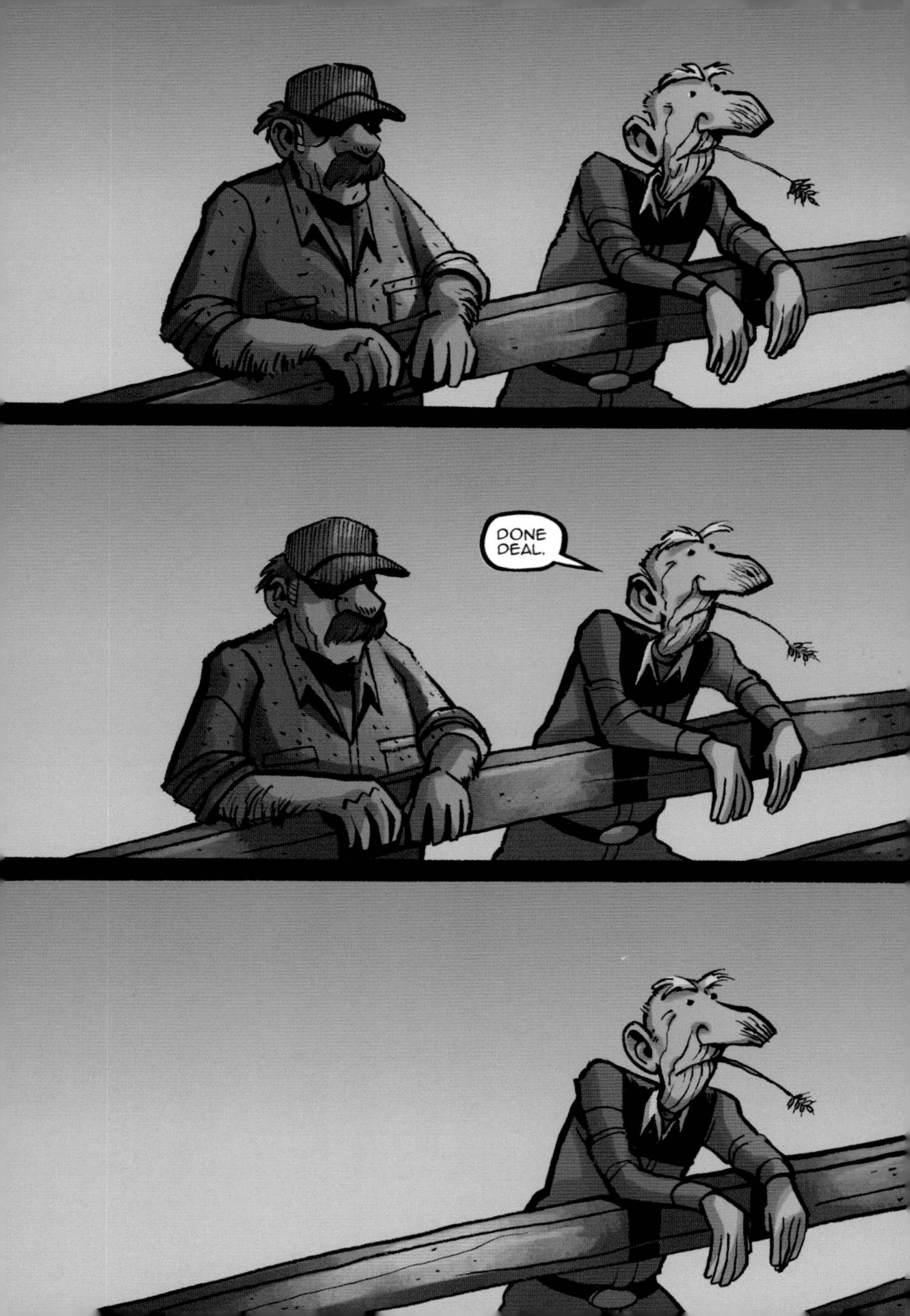
DONE DEAL.

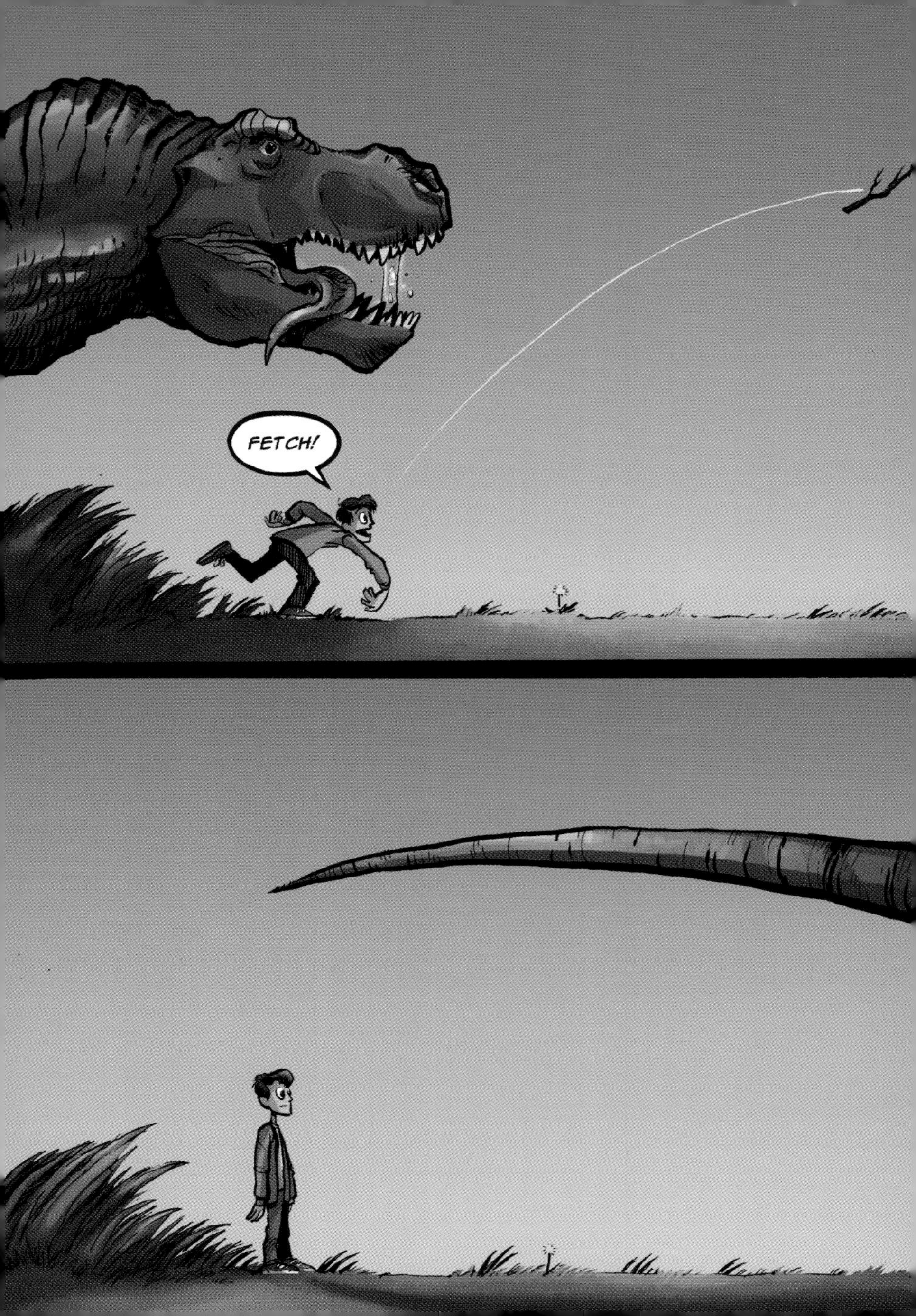
FETCH!

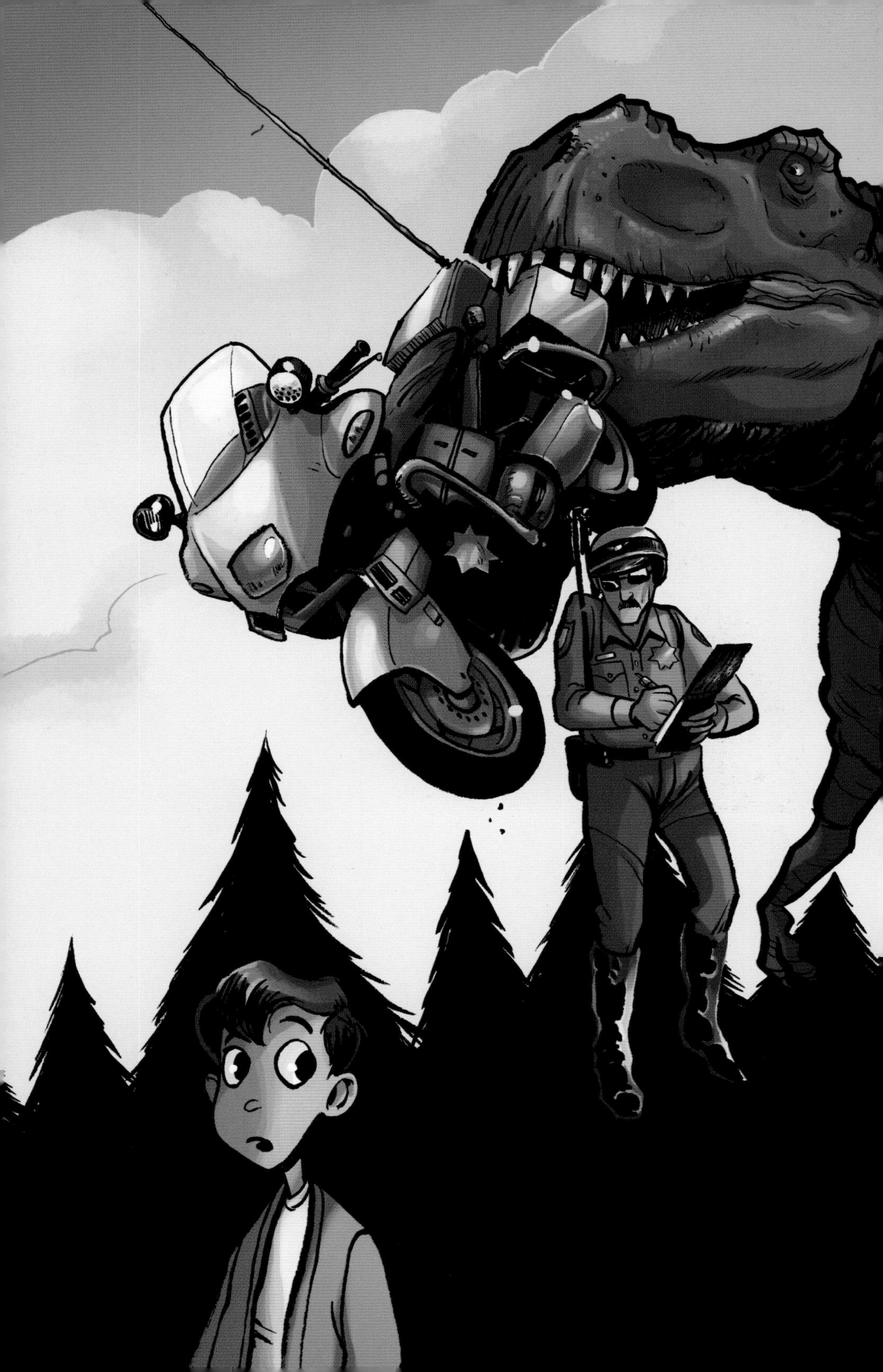

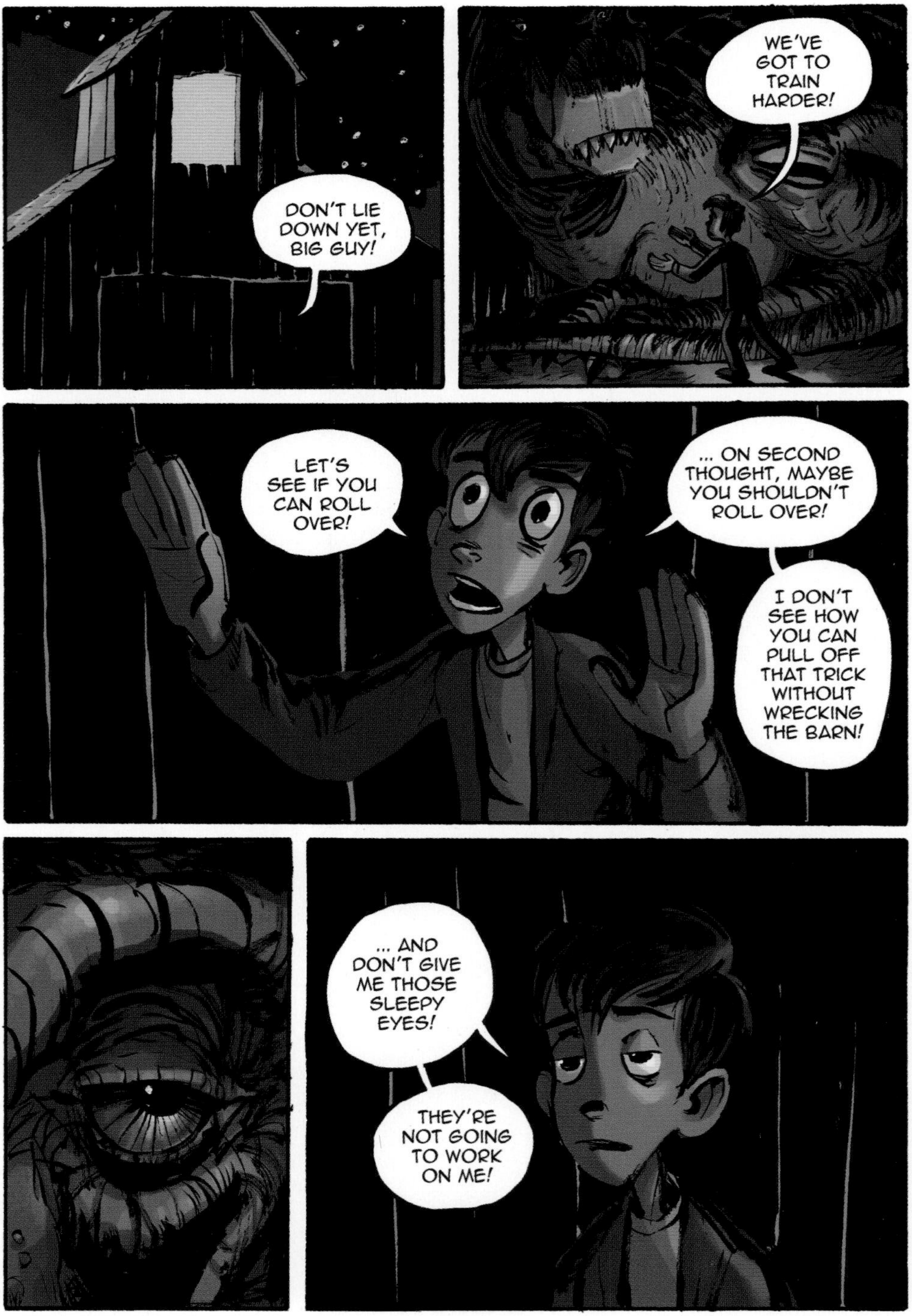
DON'T LIE DOWN YET, BIG GUY!
WE'VE GOT TO TRAIN HARDER!
LET'S SEE IF YOU CAN ROLL OVER!
... ON SECOND THOUGHT, MAYBE YOU SHOULDN'T ROLL OVER!
I DON'T SEE HOW YOU CAN PULL OFF THAT TRICK WITHOUT WRECKING THE BARN!
... AND DON'T GIVE ME THOSE SLEEPY EYES!
THEY'RE NOT GOING TO WORK ON ME!

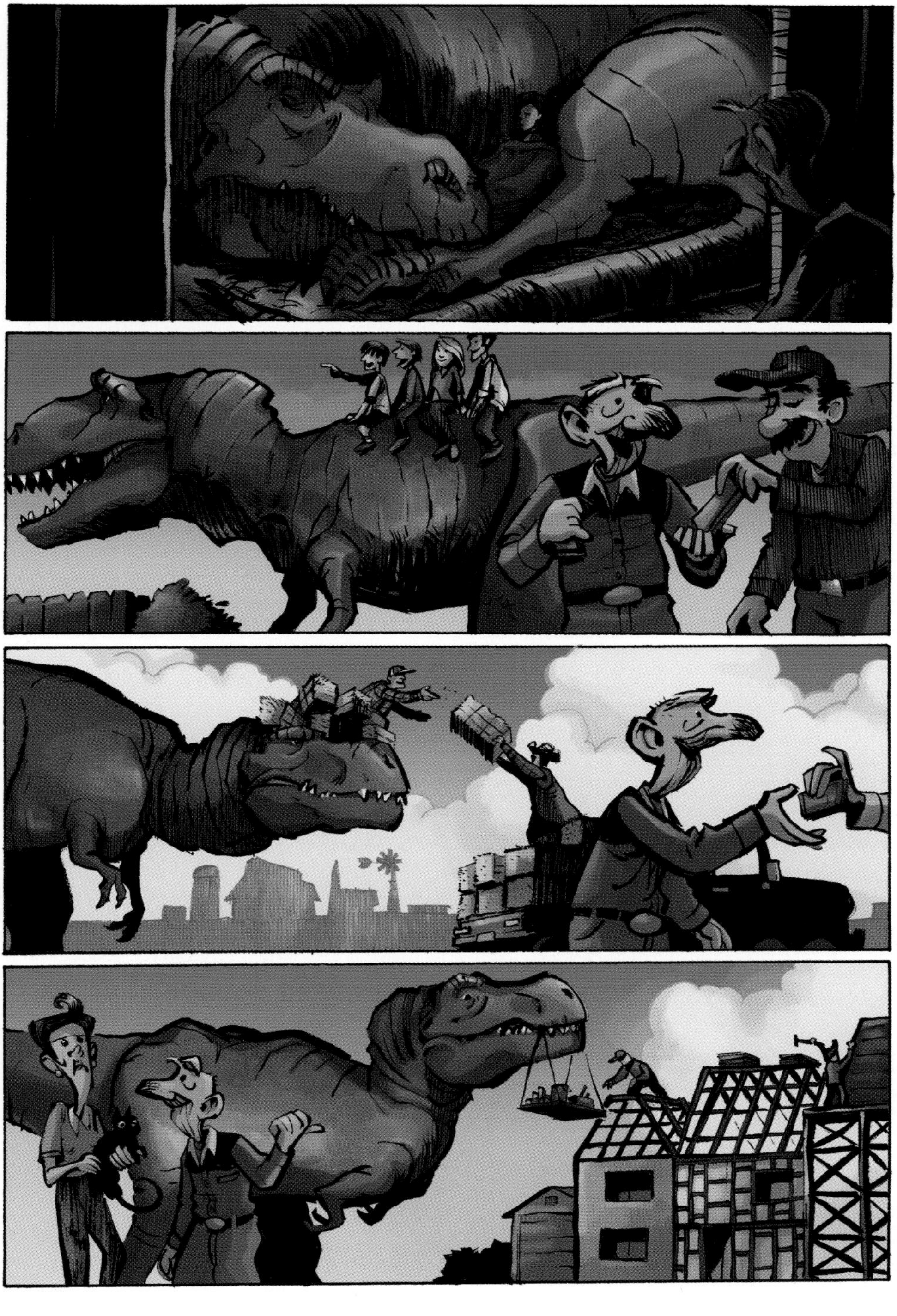

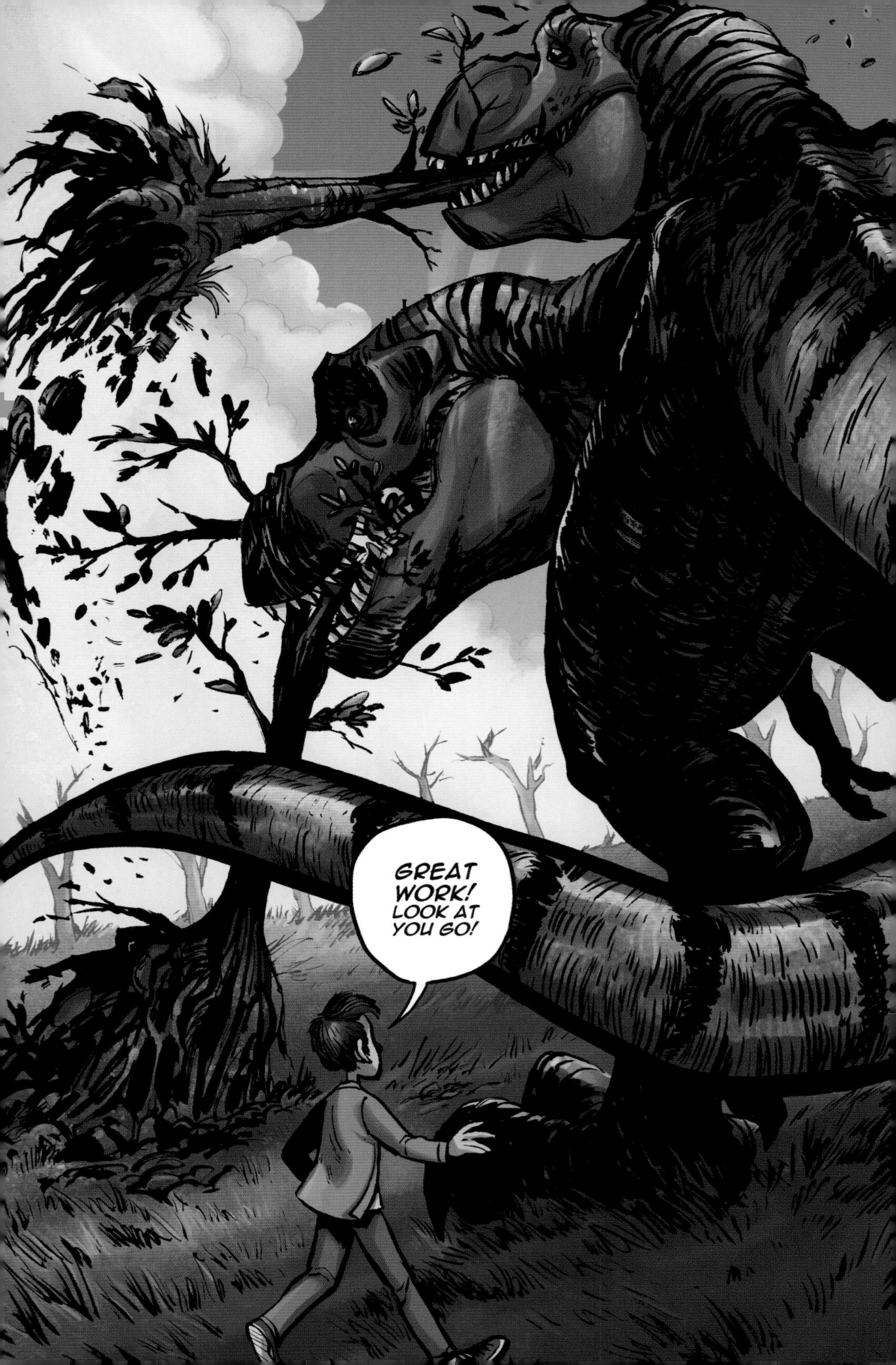
GREAT WORK! LOOK AT YOU GO!

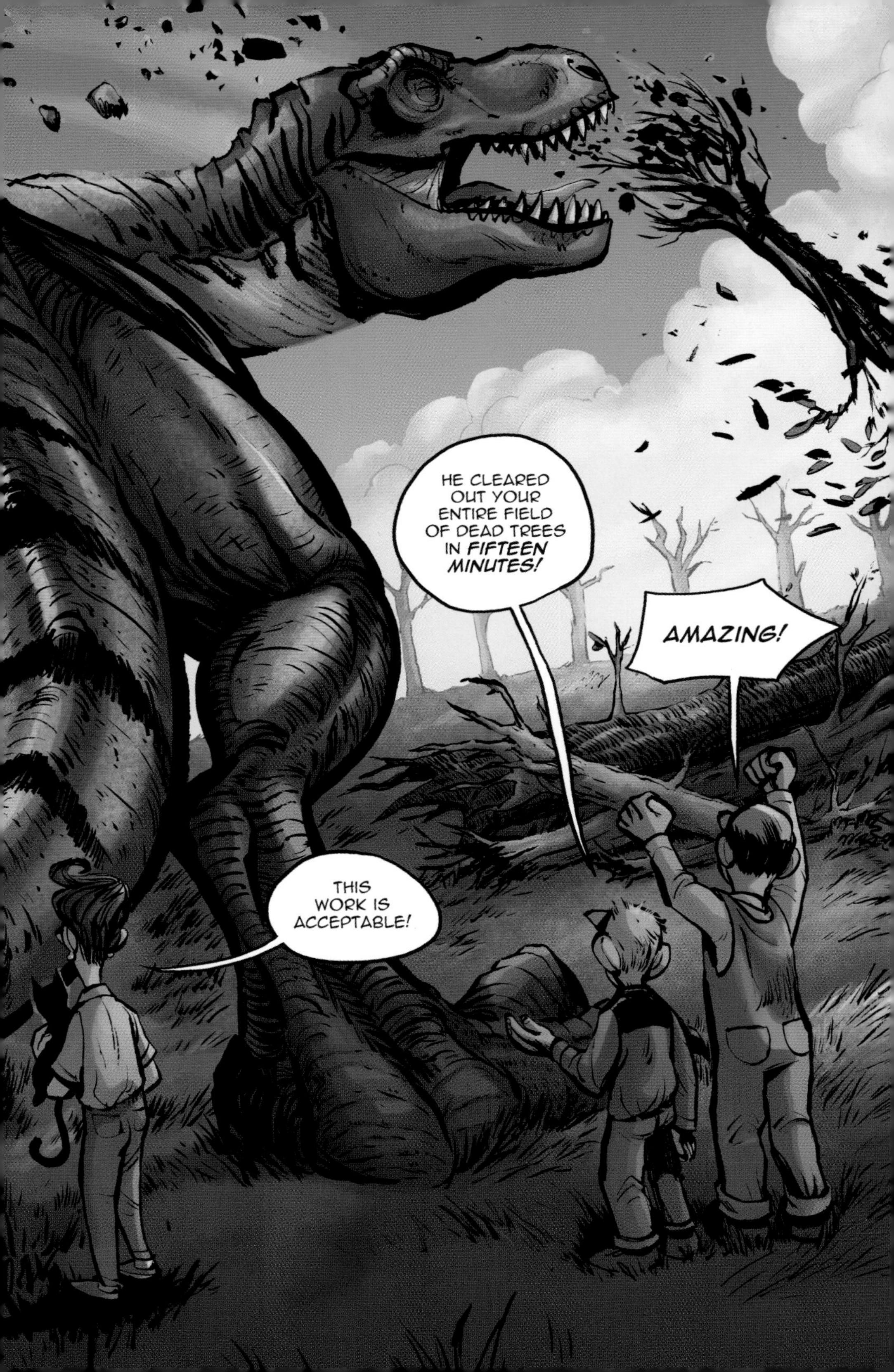
HE CLEARED OUT YOUR ENTIRE FIELD OF DEAD TREES IN *FIFTEEN MINUTES!*
AMAZING!
THIS WORK IS ACCEPTABLE!

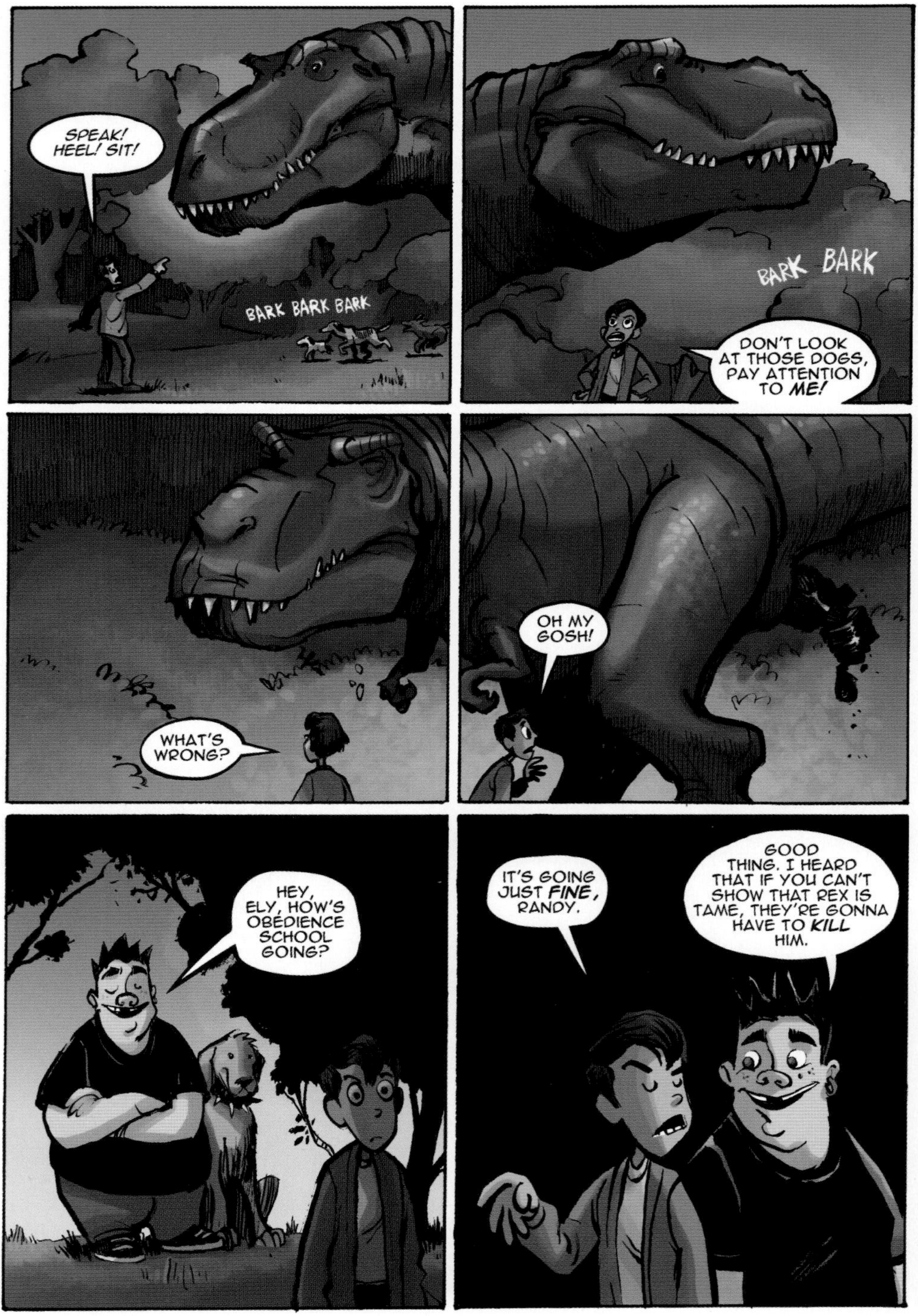
SPEAK! HEEL! SIT!
BARK BARK BARK
BARK BARK
DON'T LOOK AT THOSE DOGS, PAY ATTENTION TO ME!
WHAT'S WRONG?
OH MY GOSH!
HEY, ELY, HOW'S OBEDIENCE SCHOOL GOING?
IT'S GOING JUST FINE, RANDY.
GOOD THING. I HEARD THAT IF YOU CAN'T SHOW THAT REX IS TAME, THEY'RE GONNA HAVE TO KILL HIM.

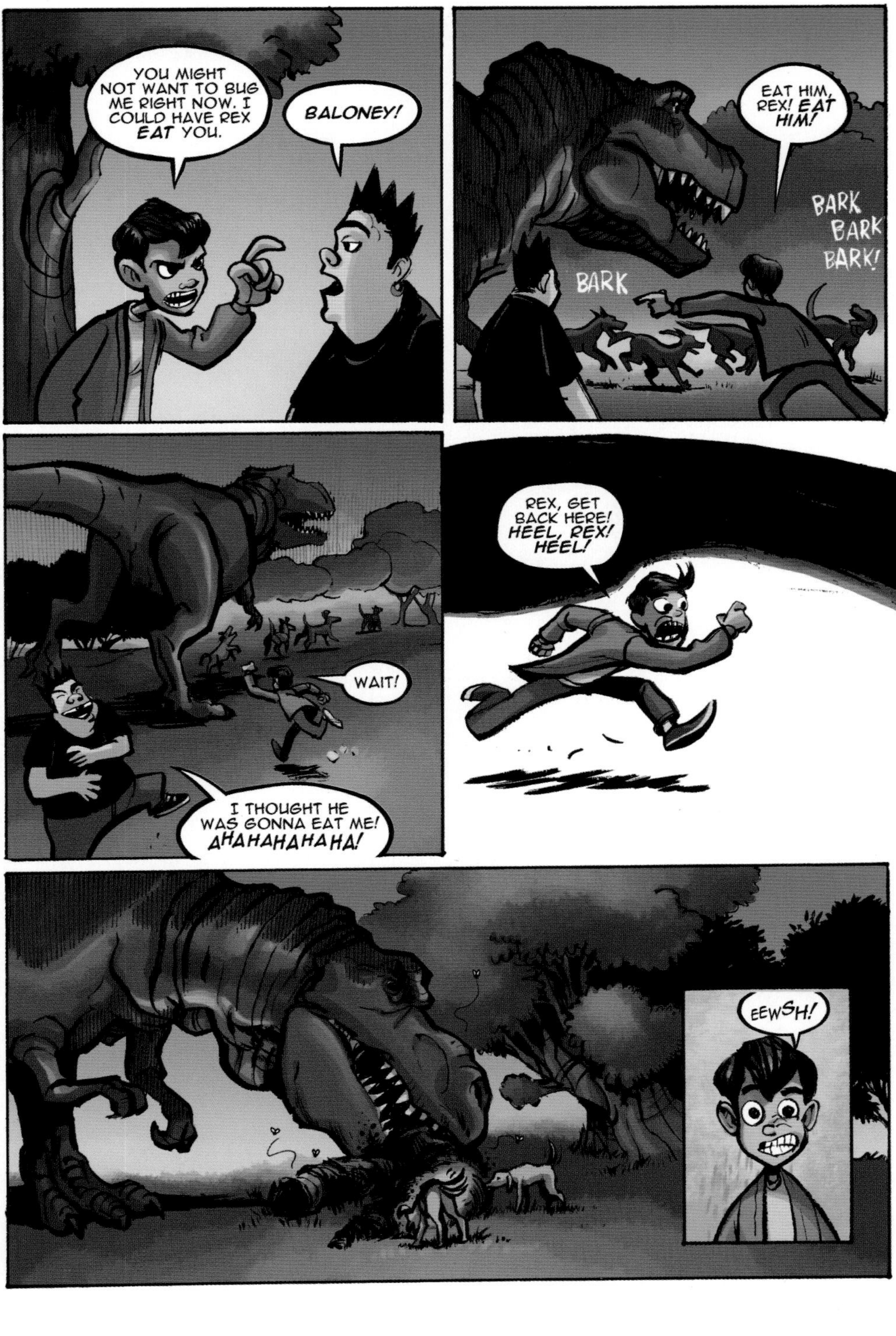
YOU MIGHT NOT WANT TO BUG ME RIGHT NOW. I COULD HAVE REX EAT YOU.
BALONEY!
EAT HIM, REX! EAT HIM!
BARK BARK BARK!
BARK
REX, GET BACK HERE! HEEL, REX! HEEL!
WAIT!
I THOUGHT HE WAS GONNA EAT ME! AHAHAHAHAHA!
EEWSH!

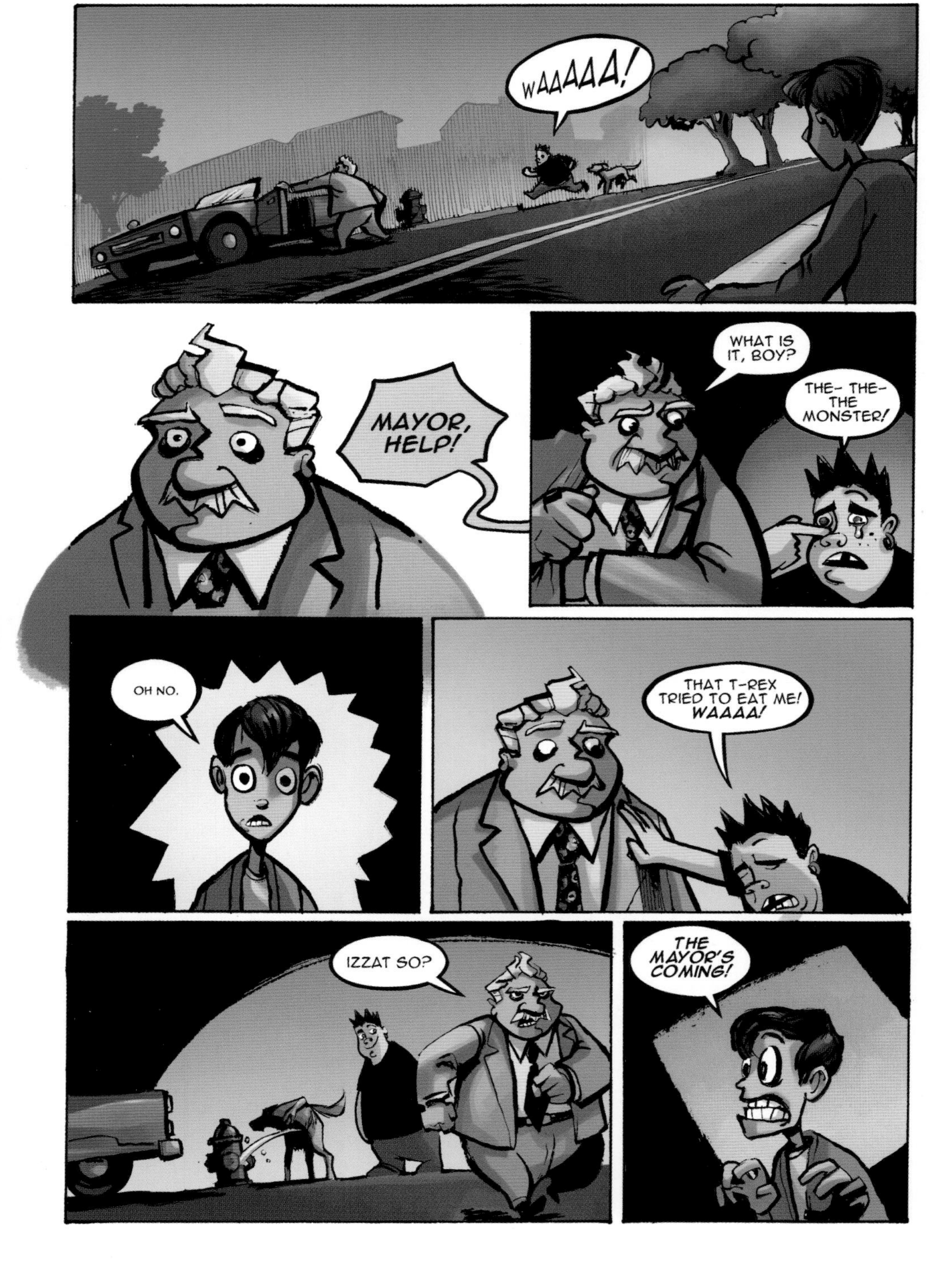
WAAAAA!
MAYOR, HELP!
WHAT IS IT, BOY?
THE- THE- THE MONSTER!
OH NO.
THAT T-REX TRIED TO EAT ME! WAAAA!
IZZAT SO?
THE MAYOR'S COMING!

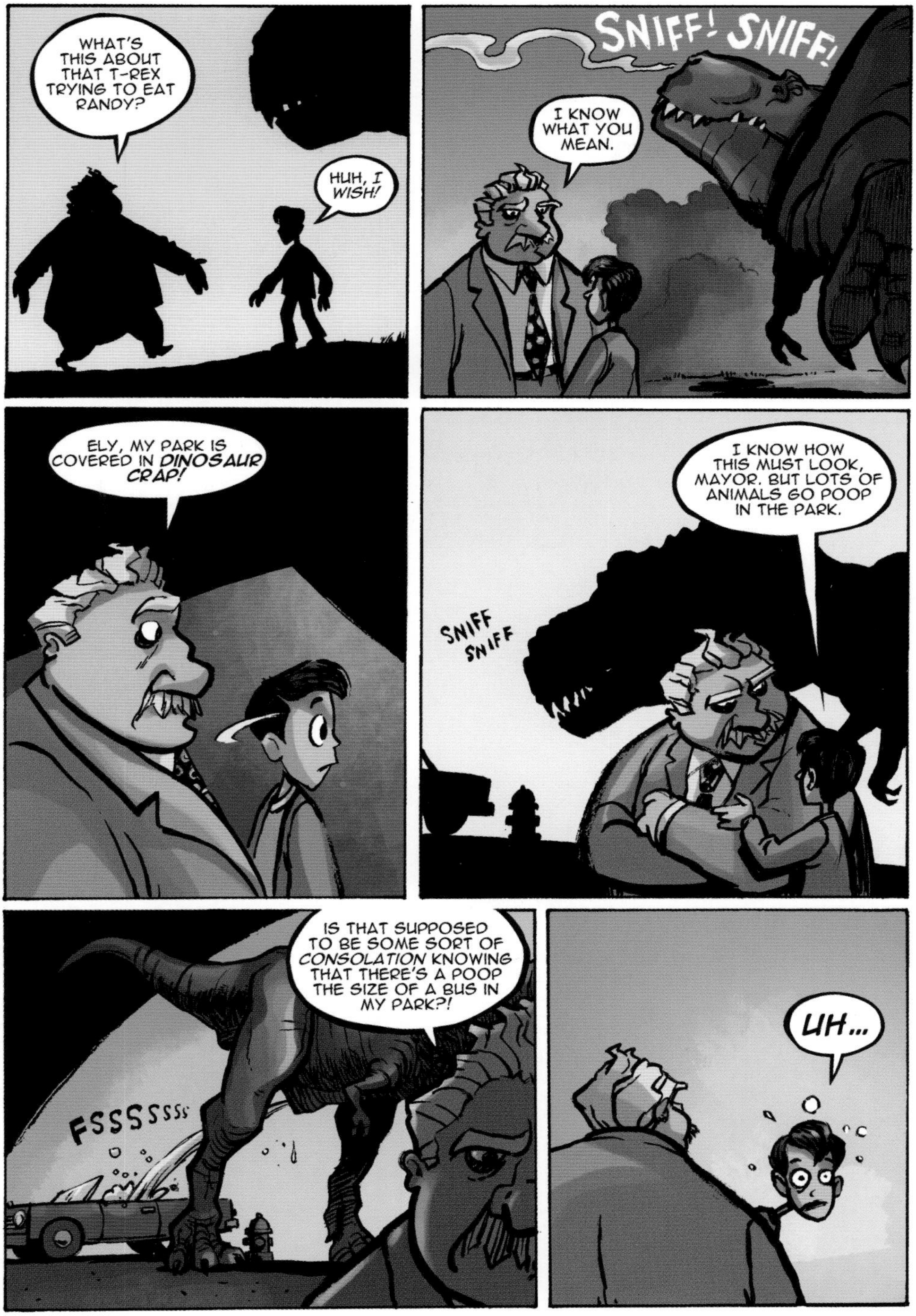
WHAT'S THIS ABOUT THAT T-REX TRYING TO EAT RANDY?
HUH, I WISH!
SNIFF! SNIFF!
I KNOW WHAT YOU MEAN.
ELY, MY PARK IS COVERED IN DINOSAUR CRAP!
I KNOW HOW THIS MUST LOOK, MAYOR. BUT LOTS OF ANIMALS GO POOP IN THE PARK.
SNIFF SNIFF
IS THAT SUPPOSED TO BE SOME SORT OF CONSOLATION KNOWING THAT THERE'S A POOP THE SIZE OF A BUS IN MY PARK?!
FSSSSSSS
UH...

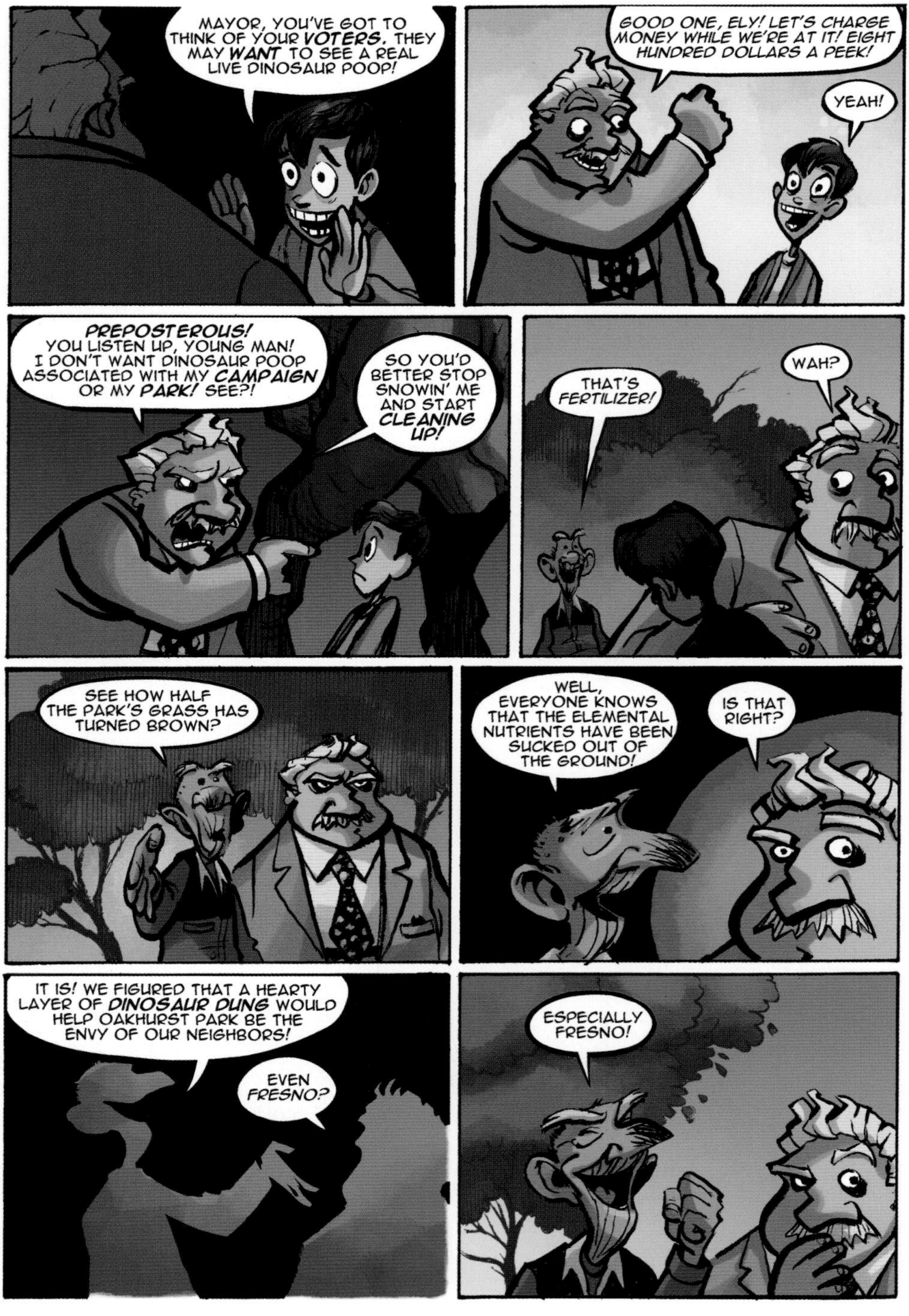
MAYOR, YOU'VE GOT TO THINK OF YOUR VOTERS. THEY MAY WANT TO SEE A REAL LIVE DINOSAUR POOP!
GOOD ONE, ELY! LET'S CHARGE MONEY WHILE WE'RE AT IT! EIGHT HUNDRED DOLLARS A PEEK!
YEAH!
PREPOSTEROUS! YOU LISTEN UP, YOUNG MAN! I DON'T WANT DINOSAUR POOP ASSOCIATED WITH MY CAMPAIGN OR MY PARK! SEE?!
SO YOU'D BETTER STOP SNOWIN' ME AND START CLEANING UP!
THAT'S FERTILIZER!
WAH?
SEE HOW HALF THE PARK'S GRASS HAS TURNED BROWN?
WELL, EVERYONE KNOWS THAT THE ELEMENTAL NUTRIENTS HAVE BEEN SUCKED OUT OF THE GROUND!
IS THAT RIGHT?
IT IS! WE FIGURED THAT A HEARTY LAYER OF DINOSAUR DUNG WOULD HELP OAKHURST PARK BE THE ENVY OF OUR NEIGHBORS!
EVEN FRESNO?
ESPECIALLY FRESNO!

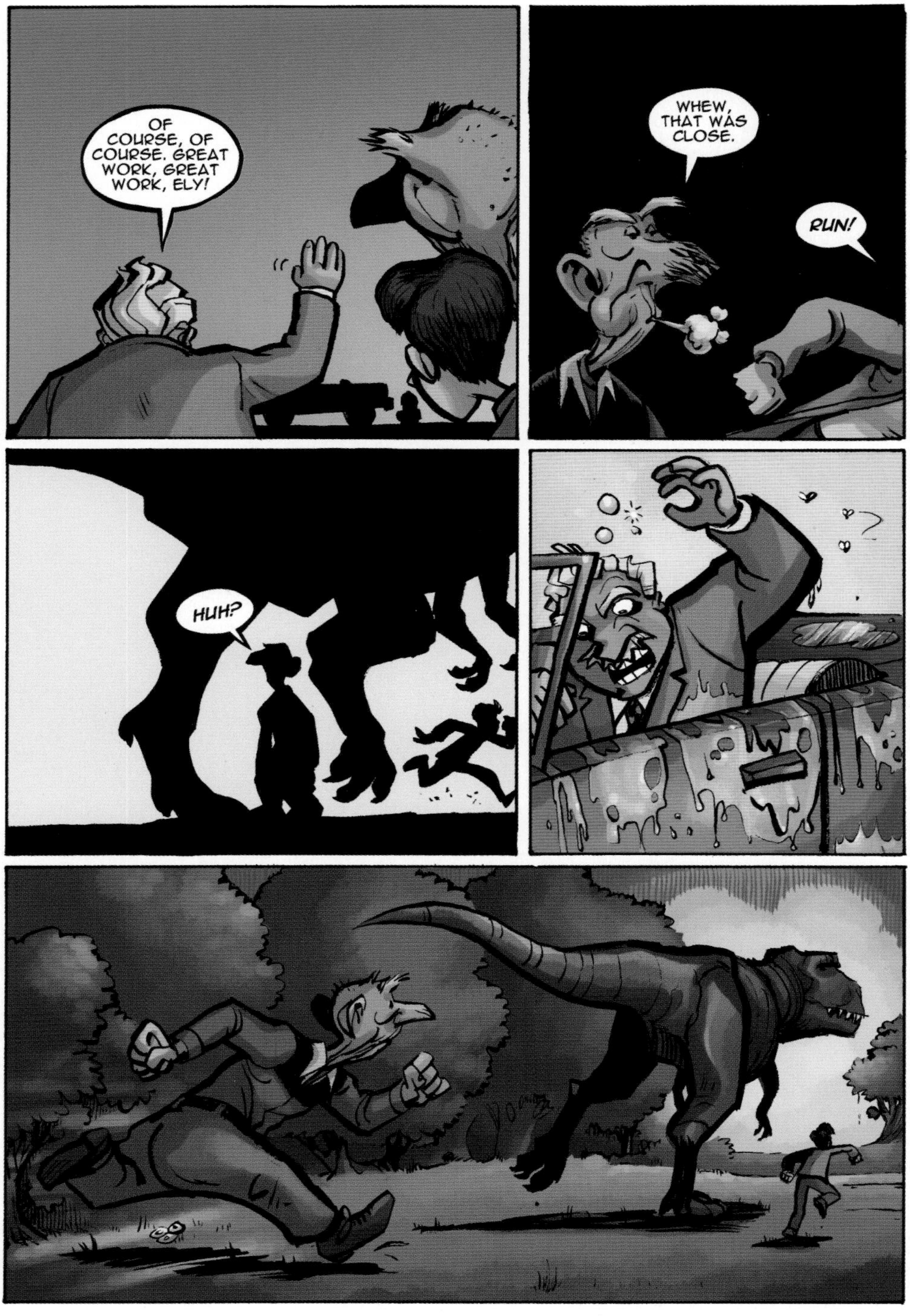
OF COURSE, OF COURSE. GREAT WORK, GREAT WORK, ELY!
WHEW, THAT WAS CLOSE.
RUN!
HUH?

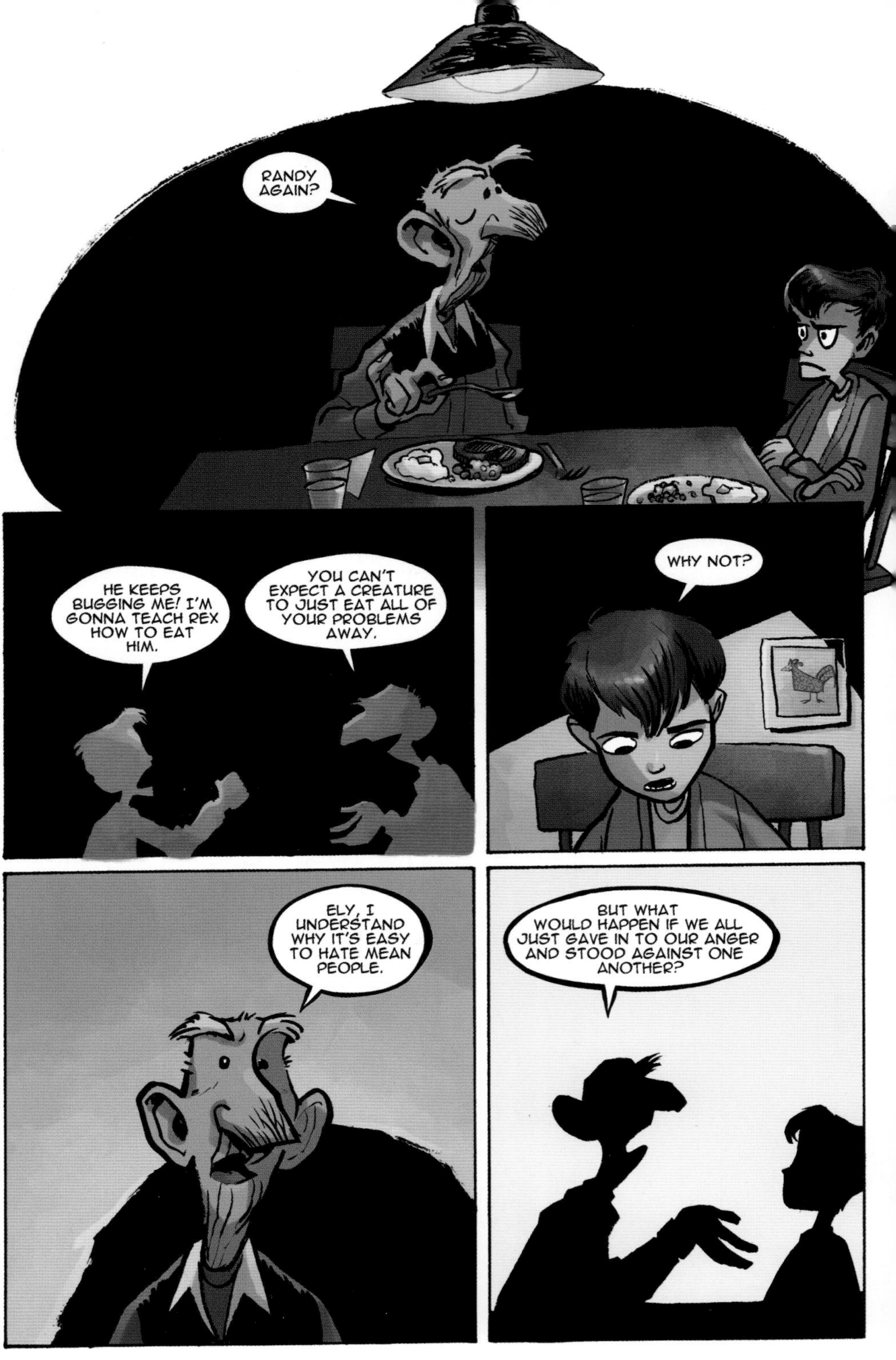
RANDY AGAIN?
HE KEEPS BUGGING ME! I'M GONNA TEACH REX HOW TO EAT HIM.
YOU CAN'T EXPECT A CREATURE TO JUST EAT ALL OF YOUR PROBLEMS AWAY.
WHY NOT?
ELY, I UNDERSTAND WHY IT'S EASY TO HATE MEAN PEOPLE.
BUT WHAT WOULD HAPPEN IF WE ALL JUST GAVE IN TO OUR ANGER AND STOOD AGAINST ONE ANOTHER?

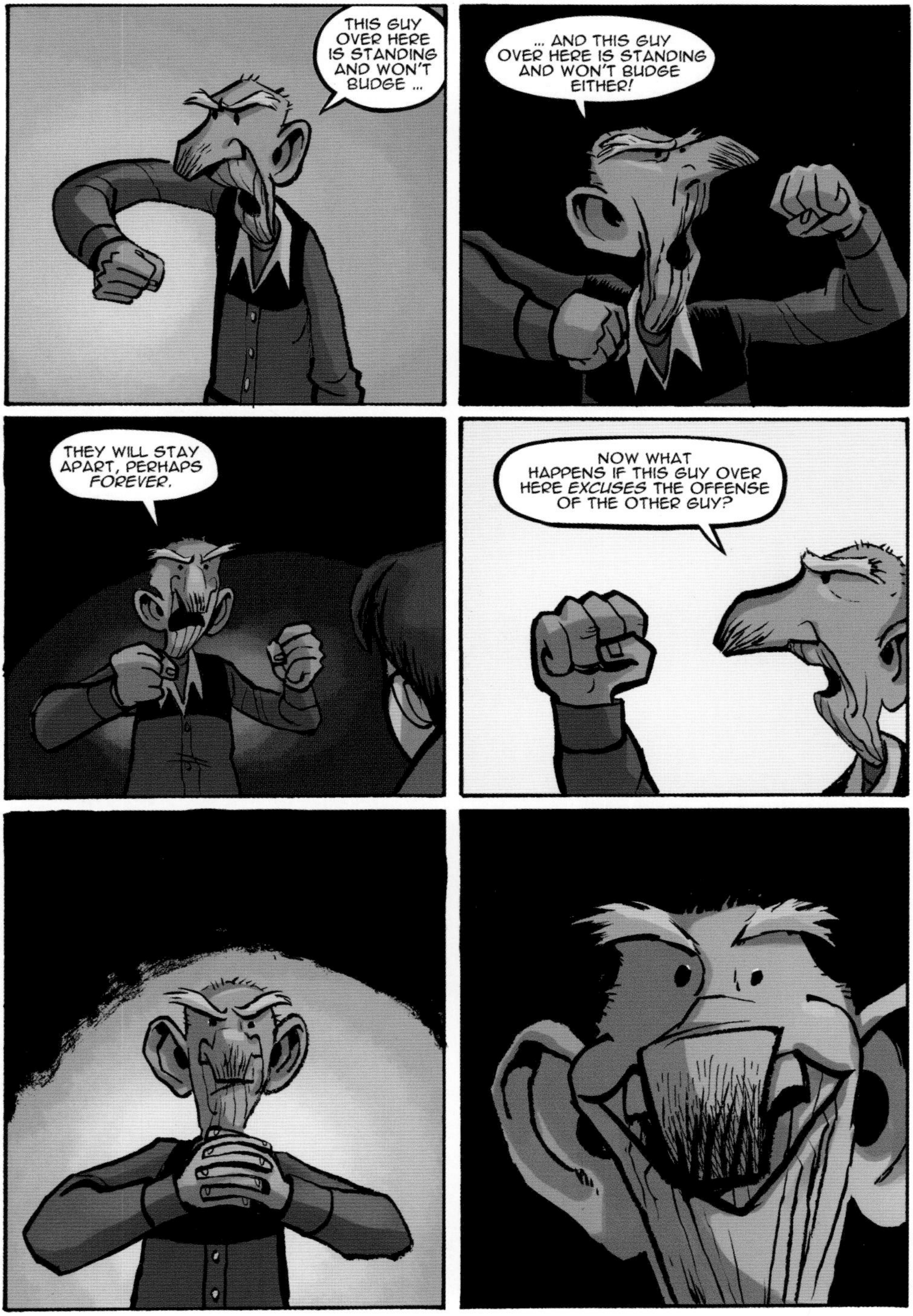
THIS GUY OVER HERE IS STANDING AND WON'T BUDGE ...
... AND THIS GUY OVER HERE IS STANDING AND WON'T BUDGE EITHER!
THEY WILL STAY APART, PERHAPS *FOREVER.*
NOW WHAT HAPPENS IF THIS GUY OVER HERE *EXCUSES* THE OFFENSE OF THE OTHER GUY?

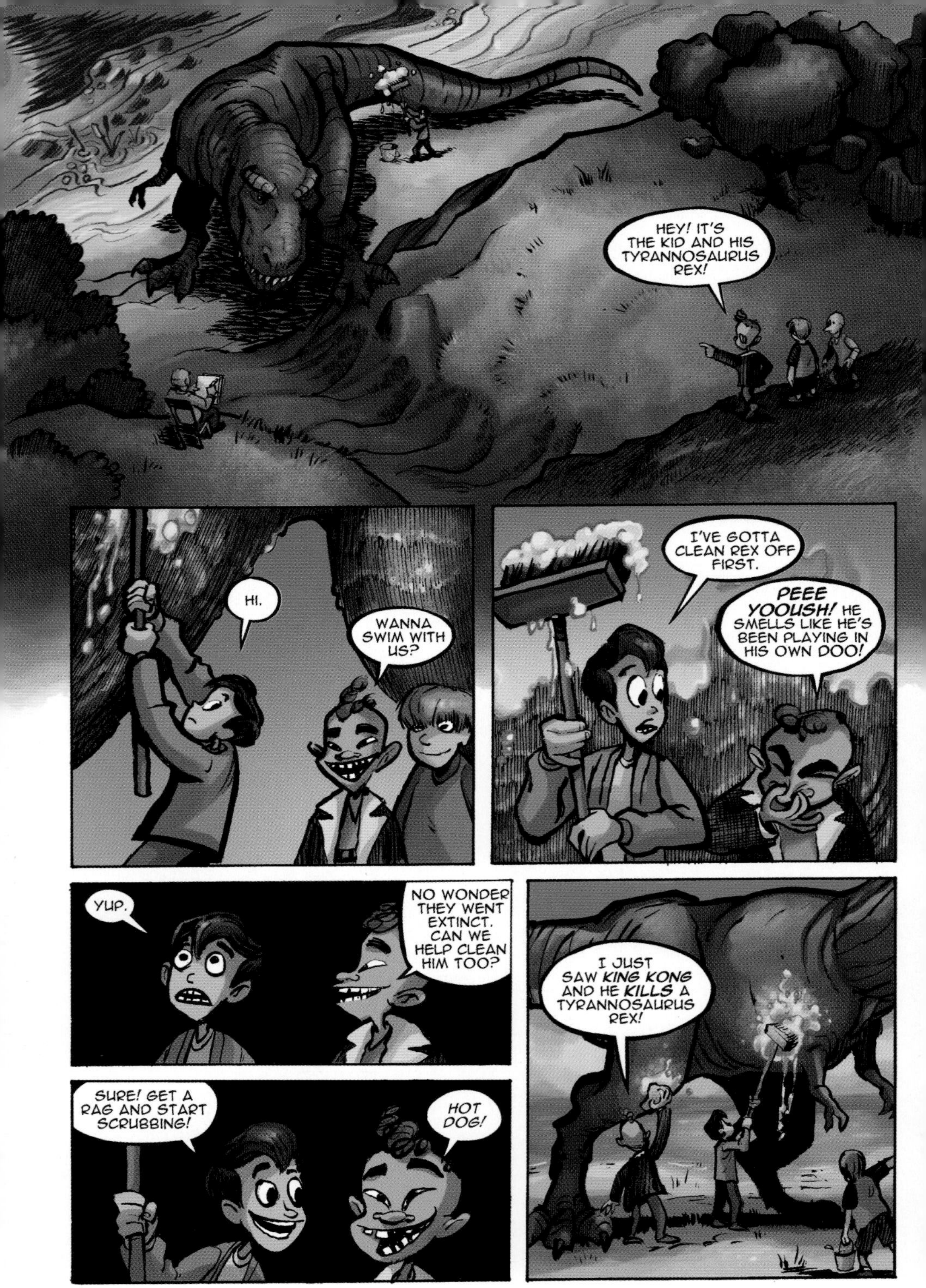
HEY! IT'S THE KID AND HIS TYRANNOSAURUS REX!
HI.
WANNA SWIM WITH US?
I'VE GOTTA CLEAN REX OFF FIRST.
PEEE YOOUSH! HE SMELLS LIKE HE'S BEEN PLAYING IN HIS OWN DOO!
YUP.
NO WONDER THEY WENT EXTINCT. CAN WE HELP CLEAN HIM TOO?
SURE! GET A RAG AND START SCRUBBING!
HOT DOG!
I JUST SAW KING KONG AND HE KILLS A TYRANNOSAURUS REX!

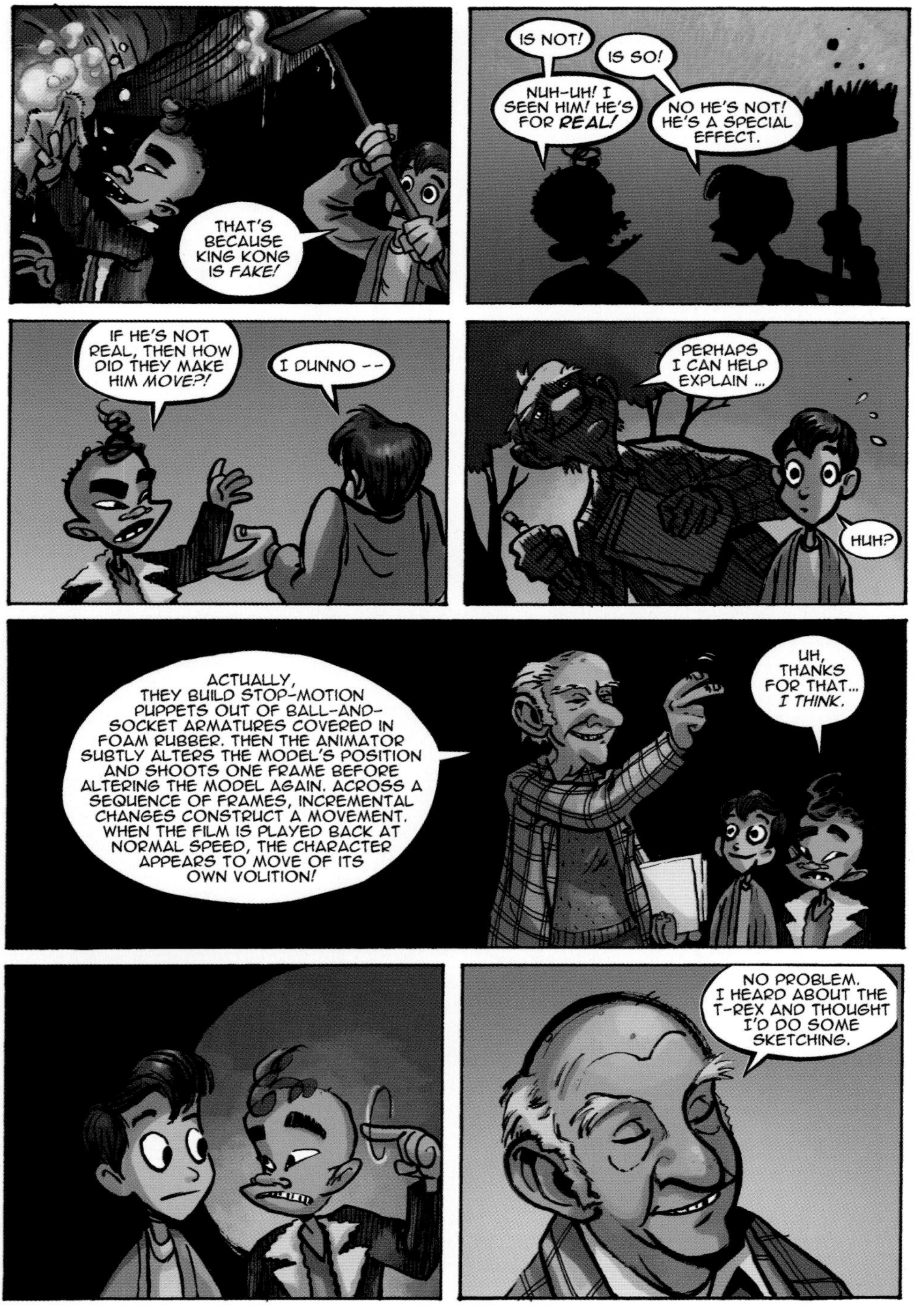
THAT'S BECAUSE KING KONG IS FAKE!
IS NOT!
IS SO!
NUH-UH! I SEEN HIM! HE'S FOR REAL!
NO HE'S NOT! HE'S A SPECIAL EFFECT.
IF HE'S NOT REAL, THEN HOW DID THEY MAKE HIM MOVE?!
I DUNNO --
PERHAPS I CAN HELP EXPLAIN ...
HUH?
ACTUALLY, THEY BUILD STOP-MOTION PUPPETS OUT OF BALL-AND-SOCKET ARMATURES COVERED IN FOAM RUBBER. THEN THE ANIMATOR SUBTLY ALTERS THE MODEL'S POSITION AND SHOOTS ONE FRAME BEFORE ALTERING THE MODEL AGAIN. ACROSS A SEQUENCE OF FRAMES, INCREMENTAL CHANGES CONSTRUCT A MOVEMENT. WHEN THE FILM IS PLAYED BACK AT NORMAL SPEED, THE CHARACTER APPEARS TO MOVE OF ITS OWN VOLITION!
UH, THANKS FOR THAT... I THINK.
NO PROBLEM. I HEARD ABOUT THE T-REX AND THOUGHT I'D DO SOME SKETCHING.

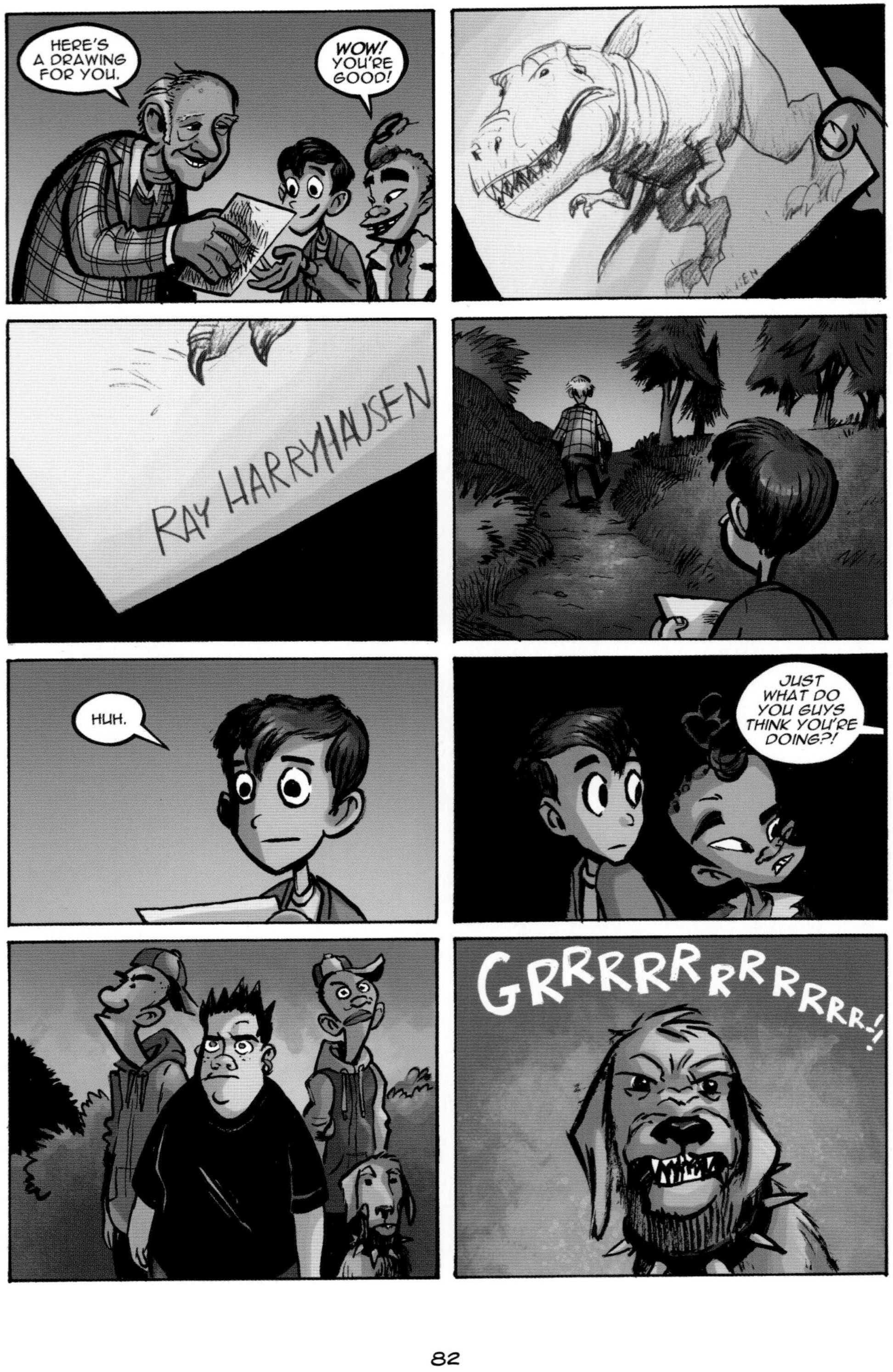
HERE'S A DRAWING FOR YOU.
WOW! YOU'RE GOOD!
RAY HARRYHAUSEN
HUH.
JUST WHAT DO YOU GUYS THINK YOU'RE DOING?!
GRRRRRRRRRRR-!

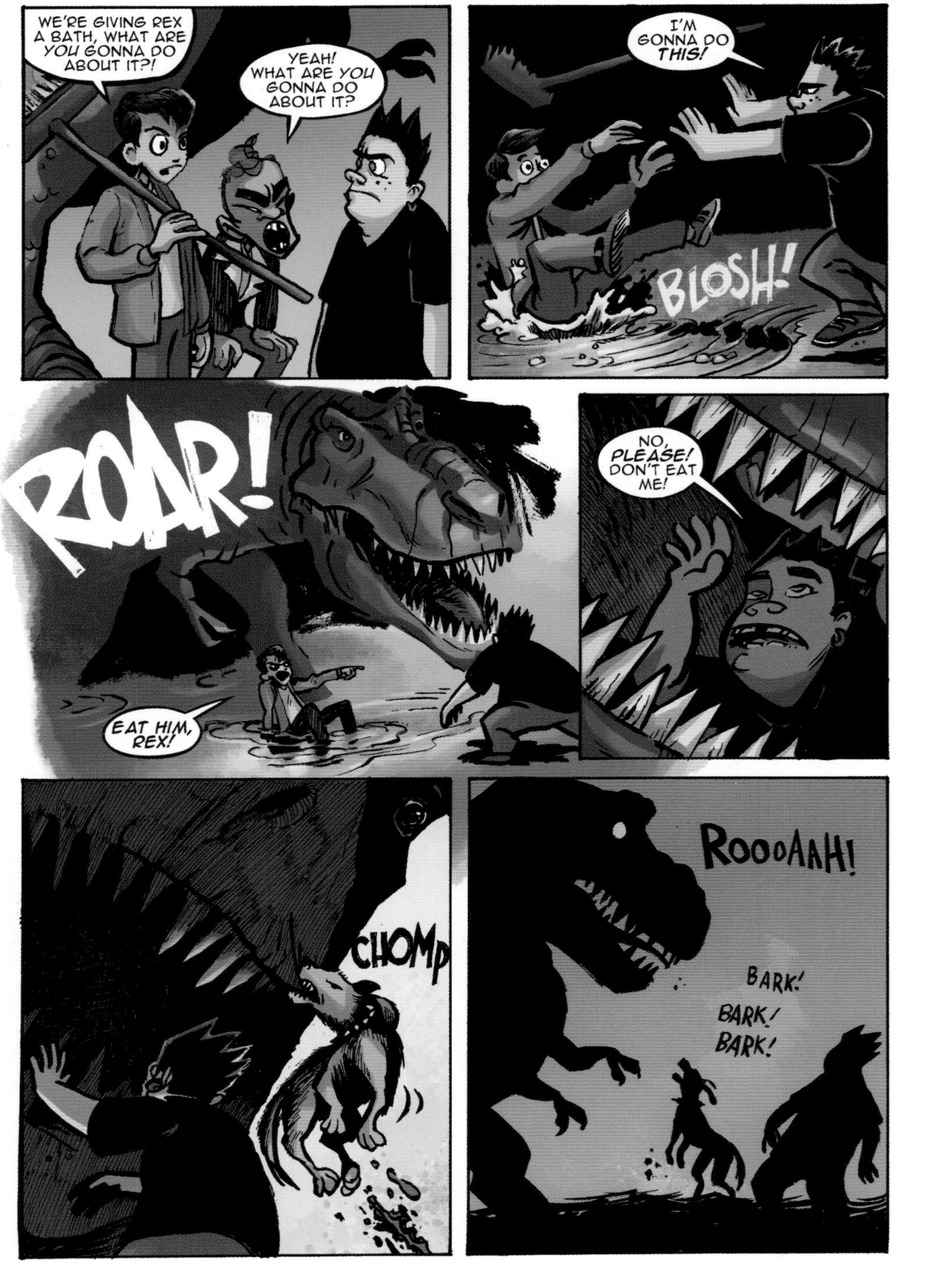
WE'RE GIVING REX A BATH, WHAT ARE *YOU* GONNA DO ABOUT IT?!
YEAH! WHAT ARE *YOU* GONNA DO ABOUT IT?
I'M GONNA DO *THIS!*
BLOSH!
ROAR!
EAT HIM, REX!
NO, *PLEASE!* DON'T EAT ME!
CHOMP
ROOOAAH!
BARK!
BARK!
BARK!

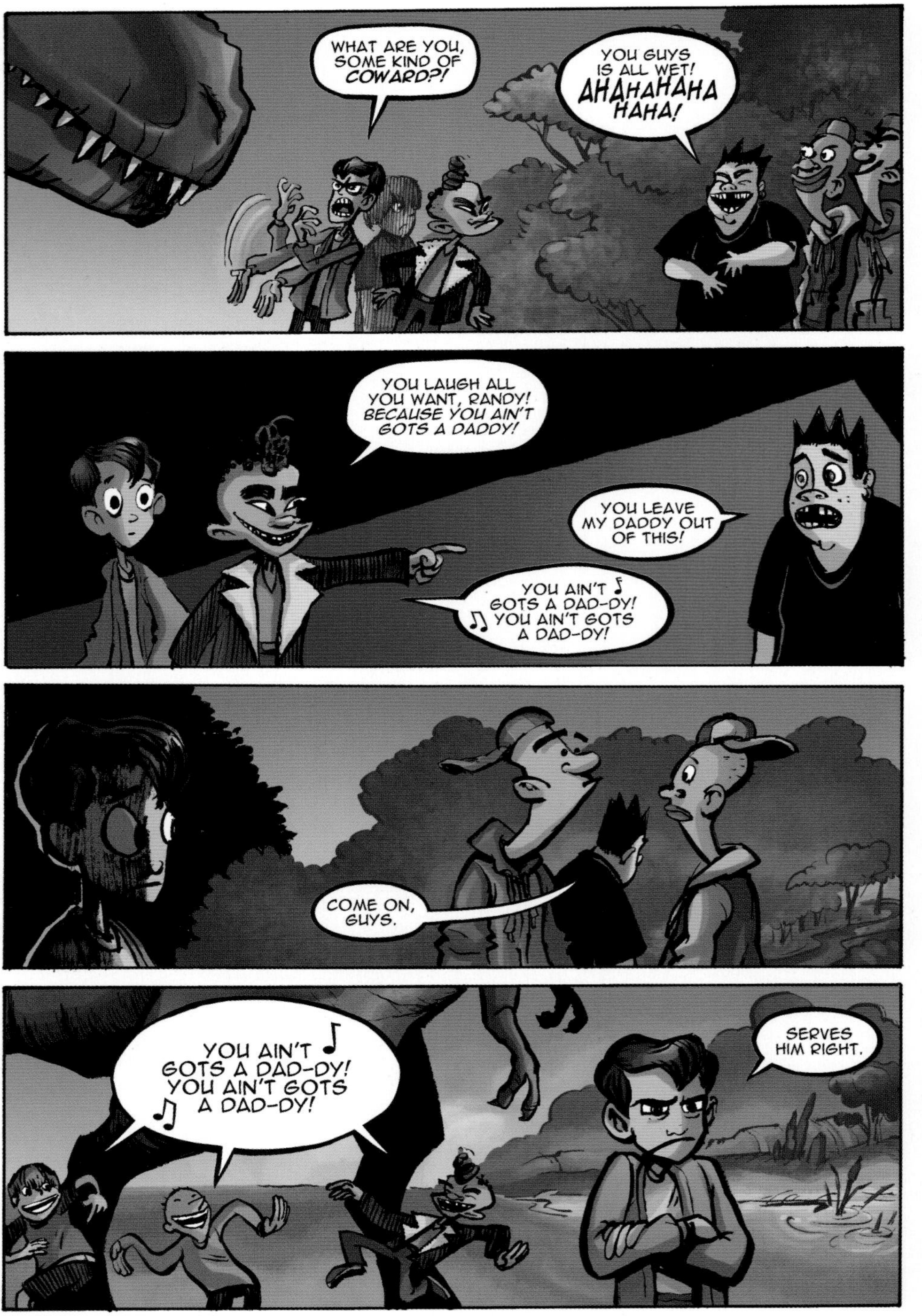
WHAT ARE YOU, SOME KIND OF COWARD?!
YOU GUYS IS ALL WET! AHAHAHAHA HAHA!
YOU LAUGH ALL YOU WANT, RANDY! BECAUSE YOU AIN'T GOTS A DADDY!
YOU LEAVE MY DADDY OUT OF THIS!
YOU AIN'T GOTS A DAD-DY! YOU AIN'T GOTS A DAD-DY!
COME ON, GUYS.
YOU AIN'T GOTS A DAD-DY! YOU AIN'T GOTS A DAD-DY!
SERVES HIM RIGHT.

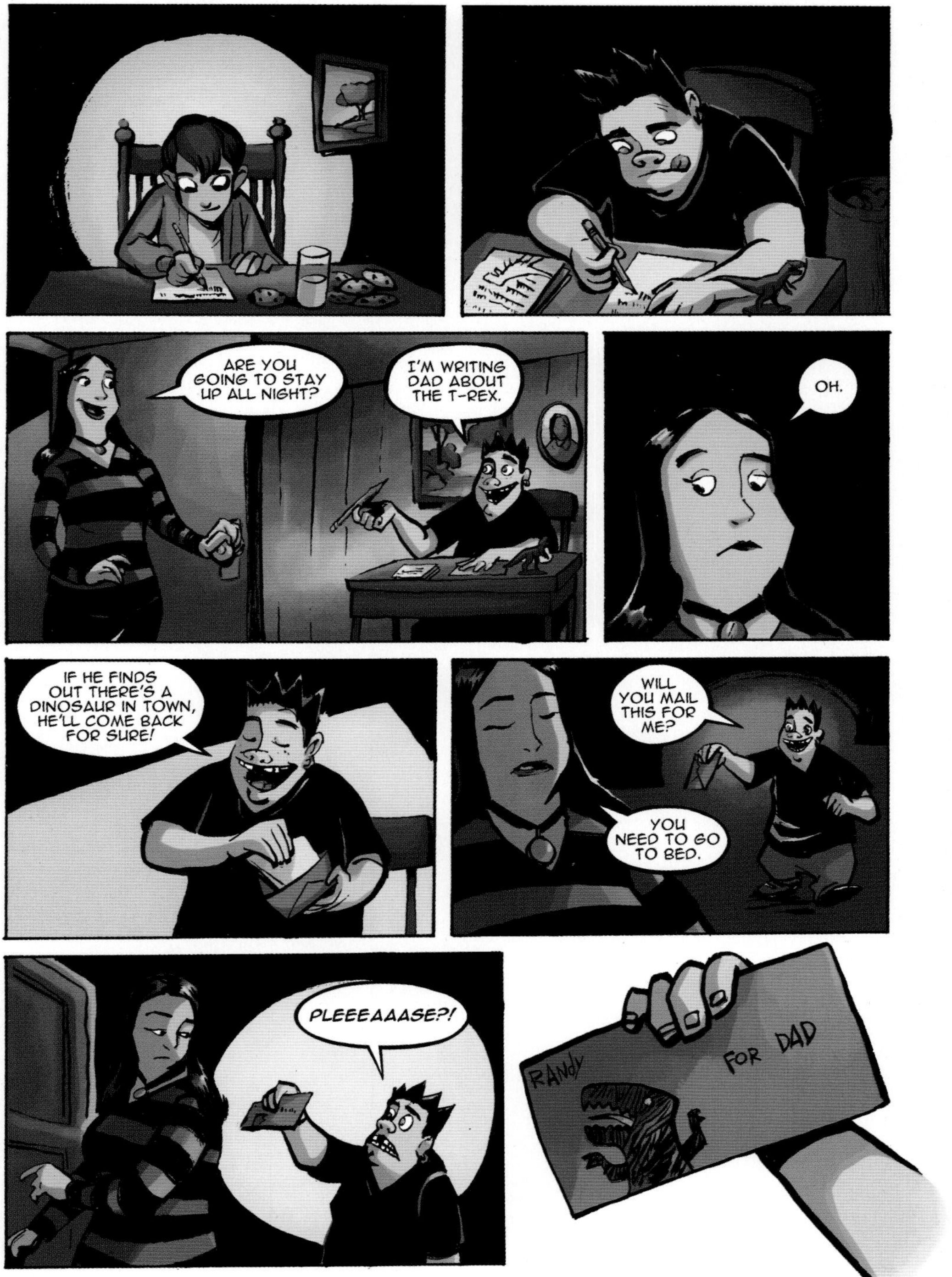

ARE YOU GOING TO STAY UP ALL NIGHT?
I'M WRITING DAD ABOUT THE T-REX.
OH.
IF HE FINDS OUT THERE'S A DINOSAUR IN TOWN, HE'LL COME BACK FOR SURE!
WILL YOU MAIL THIS FOR ME?
YOU NEED TO GO TO BED.
PLEEEAAAASE?!
RAndy
FOR DAD

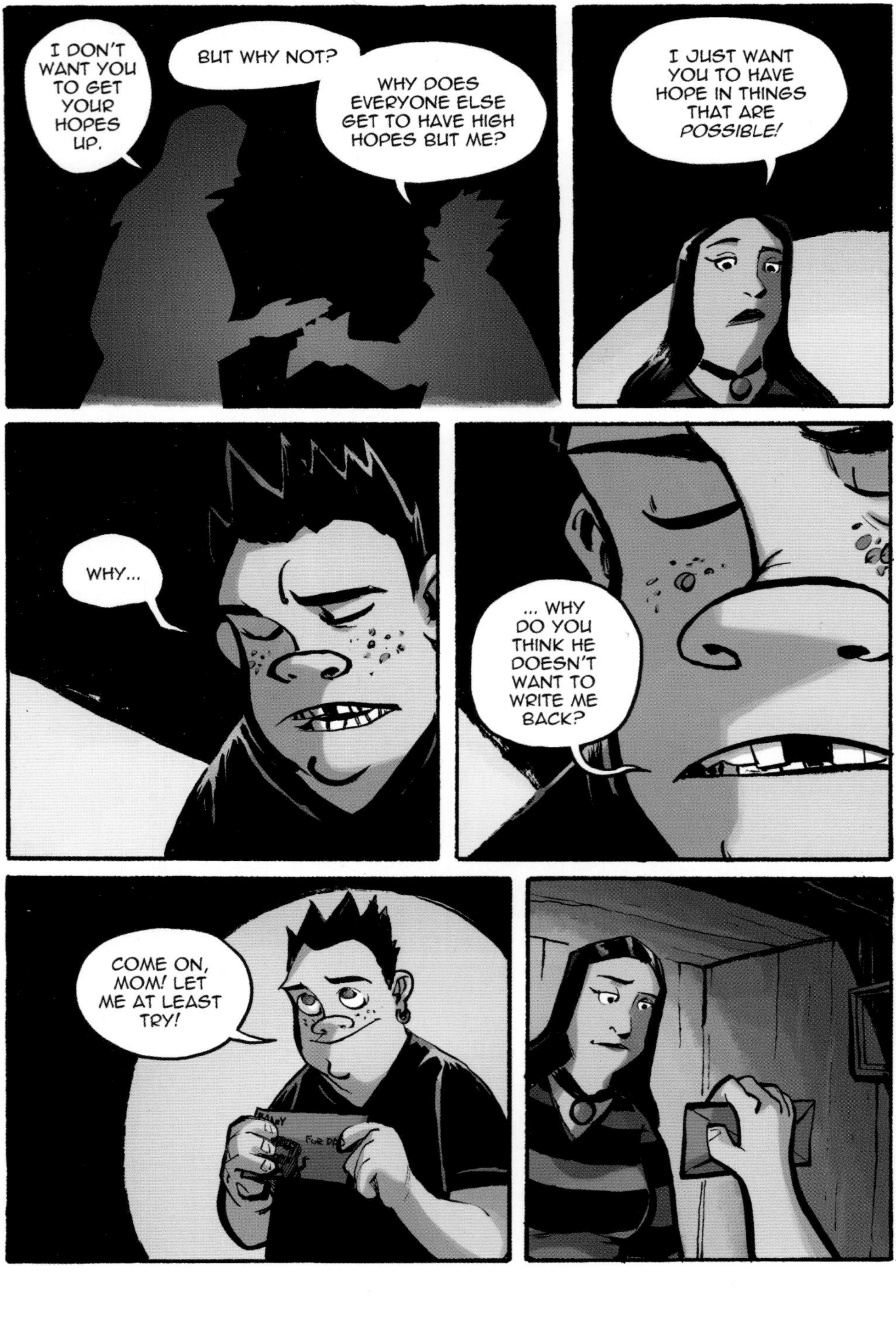
I DON'T WANT YOU TO GET YOUR HOPES UP.
BUT WHY NOT?
WHY DOES EVERYONE ELSE GET TO HAVE HIGH HOPES BUT ME?
I JUST WANT YOU TO HAVE HOPE IN THINGS THAT ARE *POSSIBLE!*
WHY...
... WHY DO YOU THINK HE DOESN'T WANT TO WRITE ME BACK?
COME ON, MOM! LET ME AT LEAST TRY!
FOR DAD

OKAY. HERE, I'LL HELP YOU WITH THE ADDRESS.
THANKS, MOM!
NOW GO TO SLEEP.
WE GOT A LETTER FROM ELY!
Dear Mom and Dad,
I'm having fun getting
lots of work done
at Grandpa's farm.
←I have a
Pet Tyranno-
saurus Rex.
Rex.
LOVE,
ELY IS SO FUNNY! WHAT AN IMAGINATION!

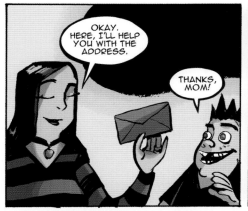

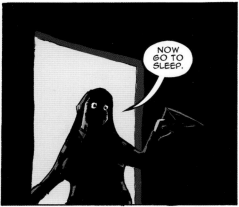

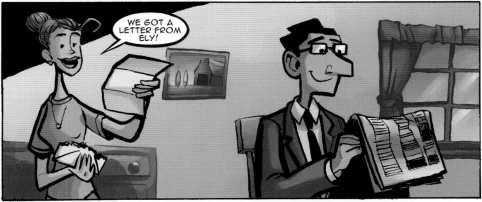

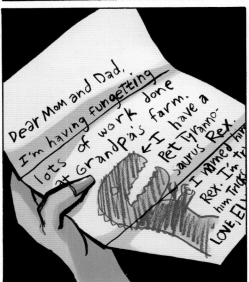

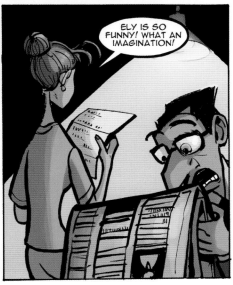

HONEY?

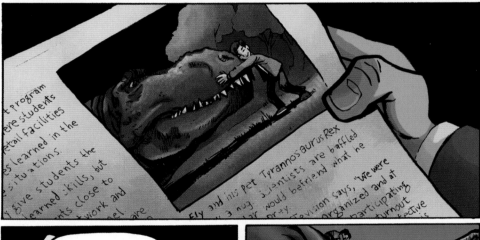

THIS IS THE HEROIC STORY OF TEN-YEAR-OLD ELY AND HIS TYRANNOSAURUS REX.

BEHOLD THEIR ATTEMPT TO DEFY ALL ODDS TO SAVE A CAT DROWNING IN A TWENTY-FOOT ABANDONED WELL-SHAFT!

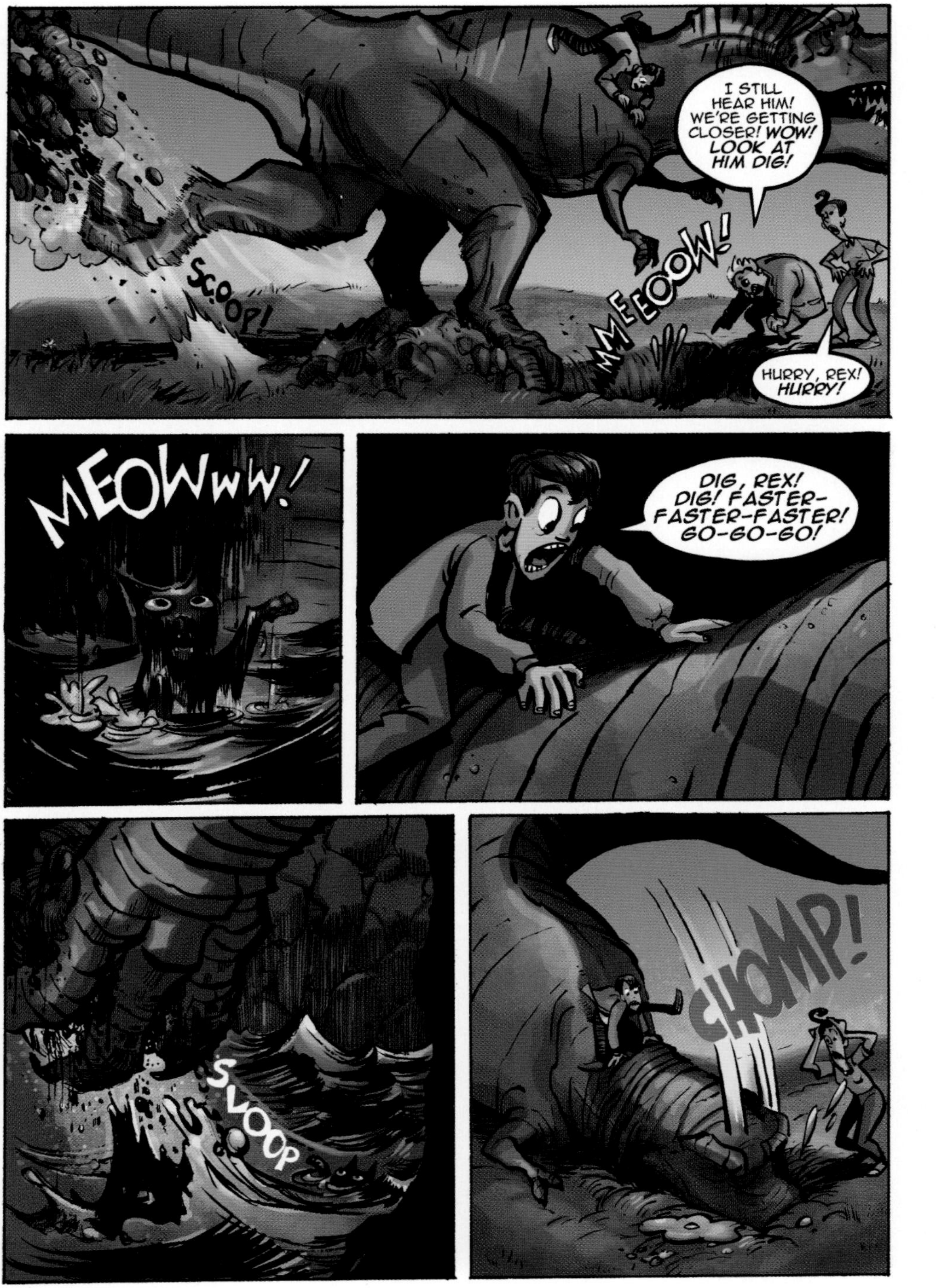
I STILL HEAR HIM! WE'RE GETTING CLOSER! WOW! LOOK AT HIM DIG!
SCOOP!
MMEEOOW!
HURRY, REX! HURRY!
MEOWwww!
DIG, REX! DIG! FASTER-FASTER-FASTER! GO-GO-GO!
SVOOP
CHOMP!

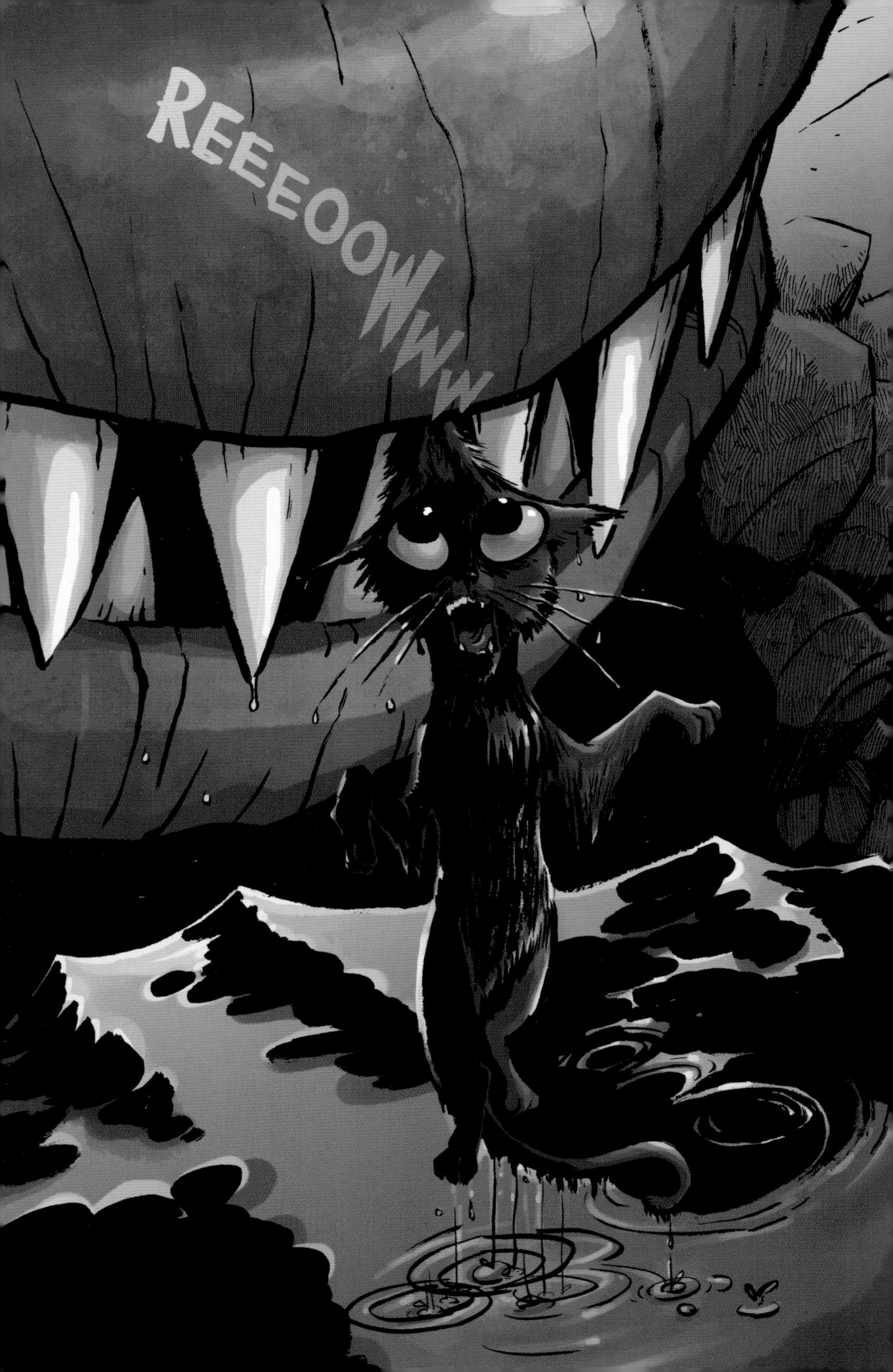
REEEOOWWWW

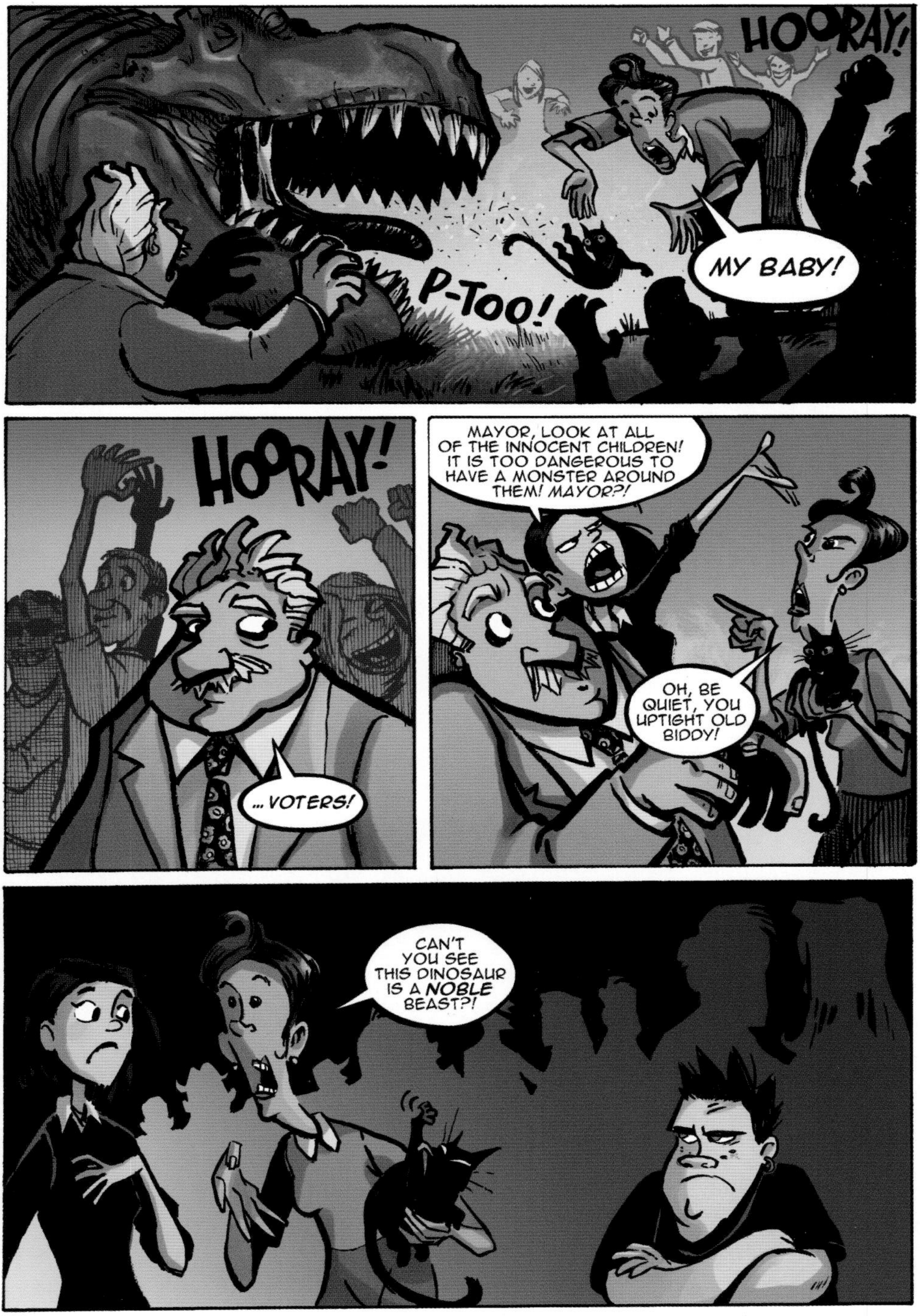
HOORAY!
P-TOO!
MY BABY!
HOORAY!
...VOTERS!
MAYOR, LOOK AT ALL OF THE INNOCENT CHILDREN! IT IS TOO DANGEROUS TO HAVE A MONSTER AROUND THEM! MAYOR?!
OH, BE QUIET, YOU UPTIGHT OLD BIDDY!
CAN'T YOU SEE THIS DINOSAUR IS A NOBLE BEAST?!

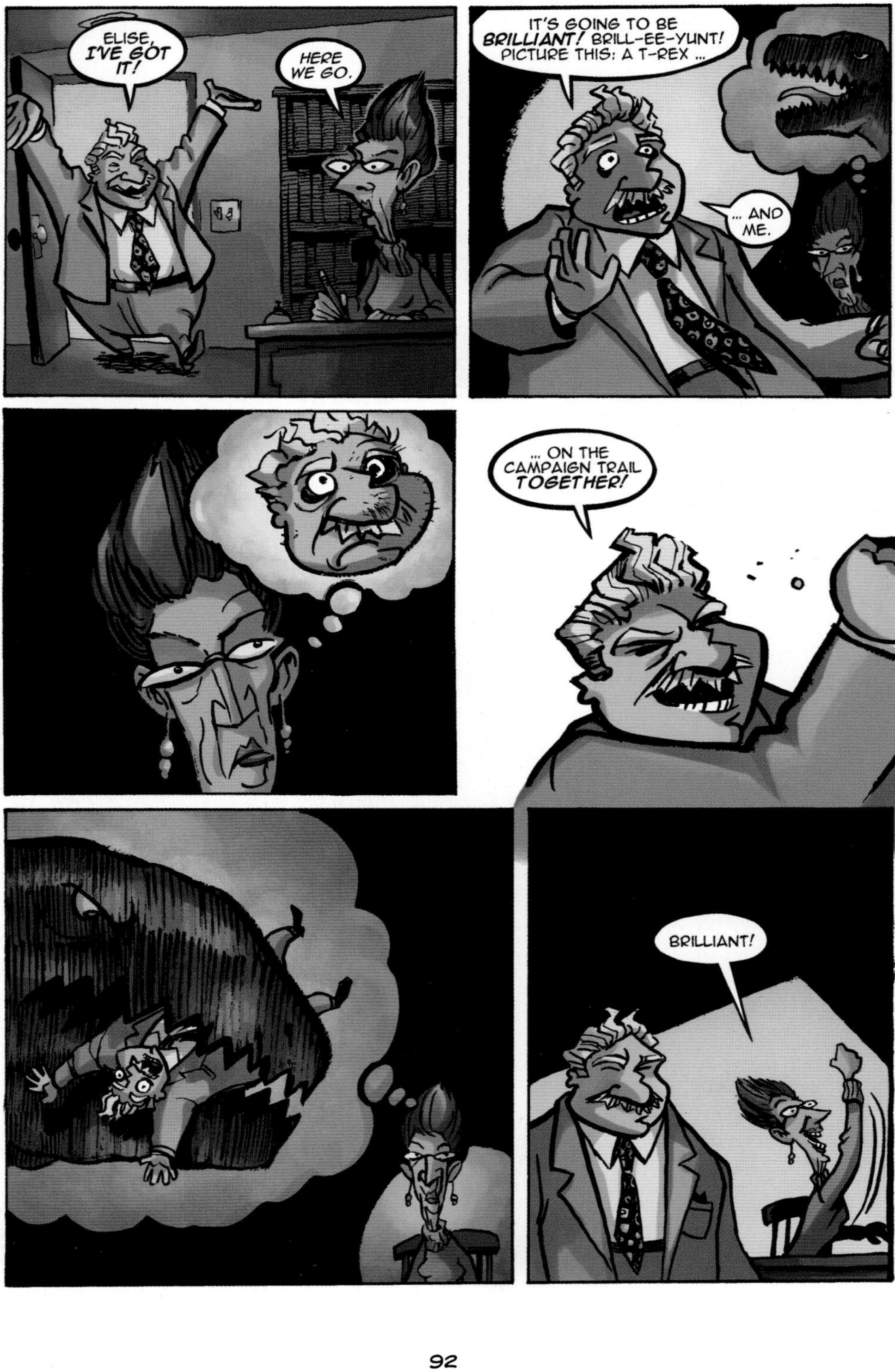
ELISE, I'VE GOT IT!
HERE WE GO.
IT'S GOING TO BE BRILLIANT! BRILL-EE-YUNT! PICTURE THIS: A T-REX ...
... AND ME.
... ON THE CAMPAIGN TRAIL TOGETHER!
BRILLIANT!

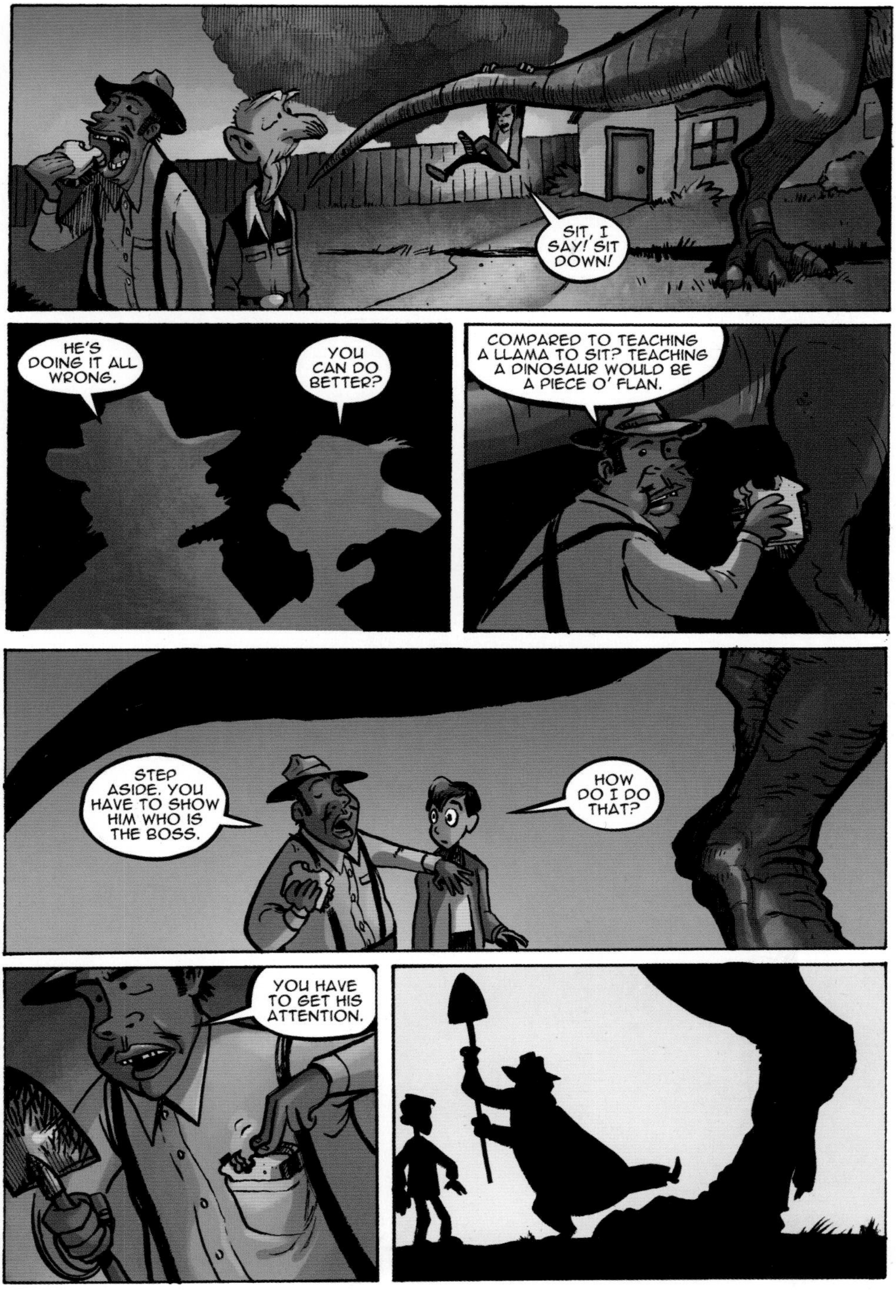
SIT, I SAY! SIT DOWN!
HE'S DOING IT ALL WRONG.
YOU CAN DO BETTER?
COMPARED TO TEACHING A LLAMA TO SIT? TEACHING A DINOSAUR WOULD BE A PIECE O' FLAN.
STEP ASIDE. YOU HAVE TO SHOW HIM WHO IS THE BOSS.
HOW DO I DO THAT?
YOU HAVE TO GET HIS ATTENTION.

K-PANG!

YOU SIT!

AAAAAA

AAAHHHHH!!

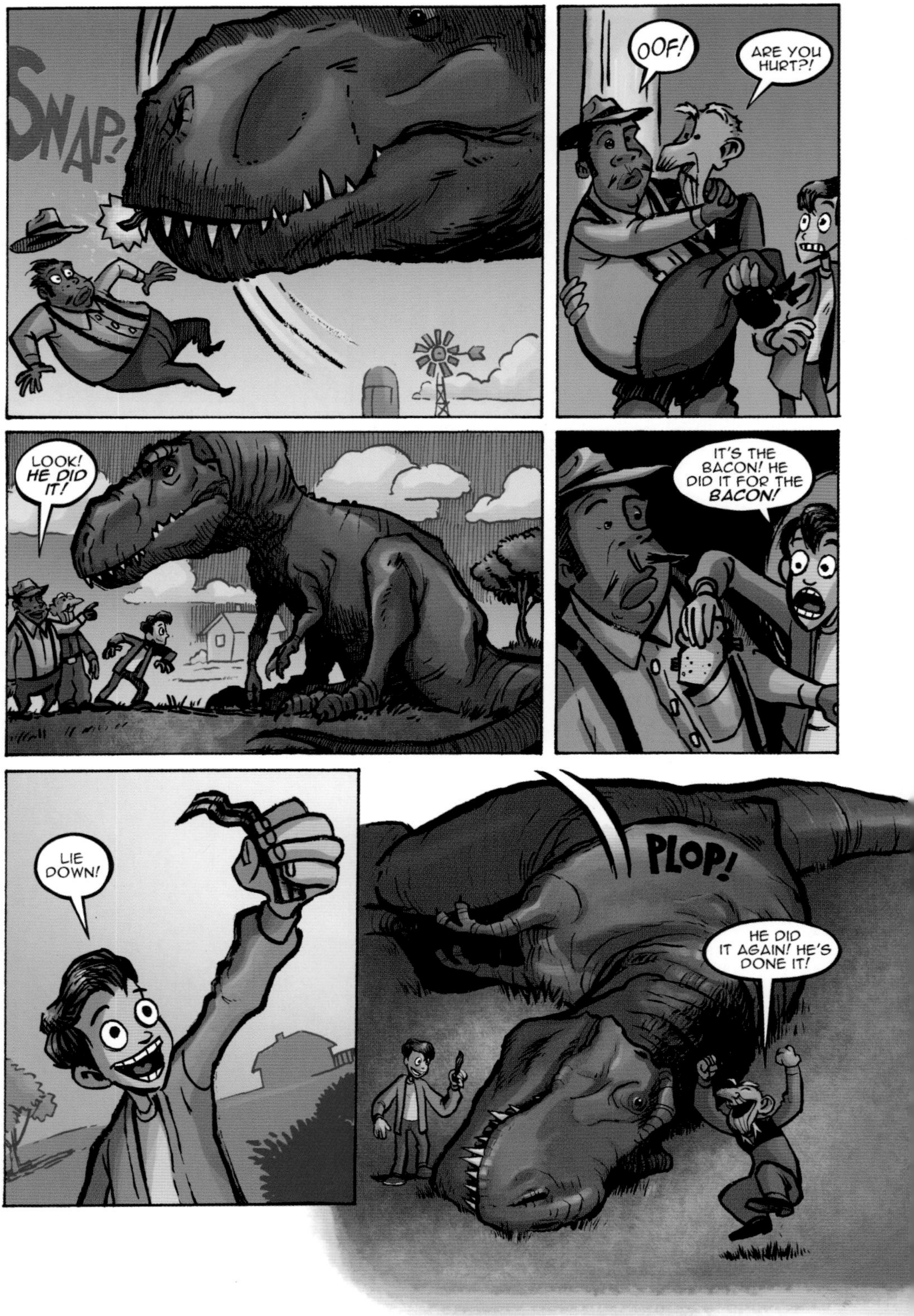
SNAP!
OOF!
ARE YOU HURT?!
LOOK! HE DID IT!
IT'S THE BACON! HE DID IT FOR THE BACON!
LIE DOWN!
PLOP!
HE DID IT AGAIN! HE'S DONE IT!

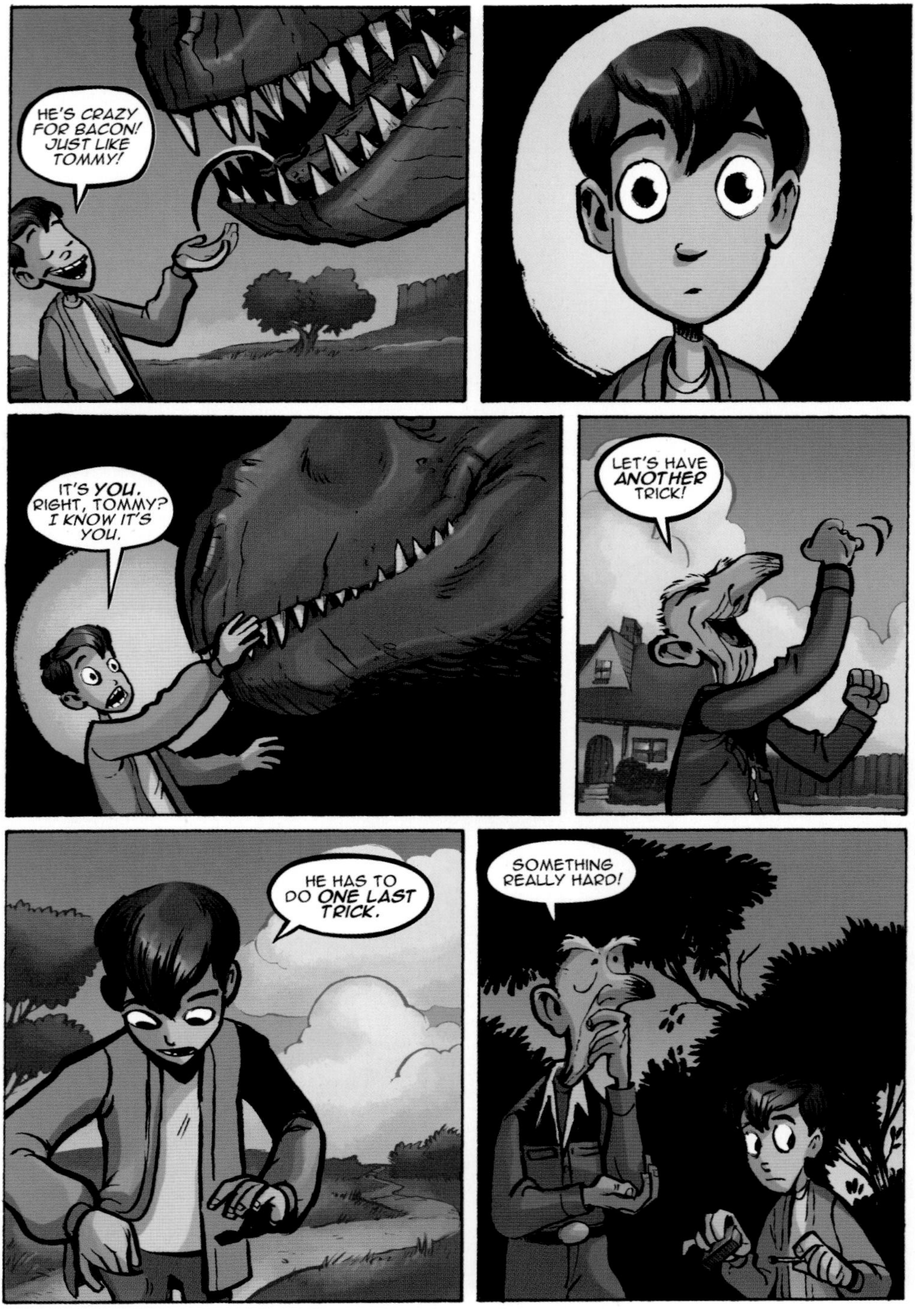
HE'S CRAZY FOR BACON! JUST LIKE TOMMY!
IT'S YOU. RIGHT, TOMMY? I KNOW IT'S YOU.
LET'S HAVE ANOTHER TRICK!
HE HAS TO DO ONE LAST TRICK.
SOMETHING REALLY HARD!

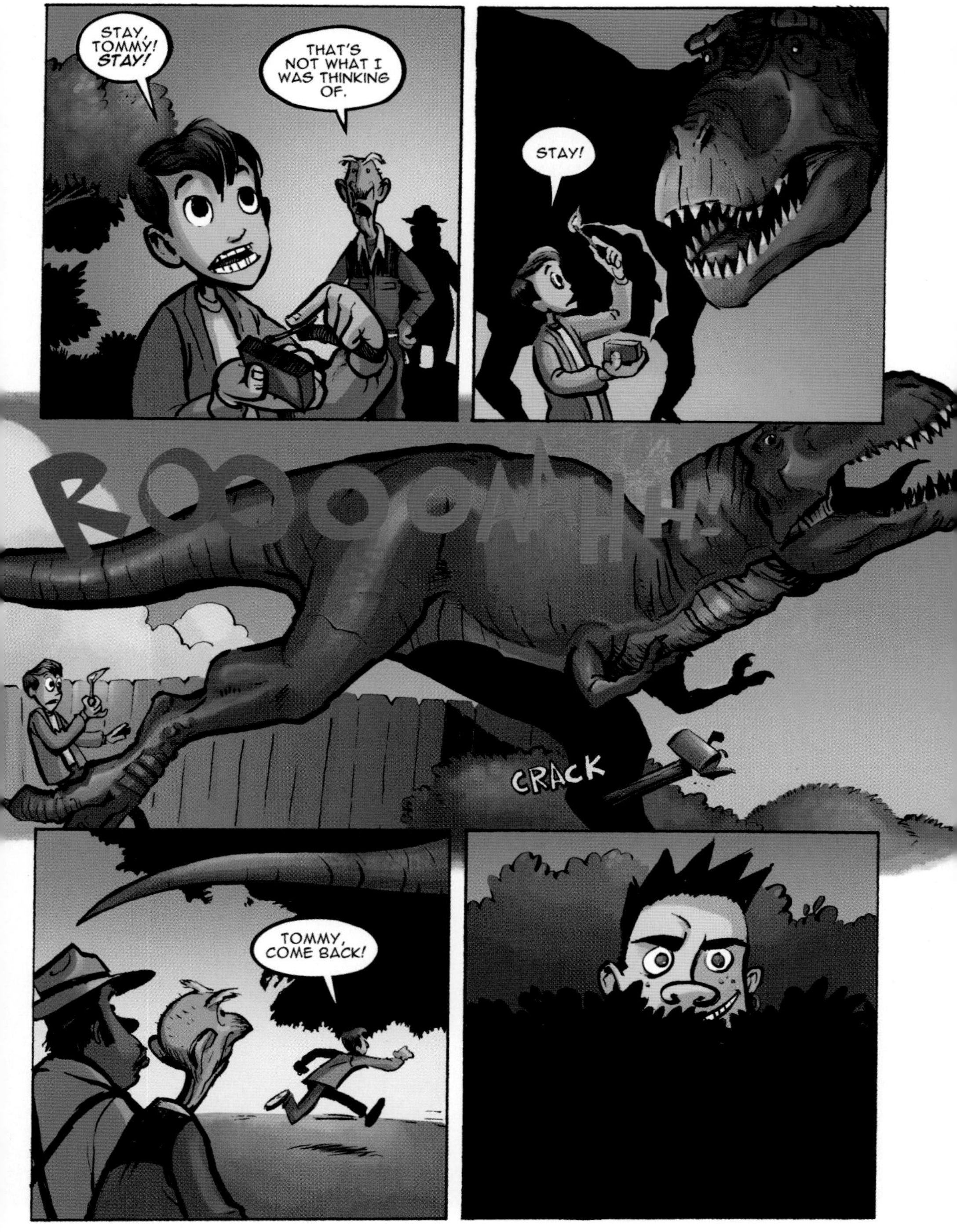
STAY, TOMMY! STAY!
THAT'S NOT WHAT I WAS THINKING OF.
STAY!
ROOOOAHH!
CRACK
TOMMY, COME BACK!

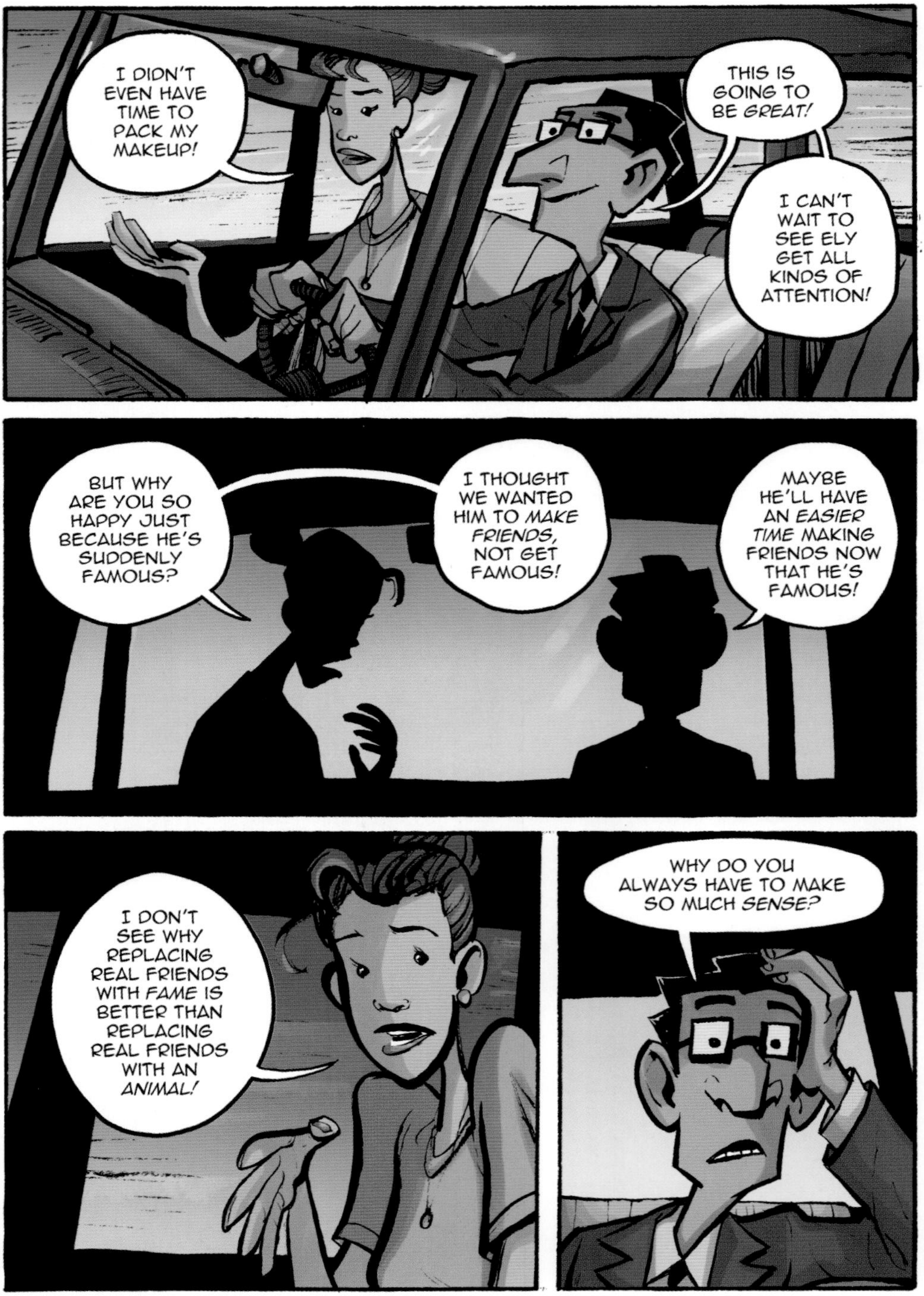
I DIDN'T EVEN HAVE TIME TO PACK MY MAKEUP!
THIS IS GOING TO BE *GREAT!*
I CAN'T WAIT TO SEE ELY GET ALL KINDS OF ATTENTION!
BUT WHY ARE YOU SO HAPPY JUST BECAUSE HE'S SUDDENLY FAMOUS?
I THOUGHT WE WANTED HIM TO *MAKE FRIENDS,* NOT GET FAMOUS!
MAYBE HE'LL HAVE AN *EASIER TIME* MAKING FRIENDS NOW THAT HE'S FAMOUS!
I DON'T SEE WHY REPLACING REAL FRIENDS WITH *FAME* IS BETTER THAN REPLACING REAL FRIENDS WITH AN *ANIMAL!*
WHY DO YOU ALWAYS HAVE TO MAKE SO MUCH *SENSE?*

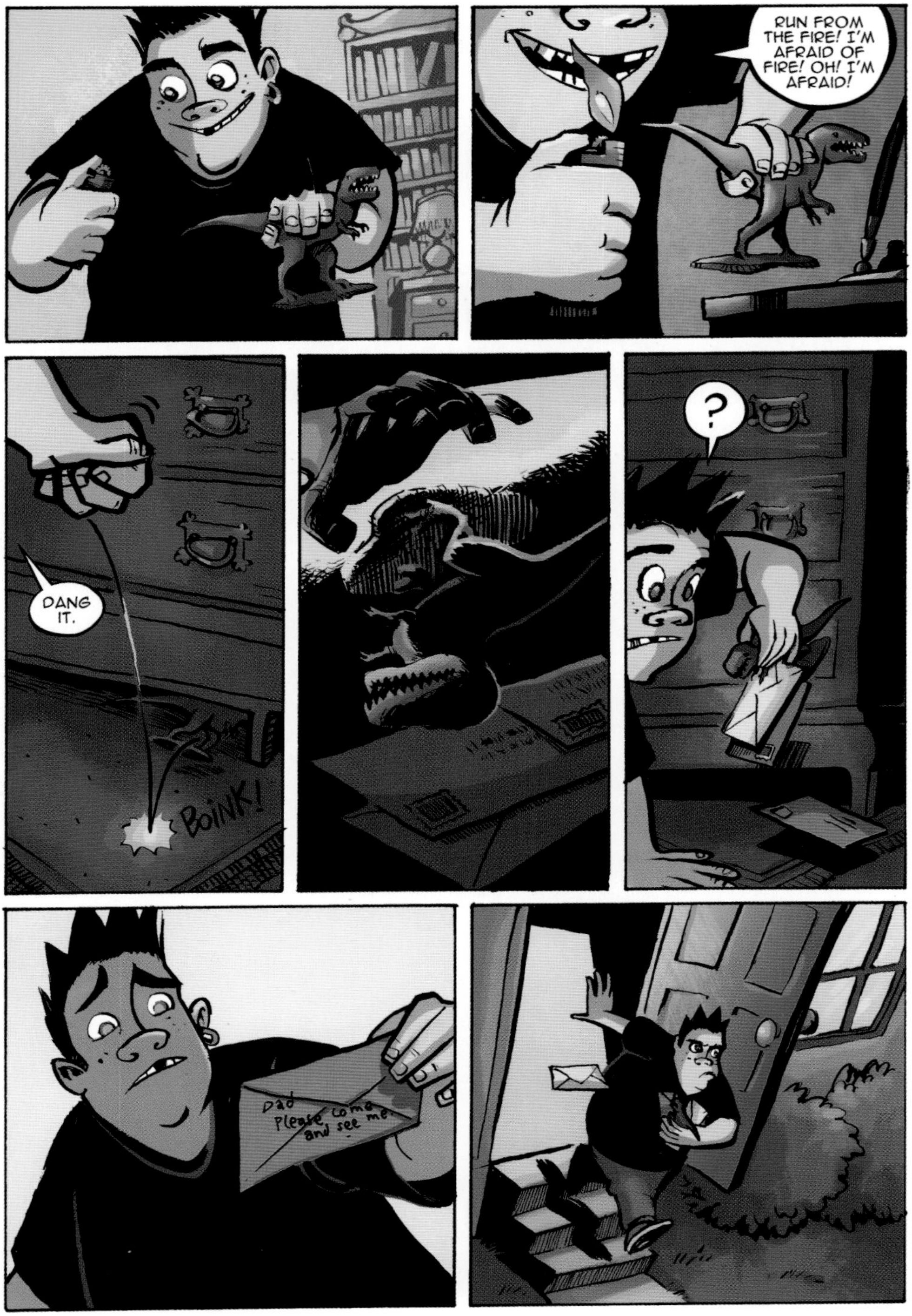
RUN FROM THE FIRE! I'M AFRAID OF FIRE! OH! I'M AFRAID!
DANG IT.
BOINK!
?
Dad
Please come and see me.

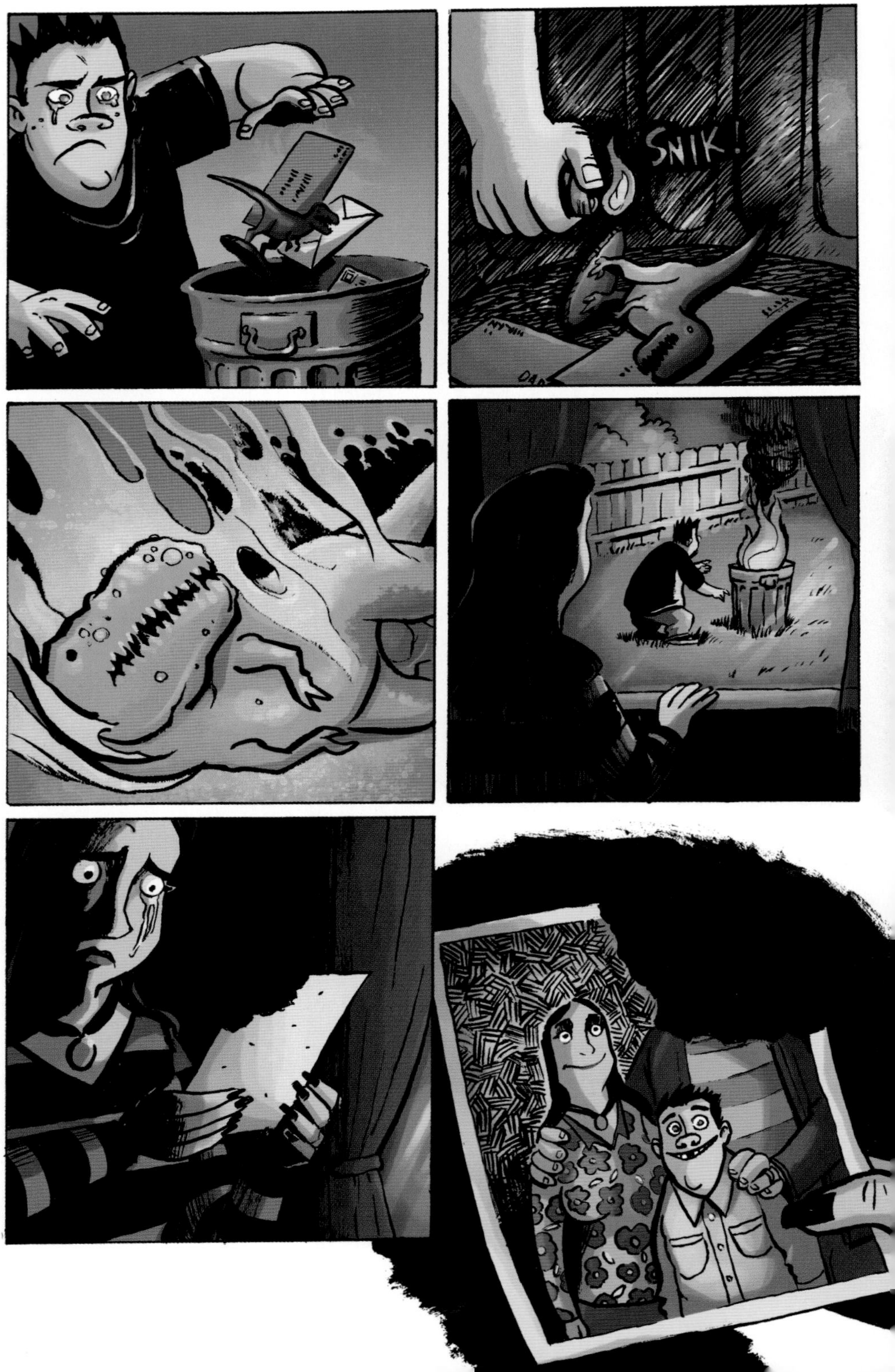
SNIK!

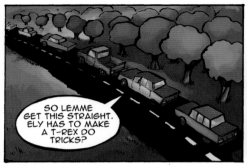

SO LEMME GET THIS STRAIGHT. ELY HAS TO MAKE A T-REX DO TRICKS?

SOMETHING LIKE THAT. I'M SO NERVOUS I'M ABOUT TO JUST EXPLODE.

OH, HONEY, WE'VE ALREADY GONE OVER THIS. IT'S GOOD FOR ELY TO BE EXPOSED TO A LITTLE RESPONSIBILITY. JUST DON'T GO ALL TO TEARS AND BABY THE BOY WHEN YOU SEE HIM.

SINGLE FILE! ONE AT A TIME! THERE'S ENOUGH FOR EVERYBODY!

Tommy SAURUS REX

DAD, WHAT'S GOING ON?!

WE ALREADY PAID OFF THE NEIGHBOR'S MORTGAGE, AND NOW WE'RE WORKING ON ELY'S COLLEGE FUND!

WHAT'S WITH THE CANE? ARE YOU HURT?

OH, I'M IN EXCRUCIATING PAIN! THINGS COULDN'T BE BETTER!

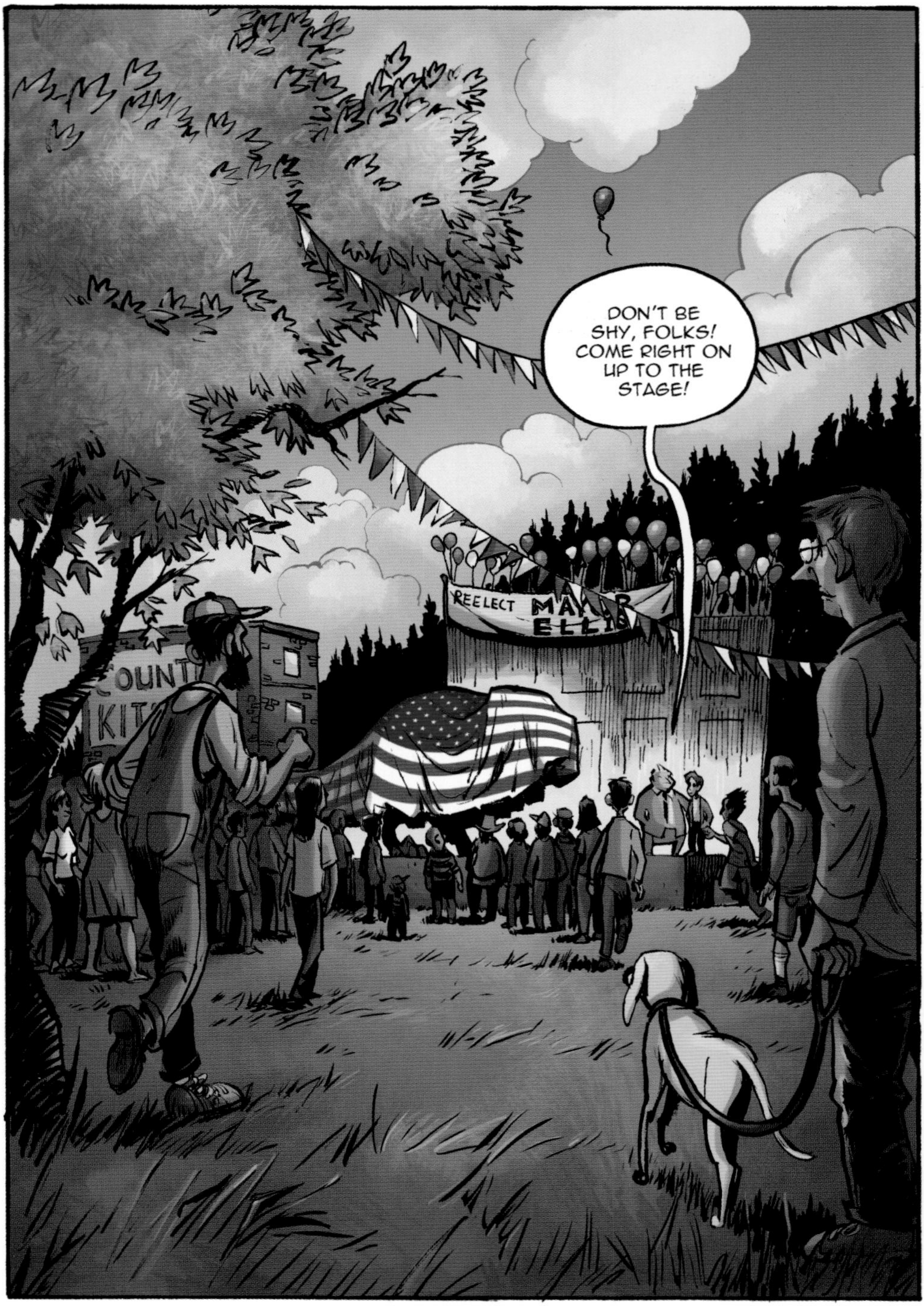
DON'T BE SHY, FOLKS! COME RIGHT ON UP TO THE STAGE!
REELECT MAYOR ELLIS

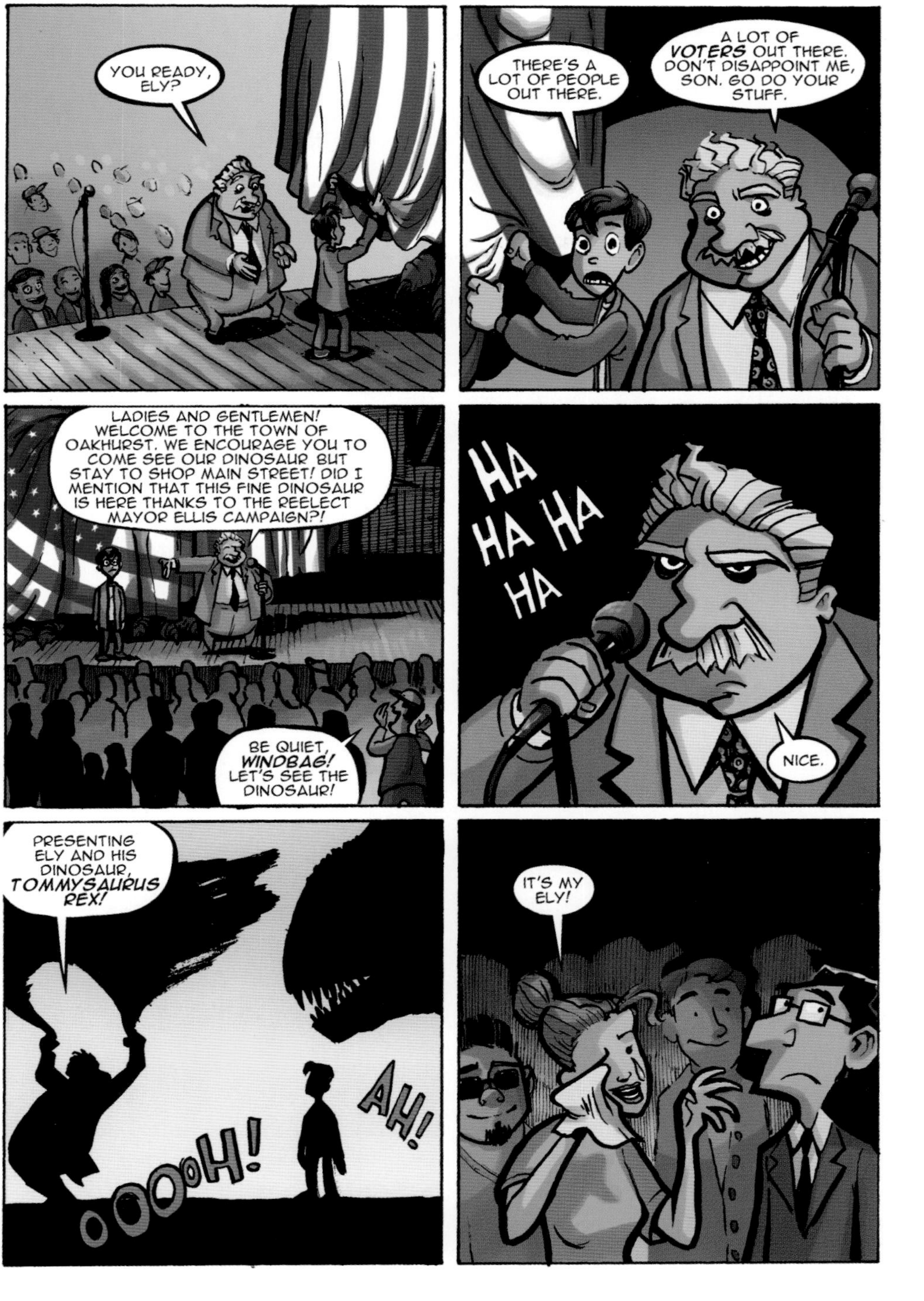
YOU READY, ELY?
THERE'S A LOT OF PEOPLE OUT THERE.
A LOT OF VOTERS OUT THERE. DON'T DISAPPOINT ME, SON. GO DO YOUR STUFF.
LADIES AND GENTLEMEN! WELCOME TO THE TOWN OF OAKHURST. WE ENCOURAGE YOU TO COME SEE OUR DINOSAUR BUT STAY TO SHOP MAIN STREET! DID I MENTION THAT THIS FINE DINOSAUR IS HERE THANKS TO THE REELECT MAYOR ELLIS CAMPAIGN?!
BE QUIET, WINDBAG! LET'S SEE THE DINOSAUR!
HA HA HA HA HA
NICE.
PRESENTING ELY AND HIS DINOSAUR, TOMMYSAURUS REX!
OOOOOH!
AH!
IT'S MY ELY!

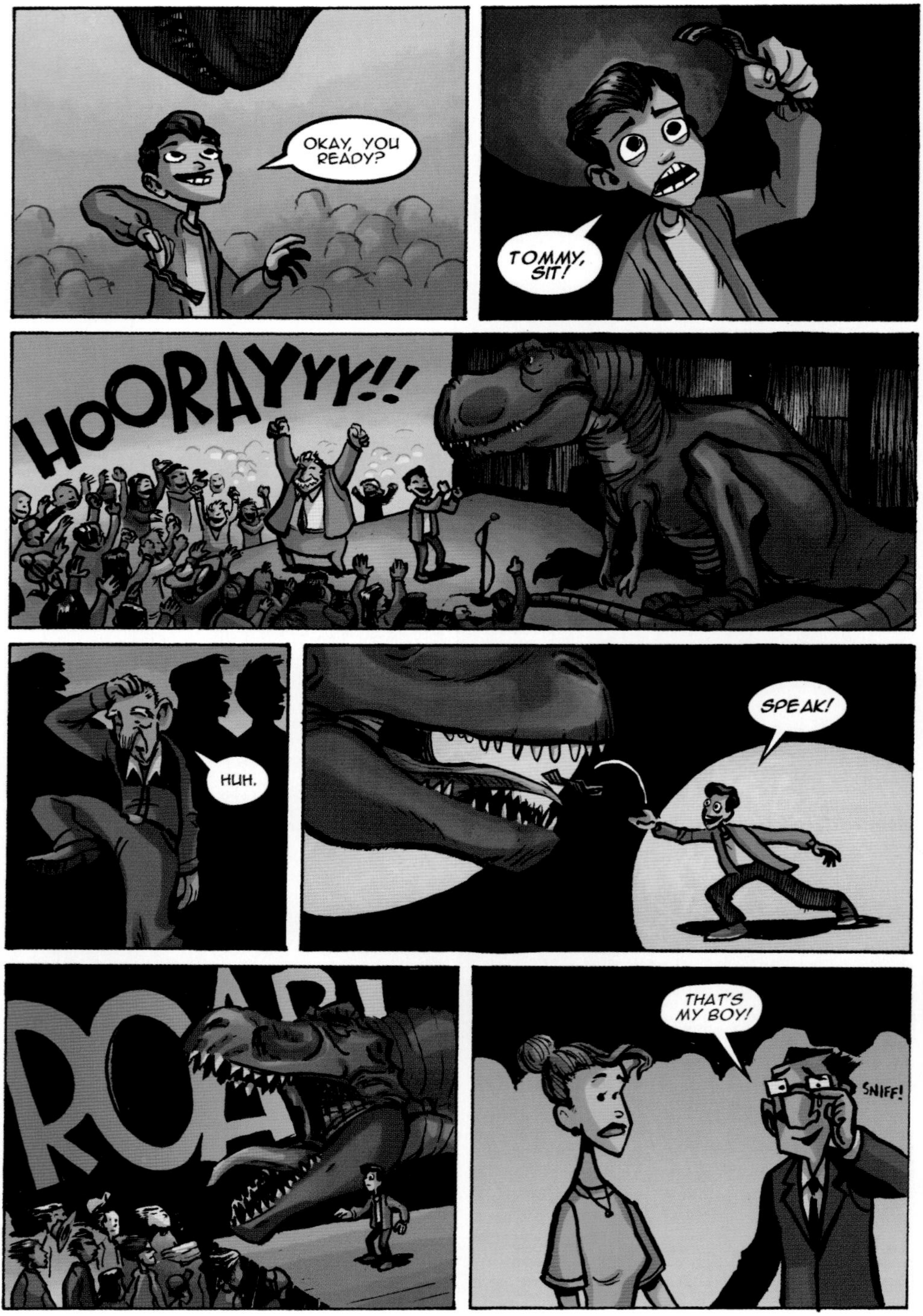
OKAY, YOU READY?
TOMMY, SIT!
HOORAYYY!!
HUH.
SPEAK!
THAT'S MY BOY!
SNIFF!

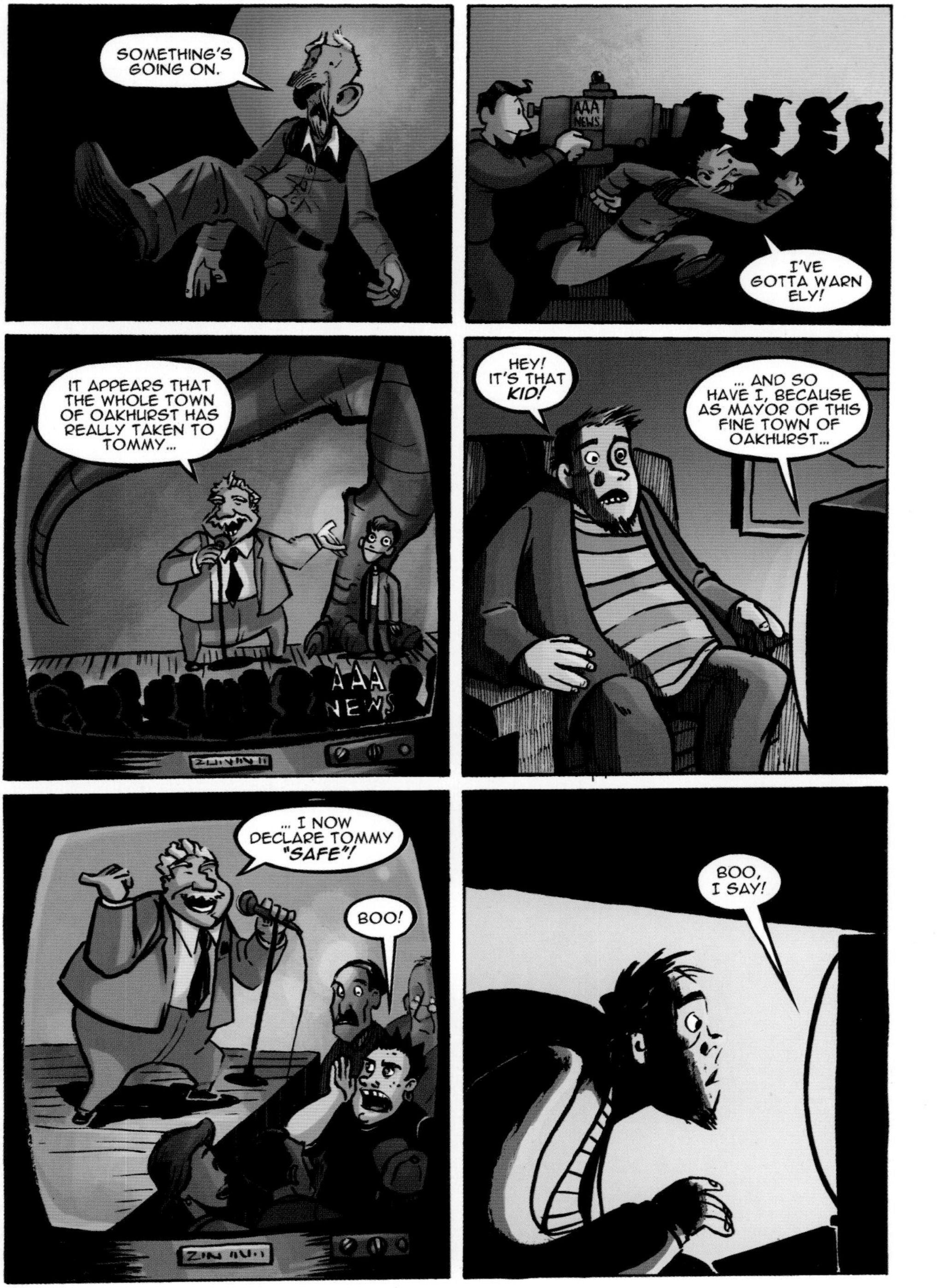
SOMETHING'S GOING ON.
I'VE GOTTA WARN ELY!
AAA NEWS
IT APPEARS THAT THE WHOLE TOWN OF OAKHURST HAS REALLY TAKEN TO TOMMY...
HEY! IT'S THAT KID!
... AND SO HAVE I, BECAUSE AS MAYOR OF THIS FINE TOWN OF OAKHURST...
... I NOW DECLARE TOMMY "SAFE"!
BOO!
BOO, I SAY!

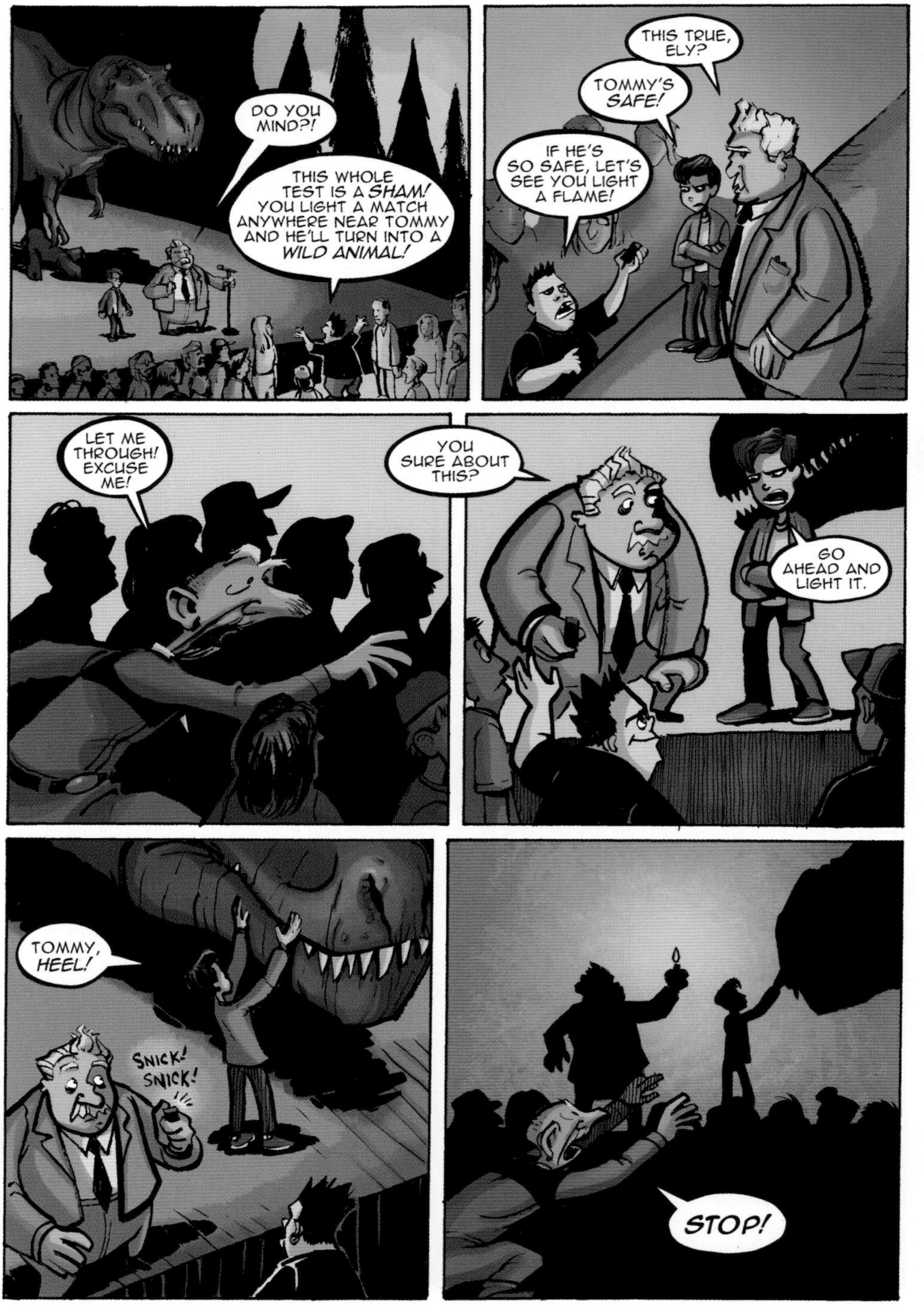
DO YOU MIND?!
THIS WHOLE TEST IS A SHAM! YOU LIGHT A MATCH ANYWHERE NEAR TOMMY AND HE'LL TURN INTO A WILD ANIMAL!
THIS TRUE, ELY?
TOMMY'S SAFE!
IF HE'S SO SAFE, LET'S SEE YOU LIGHT A FLAME!
LET ME THROUGH! EXCUSE ME!
YOU SURE ABOUT THIS?
GO AHEAD AND LIGHT IT.
TOMMY, HEEL!
SNICK! SNICK!
STOP!

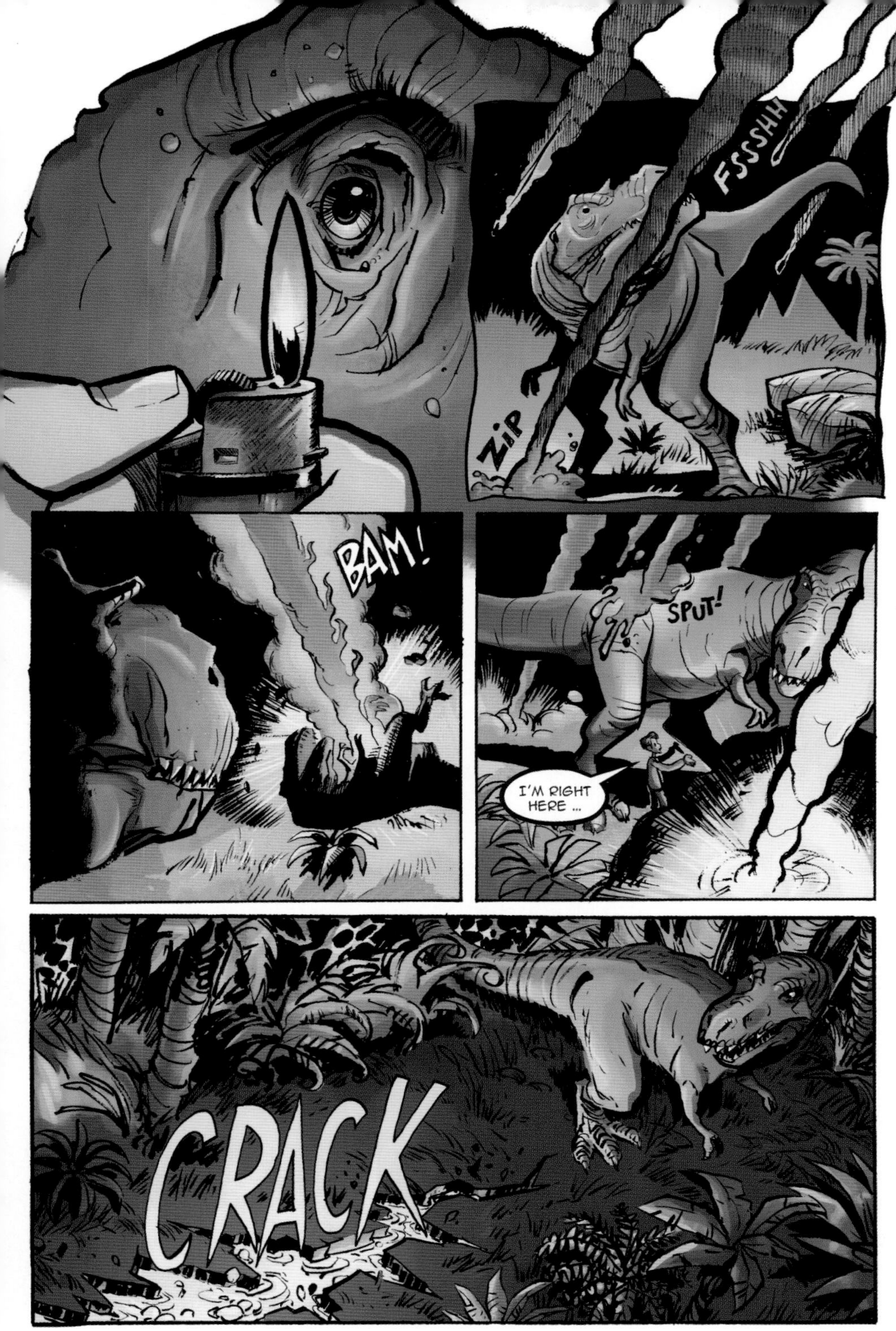
FSSSHH
ZIP
BAM!
SPUT!
I'M RIGHT HERE ...
CRACK

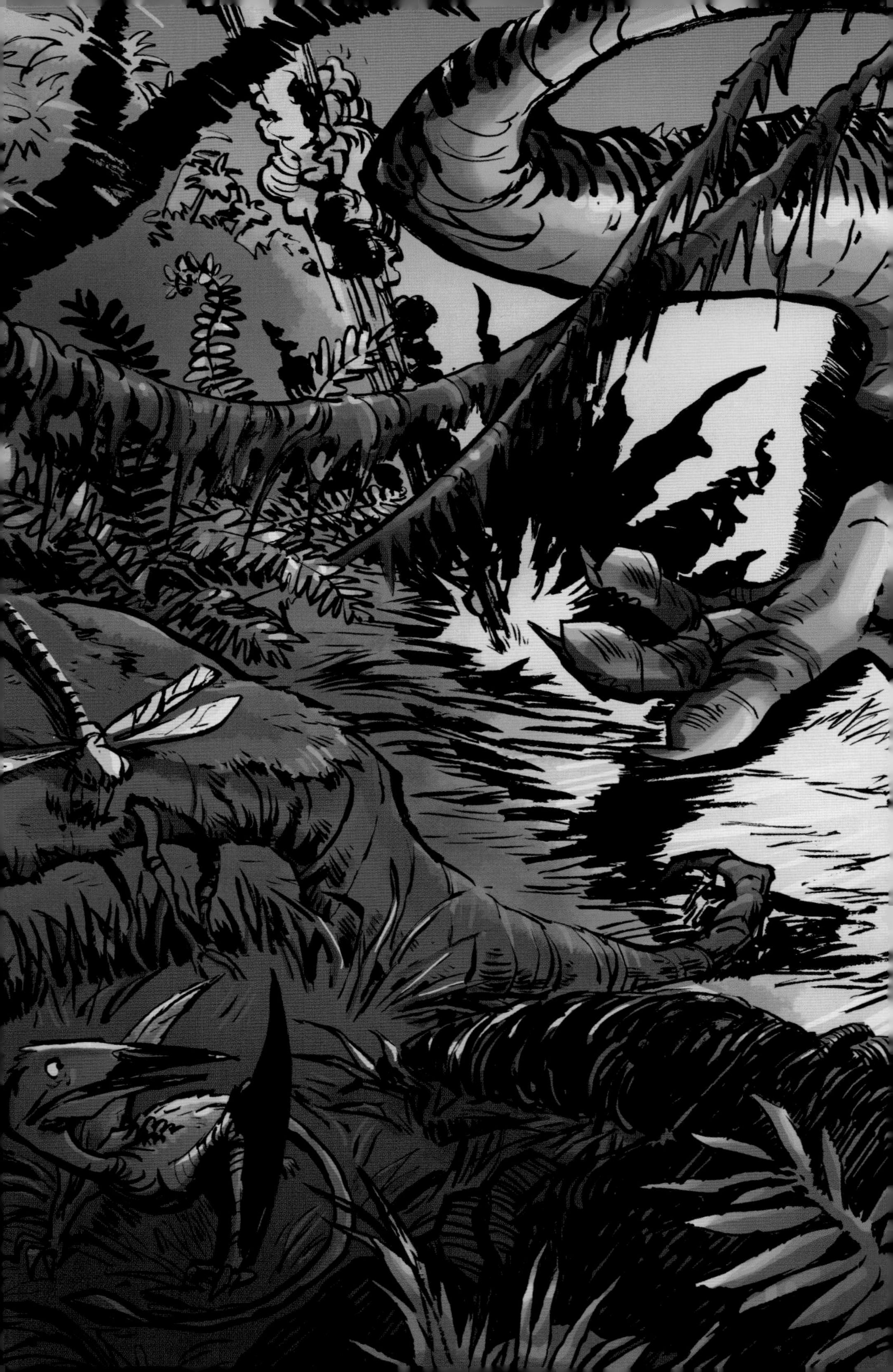

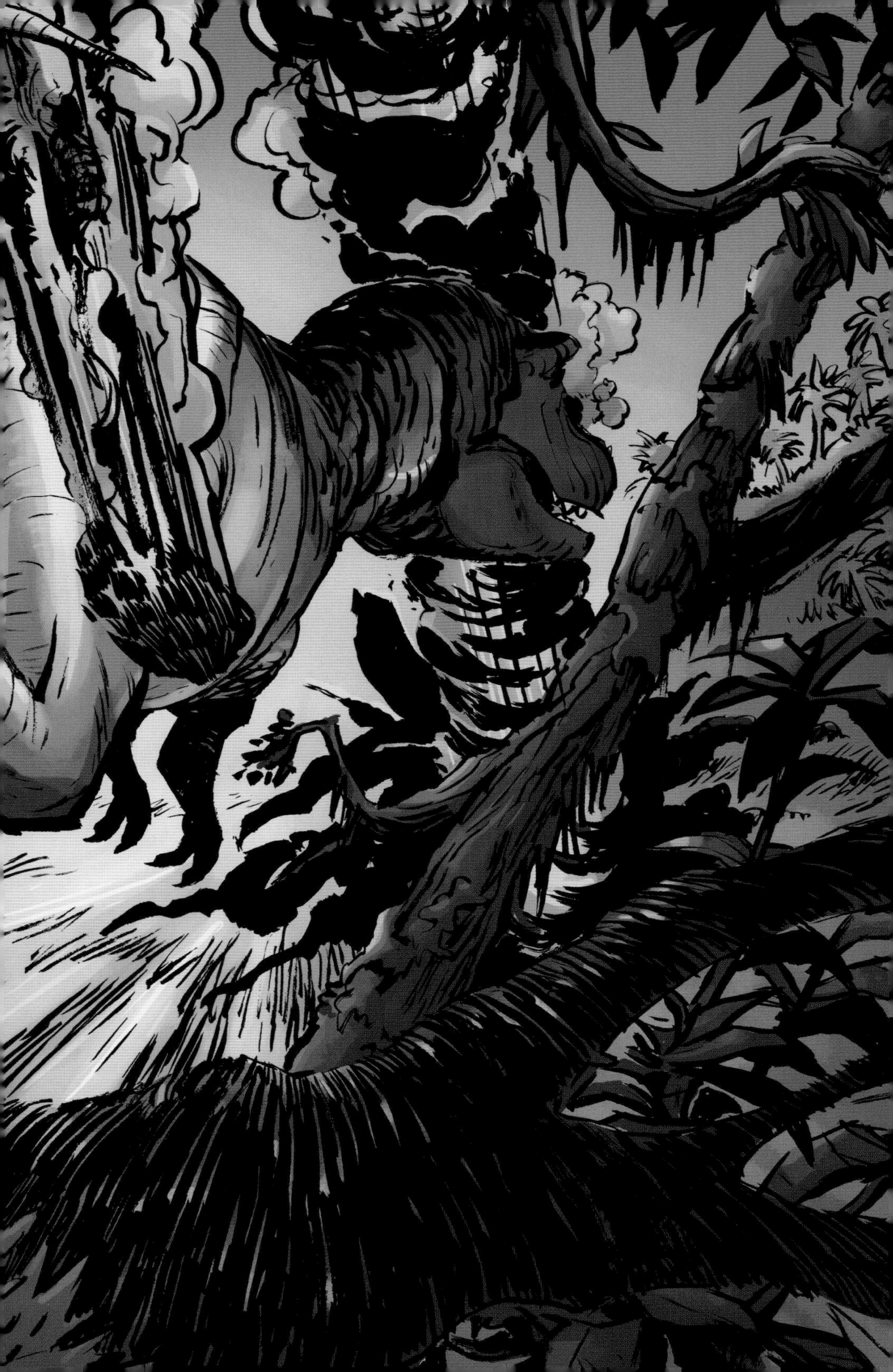

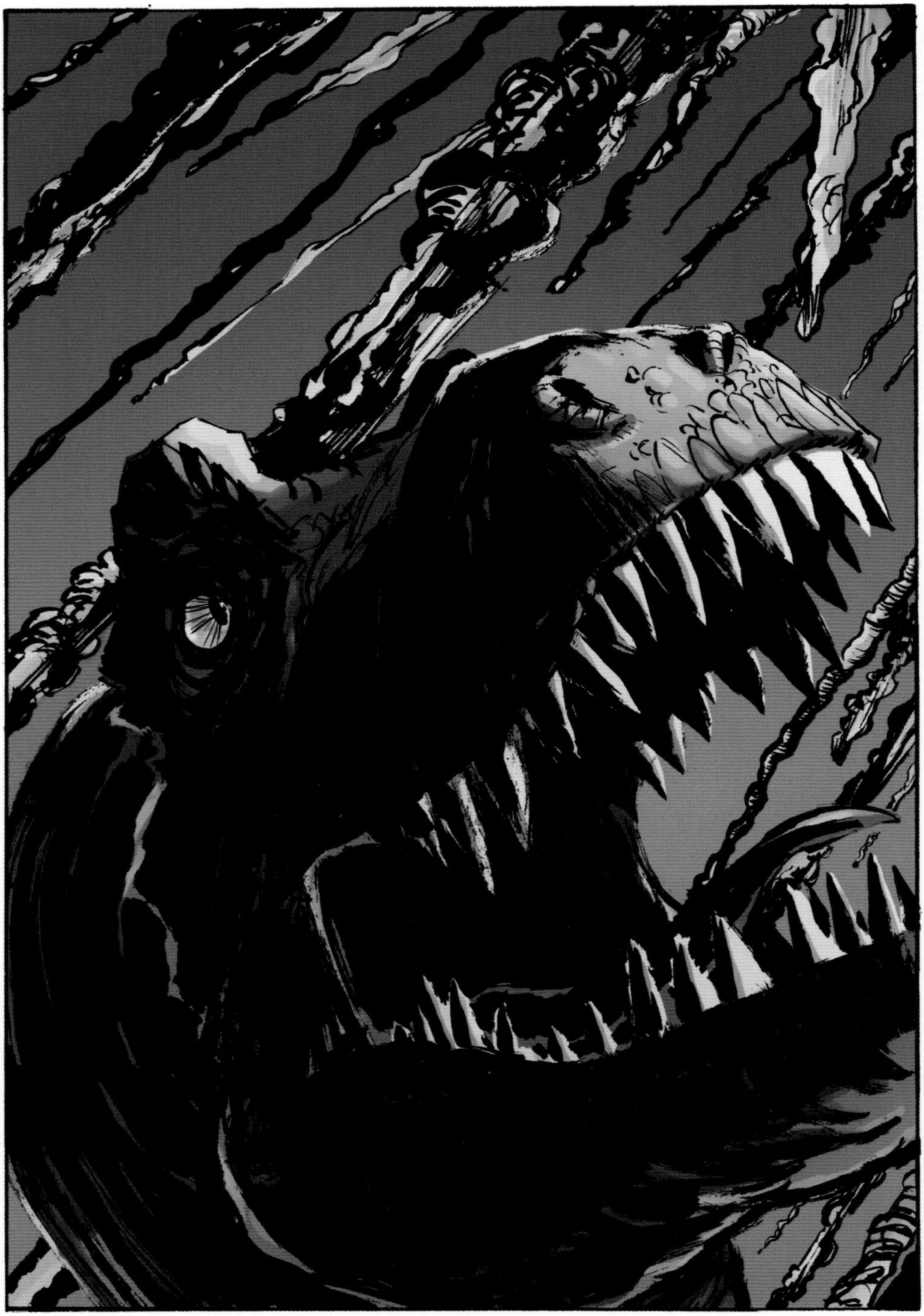

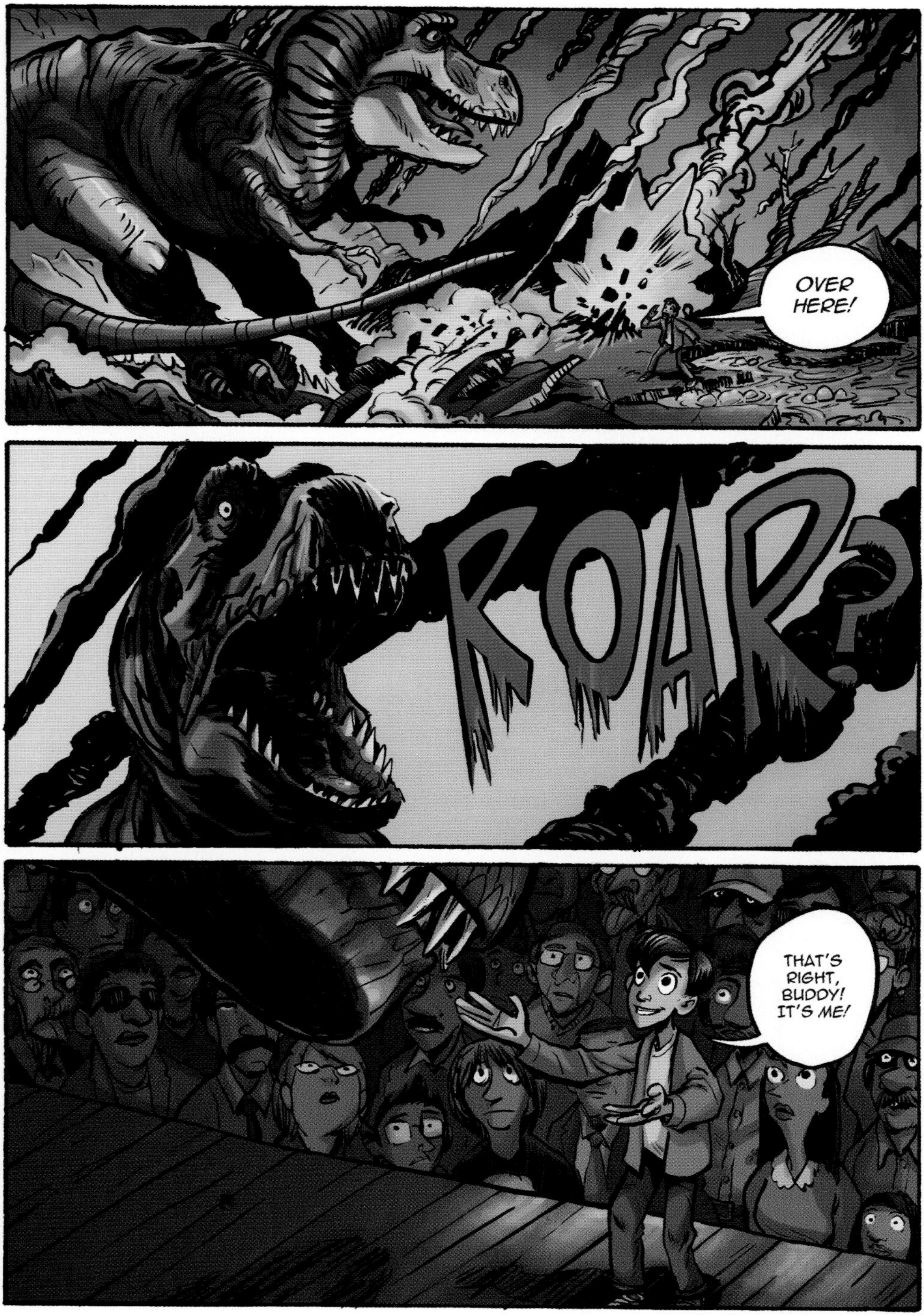
OVER HERE!
ROAR?
THAT'S RIGHT, BUDDY! IT'S ME!

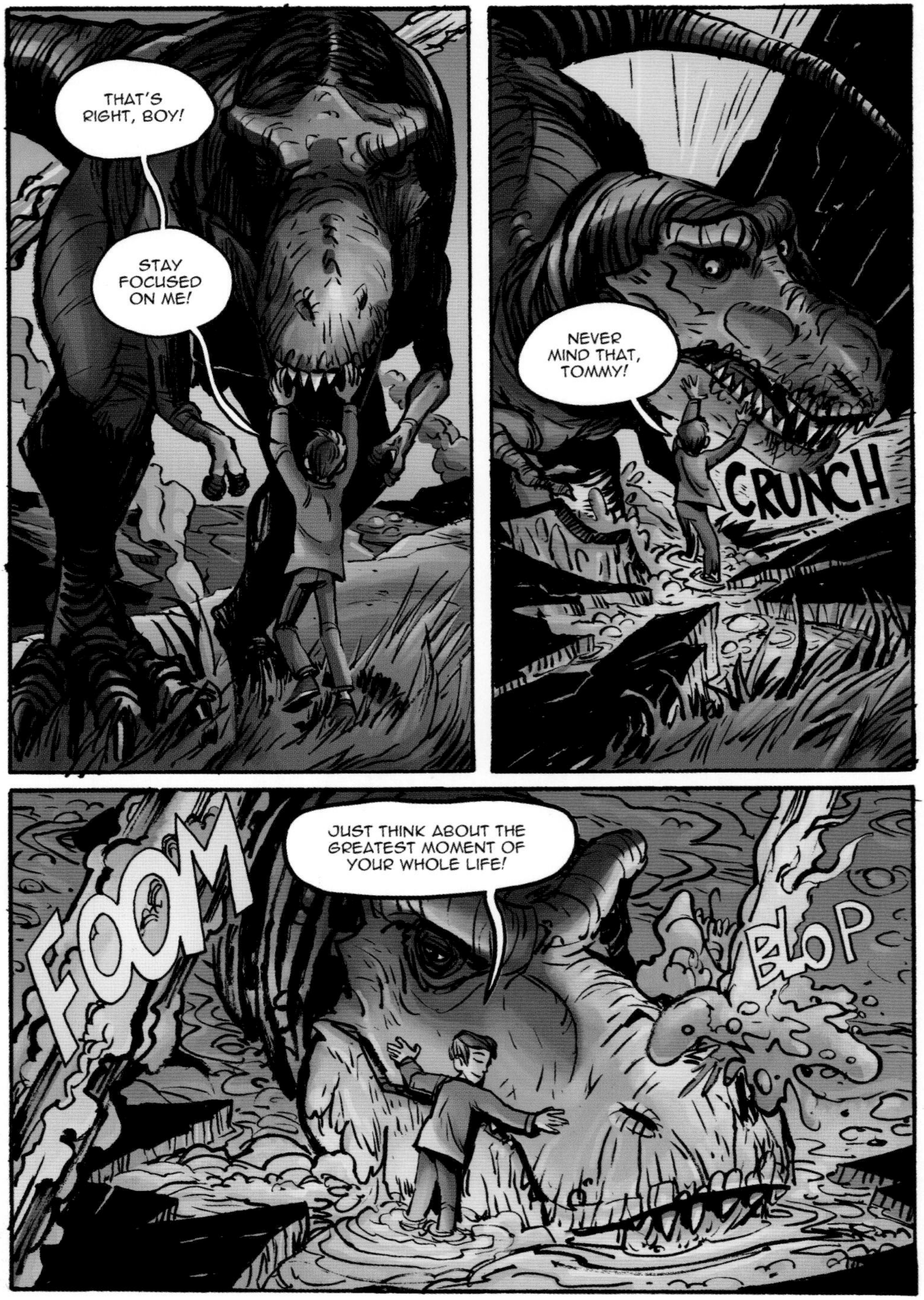

THAT'S RIGHT, BOY!
STAY FOCUSED ON ME!
NEVER MIND THAT, TOMMY!
CRUNCH
FOOM
JUST THINK ABOUT THE GREATEST MOMENT OF YOUR WHOLE LIFE!
BLOP

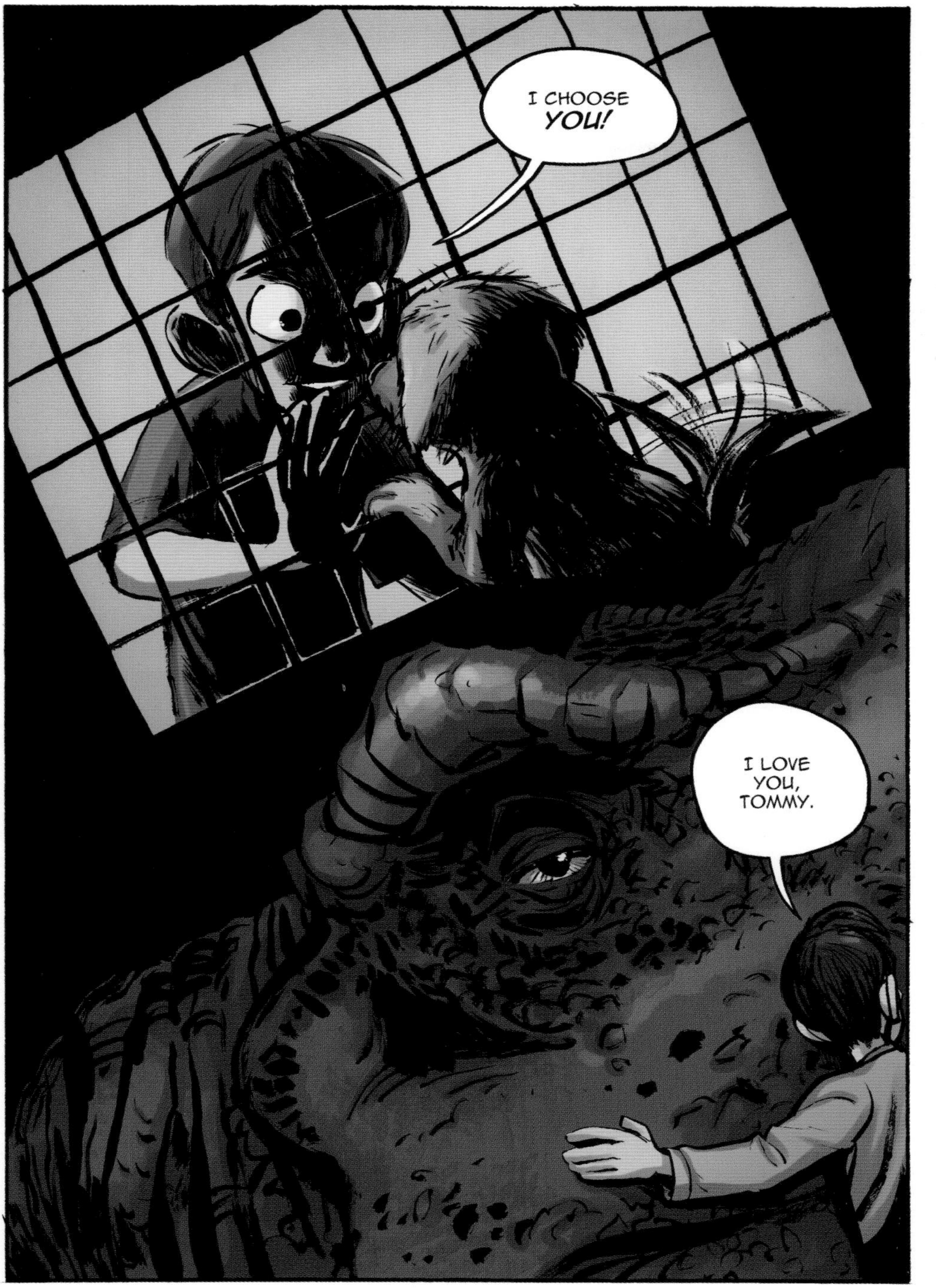
I CHOOSE *YOU!*
I LOVE YOU, TOMMY.

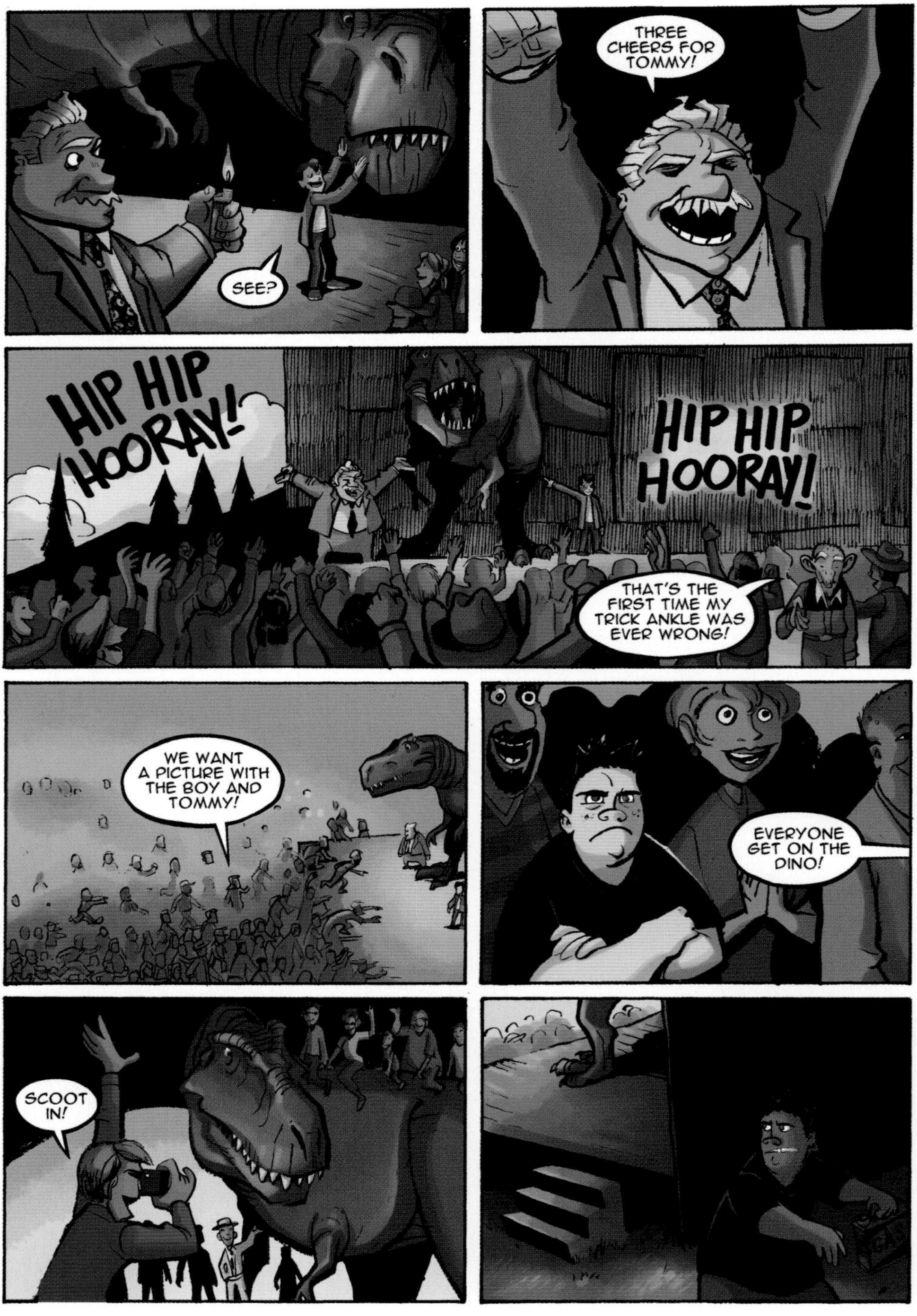
SEE?
THREE CHEERS FOR TOMMY!
HIP HIP HOORAY!
HIP HIP HOORAY!
THAT'S THE FIRST TIME MY TRICK ANKLE WAS EVER WRONG!
WE WANT A PICTURE WITH THE BOY AND TOMMY!
EVERYONE GET ON THE DINO!
SCOOT IN!

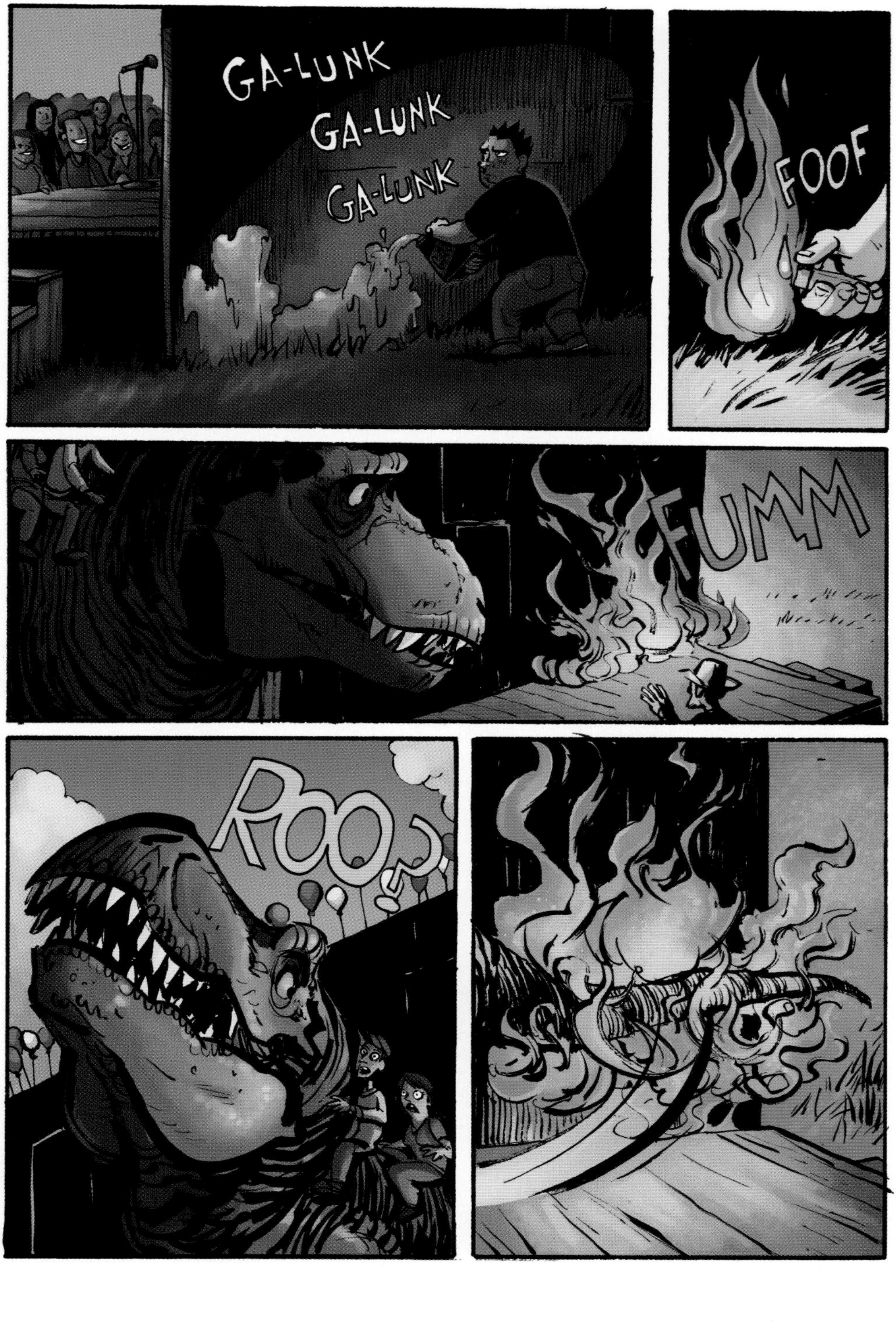
GA-LUNK
GA-LUNK
GA-LUNK
FOOF
FUMM
ROO

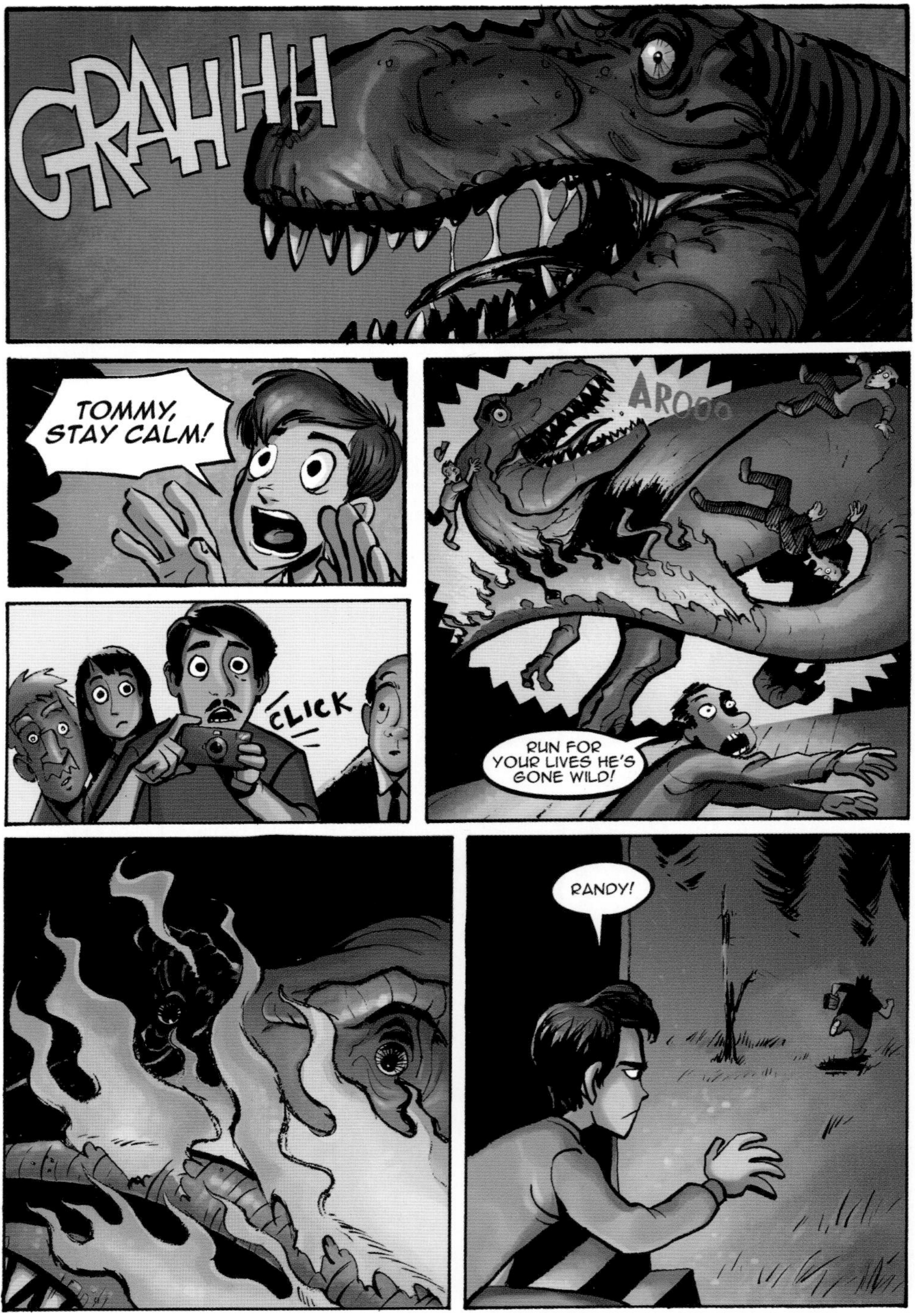
GRAHHH
TOMMY, STAY CALM!
AROOO
CLICK
RUN FOR YOUR LIVES HE'S GONE WILD!
RANDY!

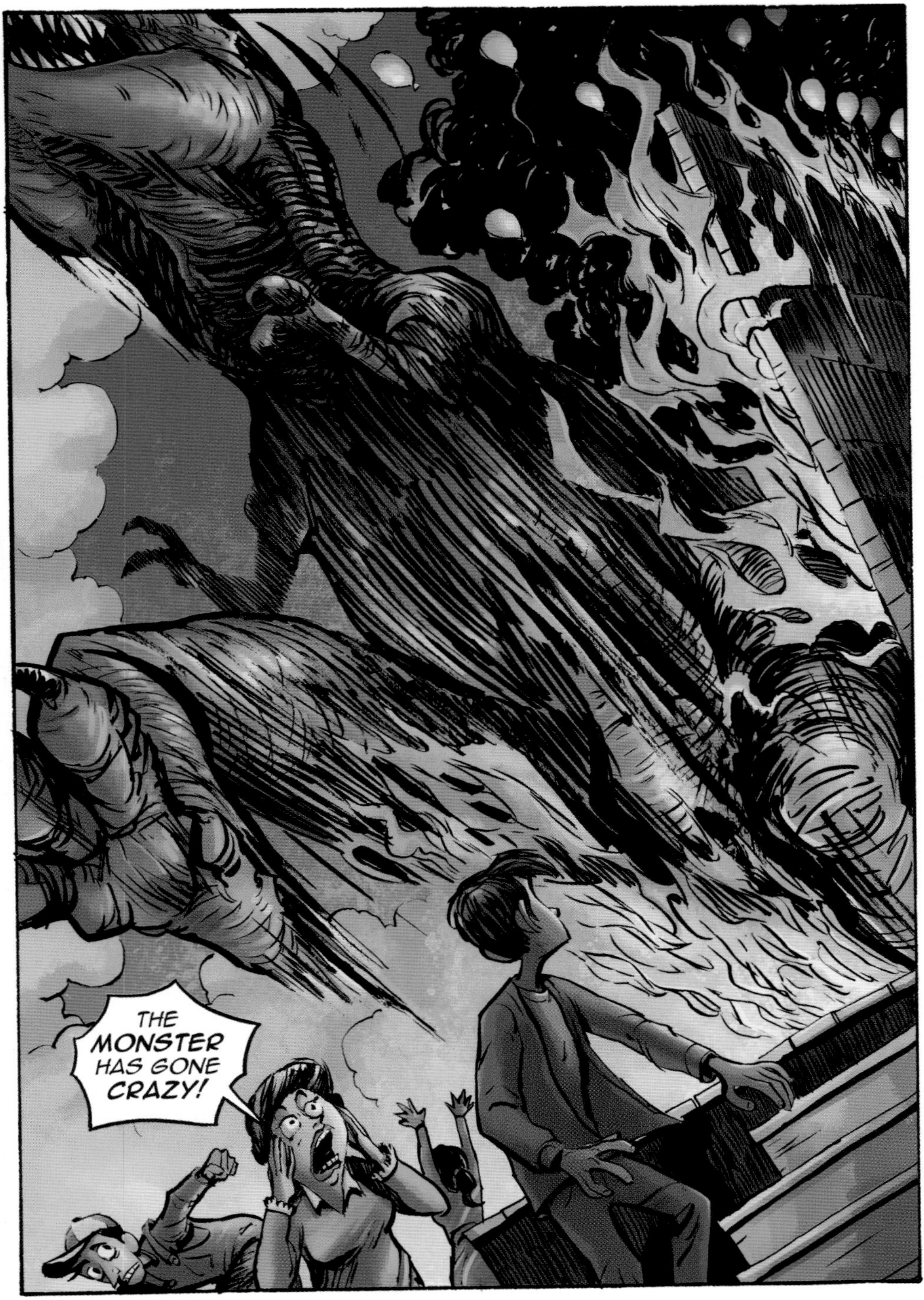
THE MONSTER HAS GONE CRAZY!

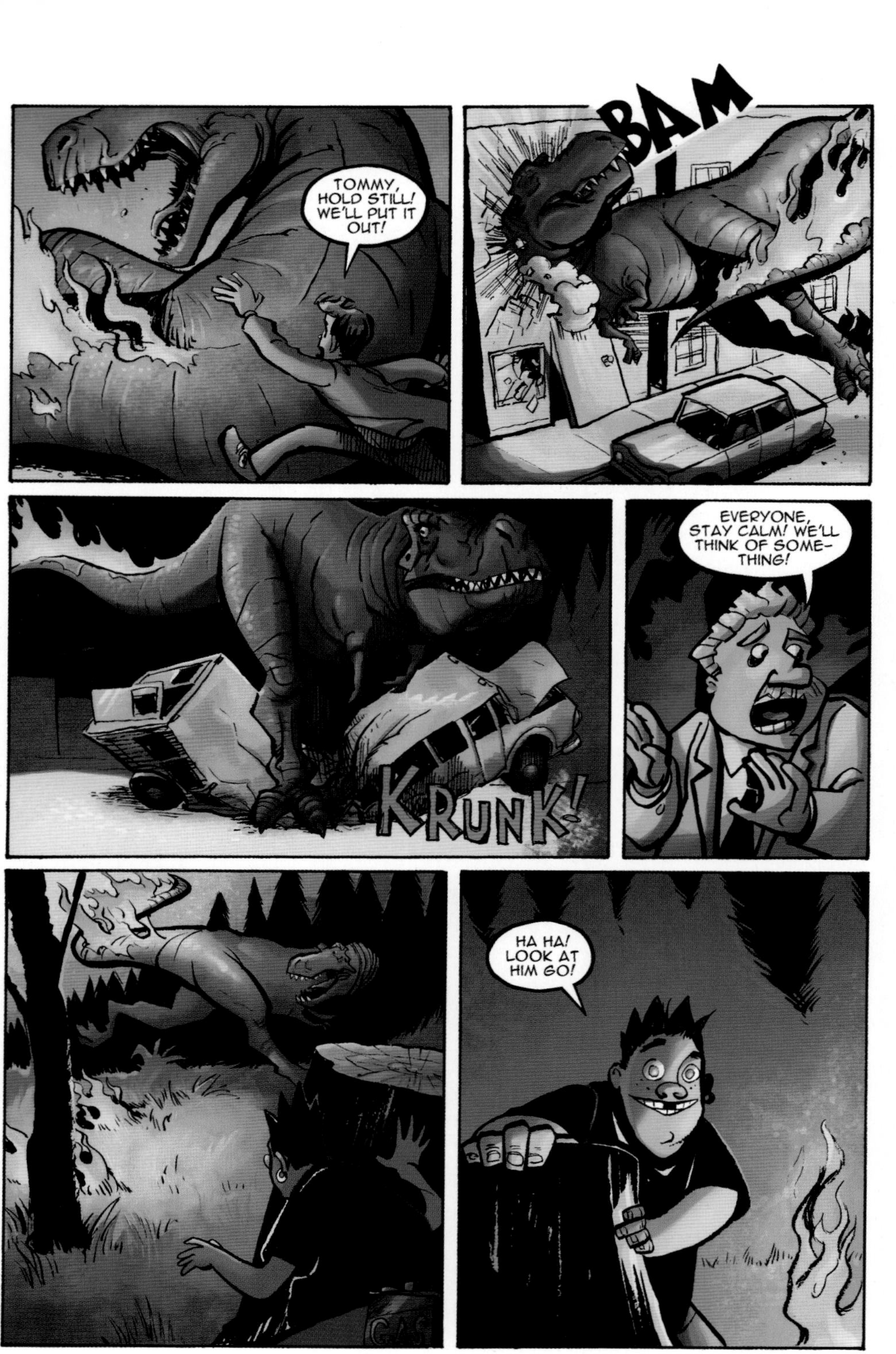
TOMMY, HOLD STILL! WE'LL PUT IT OUT!
BAM
EVERYONE, STAY CALM! WE'LL THINK OF SOME-THING!
KRUNK!
GAS
HA HA! LOOK AT HIM GO!

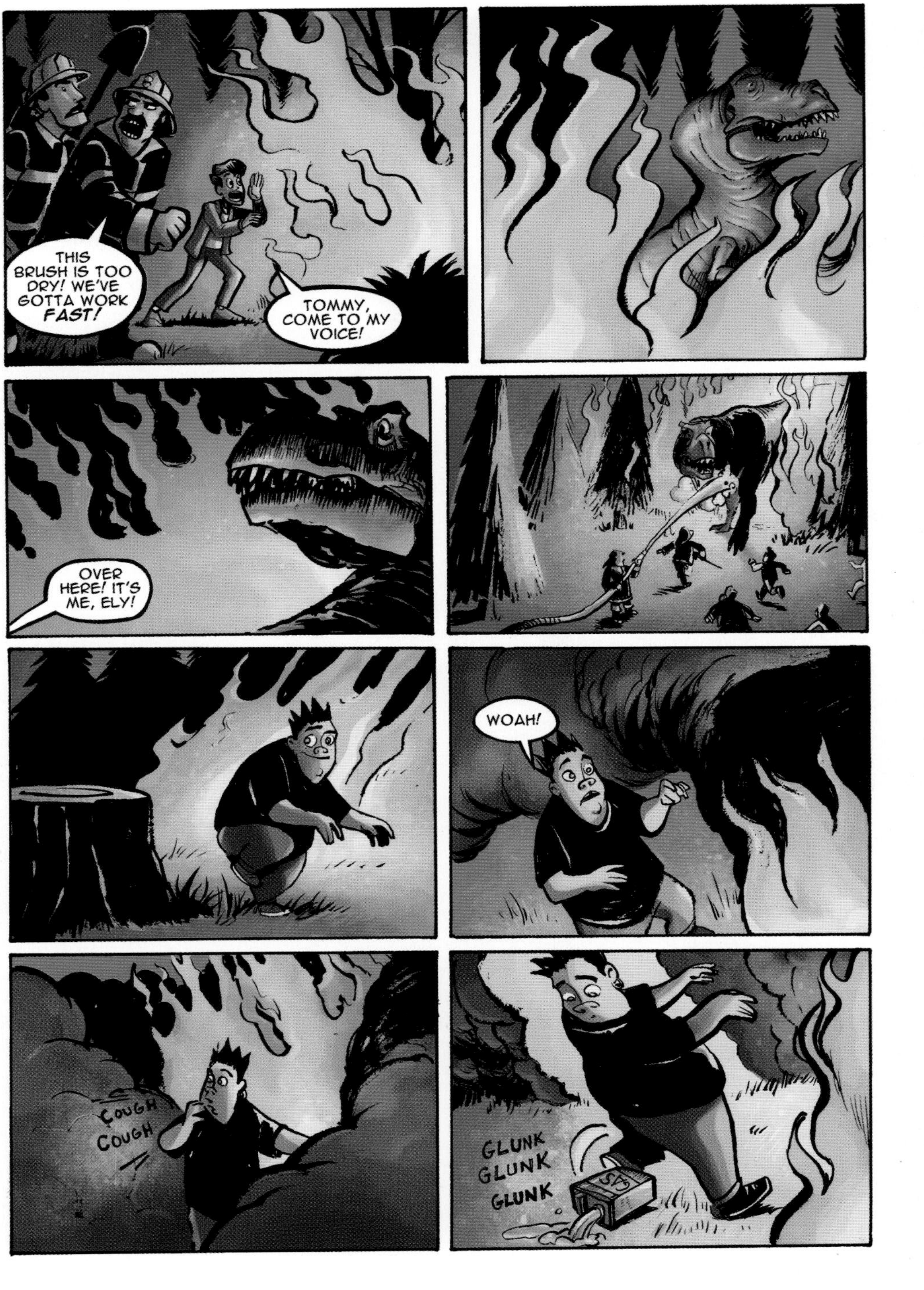
THIS BRUSH IS TOO DRY! WE'VE GOTTA WORK FAST!
TOMMY, COME TO MY VOICE!
OVER HERE! IT'S ME, ELY!
WOAH!
COUGH COUGH
GLUNK GLUNK GLUNK
GAS

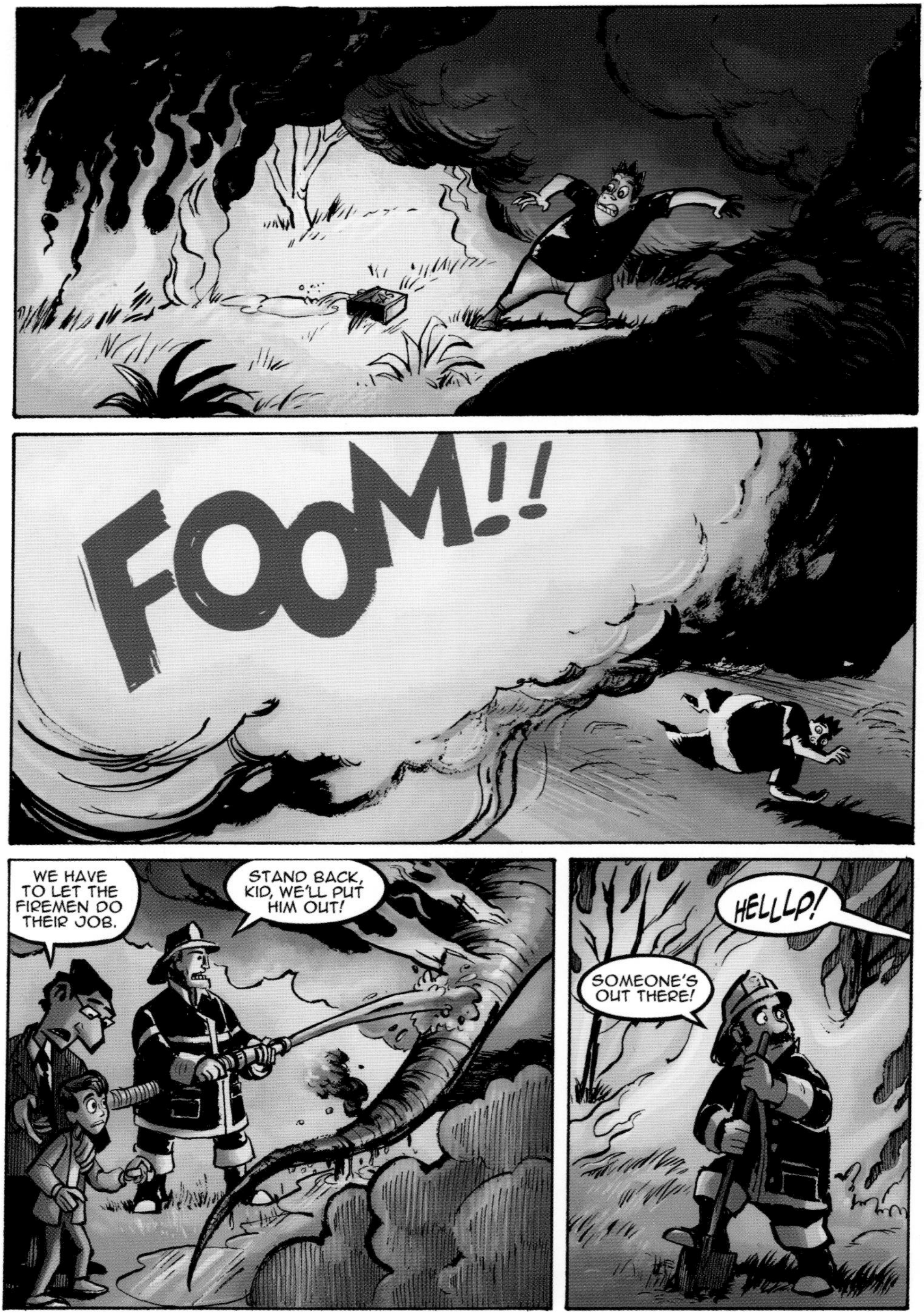
FOOM!!
WE HAVE TO LET THE FIREMEN DO THEIR JOB.
STAND BACK, KID, WE'LL PUT HIM OUT!
HELLLP!
SOMEONE'S OUT THERE!

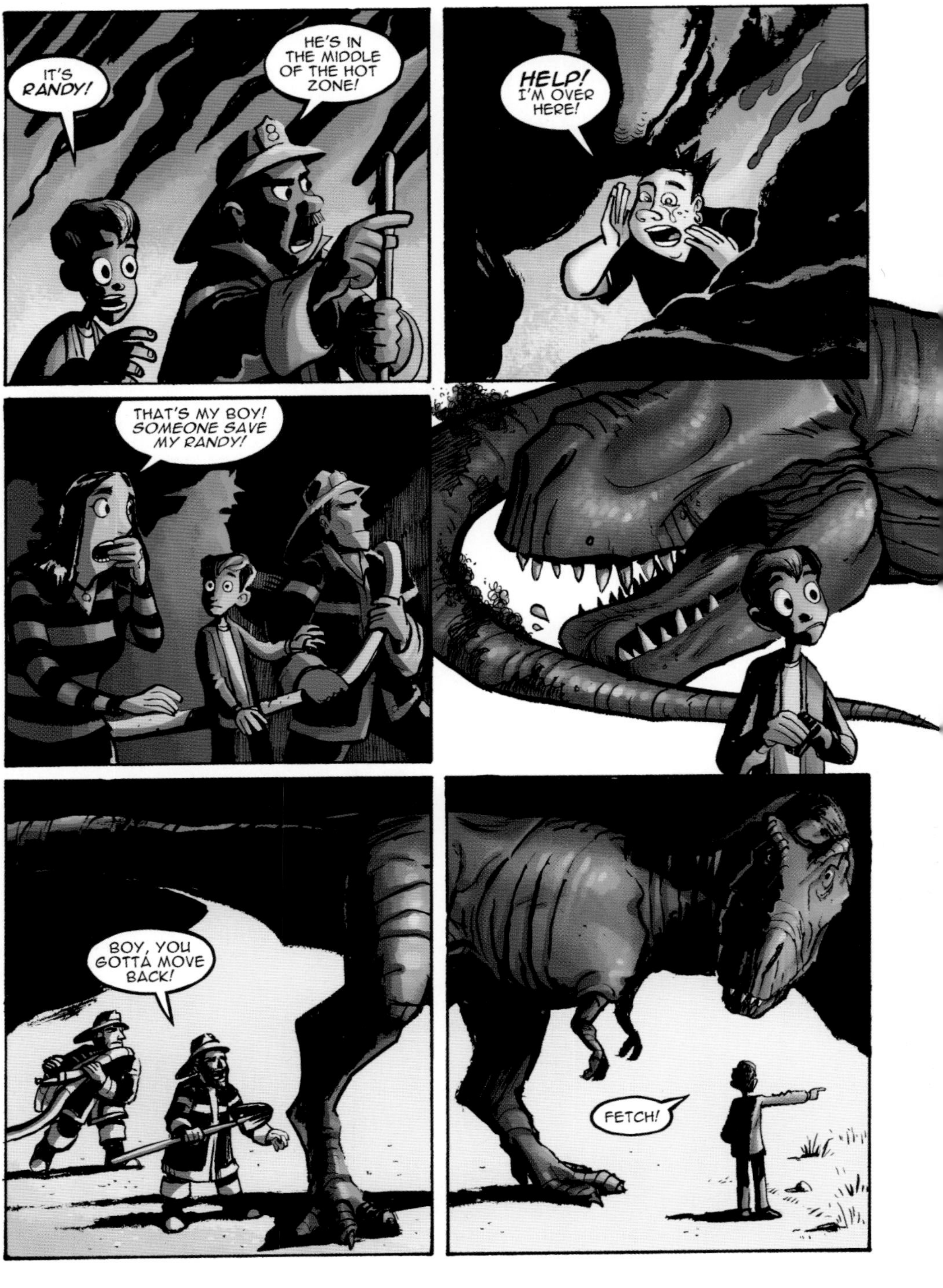
IT'S RANDY!
HE'S IN THE MIDDLE OF THE HOT ZONE!
HELP! I'M OVER HERE!
THAT'S MY BOY! SOMEONE SAVE MY RANDY!
BOY, YOU GOTTA MOVE BACK!
FETCH!

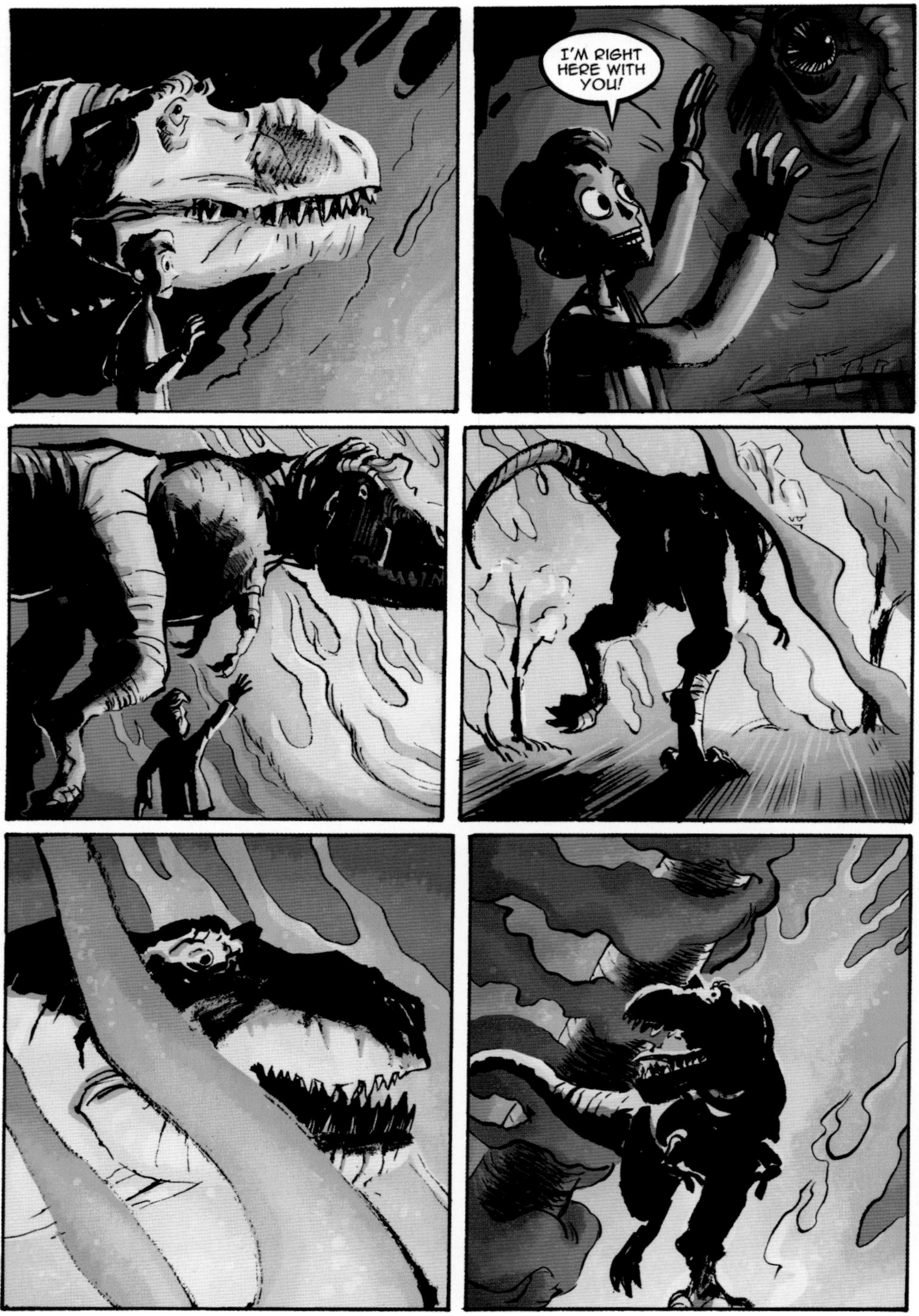
I'M RIGHT HERE WITH YOU!

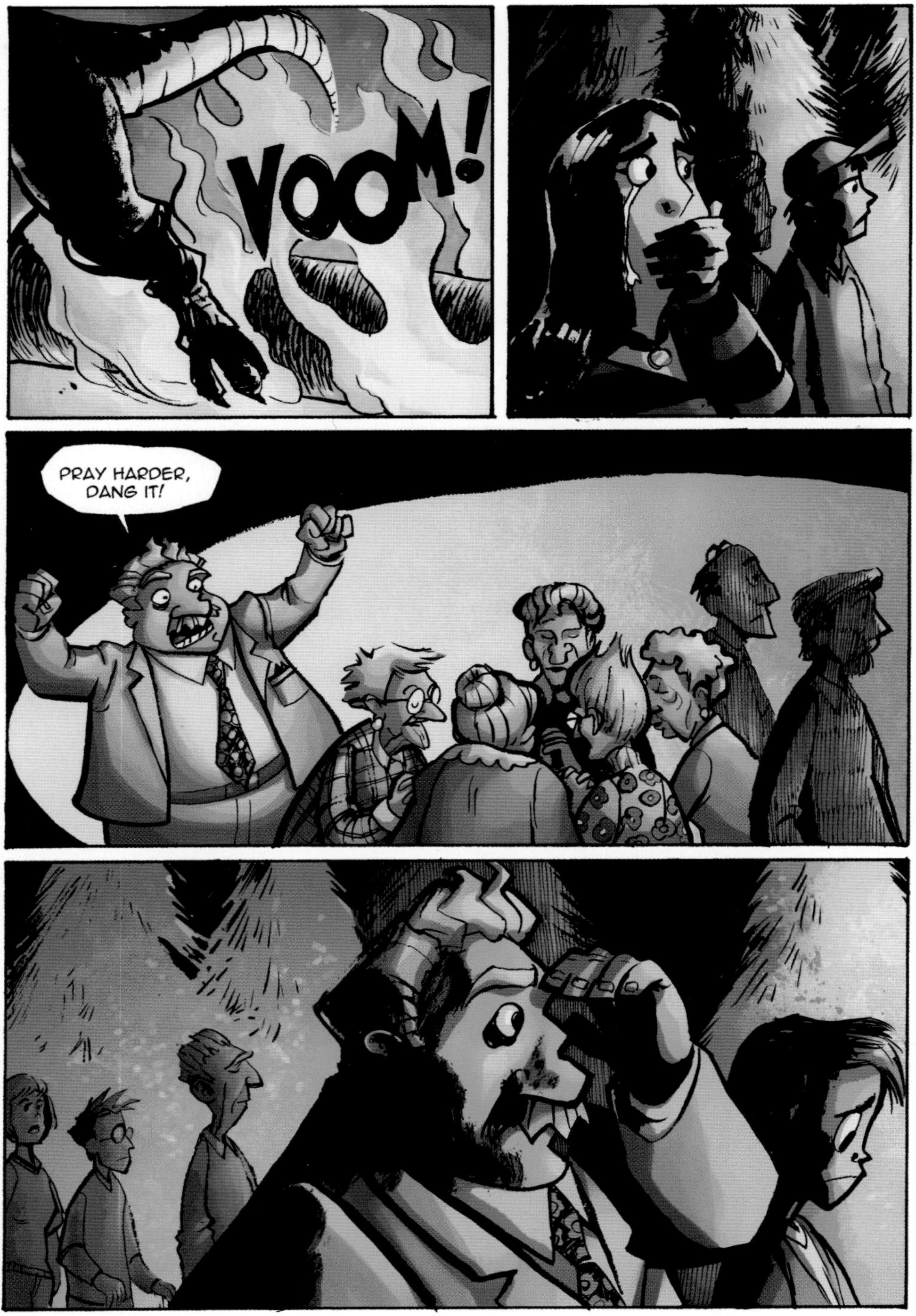
VOOM!
PRAY HARDER, DANG IT!

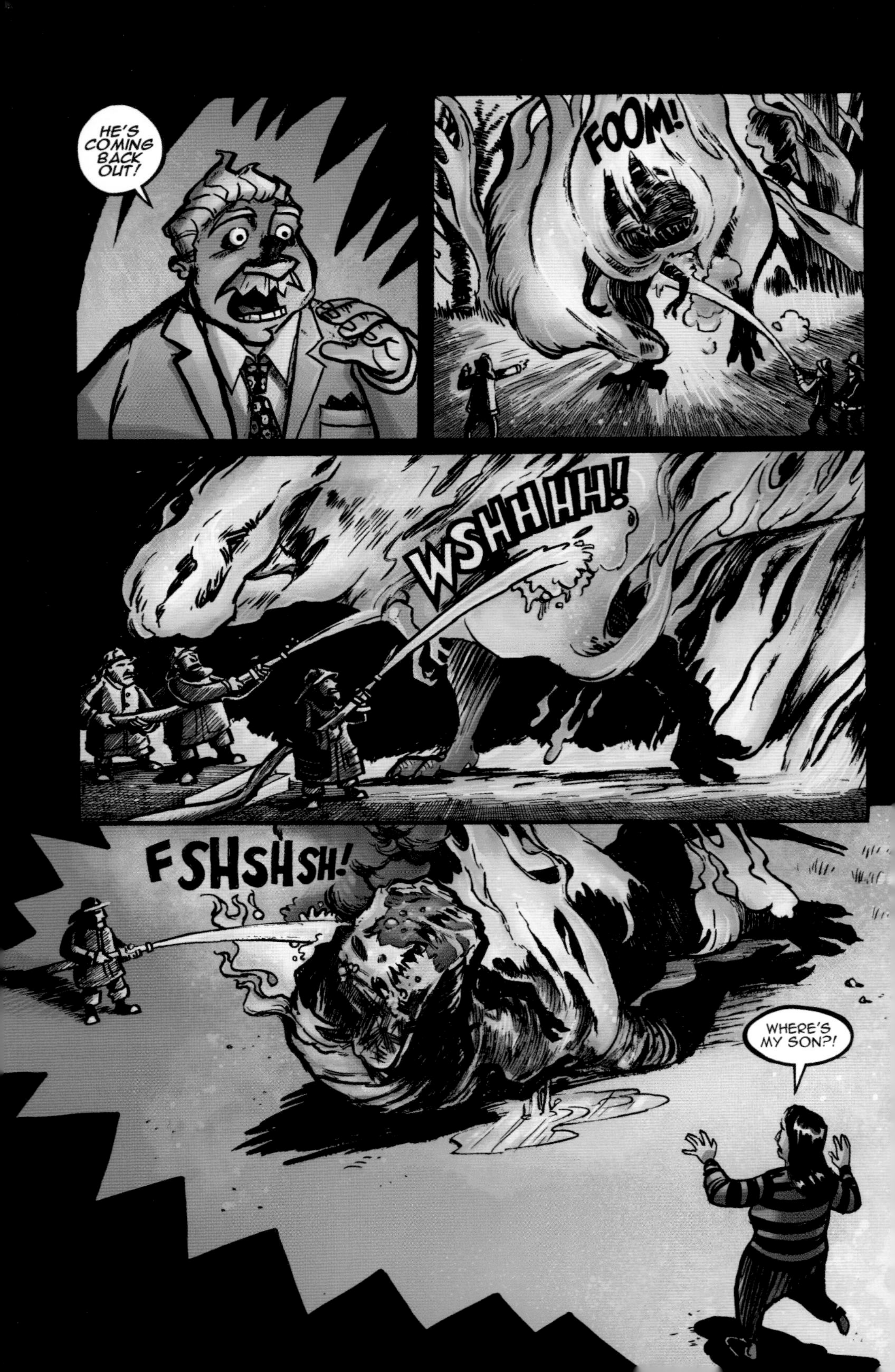
HE'S COMING BACK OUT!
FOOM!
WSHHHHH!
FSHSHSH!
WHERE'S MY SON?!

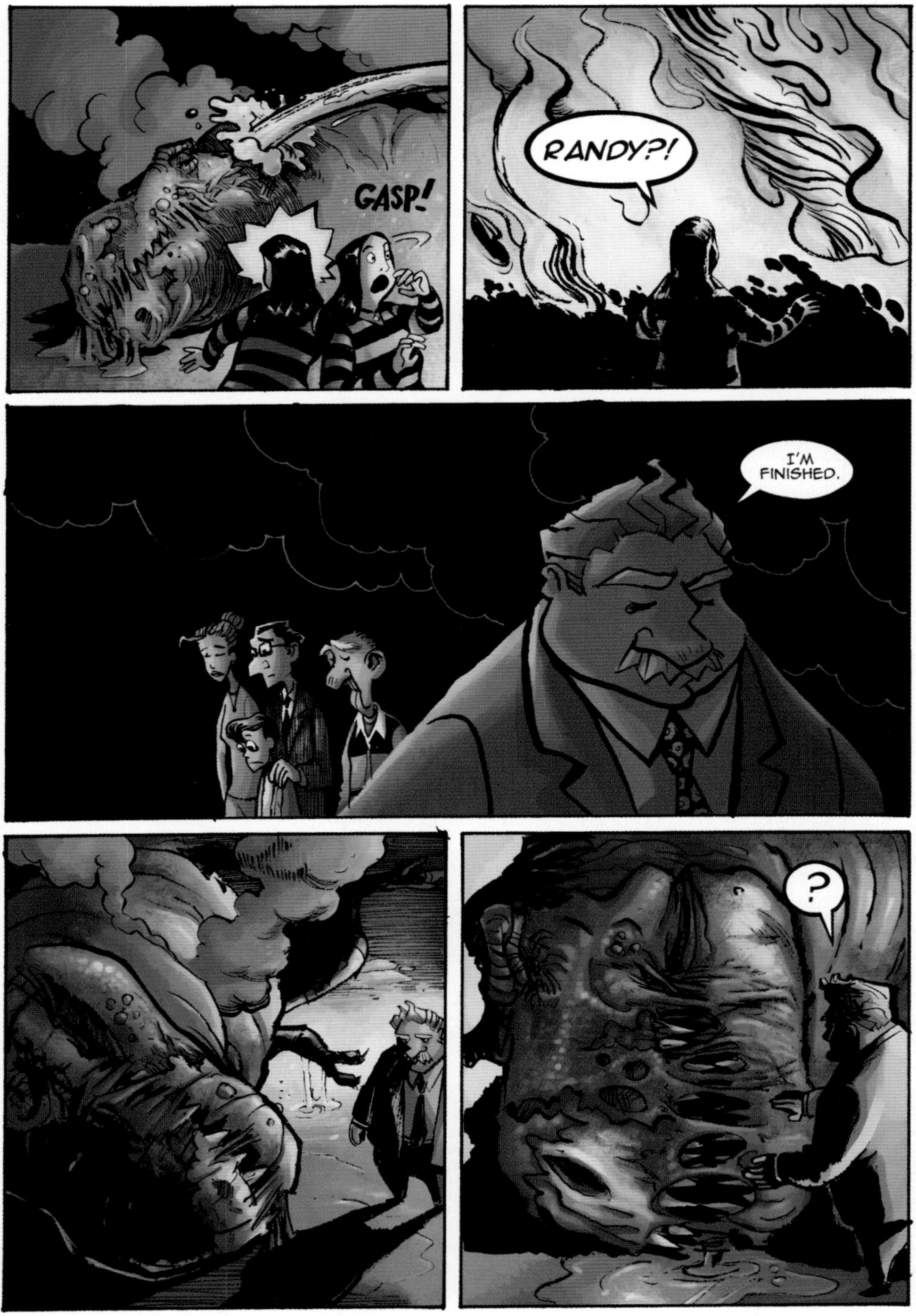
GASP!
RANDY?!
I'M FINISHED.
?

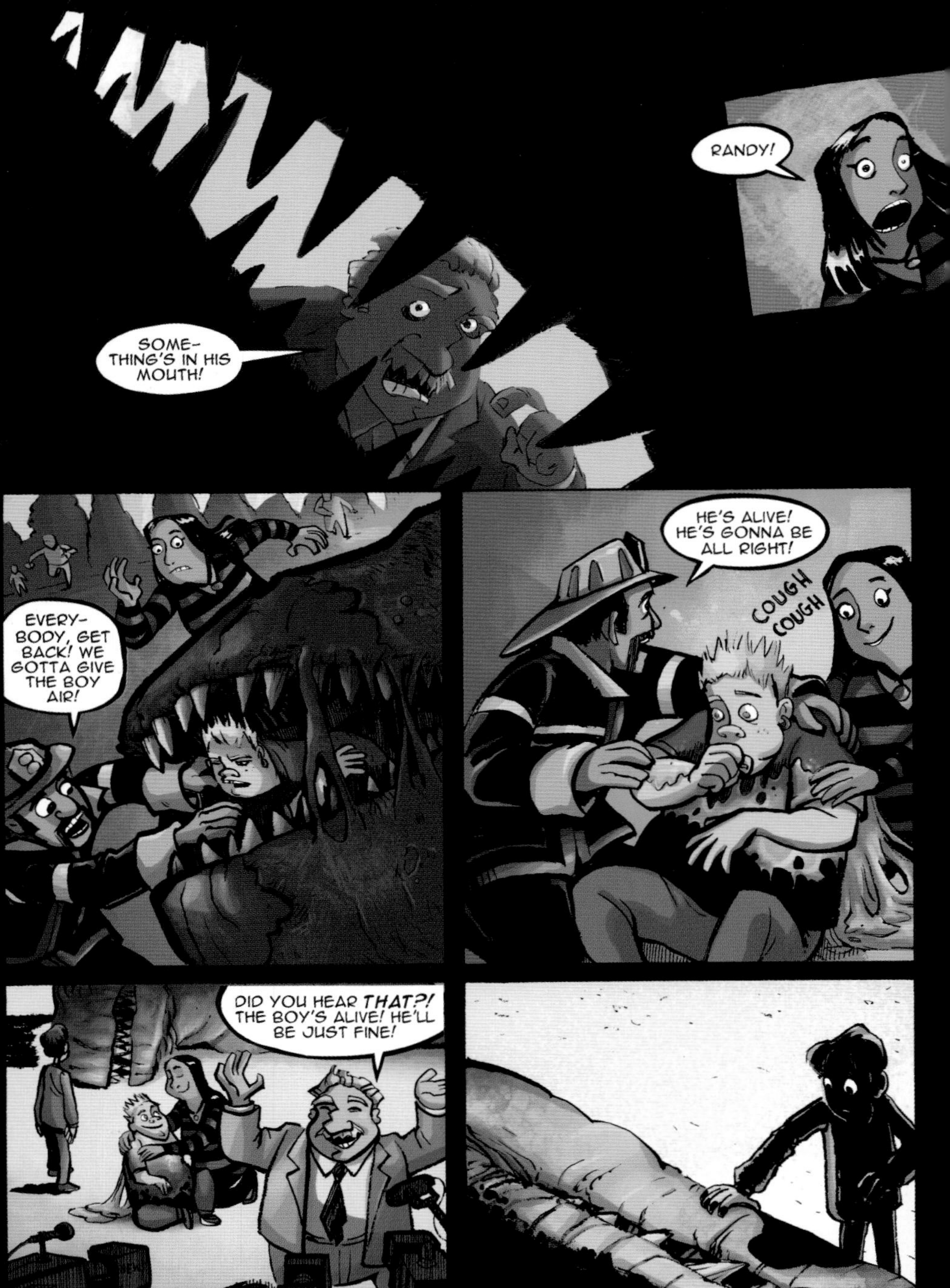
RANDY!
SOME-
THING'S IN HIS
MOUTH!
EVERY-
BODY, GET
BACK! WE
GOTTA GIVE
THE BOY
AIR!
HE'S ALIVE!
HE'S GONNA BE
ALL RIGHT!
COUGH
COUGH
DID YOU HEAR THAT?!
THE BOY'S ALIVE! HE'LL
BE JUST FINE!

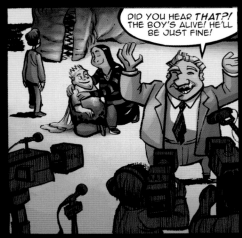

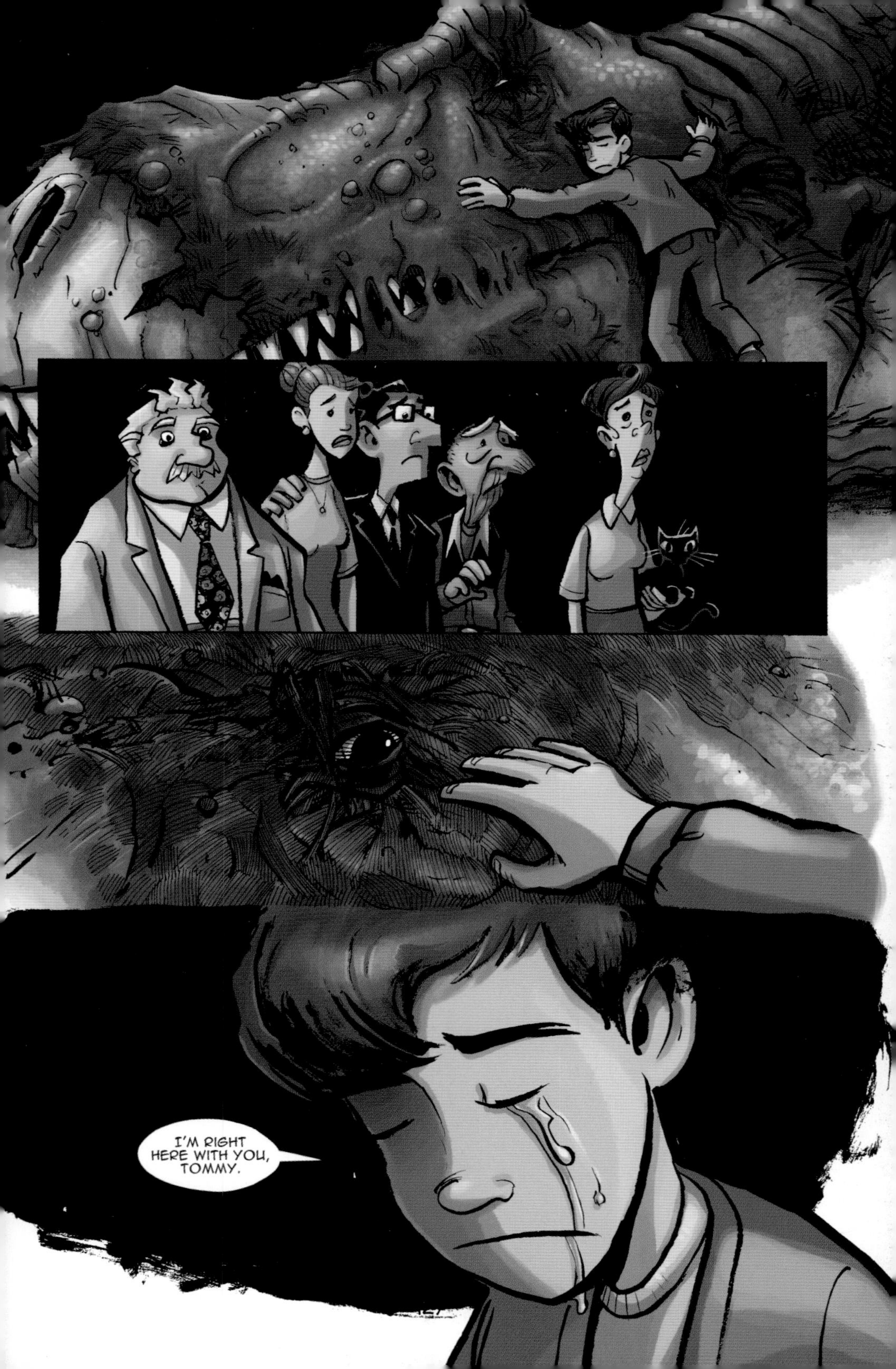
I'M RIGHT HERE WITH YOU, TOMMY.

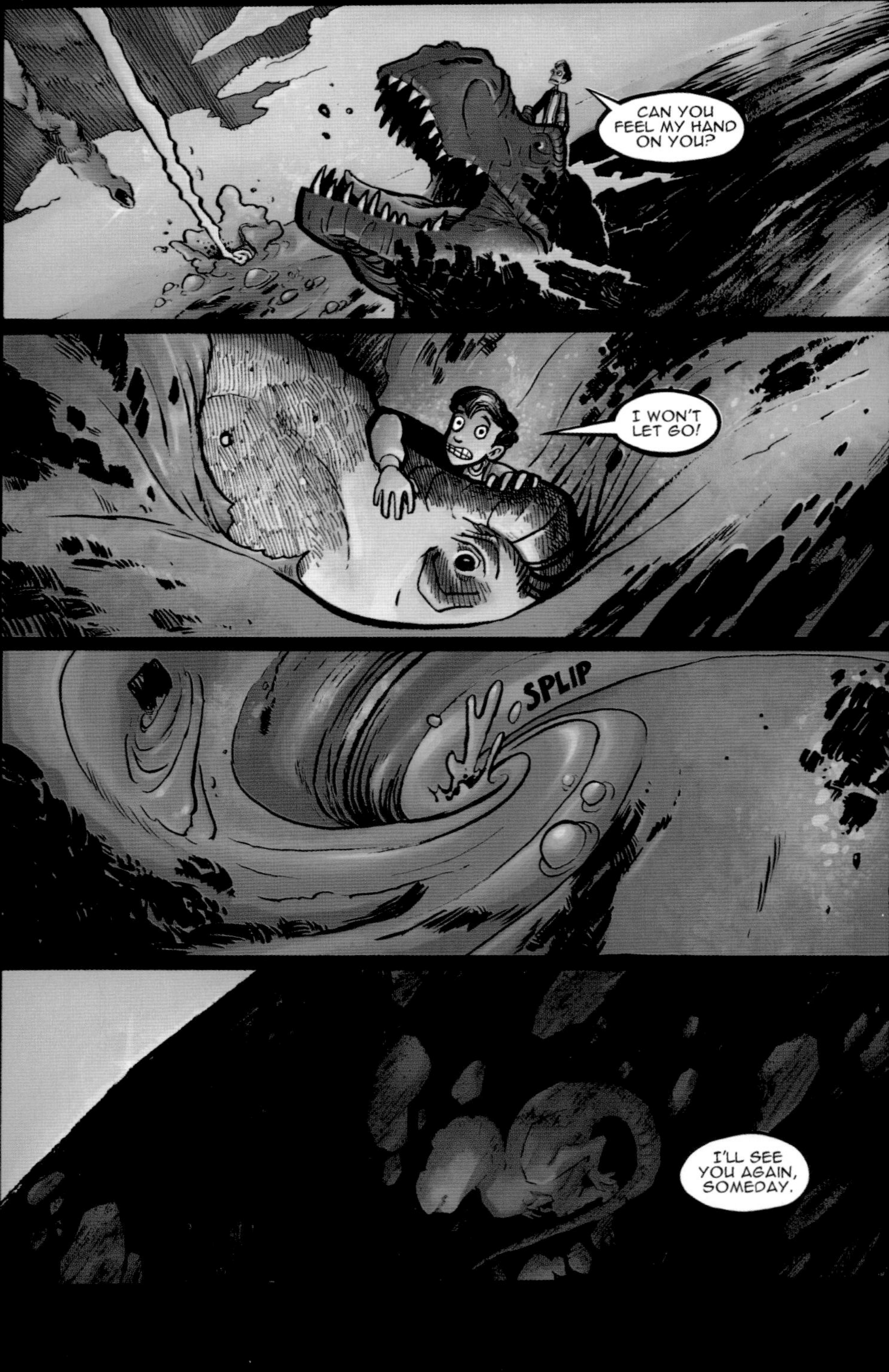
CAN YOU FEEL MY HAND ON YOU?
I WON'T LET GO!
SPLIP
I'LL SEE YOU AGAIN, SOMEDAY.

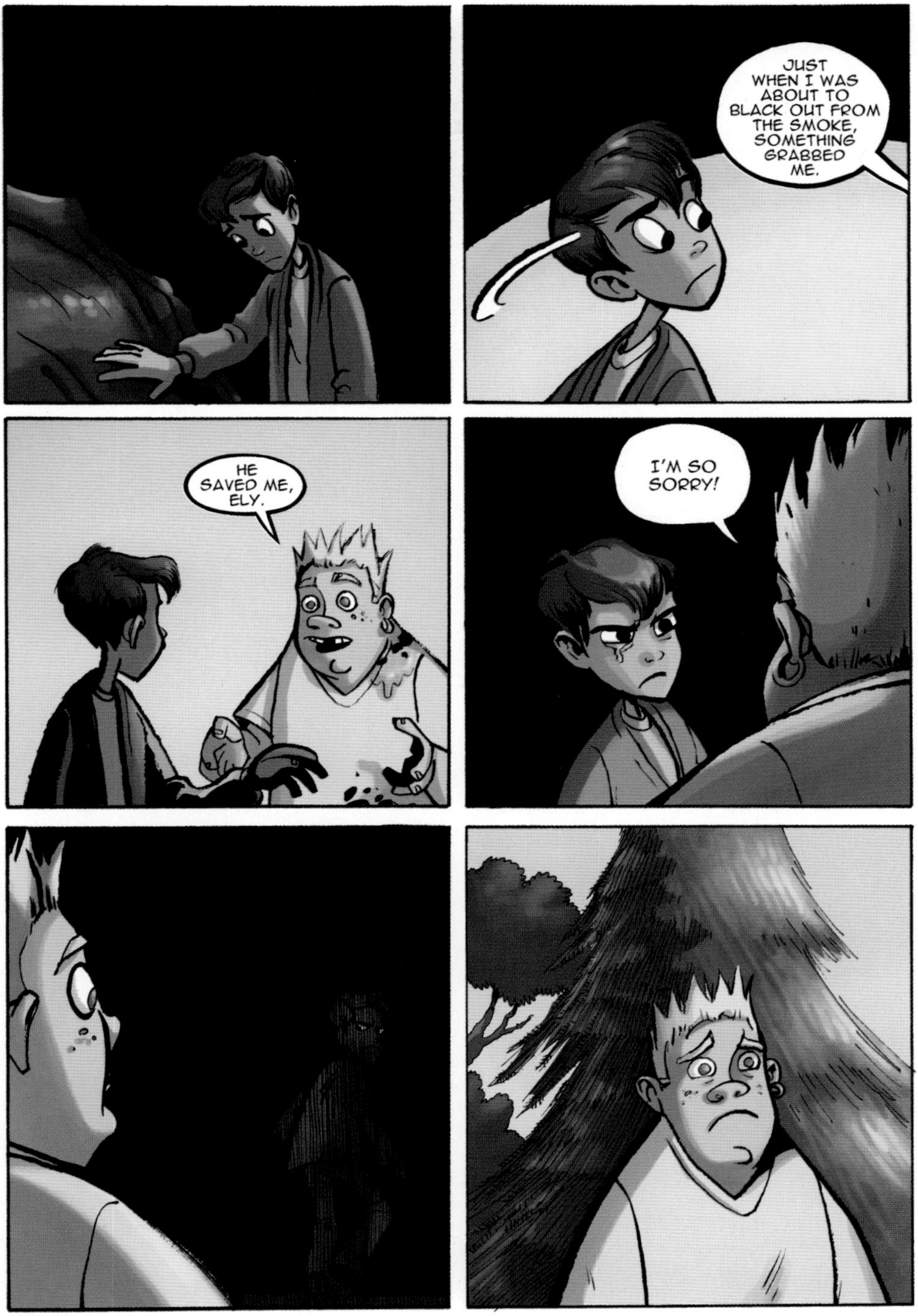
JUST WHEN I WAS ABOUT TO BLACK OUT FROM THE SMOKE, SOMETHING GRABBED ME.
HE SAVED ME, ELY.
I'M SO SORRY!

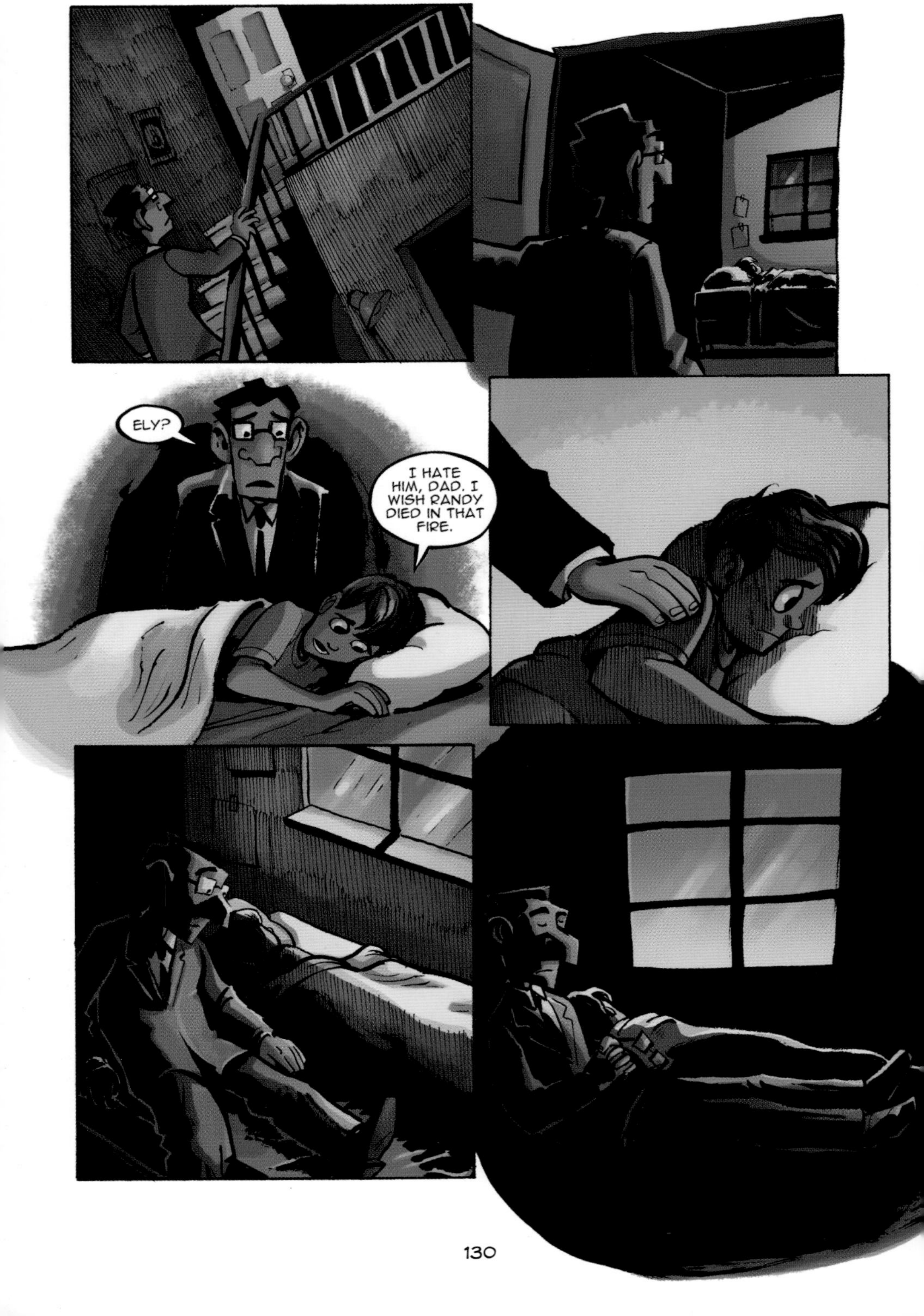
ELY?
I HATE HIM, DAD. I WISH RANDY DIED IN THAT FIRE.

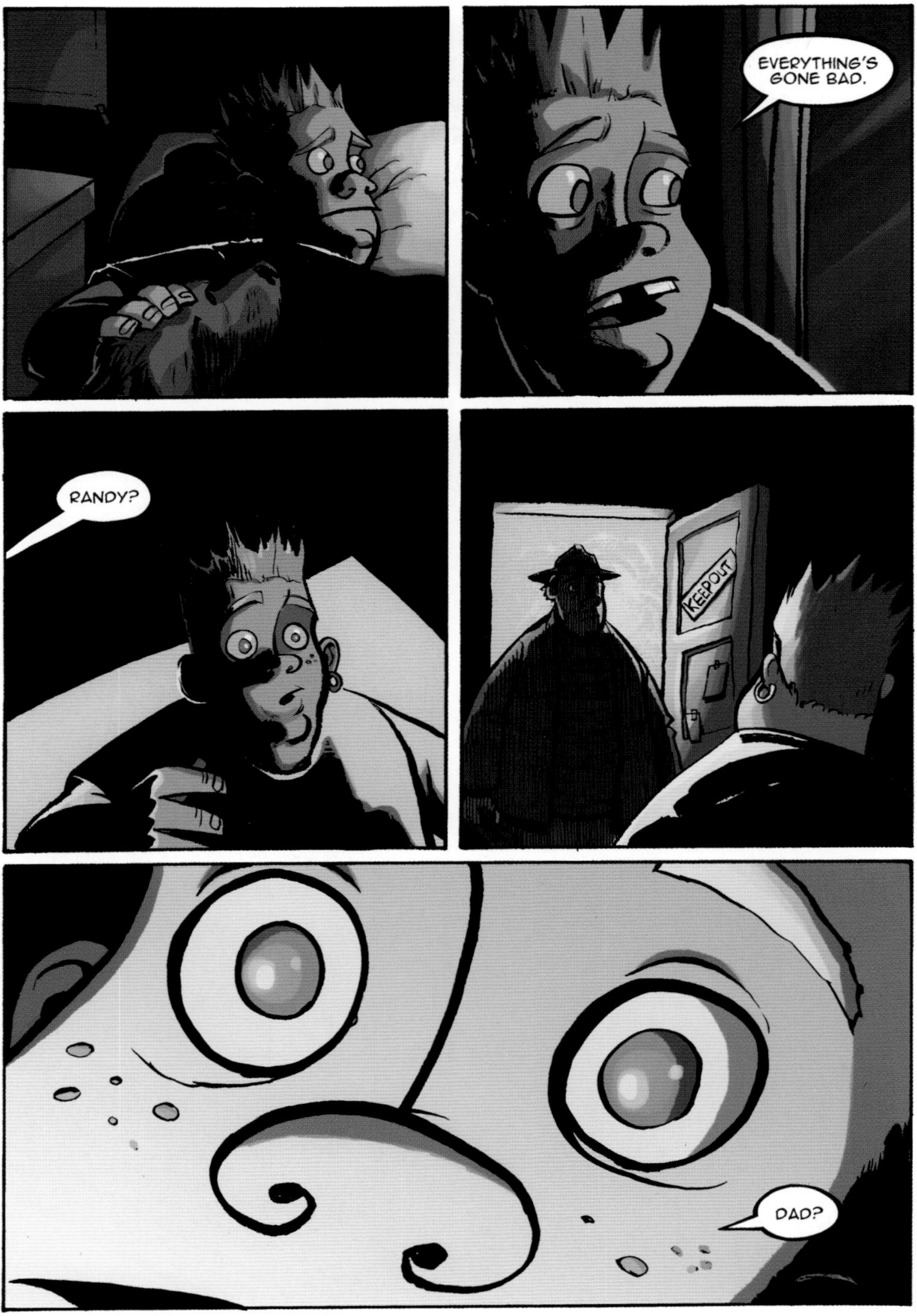
EVERYTHING'S GONE BAD.
RANDY?
KEEPOUT
DAD?

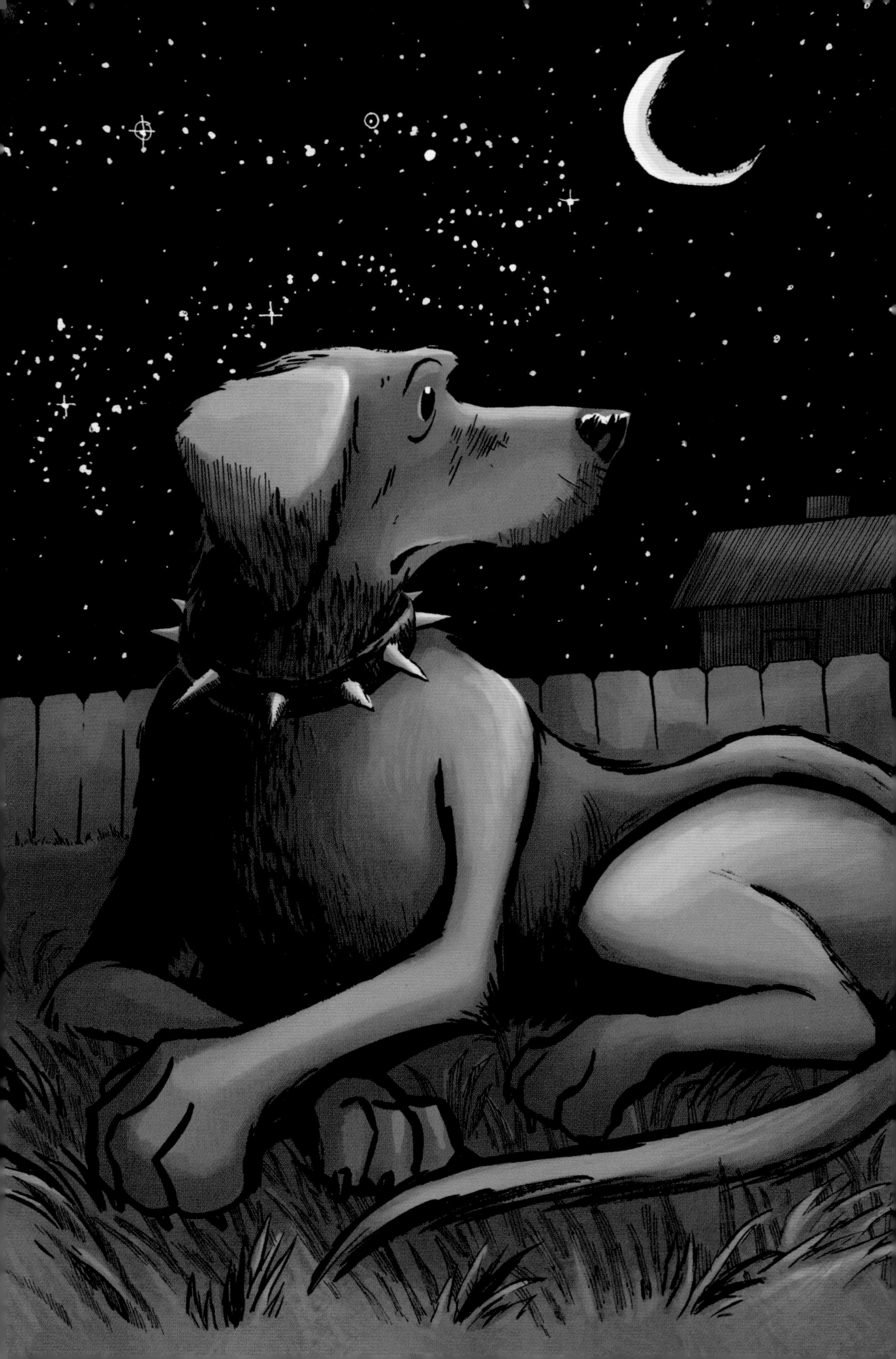

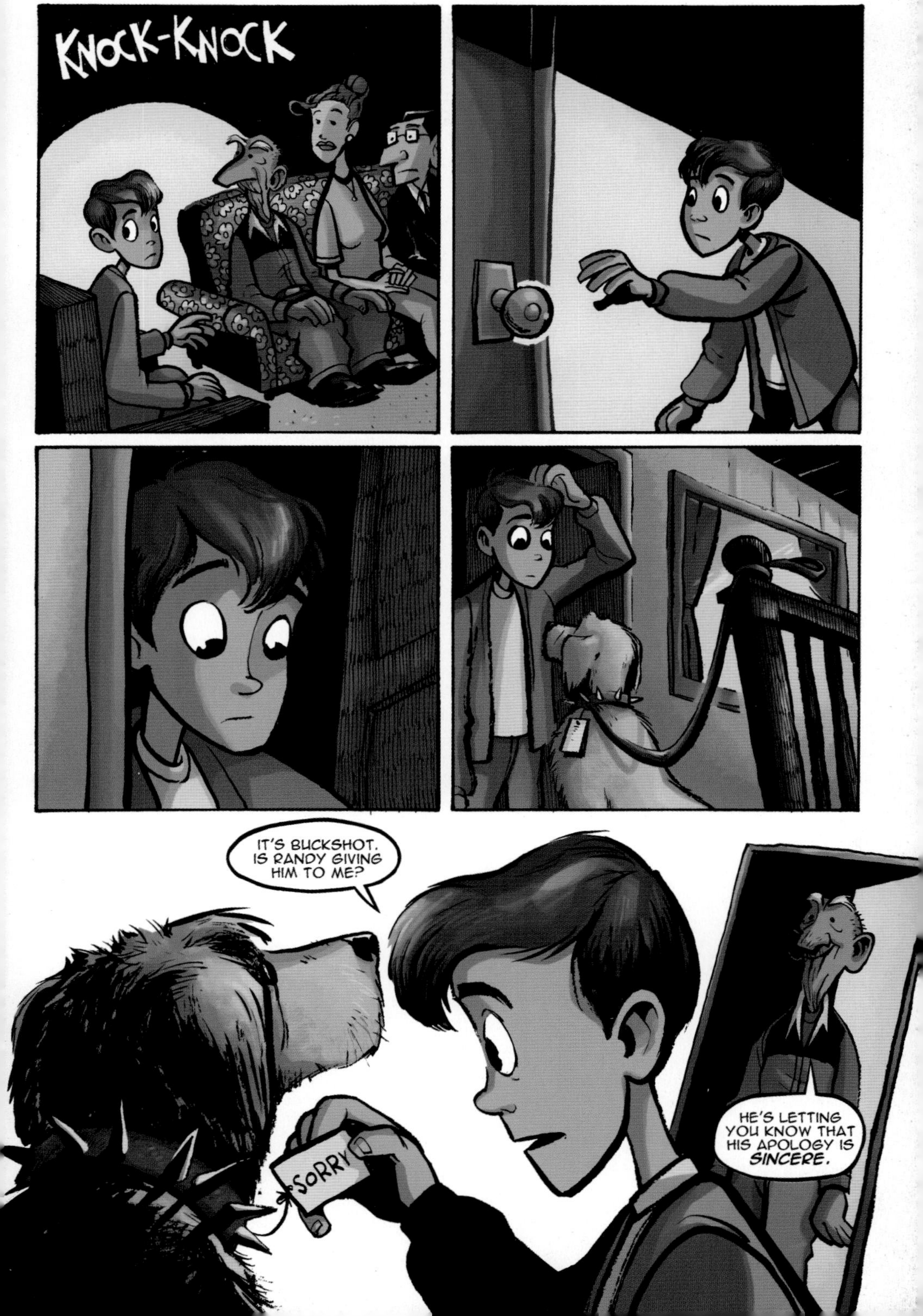
KNOCK-KNOCK
IT'S BUCKSHOT. IS RANDY GIVING HIM TO ME?
SORRY
HE'S LETTING YOU KNOW THAT HIS APOLOGY IS SINCERE.

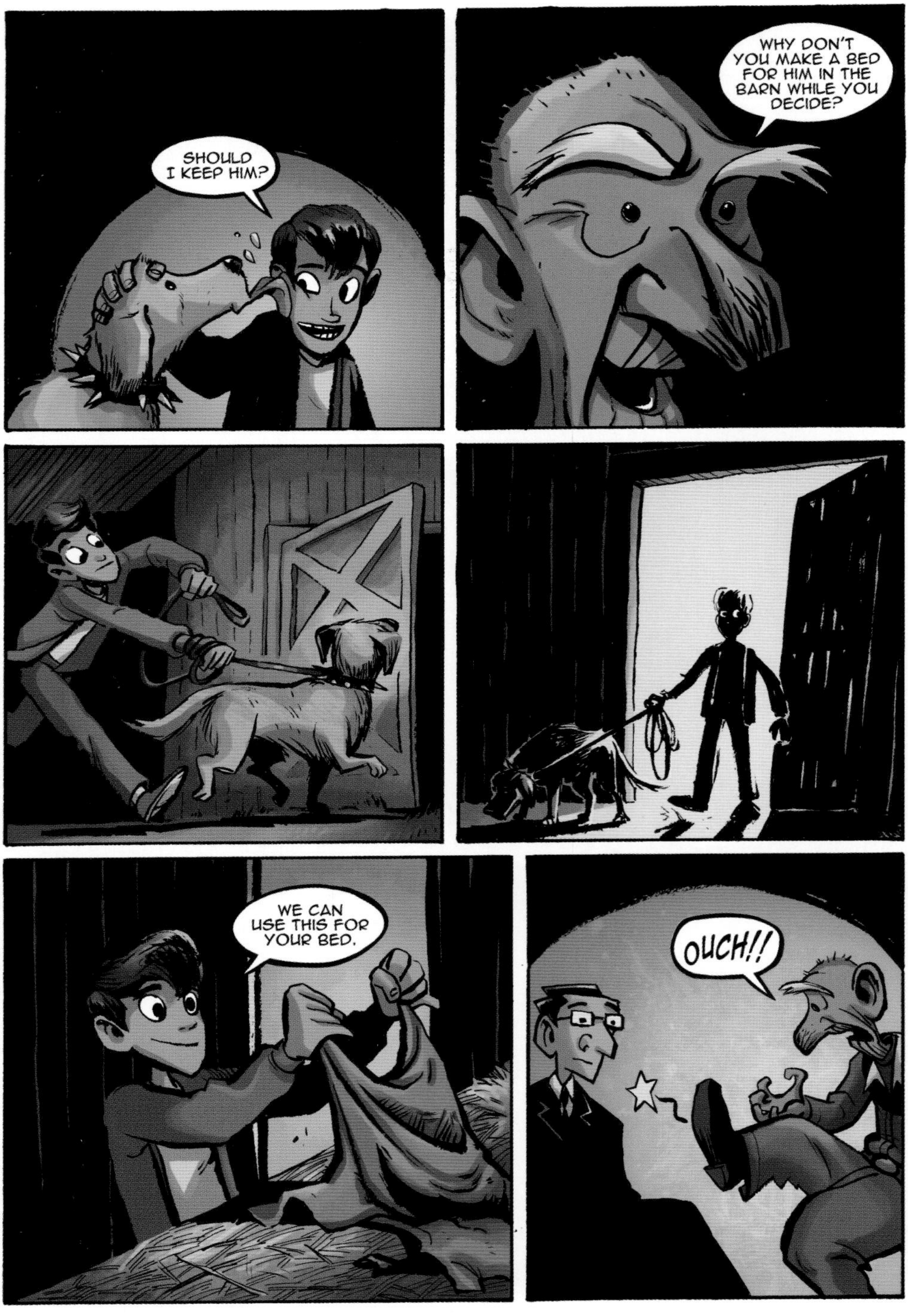
SHOULD I KEEP HIM?
WHY DON'T YOU MAKE A BED FOR HIM IN THE BARN WHILE YOU DECIDE?
WE CAN USE THIS FOR YOUR BED.
OUCH!!

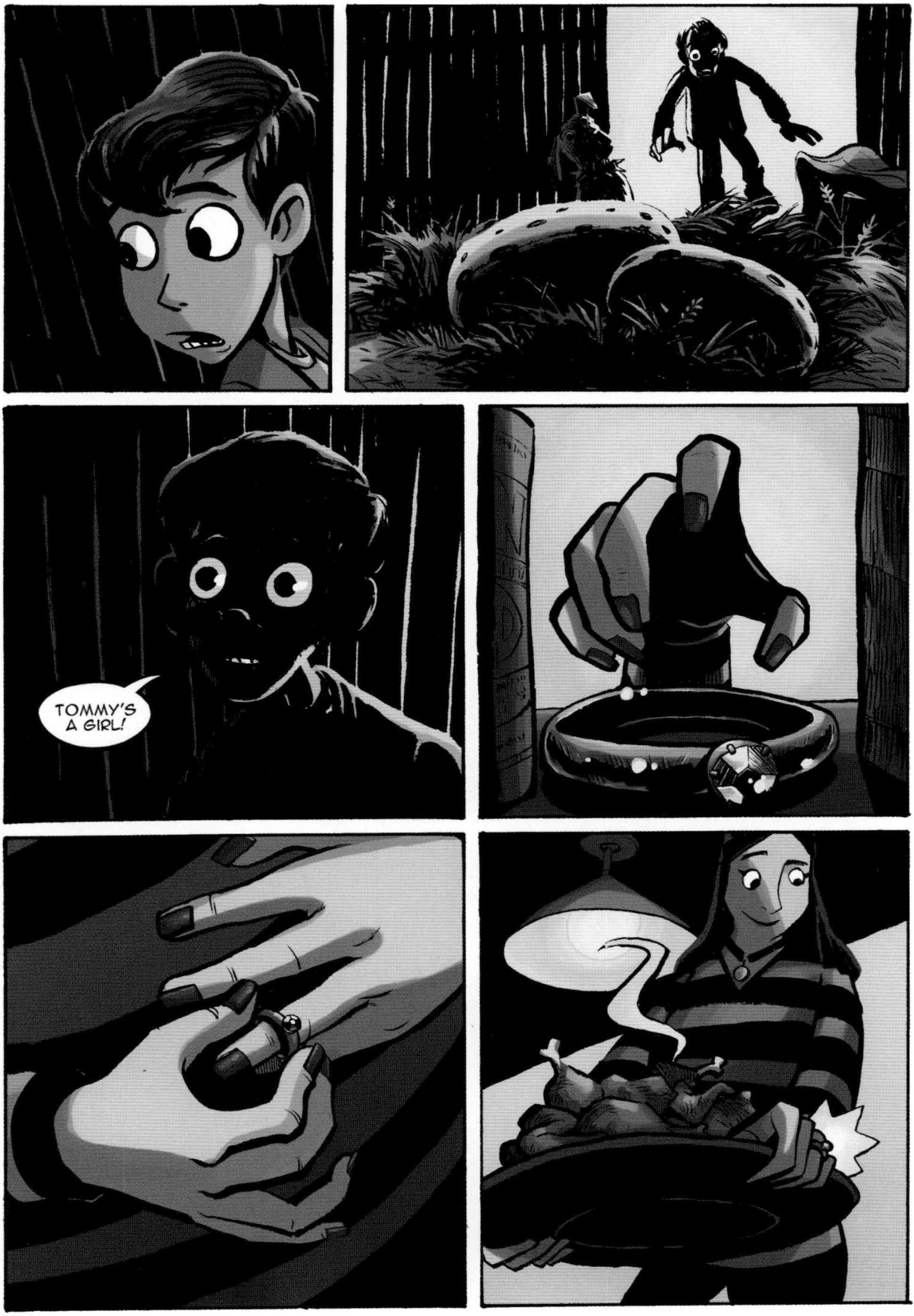
TOMMY'S
A GIRL!

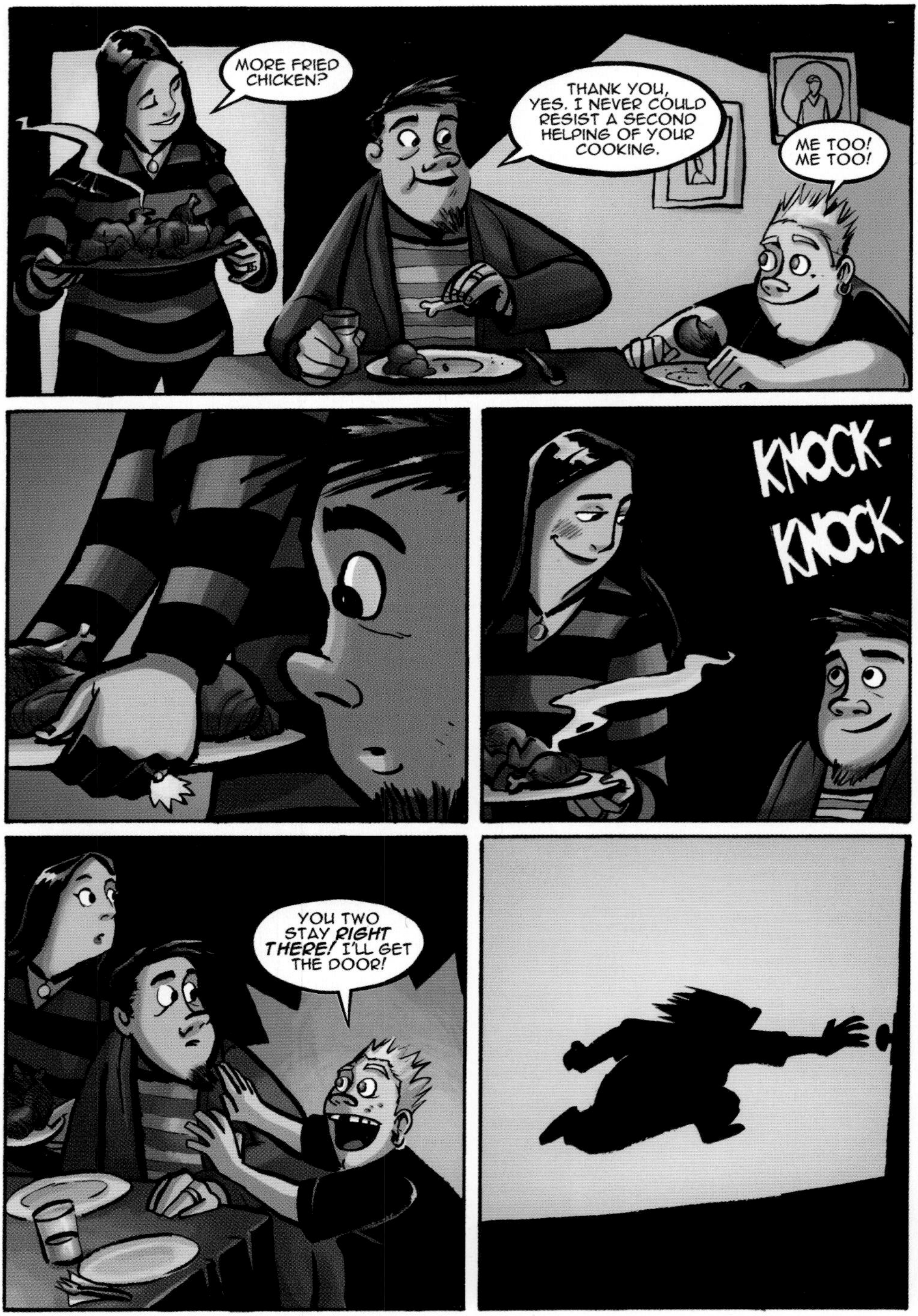
MORE FRIED CHICKEN?
THANK YOU, YES. I NEVER COULD RESIST A SECOND HELPING OF YOUR COOKING.
ME TOO! ME TOO!
KNOCK-
KNOCK
YOU TWO STAY RIGHT THERE! I'LL GET THE DOOR!

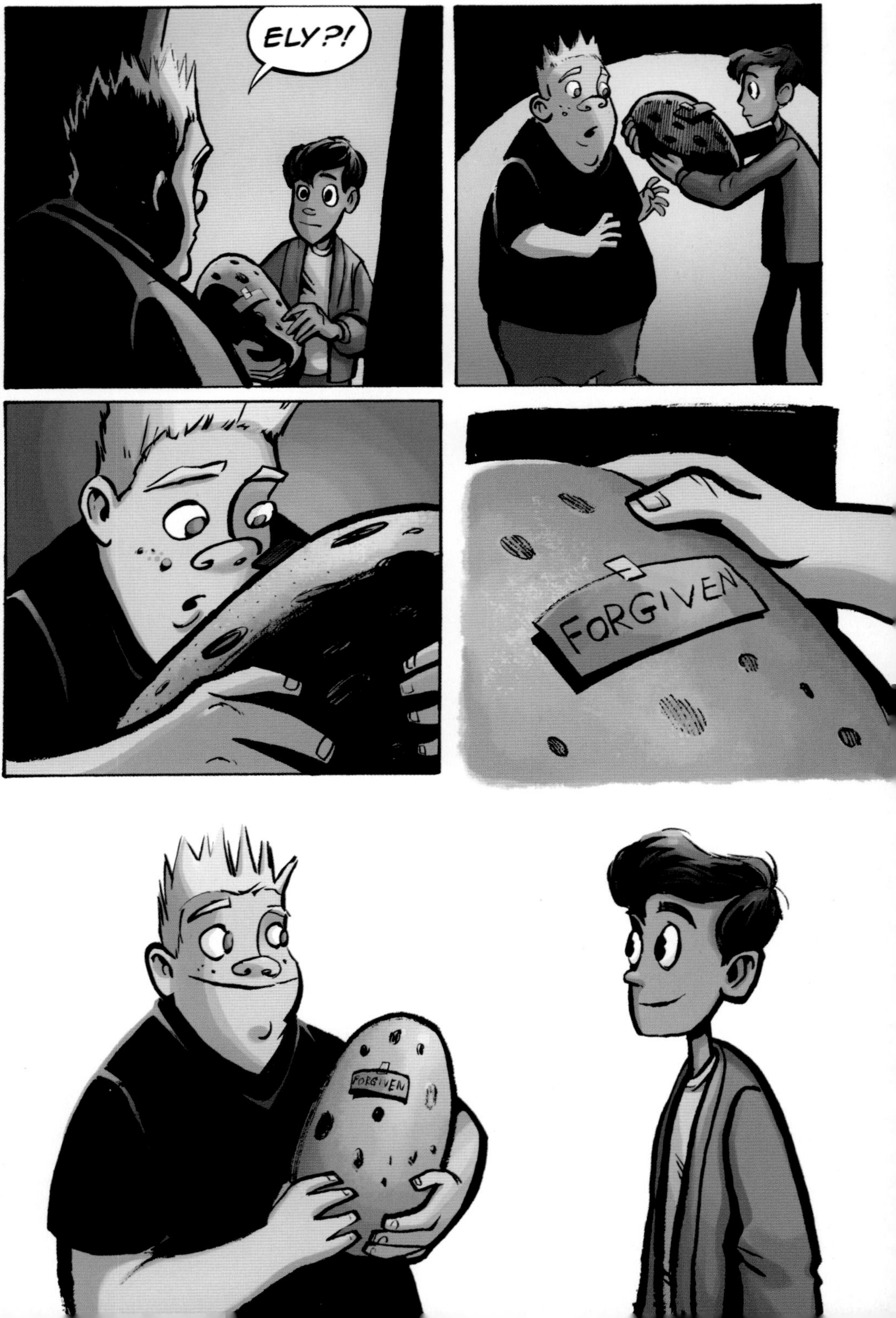
ELY?!
FORGIVEN
FORGIVEN

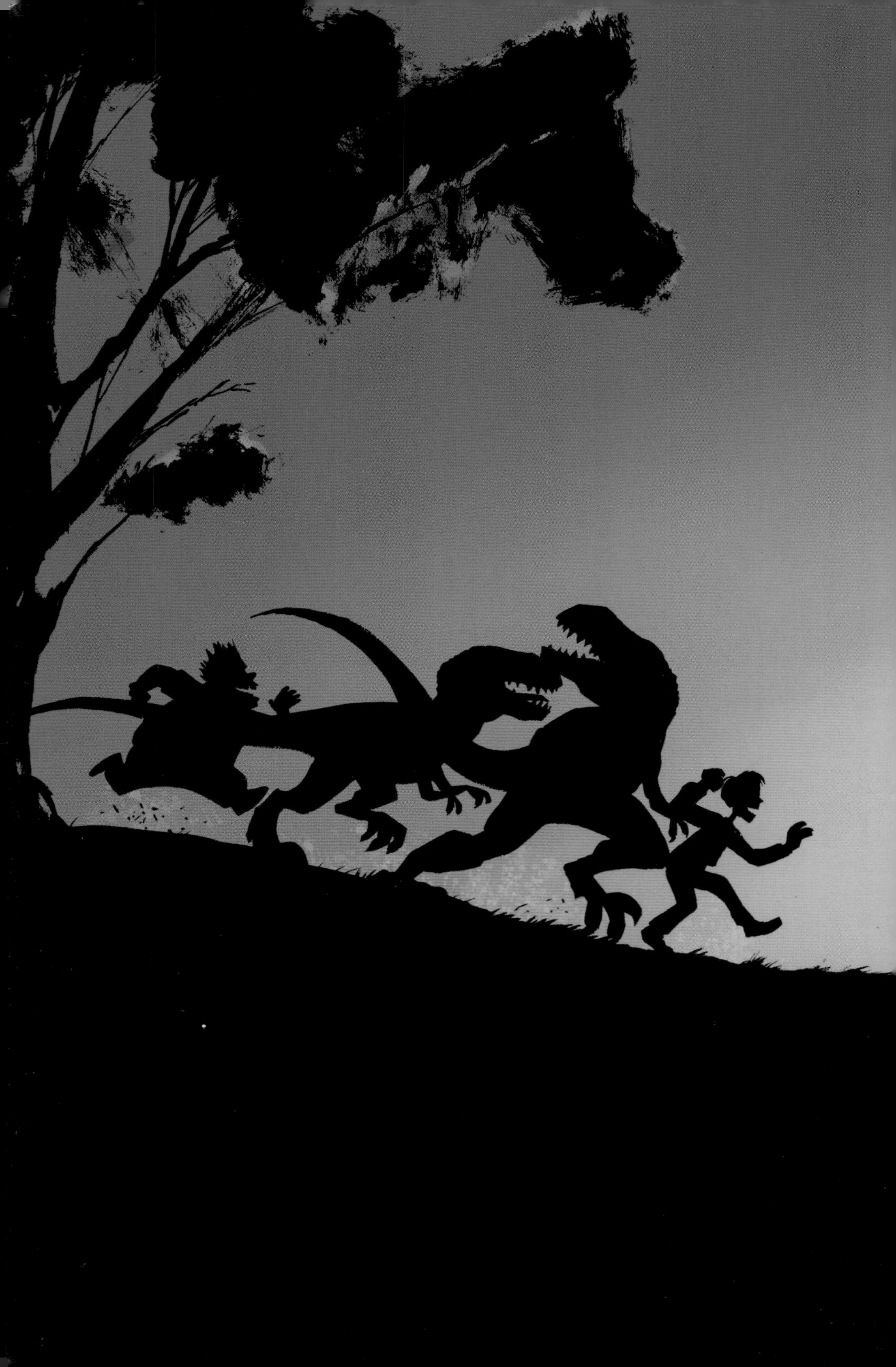

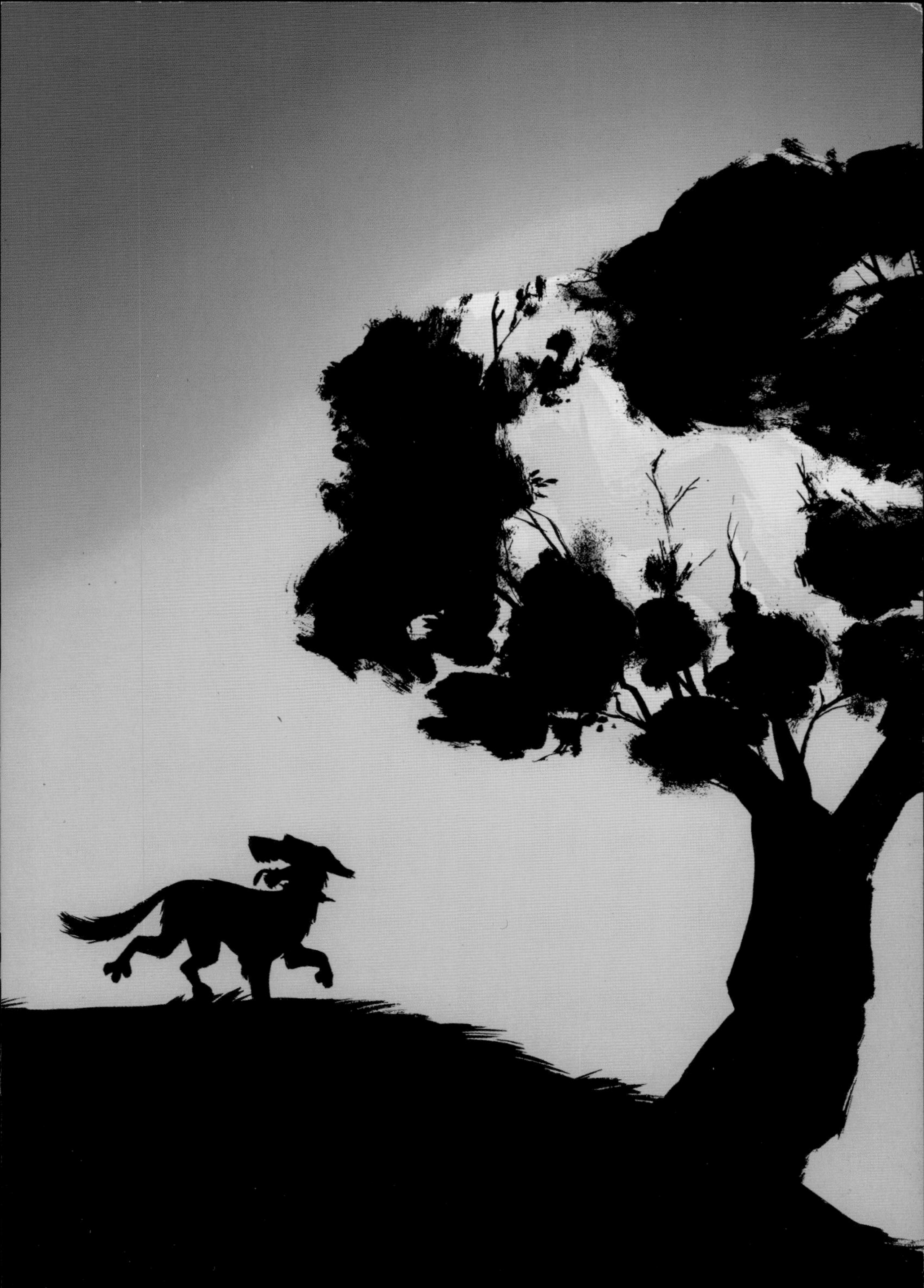

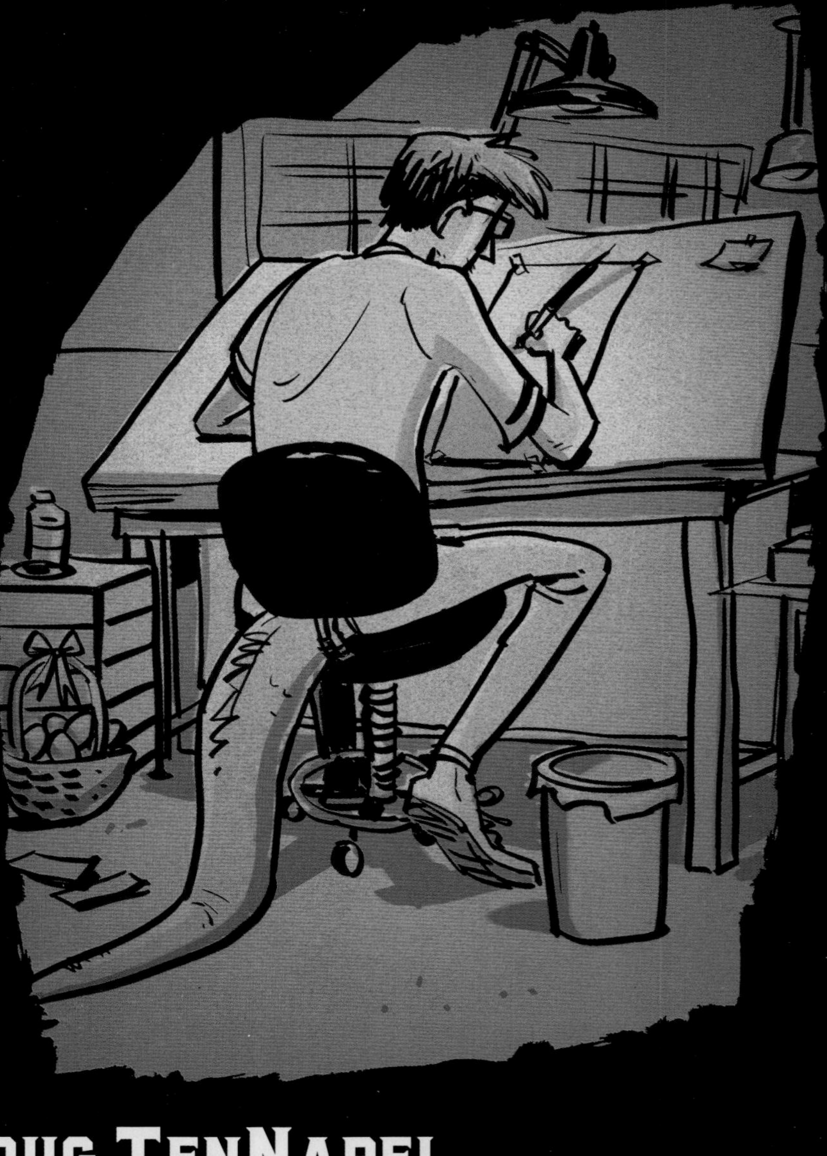

DOUG TENNAPEL is the creator of GHOSTOPOLIS, BAD ISLAND, and CARDBOARD. GHOSTOPOLIS was an ALA 2011 Top Ten Great Graphic Novel for Teens and a 2010 *Kirkus* Best Book of the Year. Both BAD ISLAND and CARDBOARD were *School Library Journal* Top Ten Graphic Novels in 2011 and 2012 respectively.

Doug is also the creator of the hugely popular character Earthworm Jim. He lives in Colorado Springs, Colorado, with his wife and four children.